LEAP

Book One of The Race Is On Series

OC Heaton

Rookwood Publishing

Join The Race is On Readers' Club

I n return, you'll receive a free novella plus loads more gifts, occasional e-mails from me about my life in rainy Leeds and first notice of when a new book will be out.

If you want to unsubscribe at any time, it's simple to do and I promise never to share your details with anyone. To join the club and receive your free gifts click on the QR code below. I look forward to welcoming you.

Contents

"Spooky action at a distance."

Albert Einstein's description of quantum mechanics in a letter to Max Born in 1947.

Route 41, South-West Iceland

13 November 2003, 18:43 hours GMT

The doomed four-by-four plumed thick fountains of spray into the darkness as it crawled along the narrow highway to Keflavík International Airport, its bright beams illuminating a hypnotic kaleidoscope of churning rain. The sight made Sally Moltex nauseous. She tried the side window, but it was mirror black, reflecting the Jeep's night-lit interior back at her. She closed her eyes, willing the vehicle to move faster as a thrill of excitement surged through her at the memory of what they'd seen that afternoon. Almost immediately, it was replaced by a prickle of fear. Everything screamed hoax: one second, they'd been stood inside the Department of Geothermal Studies, the next, they were in Ethan Rae's London Town house. They'd gone outside onto a busy Camden Town street thick with traffic. Alone. Ethan had insisted on that. They'd walked to the tube station. Bought a newspaper. Again, Ethan had been insistent. They'd asked someone where they were. And a second person. The third had shouted abuse at Sally; accused her of being an ignorant Yank. Of not knowing that she was in London. James had eventually intervened in his charming

British way, calmed the man down, and they'd returned to Ethan's office. Twenty minutes later, they were back in Reykjavík. Heads spinning at what they'd seen. Hearts beating with what Ethan had given them.

'Do you think LEAP's fake?' she asked her companion.

James Reagan didn't reply straight away. Without taking his eyes off the road, he attempted another call to his producer at News 24/7 in London. *Nothing.* He was going to miss tomorrow's deadline if he didn't get through soon. Seven million Saturday viewers was no disaster, but it was well below his Friday average.

'Nah,' he said. 'Ethan wouldn't risk it. What would he gain by misleading us?'

'That's what I can't work out,' Sally said, tracing her fingers along the cold glass of the passenger window, trying to keep pace with the streaming water.

'How do you fake what we just saw?' James said. 'Besides which, it will do him way more damage if he's lying.'

Sally wasn't so sure. She liked James. Had known him for twenty years, but he anchored a light entertainment show for a channel that needed content. Lots of content. She, on the other hand, unearthed stories. Real stories that took months to fact check before she allowed them to be broadcast. If they got this wrong, James could blame Ethan, an eccentric billionaire. She would be finished.

'I need more time,' Sally said.

'Ethan is launching in ten days. With or without us.'

'You'd broadcast on the strength of what he just showed us?'

'As of midday tomorrow,' he said. 'That's if we can take off to—'

He never finished his sentence. A loud crack from the rear of the Jeep veered it savagely left. James tried to counter by wrenching the steering hard right, but the small charge had done its job. The Jeep flipped, bleeding fuel from its shattered underbelly as it slithered off Route 41 and onto the lava below. The dead rock punctured the thin roof, ripping through plastic, metal and cables which sparked into life. Fumes met fire and a blinding explosion boiled into the sheeting rain, as long forgotten lava flows glowed red in approval.

Department of Geothermal Studies, Reykjavík

13 November 2003, 18:45 hours GMT

The axe head cut deep into the ancient oak, spuming clouds of dust into the deserted office. Andreus Grond worked the heavy blade free and paused to survey the devastation around him: books and periodicals lay scattered among smashed computers, broken chairs and toppled filing cabinets, their contents almost burying an upturned table. He glanced at his watch: 18:46.

The day's real work had just been concluded thirty miles southwest. That had been trickier, especially setting the charge. The journalists had waited in their Jeep for nearly thirty minutes before disappearing into the bowels of the building, probably to this room. That hadn't been the problem; they had returned much sooner, almost catching him underneath the Jeep, but he had planned for that as well. A loosened bumper on his Shogun, parked in the next bay, was his alibi. Baseball cap pulled low, collar high, he had knelt in the drenching rain, securing the moulded plastic with rope as the two journalists had rushed past him in their race to escape the downpour.

Otherwise, this had been one of his easiest assignments to date; the request had been made through a bulletin board buried deep within the Yahoo community pages under 'Landscaping Ideas'. However, to Andreus Grond, it meant work and, by tomorrow, freedom. As soon as he had completed this job. His last job.

The realisation energised him. Grond hefted the axe and, in a fluid movement, swung the blade back towards the last doorframe, which provided no more resistance than the other five. He detached the head, wiped it clean and collapsed the handle into three separate pieces before placing all four parts in his rucksack. As he exited the room, he stopped before a large portrait of a middle-aged man holding a steaming fountain of water in his cupped hands. Grond removed a blade from a sheath attached to his thigh and sliced the canvas twice, corner to corner. The bottom triangle of material slowly unfurled like a limp flag, covering the inscription below the picture. Satisfied, he continued down the stairs and out into the storm.

Camden Town, London

13 November 2003, 20:01 hours GMT

Ethan Rae looked up from his desk whilst CNN droned on in the background. Through the thick glass of his office, he had an uninterrupted view of the adjoining open-plan area where forty or so of his associates rushed from one task to the next. It looked chaotic, but most had been with him since the beginning and all moved with a common purpose—their biggest divestment yet. This one had been a long haul. Seventeen weeks in total. It showed. Everyone looked exhausted, but the end was near. Although Ethan couldn't hear anything, he could feel the familiar cocktail of anticipation and tension as the finishing line drew closer.

Ethan's gaze was drawn to a photograph on the edge of his desk. He didn't need the picture to remind him of the faces in the small frame, even though he hadn't seen either of them for over twenty-five years. A young couple bathed in sunlight, smiling at something off camera. Between them, a small child gazed up expectantly. Ethan closed his eyes, savouring the memory of that rare summer's day in Aberdeen: the softness of his mother's skirt on his cheek, the air still heavy from a thunderstorm that morning, the pungency of his father's cologne tickling his nose. A wave of contentment washed over Ethan like a warm blanket, and he sat there bathing in its fleeting embrace, even as he remembered his father receiving a phone call that same afternoon, one that would send them all overseas and —.

Right on cue, his leg began to ache. Resigned, he braced himself for what was to come. Hot flicks of pain across his back, moving slowly at first, but he knew the drill. They would quicken. They always did. And they wouldn't stop until the count of fifty. He leant forward in his seat, hands gripping the table, eyes closed, fighting the urge to cry out as the final ten flashes of pain began. They cut deepest, slicing through flesh until he could feel warm blood run freely down his back, the memory still raw after all these years. When the pain stopped, he stood up gingerly, his shirt bathed in sweat, willing the memory away, but it wouldn't be hurried. Finally, he opened his eyes, collapsing back into his seat, where he stared blankly at the TV on his desk.

It was some seconds before the images on the screen registered. The couple looked familiar, but he couldn't work out why. And then recognition dawned: It was James Reagan and Sally Moltex!

As he watched, England's most celebrated TV journalist and the US' current hot investigative TV reporter faded to the familiar glass frontage of Keflavík airport. Ethan grabbed the remote, his pain forgotten.

'... Jeep Cherokee crashed on the way to Iceland's International Airport in the middle of a violent November storm. The vehicle was discovered by a road crew who had come out to investigate the loss of power in one of the many thermal generators that line Route 41. Apparently, the four-by-four left the road less than a mile from the airport. Although the cause of the accident is unknown, rescuers have already dismissed the possibility of survivors due to the ferocious diesel fire they discovered at the scene. Early indications are that the force of the impact must have caused the vehicle's fuel tank to explode, which would have given its occupants no chance of getting out alive, even if they'd escaped the fifteen-foot drop onto the lava flows below. Sally Moltex and James Reagan are two of the—'

Ethan muted the presenter, the TV rushing away from him as if he were viewing it through the wrong end of a telescope. He'd only met Sally and James a few hours ago. Had organised the meeting. Shown them LEAP. His chest suddenly tightened at the realisation that he may have led them to their deaths. The timing was too great a coincidence and that meant someone knew about their plans.

More worryingly, Uma might be in danger.

The thought catapulted Ethan out of his chair and into the deal room. As he passed the first row of workstations, Pike, Head of Deals, his face etched with fatigue from too many late nights, stepped forward to intercept his boss.

'Ethan, Chandler's sticking on the retentions. They want one percent of the purchase price.'

'Give it to him.'

Pike stopped in his tracks. 'That's one hundred million!' he exclaimed. 'We've never gone this high. Why start now?'

'Time's not on our side. We launch Green Ray within the month.'

'That's my worry. They might smell a rat if we cave in too readily.'

'No chance,' Ethan said, continuing to the back of the room, where he paused in the doorway that led up to his living quarters. 'This deal is past the point of no return. It will cost them the best part of their £25 million exclusivity fee if they walk now. Not to mention advisor fees. Give them the point and close the deal.'

Pike looked crestfallen. He wasn't used to selling. None of the team were. Until twelve months ago, they had prided themselves on being the most acquisitive private corporate finance team in the country, with over £20 billion worth of deals under their collective belts. But that had all changed overnight when his boss had announced a fire sale of his entire holdings. Every last penny was being channelled into Green Ray. Despite the obvious reference to the environment, no one knew exactly what it was. The entire project was shrouded in secrecy, but it was big. To date, over £30 billion was now sat in the fund.

Ethan disappeared through the door and as it swung shut, the clatter of the office was suddenly muted. He pressed the VoRec implant in his right ear.

'Jill, get me Uma.'

'Yes, Ethan. Do you want her home, office or mobile?' the auto attendant asked in a reassuring, but manufactured tone.

'Home,' he guessed.

Seconds later, Uma answered.

'Uma, thank God. Have you seen the news? Sally and ...'

His voice trailed off as he heard the familiar click of Uma's voice-mail.

'Jill, try all three numbers.'

Ethan continued up the wide oak staircase of the restored Victorian terrace. In the absence of family photos, Ethan's housekeeper had hung framed magazine covers in clutches of four above each step. *Technology Monthly* sat alongside *Forbes* and an assortment of other, similarly titled publications, all of which contained smiling images of Ethan staring miserably into the camera. On the first landing they petered out, replaced by homeless frames which lay ten deep on the thick carpet. Propping up one of the piles were several Business Person of the Year awards, stacked on top of each other like abandoned Lego bricks.

Past the first floor-landing, the steps were set much closer together, allowing Ethan to take them in twos, until he reached the top floor of the old house. A smooth stainless steel door faced him, a black mat beneath. On each side, protruding from the walls at waist height, were two solid blocks of dull grey plastic. There was no handle or apparent means of opening the door. A small inscription on the bottom right corner read 'Gatekeeper. Rae Security Group'.

Ethan positioned his feet on the black mat and flattened both palms on the blocks. A thin rod, the width of the doorframe, emerged from the ceiling and slowly descended. As it drew level with his hair, a band of light lit up his forehead, flashing once as it reached his eyes. Jill's comforting voice confirmed the results.

'Optical scan, successful. Palm and finger scans, successful. Please state your name for the record.'

'Ethan Rae.'

'Voice authentication successful. Ethan, please maintain your position,' instructed Jill as the black rod slowly completed its patient descent and soundlessly disappeared into the floor.

'Body X-Ray and scan matches medical records. A one hundred and fifty millimetre titanium rod and two screws in right femur. Amalgam filling in upper right rear molar. Correct scar tissue density, length and width on right thigh. Body mass is within acceptable parameters. You have been cleared for personal profiling. Which school does your son go to?'

'I don't have any children.'

'Please provide the birth date of your wife.'

'I'm not married.'

'How much did you give to charity last year?'

'£250 million.'

'Personal profiling, complete. You have been cleared for entry.'

As the door slid open, a familiar voice in his ear stopped him from entering the empty room beyond.

'Ethan?'

'Uma! Where are you?'

'I'm at the lab.'

'What are you doing there? I thought you'd be home by now.'

'I was. The university's security office called me in, about half an hour ago. It's a disaster in here. Someone's completely wrecked the place.'

'Christ! When did this happen?' he said.

'I'm not sure. Whoever broke in must have struck shortly after we left this evening.'

'Did they take anything?'

'All the doorframes have been destroyed.'

Ethan swallowed hard.

'Do you think someone found out about our meeting with Sally and James?' she said.

There was a long silence.

'Uma,' he finally said. 'They're both dead.'

'That's not possible.' Her voice was tight with incredulity. And something else—fear. 'I just saw them off. How do you know?'

'It was on the news. Their Jeep crashed on Route 41.'

'They're dead?'

'There was a fire. The Jeep exploded. Nobody survived.'

'Ethan, what's going on?' She sounded panic-stricken. 'How could this be? Has someone found out what we're doing?'

'I don't know. None of it makes any sense. I was thinking of coming over. Once the police make the connection, they're going to be all over you and the lab.'

'They were already here when I arrived.'

Ethan groaned inwardly. How had they moved so fast?

'I'll go to your father's house then. When can you get there?'

'That might not be possible.' Uma's voice had acquired a note of caution. He could hear muffled voices in the background but, seconds later, she was back on the line. 'The police are there as well. They came to pick me up after I got the call about the offices. I thought it was strange at the time, but maybe they already know I was with James and Sally this afternoon.'

'Just stay put. You're in the best place,' he said. 'I'll still head out now. If I leave for the airport in the next thirty minutes, I can be in Reykjavík by midnight.'

'What do I say if they ask about James and Sally?'

'The truth. We were helping them with an Anglo-American story on Internet security. That's perfectly feasible considering my current profile, plus they must know that you and I have been working together for twelve months now. We've absolutely nothing to hide.'

'You're right.' She sounded more relaxed. 'Where do I go afterwards? Suppose I'm next on the list.'

'Unlikely,' Ethan said. 'If whoever is behind this wants to hurt you, they have had plenty of opportunities already. They're either trying to scare us off or slow us down. I think we're both safe for the time being.' Ethan sensed Uma was not reassured and tried a different tack. 'Call Baldursson.'

'Fredrik?'

'He was a close friend of your father's.'

'I'm not sure it's his area.'

'Who cares? He said his job was to protect you, that he owed that much to your father. Now's his chance.'

'OK, that makes sense.' Uma sounded relieved. 'I'll try him now.' The phone line went quiet again, but almost immediately, Uma was back. 'Ethan, I have to go. The police want to talk to me.'

Ethan shut his phone and stared at the smooth metal door that had slid silently back into place during their brief conversation—there was no way he could use LEAP if the offices and the house were swarming with police. They might be there for hours. His back prickled at the thought of something happening to Uma whilst he was here, sat in London, waiting for them to leave. It was that same feeling of helplessness after he'd lost his parents. That he could have done something differently but hadn't. The problem was that if he flew now, he wouldn't get to her until after midnight. At least she was with the police, but he couldn't help thinking that whoever had the resources to kill off two of the West's most recognisable journalists would probably not be deterred by local law enforcement. Baldursson had been a good idea; he ran a Special Unit that supported the police on dangerous operations. If Uma managed to get hold of him, he might be able to provide an armed escort for her. The thought of guns made his mind up. He hurried down the steep steps, two at a time, firing off instructions to Jill.

'Call Brett Adams. I need a ride to the airport. Then get hold of Robin Greg. Tell him to ready the Challenger for an immediate trip to Iceland. I want to leave within the hour.'

By now he was standing in a tiny room at the end of the first-floor landing. It was dominated by a black-and-white photograph hung opposite a thin mattress that lay against one wall. The picture was over five feet across and depicted a couple in their early thirties staring into the camera. Both were laughing, their eyes almost shut tight with merriment. Ethan couldn't bring himself to look and instead busied himself with his mattress, removing the thin sheet and rolling it up before tying the light foam with twine. He tucked it under one arm and swiped his thumb over a blank light-switch plate. A vertical crack appeared in the wall, which soundlessly enlarged as two partitions glided apart to reveal the rest of Ethan's bedroom. A battered writing desk sat in the large bay window overlooking the main road and he made his way over to the only other piece of furniture in the room, an early Victorian combination wardrobe that the outgoing owners had sold him seven years earlier. He grabbed a small leather holdall, into which he threw jeans, several shirts, underwear, socks, a thick waterproof fleece and gloves. As he finished, there was a timid knock on the open door. It was Georgina Carr, his resident caretaker, chef and housekeeper, come to tell him that his ride to the airport had arrived.

Traffic out of central London was in its usual state of crawling indifference to the collective impatience of both early evening commuters and one particularly anxious passenger. Ethan forced himself to concentrate on e-mails and missed calls whilst he fought with visions of Uma surprising the intruders that had wrecked her offices. It never seemed to end well. Each outcome left him with a knot in his stomach and nursing a cold sweat. He willed time to move faster, but it seemed to stand still, along with the cars ahead.

At 21:18, the limo pulled up outside the gates of PCA, a private charter company that leased Rae Enterprises a berth for the Bombardier Challenger 800. Ethan was soon twisting and turning through a maze of metal and concrete that the driver of their small two-seater electric buggy navigated with weary familiarity. Eventually, the buildings gave way to open tarmac and shortly he was standing inside a cavernous hangar, shaking hands with Robin Greg, his pilot. Conversation was impossible above the roar of two rear-mounted GE CF34-3B1 turbo-fan engines, so they walked in silence over to the mobile stairwell, where an immigration official cleared their paperwork. The two men hurried up the narrow metal stairs into the sleek interior of the business jet airliner. As the door locked shut, the sudden silence calmed Ethan. They would be in Iceland within three hours. His optimism was short-lived.

'Boss, we may have a problem,' Robin announced. 'There's a nasty weather system heading towards southern Iceland. All flights into and out of Keflavík are moving freely at the moment, but it may not last.'

Ethan groaned with frustration. Had he made the wrong decision? Should he stay in London and wait till the storm cleared?

'What do you suggest we do?'

'There's not much we can do, other than monitor air-traffic control for further updates,' Robin said.

'Can we beat it?'

'We might slip through if we leave now.'

'Let's do it,' Ethan said, heading towards the rear of the plane, through the office-cum-meeting room and into the dining area, where he threw his travel bag and mattress into a corner before settling into a large, soft, brown-leather armchair.

'Can I get you anything more substantial to eat, sir?' enquired his flight attendant, who placed a selection of canapés beside him. Ethan suddenly realised how hungry he was and ordered a tuna salad before booting up a recessed screen that silently dropped to eye level. Already, his inbox was groaning under the weight of yet more e-mails, but once again he found work impossible. Instead, his thoughts drifted twelve hundred miles north to the woman who had changed his life forever in the twelve short months he had known her.

Reykjavík Technical College, Reykjavík

Thirteen Months Earlier

4 October 2002, 15:00 hours GMT

Whenever she looked up from the lectern, her dark green eyes burned a swathe across the audience. Ethan glanced down at his programme notes.

"Think Big, Dream Bigger. Presented by Uma Jakobsdóttir, Head of Geothermal Studies, Reykjavík University."

The name sounded familiar, but he couldn't recall where he had seen it before. It was obviously Icelandic. So was her accent. With a hint of somewhere else?

"Geothermal" sounded interesting, though. He ringed the word and scribbled, "investment opportunity?" beside it, before turning back to the lecture.

'It sounds crazy, but you've only got two choices with this sort of science. If I wanted to get from London to New York for a dinner date, I'd either have to make a copy of myself or somehow transport everything. Personally, I don't like the copying idea. For a start, it wouldn't be very practical to have hundreds of "me" charging around. I'm sure my dinner date wouldn't appreciate it either.'

Laughter rippled around the packed auditorium. Uma Jakobsdóttir glanced up from her podium position in the main lecture hall of the Reykjavík Technical College. Her unseeing gaze swept over Ethan, who, as one of the judges, was afforded a front-row seat at the launch of the fifth annual I-ce Fest competition—a fund-raising event for Iceland's burgeoning ranks of tech entrepreneurs.

'On a more serious note, it's not remotely practical to follow the copy route—if you provided every man and woman in the Western World with the means to travel to and from work using teleportation, within twelve months you would add another hundred billion people to our planet. That's a sixteen-fold increase in our population. In just one year! Regardless of which option you choose, both present some considerable challenges. Not least, the quantity of information to be scanned and sent. Take me, for instance. I weigh about one hundred and ten pounds or, approximately, fifty kilos. That represents about ...'

Uma half turned towards the screen behind her, where a number appeared: 280,000,000,000,000,000,000,000,000,000.

'That many atoms of matter. For those of you who can't count that fast, I will save you the trouble. That's two hundred and eighty, followed by twenty-seven zeros. That's octillions of atoms which are "me" and have to be transported. To put this into perspective, if we performed the transport using the fastest broadband on the market, it would take over one hundred million centuries to transport me from London to New York. By the time I got there, my dinner guest would have long departed this earth, as would the restaurant, probably the Big Apple and maybe even the continent we currently call North America!'

More laughter echoed round the cavernous room, its steep sides carrying the audience high into the roof structure. As they settled down, a loud ping in the front row caused people on either side of Ethan to glance over, some shaking their heads. He quickly turned the phone to vibrate as the text announced itself again.

'Jarvis knows about 4Tel.'

As Ethan absorbed the message from his deal manager back in London, he could feel Uma's stare pinned to his forehead.

'Offer him London,' he typed, and as he pressed send, Ethan finally risked a glance towards the lectern. As their eyes locked for the briefest moment, he knew she had been waiting for him to look up, willing to delay the lecture until she had communicated her contempt for his interruption. Message delivered, Uma continued as if nothing had happened.

'Let's assume for one second that speed of teleportation isn't an issue. We still have to get me there in one piece, which is no easy feat. Whatever scans me and reassembles me has to locate the position of every single atom in my body to ensure that it replicates them at the other end. That represents a massive amount of computations, since each one of my 280 octillion atoms will require three measurements to ascertain its position. Currently, the fastest known supercomputer, IBM's Blue Gene/L, can perform 70.7 trillion simultaneous calculations per second, but it would still take five thousand years to process all the information that constitutes "me".

'Besides which, the real issue here is neither the speed of transmission nor computational power. The big challenge is overcoming a very long-standing principle of quantum mechanics, called the Uncertainty Principle. It was first proposed by Werner Heisenberg, who worked out that no one can know both the position and the speed of an atom simultaneously. In a teleporting sense, this is very problematic since it means you can never perform a perfect scan of my body. The very act of scanning me to find out the location and speed of every particle in my body would disrupt the original state of each particle, to such a degree that it would be impossible to extract sufficient useful information about each particle. If you can't extract sufficient information to make a perfect copy of me, then, the thinking goes, it would be impossible to make a perfect copy. In other words, the copy would be subject to errors. So, whilst I might arrive at my dinner date, I could look like Seth Brundle in *The Fly*.' A black-and-white still of Jeff Goldblum appeared behind Uma. Or at least what was left of him following his transformation in the famous movie of 1986.

As the audience once again erupted into laughter, Ethan felt his phone vibrate with a new message.

'He wants the South.'

'No. Just London.' He tapped out.

'Fortunately, scientists have overcome Heisenberg's predictions—quite some time ago, in fact. Einstein first observed it back in the 1930s and, for a long time, we knew it as the EPR effect, after the three individuals who discovered it—Einstein, Podolsky and Rosen. Einstein called it *"spooky action at a distance"*. He was referring to entanglement, a quirk of quantum theory he himself admitted, defied explanation using the classical laws of physics. In brief, they discovered a way to scan out part of the information from an object they wanted to transport. Not all of it, so that it didn't contravene the Uncertainty Principle, but enough to ensure that the information about its state was preserved intact.

'This is the "spooky" bit that Einstein referred to—the fact that entanglement could occur over any distance. From a teleportation perspective, this is really very useful. If I was trying to get from London to New York and went to my teleportation pod, it would scan me to measure the position and speed of each of my particles. That information could be transmitted to New York and instantly recreated in the entangled particle in New York. If this was subsequently entangled with further atoms, my atomic state could be recreated in New York.

'However, there is one unfortunate downside with entanglement. At the point the second pair of objects are entangled, the original object—me, in this instance—is destroyed. In one sense, that is clearly a good thing. It solves the inherent and practical problem of zillions of copies of me and others populating the earth.'

Ethan saw the reply as his phone vibrated silently.

'The South or he walks.'

Ethan smiled. Even over text he knew Jarvis was bluffing. It didn't matter that they'd discovered he was also buying their biggest competitor, effectively handing Ethan control of the UK market. Jarvis was short on cash. By Ethan's calculations, they had twenty days left. They couldn't afford to walk.

'Let him,' he replied, before turning back to Uma.

'Having said that, it causes all sorts of ethical issues. First, has the teleportation company committed murder, and second, if the original is destroyed, what has happened to my soul? Is that also reproduced in the person who has been reassembled in New York or is the new me purely a physical copy? If just a physical copy, then has something essential been lost in the transfer? Something that is not atom based, and the loss of which makes the New York "me" a lesser being than the original?'

Uma paused for dramatic effect. No one was laughing now. In fact, you could hear a pin drop in the enormous lecture hall as she continued.

'Arguably, murder would be very difficult to prove, especially if I suddenly presented myself to a police station in New York within seconds of disappearing in London. Even using the latest identification techniques, you would be hard pushed to deny the New York "me" was not the original London "me". My DNA would match, as would my fingerprints. If you performed an iris scan, you would find they matched, as would all other visible means of identification, such as a tattoo or even an appendix scar. All would be faithfully and perfectly reproduced by the transportation. As for my soul, how do you prove that something has been destroyed, or transferred when it still has not scientifically been proven to exist in the first place?

'I would argue there is no soul. We are just a bunch of atoms, like every other thing on this planet. There is nothing unique about us at all. We are comprised of just three elements: oxygen, carbon and nitrogen. In fact, I would go even further—' As Uma took a long drink of her water, Ethan's phone lit up.

'Jarvis has left the building!'

'He'll be back,' Ethan tapped out, impressed at the double bluff. He could imagine the argument unfolding amongst the Jarvis team as they debated their choices: either lose the entire business or accept thirty million, a seventy-five percent discount on its book value. No wonder they wanted to keep the South. It was the only profitable part of the company.

'—there is no higher being at work dictating what is happening on earth. It's our atoms doing that, and the things that define us individually, to ourselves and others, have nothing to do with God. At an atomic level, their composition is straightforward. They're just cells. Cells contain molecules which, in turn, comprise atoms. Whatever you choose, we return to atoms. They're the building blocks of everything, not God.'

'It's an abomination!' The shout came from the right-hand side of the lecture theatre and, as one, everyone turned to see who was making the disturbance. 'It's an abomination. What you suggest is an abomination. It's an affront to the grace of God.'

The voice had suddenly been magnified tenfold, thundering off the steep sides of the theatre. It made everyone jump, including Ethan. As excited chatter swept the auditorium, he stood up along with half the audience to get a better glimpse of who had interrupted the lecture. A long-haired man appeared in the central aisle. Dressed entirely in white, he ran towards the stage holding a microphone. As the man reached the front row, he leapt onto the low stage and, within three bounds, stood towering over Uma.

'Ladies and gentlemen, don't listen to this poison. It's the work of the Devil,' the man thundered at the audience before turning to glare down at Uma with wild eyes. 'She is one of Satan's messengers,' he continued, pointing at her. 'Only God has the power to appear before anyone, anywhere, at any time.'

Uma glared up at the intruder, her fists curled into tight balls. As the man turned towards the audience, she took a step towards him. *Christ, she's going to hit him,* Ethan thought, as a giant of a man appeared in the main aisle with two attendants. He was powerfully built, with jet-black hair, buzz-cut short, and dressed in faded military fatigues. All three of them leapt onto the stage, surrounding the invader, who continued to rant.

'We are not spirits or wraiths who can move at will around the earth. That was never intended by the Almighty. We are—'

His booming voice was suddenly cut off as one of the attendants grabbed him from behind. The man jerked his head back into the attendant's face, who collapsed to the stage with a howl of pain. Uma leapt at the man, catching him a glancing blow with her fist. With a scream, he pushed her away and drew his arm back to punch her. A guttural roar echoed through the auditorium as the giant grabbed the intruder by his coat and swung him in a wide circle off the stage.

Ethan never stood a chance as two hundred pounds of flailing limbs smashed into his midriff. He felt a blinding pain across the back of his skull as they both crashed to the floor, scattering chairs, glasses, bottles and fleeing bodies like bowling pins. Snowflakes whirled across his vision as Ethan curled into a ball. It was instinctive, driven by muscle memory from another lifetime: get hit, go down, curl up. It would lessen the beating, limit the damage. He lay there, eyes screwed shut, arms shielding his face, but he felt no kicks to the head. No blows rained down on his back or legs.

Just the scorch of the midday sun burning his skin.

Hot sand scratching his face.

The ever-present dust choking his lungs.

Seconds passed, before Ethan peered through his fingers, searching for his attackers. They always attacked in pairs, waiting until he was alone: in the toilets, sometimes the shower block or even the medical centre.

Get hit, go down, curl up. It was good advice.

But he couldn't see them. He could only see a giant dragging a thrashing figure by one leg down a central aisle towards the rear of a large theatre. A woman was standing over him. She looked familiar. Sparkling eyes, framed by a riot of jet-black hair. She was saying something. Ethan frowned, wondering what she was doing there.

Ethan struggled into a sitting position as Uma knelt down beside him.

'Mr Rae, are you OK?'

Ethan stared at her stupidly, wondering how she knew his name. Behind her, on a raised dais, a man with a microphone was announcing that the lecture had finished. Around him, groans echoed out as people began leaving their seats. A phone vibrated on the floor beside Ethan and the familiar buzz jolted him back into the auditorium: the lecture, Uma, the crazed attacker, Jarvis!

He grabbed his mobile but then thought better of it. The deal could wait for now. He needed to clear his head. Ethan hadn't had an episode like this in years, and the experience was deeply unsettling. He'd worked hard to bury his past, but getting hit had shaken something loose, the memories bubbling up from the deepest recesses of his mind like an awakening leviathan.

'Umi,' a voice boomed behind them. Ethan turned with a start, whilst Uma jumped to her feet with delight as an imposing figure came barrelling towards them—the giant. He gathered Uma up in a bear hug.

'Fredrik,' she said. 'Are you OK?'

'Of course,' he bellowed, putting her down. 'But what about you?'

'I'm fine, Fredrik.' She clenched both hands into tight fists like a shadow boxer.

'And him?' the giant nodded at Ethan.

'Just winded,' Ethan said, struggling to his feet with the help of Uma, who had a surprisingly strong grip. He lingered, suddenly aware of her soft skin, cool on his flustered skin.

'Can I have my hand back, please?' he heard her say, but she didn't withdraw it either.

'Of course.' Ethan let go and their eyes met. She was smiling at him, her lips pursed mischievously, as if she knew what had just happened. Ethan glanced at the giant who seemed completely oblivious to their exchange. What had just happened? He felt different but couldn't understand why and then suddenly, he realised: the memories had faded away. How had she done that? An attack would normally stay with him for hours, lingering on the outskirts of his mind, waiting to pounce again.

'Mr Rae, can I introduce you to Chief Inspector Baldursson,' Uma said. 'He's an old friend of my father's.'

'And you are?' The enormous man glared down at Ethan.

'Ethan Rae,' he said, pulling his gaze away from Uma, 'I'm an investor.'

The large man looked unimpressed.

'He's not another environmentalist, is he?' Baldursson said, turning to Uma in alarm. 'Please tell me you're not going to be chaining yourself to any more whaling ships?'

'Of course, he isn't,' Uma said, blushing slightly. 'Besides, that was a long time ago.'

Baldursson visibly relaxed and shook Ethan's hand with a vice-like grip.

'I'm sorry. Old habits die hard. You know how responsible I feel for you. Always have and always will. I owe Jakob that much.'

The name sounded familiar to Ethan, but he couldn't pin it down.

'Who's Jakob?' Ethan said.

'He's a legend in Iceland, that's who he is,' Baldursson said. 'I, on the other hand, am an overweight public servant whose best years are behind him.' He patted his ample stomach and guffawed.

'Rubbish, Fredrik. Papa said you were the sharpest mind he had ever met outside academia. President Reagan certainly seemed to think so.'

'Reagan?' Ethan's brain was behaving like a deflated balloon.

'The one and only. He tried to recruit Fredrik into the CIA.'

Baldursson grinned from ear to ear as Uma continued.

'Papa helped broker the Reykjavík non-nuclear arms proliferation summit between Russia and America back in '86. Fredrik and his team were in charge of co-ordinating security for the weekend and worked closely alongside Papa.'

Ethan's phone buzzed again, but he ignored it, trying to piece the conversation together. The words meant something important, but they were scattered across his mind like an unfinished jigsaw: the nuclear connection, Reagan, his Christian name, Jakob, the '86 talks.

'Mr Rae, you're hurt,' Uma exclaimed, pointing at his hand. 'It's covered in blood.'

Ethan looked down and, sure enough, there was a deep cut in his left palm. He hadn't even noticed it but now she'd pointed it out, he began to hurt like hell.

'Here, let me look at that.' Uma inspected his hand.

Ethan stood there, remembering their last touch, although this time it felt different. Uma was business-like, binding his hand expertly with a handkerchief from her pocket.

'There. You'll live,' Uma said. She was staring at her fingers and Ethan could have sworn a smile flickered across her face before being replaced by a concerned frown. She wiped her hand with a tissue from her jeans, which she pocketed. 'But it needs cleaning,' she continued. 'I have a first-aid box in my office.'

'It's fine,' Ethan said. He suddenly felt exhausted and remembered that he still had to close the deal. 'I think I'll just go back to my hotel. It's a tiny cut. They can treat it there.'

'OK, but where are you staying?' Uma sounded slightly panicked.

'The Saga.'

'That's right across town. My office is directly opposite the lecture theatre.'

Ethan made to protest, but Uma cut in.

'Nonsense, Mr Rae. I feel responsible for this. It's no problem.'

'If it's all right with you two, I've got someone to interrogate. You,' Baldursson growled at Uma good naturedly, 'please stay out of trouble. Mr Rae, it was a pleasure.'

He turned and bellowed some orders at two men by the entrance before striding purposefully down the aisle.

Ethan stared at Uma. He really didn't have time for this. The Jarvis deal still needed closing, but something made him pause. He couldn't put his finger on it. One of his famous hunches, maybe? They'd served him well over the years. Besides which, something about this Jakobsdóttir woman intrigued him. Particularly the whole teleportation thing. What had that lecture really been about? And then their connection just now. It hadn't just been him. She had noticed it as well. He was sure of that. The thought of being around Uma filled him with an anxious anticipation that he hadn't felt before.

'If you're sure?'

'No problem at all.' She seemed nervous, as if afraid he would change his mind.

His phone buzzed like an angry bee.

'Are you going to take that?' she said, her voice challenging him.

Ethan smiled.

'No, it can wait,' he said, pocketing the mobile.

'Good. Let's go then.' Uma grabbed Ethan by the forearm and led him away towards the back of the stage.

Department of Geothermal Studies, Reykjavík

4 October 2002, 16:00 hours GMT

E than peered out of the doorway into the dark street. The building opposite was barely visible through the sheeting rain, which was bouncing waist high off the road in front of him. Returning to the hotel in a taxi was beginning to look like the better option, but Uma had other ideas. With a shriek, she grabbed his hand and plunged into the storm. It was like stepping into a shower and his grip on Uma's hand, suddenly slick wet, was lost as she raced across the street. By the time he had followed her up the steps and through the door, he was soaked through. What's more, Uma was nowhere to be seen. As his eyes adjusted to the gloom, he could just make out a wide staircase, at the foot of which was an ornate table covered in office equipment. To his right, an open door spilled weak light onto hard marble. However, the strangest sight was in front of him. A shimmering column seemed to hover just above the floor. Its base was wide, maybe five feet across, but as it rose upwards, it tapered off like an inverted ice-cream cone to a point that Ethan couldn't see in the blackness above.

'Are you there?' Ethan called out, but the only reply was his echoing voice. Where the hell was she? Suddenly, the great hall lit up, and seconds later, Uma appeared through the open doorway. As she approached, Ethan realised her clothes were just as sodden as his. The cotton of her white shirt was plastered tight against her skin, the outline of her breasts clearly visible through the translucent material.

Ethan dropped his gaze hurriedly, unsure where to look.

'You're drenched,' he mumbled to the floor.

'I'm fine.' Uma tugged at the sodden black beret under which she had crammed her thick hair. Liberated from the tiny hat, it sprang out in all directions. 'I'll soon dry out.'

Ethan busied himself with a detailed study of the cone in the centre of the hall. It was even taller in the harsh glare of the lights, perhaps thirty feet high, tapering off to a sharp point, its tip almost level with the second balcony. On the plinth surrounding its base was an inscription: *The Age of Man*.

'How does that represent man?' he said.

'It's one of Papa's little jokes. The age of the earth is represented in white and man's in red.'

'But there isn't any red!'

'I think that was his point.' She motioned for Ethan to follow her up the broad stairs and as they climbed, he tracked the progress of the tall statue. It appeared to be metallic, painted white, its matt surface gleaming dully in the bright lights. As they reached the second-floor landing, Ethan realised its tip was just twelve inches below the level of the railing. He could easily have leant out and touched it. But he still couldn't see any red. Just a razor-sharp point.

Uma stopped in front of a large oak-panelled door on which the name "Uma Jakobsdóttir, Head of Geothermal Studies" was inscribed in large, gold lettering. To their left was a large portrait of a middle-aged man gazing out towards the cone. His face was partly obscured by steam pouring from a geyser held in his outstretched hands. Ethan read the caption.

'The springs of life—from one generation to the next. In fond memory of Jakob Arnasson. Head of Geothermal Studies. Reykjavík University. 1925-2001.'

Suddenly, the pieces of the jigsaw that had puzzled him earlier snapped into place. How could he have missed it?

'Your dad was Jakob Arnasson?'

'You knew him?'

'Not personally, no. I've been researching geothermal to understand the commercial viability of green projects. Your father was a pioneer.' Ethan's instincts had not let him down. The fact that Uma was related felt like the icing on the cake.

'Is that why you're here at I-ce Fest?' Uma said.

'Partly. Green energy will be the next big thing, so that's my focus.'

'Are you looking for a fast buck, like every other VC here?'

'Not really. I prefer the long game.'

'Well, from what I've seen, that makes you quite an unusual breed, Mr Rae,' Uma said, her face lighting up with a wide smile. 'Come, let's get that cut seen to.' She swiped a card across a small panel beside the door. There was an audible click, and they stepped inside.

'Wait here whilst I get the first-aid kit.'

She disappeared through a door at the far end of the room, leaving Ethan alone again. He suddenly felt bone weary and made his way over to an oversized office chair beside a large desk littered with office paraphernalia. As he collapsed into the soft leather seat, his phone buzzed angrily, and as he pulled it from his pocket, the thought of Jarvis revived him slightly.

'The Jarvis team has just appeared in reception.'

Ethan smiled, despite his fatigue. Once he combined their business with 4Tel, he would control the UK market. It would add millions to his net profit and, in turn, feed the charities. A brief surge of contentment washed through his veins, even as he realised it would never be enough. But what choice did he have?

As he pocketed the mobile, a familiar logo caught his eye. Frowning, he picked up a Rae Enterprises brochure from a pile of papers on the desk. Beneath it was a folder with his name scrawled on the cover. That was strange. He glanced in the direction that Uma had disappeared before leafing through the thick file. It was stuffed with press cuttings about his various companies, including several interviews he had given last year about his new focus on the environment as an investment opportunity.

An icy chill slid through his guts. Why was this woman stalking him? Grabbing the folder, he stormed across the office then paused at the door. It was slightly ajar and through the crack he could see Uma sitting at a desk, tapping away on a computer keyboard, the bloody tissue by her side. She looked round as the door creaked open and gasped as Ethan held up the file.

'What the hell is this?' he said, stepping into the room, but he didn't get far. Something was restraining him. It felt as if he had been submerged in a bath of thick molasses. Ethan glanced down to see what was holding him back, but there was nothing. He was now completely unable to move, his neck inclined at a forty-five-degree angle towards the floor.

Black specks danced across his eyes as he desperately tried to move, but it was no use and he felt himself falling, except that he wasn't falling. He was frozen to the spot, his heavy limbs unable to respond.

The memory of a clear summer evening flooded back to him. He was in a Jeep. It was dark. He was laughing at something his mum had said. He couldn't remember exactly what. A blinding light appeared. And then, suddenly, he was flying through the air. Ethan's silent trajectory had carried him high into the night sky. Towards the warm white surface of a full moon before, finally, losing momentum. The black earth had rushed up to meet him as he plunged towards the cold, hard tarmac below and then ... nothing. Just blackness.

Unknown Destination

4 October 2002, 18:10 hours EDT

When Ethan came to, he was lying on a couch in a room he didn't recognise. Through the partially drawn blinds, he could see the warm glow of a setting sun. Not the dark wet night he had experienced less than ... he glanced at his watch. Ten o'clock? He had entered the Department with Uma at about nine. One hour ago. That didn't make sense: Iceland was in virtual darkness twenty hours a day at this time of year. He attempted to sit up but collapsed back onto the couch as waves of pain split his skull in protest at the sudden movement. He groaned in submission and shut his eyes, massaging his throbbing temples. That was strange; his fingers traced the outline of a thick gauze bandage wrapped around his head. He winced as he felt an egg-shaped lump just above his right ear. He closed his eyes to regulate the pain, which seemed to work.

The last thing he remembered was walking through a doorway in the lab, holding a folder stuffed full of articles about him and then ... nothing. As hard as he tried, he couldn't recall the last hour. Maybe he had blacked out or fainted? That seemed likely, given his aching head, but it didn't explain where he was or how he had got here. He heard a door open and close softly. Footsteps coming towards him. Ethan opened his eyes, wincing as the dim light burned his sore retinas.

It was Uma. She had changed out of the sodden clothes from earlier and was now dressed in jeans, biker boots, and a pale cotton shirt.

'Thank God you're awake.' She sounded relieved. 'I was beginning to worry you had a serious concussion.'

'Why are you stalking me?' Ethan demanded. 'Where am I?'

'I'm not stalking you. What you saw in my office was research to identify the best investment partner to take my discovery to market. As for your second question, see for yourself.' She nodded at the window. Ethan stared at the light seeping into the office and tried to stand up, but immediately sank back down onto the couch, groaning in pain.

'OK, Mr Rae. Steady on. You need to take it easy for a while. Let the effects of the jump wear off.'

Ethan ignored her and hauled his lanky frame off the couch. Bad idea. His head spun. He felt nauseous. Uma tried to help him, but he waved her aside and slowly made his way over to the window. Uma followed him and drew the blinds back.

They were high up. Fifty floors at least, with views of a river in the foreground, framing the unmistakable outline of the Statue of Liberty in the distance. Ethan frowned. Directly below them was a vast construction site covering three, maybe four blocks. On the far side, a large ramp sloped steeply into a chaos of concrete, cranes and metal that littered the vast crater. A procession of enormous trucks slowly snaked their way towards the base of the ramp, whilst construction workers, the size of ants, swarmed everywhere. Even from this distance, Ethan recognised the site as Ground Zero on the southern tip of Manhattan Island. He staggered back to the couch, his mind whirling. How had she transported him to New York City?

Uma remained by the window, staring at the scene below. A full minute passed before Ethan spoke. 'That's impossible,' he said, nodding at the vista. 'The last thing I remember was standing in your office.'

'And then you walked through a door before I was ready. And fell over. You caught your head on a table.'

Ethan scowled at her.

'Look, lady, I'm not in the mood for your games. I've a splitting headache and feel like shit. What the hell is going on?'

'It's the only way I could demonstrate my discovery to you. By actually having you use it for yourself. Otherwise, you would never have believed me.'

'What are you talking about? How did you even get me here?'

'I teleported you,' she said simply.

It was Ethan's turn to laugh. She was mad. A mad stalker.

'You're serious, aren't you?' he said. 'How do you expect me to believe this nonsense?'

Uma glanced at the window.

'So what?' he said. 'That doesn't mean a thing. You could have flown me over from Reykjavík after I knocked myself out last night. Flights into Manhattan leave regularly from Keflavík airport and take, what, five hours?'

'But you knocked yourself out here in New York. You were conscious when you left my office. But let's say I flew you over without you realising any of it. How do you explain that it's still Friday, 4 October? If I had flown you, it would now be Saturday afternoon. It's still Friday afternoon here in New York—six fifteen to be exact; ten fifteen in Reykjavík. Look at your watch if you don't believe me.'

He didn't need to.

'You could have changed it,' he said.

'What about your hand? It's still bandaged from your fall in the theatre. That's a fresh cut. How much more proof do you need?'

Ethan looked down. Sure enough, Uma's bloody handkerchief was wrapped round his aching hand. Uma sensed a chink in Ethan's resistance and grabbed a remote control from the table. The TV in the corner of the room sprang into life and she changed channels to a local news station.

'You could have recorded that yesterday.' Ethan was getting impatient. During their exchange, he had remembered the Jarvis deal. It was going to close today, and whilst his team back in London were more than capable, he always liked to attend the completion meeting. It was the only time he felt any sense of satisfaction, until it had ended, of course. And then he would focus his mind on the future, the deal already forgotten. Consigned to the past. He never dwelt on the past. It was too painful. He just kept moving forward to the next deal.

Ethan stared at Uma, wondering if she was a part of his future. Earlier, he had definitely felt a connection, and the memory both excited and terrified him in equal measure. But now that possibility seemed remote, given her deception and what she had just done to him. Either way, he needed to move on. That was what he was good at, and there was a simple way to prove that this was nothing more than a stunt. A very well executed one, but a stunt, nevertheless. Why was a different matter. He could solve that problem later.

'OK, then,' Ethan said. 'Let's assume you have cheated the classical laws of physics and can hop around the globe at will. Return me to Reykjavík now. That should be possible, right? If you can, then you have my full attention. If not, let me clean myself up. I will walk out of here today and you will never see me again.'

Uma beamed at him.

'Ah. Now you're thinking. I was beginning to think I had got the wrong Ethan Rae.'

The Interior, Iceland

4 October 2002, 23:00 hours GMT

Uma had carefully briefed Ethan this time, warning him about the gradual fade as the system prepared his body and also the risk of falling due to the transfer being instantaneous. Even so, the experience still took him completely by surprise. Suddenly, he found himself in a completely different room from the one he and Uma had entered shortly after their standoff in New York. One moment, he had been walking through an empty office and then he was somewhere else. The recovered momentum of his interrupted stride caused him to stagger forward as he entered the new room. Uma was ready this time.

Ethan fell into her arms, and once again he lingered, this time savouring the moment. He couldn't remember the last time he had been this close to a woman and was suddenly aware of all the wrong things. Her body pressed against his. Those thick curls tickling his face. His hand tightly gripping her shirt, which hours earlier, soaked through by the rain, had revealed more than he had seen in a long time. He was sure that Uma didn't resist, or maybe it was his wishful thinking. Either way, it suddenly felt way too awkward, and Ethan straightened up before turning away to examine his new surroundings. This room was nothing like the office he had recently vacated. It had been spacious, with a landscape view of the East River. This was windowless, with white walls that had a prefabricated feel to them. A row of bright fluorescent tubes bisected what was clearly a suspended ceiling. Ethan shivered involuntarily. The room was chilly after the warmth of Uma's Manhattan offices.

'Where are we now?' he said. Had she tricked him again? 'This doesn't feel like the Department of Geothermal Studies.'

'It isn't. We—'

'What do you mean?' Ethan said. 'You promised me no more tricks.'

'We're in Iceland. That's what I promised,' Uma said. 'I've brought you to the labs I set up with my father to fine-tune his discovery.'

'Your father! What's he got to do with this?'

'One thing at a time, Mr Rae. I will answer all your questions. But first we need to change into something a little warmer.'

Uma made her way down a short corridor into a much bigger area that contained an assortment of warm winter clothing, hung up neatly in designated bins. She expertly sized Ethan up and pointed him towards a changing stall hung with a selection of garments.

'My God,' Ethan said from behind the curtain, as he sorted the pile of clothes she had given him. 'Where are we? The Arctic Circle?'

'Not far off,' Uma said. 'It's called the Interior.'

'The where?'

'The Interior; it's a vast wilderness of lava and ice that continues for hundreds of miles right across Iceland. At this time of year, temperatures fall well below minus thirty degrees Celsius. So, I suggest you wrap up well.'

Ethan restrained himself. Although he couldn't deny they'd moved from one room to another, he hadn't been presented with any proof that she'd managed to jump him halfway across the world in the blink of an eye.

'So, why build it here, then?'

'Privacy. The Interior is virtually impassable for most of the year. What better place to hide a big secret?'

'Why hide it? A discovery like this?'

'There you go again, Mr Rae, with your questions. Let me show you your evidence, and then we can talk. Are you ready?'

Ethan was fully suited up and waddled unsteadily after Uma. By the time they reached a large circular revolving door cut into the fabric of the building, he was sweating freely. Uma hit a button, and the door smoothly disappeared to reveal a circular chamber into which they crowded. The door silently closed and dim halogen lights flickered into life above their heads. Seconds later, the external door slid open and they shuffled outside.

Ethan had not really been sure about what to expect, but the sight made him pause in mid-stride. It was as if he had entered the wrong room by accident. His first reaction was to turn round and re-enter the chamber, but the door had closed, forcing him to look back.

The clamour of the busiest city on earth had been silenced by a howling gale. The clutter of Manhattan's skyscrapers had been replaced by the endless expanse of open desert. The 700-foot elevation of Uma's office had been flattened to ground level.

Day had become night.

Sun had become moon.

Stars had replaced clouds.

The mosaic of colours, shapes and sounds visible from Uma's window, less than five minutes ago, had diminished to a dull icy grey that stretched beyond where white earth met black sky. The autumnal warmth had been frozen out by the chill of mid-winter. Snowy ghosts swirled across the exposed plain before them—some, slowly twisting and turning; others lazily floating just above the frozen landscape, whilst yet others scurried across the surface.

Ethan shuffled forward into the unforgiving landscape. Above him, the harsh lunar glow had turned darkness into an eerie half daylight. He slowly turned, absorbing the contrasts of the two environments half a world apart, and stopped to study the building they had just emerged from—the white single-storey structure was maybe forty feet in length and almost invisible against the icy backdrop of the desert plain.

He felt a sharp tug on his arm and turned to face Uma, his own image eerily reflected in the black mirror of her face mask. She was gesturing back towards the chamber and, once she was certain Ethan had understood, she awkwardly made her way over to the door and banged against the side of the unit. A hole appeared, and she stumbled in, Ethan close behind.

Back inside the changing room, they removed their garments in silence. Ethan's mind whirled with unanswered questions. He didn't even know how to phrase the technical ones and felt quite certain he wouldn't be able to understand the answers. It didn't matter: early man didn't understand the properties of fire, but it didn't stop them enjoying the benefits.

Unbidden, an image of his mother's laughing eyes appeared. She had loved science fiction and would endlessly read to him as a child. They had covered all the greats: *The War of the Worlds; 1984; I, Robot; Brave New World; The Day of the Triffids*. As he got older, they would read together, curled up in his parents' bed whilst his father was absent on one of his long trips. Or in front of a roaring fire wrapped in a thick blanket, snug against the worst a Scottish winter could throw at them. They read as one, finishing the page together and taking turns to flick over to the next. Afterwards, they would spend hours discussing what they'd read. His mother's favourite game was to imagine what they would have done if it was all real. How would they have escaped HG Wells' Martians? Or cope with Huxley's parentless nightmare? Or use Asimov's robots. He struggled to recall one about teleportation. She would have loved this moment. Fiction made fact. He felt a flush of shame at the memory—she was dead. Hot flicks of pain began to burn his back. Normally, he fought them, but today he embraced the familiar cuts with weary resignation. A fitting punishment for his foolish mistake. Dead is dead. The words sliced far deeper than the fifty cuts he had endured.

Uma looked on in horror as Ethan gripped the metal door of his locker, every sinew taut with pain.

'Mr Rae, are you OK?'

Ethan opened his eyes.

'Of course,' he said, straightening up.

'I just feel a little nauseous. It must be the jump.' He turned away and pulled a thick fleece up over his head. Uma gasped with shock; his back was a chaos of angry red scar tissue, some raised high, others running deep.

'Your back,' she managed.

'What about it?' he said, pulling his shirt down.

'It's—'

'It's nothing.' He turned away from Uma, steadying himself. 'I'm sorry,' he continued softly. 'I would rather not talk about it, if that's OK?'

'Of course,' Uma said, too shocked by what she had seen to argue.

'Good.' Ethan attempted a smile, but his face resisted, his lips contorting into a half-grimace. He shut out his mother with a practised determination and forced himself to think of the possibilities. The limitless uses to which he could put this ... discovery. He immediately felt better. It had become his mantra over the years: Look forward, never back. Back is bad. He couldn't change the past. But he could control the future. And Uma had just shown him the brightest one imaginable.

One Liberty Plaza, New York City

4 October 2002, 20:30 hours EDT

Ethan was standing in front of the huge office windows on the fifty-second floor of One Liberty Plaza. Vertical columns of shimmering lights surrounded them on all sides, in sharp contrast to the black horizontal void of the Hudson River that stretched away to the bright lights of Jersey City in the distance. Below, he could just make out the streaming red pinpricks of nose-to-tail traffic on the West Side Highway. The northbound vehicles were blocked by the sheer volume of their combined exodus into the Holland Tunnel, whilst the opposite carriageway was similarly motionless, also gridlocked by the bottlenecks around the Brooklyn Battery Tunnel. From this distance, that was the only evidence of human activity on the ground, but as Ethan and Uma had discovered on their short walk back to the office from their hurried hotdog, the city was bustling with activity. As they'd slowly made their way down Fulton Street, early evening crowds had thronged the pavement. Conversation had been impossible, and they'd not really spoken until now. Ethan turned to face Uma, who was watching him from the couch where he had recovered consciousness less than three hours earlier.

'Why me?' Ethan said.

'You're right, Mr Rae. I could have chosen any number of people to help me, but I like the way you do business.'

'In what way?'

'You've geared your entire business to helping others less fortunate.'

'Go on,' Ethan said, experiencing the familiar unease whenever someone talked about his charities. If only she knew the half of it.

'It's unusual to give away nearly everything you make. Especially for a VC.'

Ethan stayed silent as eels of pain slithered up his back.

'It's why I approached you, Mr Rae.'

'And how does my charitable giving relate to—' Ethan paused, realising he didn't have a name for what Uma had just shown him.

'Papa christened it LEAP.'

'LEAP,' Ethan repeated. It had a nice ring.

'I want you to get this technology to as many people as you can in as short a time as possible.'

'And how do you expect me to do that?' he said. 'Give it away?'

Uma nodded.

'That's an unworkable business model,' he exclaimed.

'It seems to have worked well for you,' Uma said, frowning. 'How much are you worth, Mr Rae? Thirty billion pounds?'

'You've got this back to front. To give away money, you need to make money. One feeds the other, and I would approach LEAP in the same way.'

'Well, this needs to be free.' Uma folded her arms, her eyes now narrowed dangerously, lips pursed. Ethan had seen that look earlier, in the auditorium, when she had confronted the stage invader.

'But there's no need to,' Ethan repeated. 'I already have a few ideas about how we can launch this out to the market. You will make billions. No one will be able to compete.'

'This isn't about making money, Mr Rae,' Uma said. 'I want to stop mankind from destroying the planet.'

Ethan couldn't believe he hadn't seen it earlier. That blow to his head must have really scrambled his brain. No wonder she had chosen him, with his new found green credentials.

'I never took you for a greeny.' But even as he said it, he remembered Uma's exchange with the fat policeman in the auditorium. Something about being chained to a whaling ship. And her father's focus on renewable power. Of course, she was green. As green as they come.

'This isn't the '60s,' Uma said. 'The Green movement has moved on. Besides, you hardly fit the profile of a committed environmentalist.'

'Because I'm not,' he said.

'But why else would you get involved in all this green technology?'

'So I can—'

'—make money.'

'Its time has come,' he said. 'The vast majority of people are locked into their carbon-based lifestyles, even if they care about the environment. The only way you can wean everyone off carbon is if we price the alternatives low enough—look at what your father managed with geothermal.'

'Precisely. That's why we need to give it away. In that way, every person and business on this planet can travel anywhere, any time of day, without ever having to set foot inside a plane, train, ship or car ever again. We will also give it away to every manufacturer and distributor so—'

The double doors to the office suddenly flew open and a woman burst in, followed by Uma's secretary.

'I'm sorry, you can't come in here,' fussed the PA. 'Miss Jakobsdóttir asked not to be disturbed.' She placed a restraining hand on the arm of the surprise guest, who whirled round.

'Don't you dare touch me!' the woman screamed at the PA. 'I swear to God, I'll have you arrested if you do that again. Now, where's my sister?'

As she turned, Ethan was provided with his second shock in as many minutes. The intruder was the exact double of Uma; she had the same thick mane of black hair, green eyes, and diminutive stature.

The resemblance was uncanny, but so were the differences. Whereas Uma was dress-down casual, her twin was a study in sophistication in a full-length black suede coat with a high collar, open at the front to reveal a close-fitting grey silk trouser suit. Her hair was scraped back tightly by a huge silver clasp from which it burst out behind her shoulders. A sparkling necklace of bluish-purple stones offset the dark colours. They looked expensive. Everything did, including an oversized black leather handbag that she abandoned on the carpet. The effect accentuated her striking features, which were currently directed at Uma's PA.

'Look, if you don't leave, I will have to call security,' the secretary said, clearly uncertain whether she had overstepped her authority.

'Why, you little twerp!' the woman shouted, making as if to strike her. 'I'll see to it that you never set foot in this building again.'

Uma stepped forward.

'It's OK, Fran. I'll take care of this. And thank you for following my instructions. You were quite right not to let her in.'

The young woman nodded and retreated from the room, carefully closing the doors as she left. Eva scowled after her before embracing Uma.

'Darling, did you hear what that little woman said to me? It's preposterous. Make sure she never enters this building again.'

'I'll do nothing of the sort,' Uma said, steering her sister away from Ethan towards the other end of the office. 'Now, to what do I owe the honour of this visit?'

'I wanted to see you. It's been months. You never return my calls. So, here I am.'

'I've been busy,' Uma said.

'You're always busy. You know what they say, Uma, darling ... all work no—'

'Not now, Eva,' Uma cut in. 'I haven't got time for this. I'm busy.'

'Where is he?' her sister shrieked, whirling round. 'Oh!' she exclaimed, catching sight of Ethan. 'Who do we have here?'

Before Uma could stop her, Eva marched to the end of the room and began inspecting a bemused Ethan as if he was a broodmare for sale.

'Uma, darling, your taste in men is as desperate as your dress sense. Where on earth did you find him? Down at the 11th Street shelter? And why is his mouth open? Has he never seen identical twins before?'

Ethan had forgotten what a mess he was, but stepped forward to introduce himself.

'Hello, I'm—'

'Eva, this is not a good time,' Uma interrupted. 'I'll call you tonight as soon as I've finished my meeting. I promise.' She tried to steer Eva towards the door, but her sister wasn't listening. She was staring at Ethan, a strange look on her face.

'Don't I know you from somewhere?'

Again, Ethan didn't get the chance to respond. This time, Uma physically took her sister by the arm and half-frogmarched her out of the office.

'OK, I heard you. You're busy,' Eva said, looking back towards Ethan. 'That man looks awfully familiar, Uma. Are you sure I don't know him?'

'Quite. He works for one of Papa's old contacts,' Uma said. 'Now, please. Leave me. I've work to do. I'll call you tonight.'

Uma shut the door on her twin before turning back to Ethan.

'Who on earth was that?'

'Who do you think it was, Mr Rae?'

'No, I didn't mean it that way. I meant, she isn't anything to do with this, is she?'

'No, of course not. She's never been near my father's work.'

'No. What I meant to say is ... is she a ... a result of this technology?' Ethan said, his mind spinning.

'Mr Rae, you've watched way too many science-fiction movies.' Her green eyes gleamed with amusement. 'Eva has no idea any of this even exists. She is a natural twin, born two minutes after me.'

Ethan looked doubtful.

He was thinking about Eva. Knowledge of LEAP made him see her with new eyes. No longer a twin, but a replica of Uma. He hadn't even considered that possibility back in the Interior.

'But you could copy yourself?'

'Why on earth would I want to do that?' Uma said.

'I don't know. Having two of you running around would be useful, don't you think? You'd get twice as much done. Hell, have three or four, or even an entire army. All carrying your exact values. Imprinted with the same intellect. Thinking as one.'

'Were you not listening to my lecture?' Uma said. 'Oh, I forgot, you were on your phone!'

'But you'd be unstoppable,' Ethan said.

'You're not allowed to make copies: the LEAP Laws prohibit it.'

'The LEAP what?'

'The LEAP Laws,' Uma said. 'I drew them up to prevent the sort of chaos that would ensue if people were allowed to mess around with technology like this.'

'Makes sense,' Ethan said. 'So, you've got a no-copying rule. What else?'

'If your physical body dies in the natural world, your LEAP file must be deleted from the system. Otherwise, somebody could just regenerate you.'

'Wait a minute,' Ethan said. 'You're telling me you don't need the actual person to teleport them?'

'That's right, yes,' Uma said. 'Once we've scanned your atomic structure into the system, we use the scan—the blueprint—if you will, to rebuild you at your destination. The original "you" is disassembled.'

Ethan blew out his cheeks, eyes widening in surprise. 'Somebody could live forever.'

'Not exactly,' Uma said. 'Remember, the blueprint is simply a snapshot in time of everything that comprises you. Not only your body, but your brain, including all your memories. So, whilst in theory, you could regenerate an earlier, younger copy of yourself, your memories would be those of the earlier version. It'd be like groundhog day. Not very useful for an eternal life, wouldn't you agree?'

Ethan was silent, absorbing what Uma had just told him.

'Besides which, the next law forbids it. You can't alter memory.'

'What do you mean?' Ethan said. 'I thought you just said that memories were frozen at the point of scanning. Doesn't that make your law obsolete?'

'Well, yes, in practice. But in theory, you could implant memories from different copies. It would be fiendishly complex, but possible. Say, for instance, someone lost an arm in an accident. We could restore it from a previous copy. The same would go for memories.'

'So, what you've just said, about memories, isn't necessarily true?'

'I don't think so. It's never been attempted, but I've tried to anticipate the possibility. Can you imagine the impact of people living for hundreds of years?'

Ethan had considered none of this in his initial excitement. He could live with these conditions, but could others? LEAP was not simply a teleportation system. It was all powerful. Just like the student's god. Ethan wasn't a religious man. His parents' death had put paid to that. No. There was no god. Of that, Ethan was certain. Not after what he had been through. What God would make anyone suffer like he had? But for many people, Uma's system was God-like in its potential to trample over diseases. Life-threatening injuries. Even death itself. No, God wasn't Ethan's concern. What Uma had just told him raised more earthly matters around who got to enforce the Laws. Who got to decide if you could recover someone's memory from their LEAP file if they lost it in an accident? What did 'alter' mean, anyway? What did death mean? A person in a long-term coma? What happened if someone recovered consciousness after dying and had permanent brain damage? Why not resuscitate their LEAP programme if it meant continued life? Who got to decide? Uma?

Suddenly, the enormity of LEAP hit him. It was joined by yet more questions that swirled around his head like autumn leaves, demanding answers, but every time he reached for one, yet more arrived until he felt like his cranium would split in two from their sheer number. His hand began to throb again, and he forced himself to focus. They would all have to wait for the time being. There was a deal to be done. Too much detail always derailed things. The effort left him feeling weak, and this time he risked the short steps to the couch and sat down heavily. Despite his earlier retort, he knew he couldn't walk away from this opportunity. No one could. Except for Uma. He had seen enough of her to realise that she might. She held all the cards and knew it. If they did part ways, the reality was that no one would believe him. It was now or never.

'You said there were four laws.'

'Yes. One more—you can't merge any other species.'

The last law hung between them.

'You can do that?'

'Theoretically. Yes. Every earth-based life form is constructed with atoms. Given time, you could do anything. Give someone gills. Fur. Night vision.'

Ethan stared at her in shock as the implications of what she had just said sank in. The ethical conundrums had just multiplied a thousand-fold. Ethan steadied his racing mind. This was just detail. He had to focus. There was a deal to be done.

'So, let me get this straight. You want to give LEAP away—for free—to speed its rollout to billions of people so we can reverse global warming.'

Uma nodded.

'And I don't think we can afford to do that. I don't have enough to achieve what you want to do. I could start it off with seed capital to attract more money but, at the end of the day, anyone else we turned to would expect a return on their investment.'

Uma started to interrupt, but Ethan ploughed on.

'In fact, you don't have too many choices; you can either approach someone like me, or you could go to the markets, but they will tear you and your precious Laws apart. If you think my motivations are driven by money, wait 'til you've met those barbarians. Before you'd know it, they would own it all and you wouldn't know it had happened until it was too late.'

Uma's spirits sank. She had not expected this reaction. In her mind, the benefits of LEAP were self-evident, as was the sense of the LEAP

Laws. She hadn't really thought beyond releasing LEAP to the world and watching CO2 levels tumble.

'However, we can achieve both our aims here without getting them involved.'

'OK, Mr Rae,' Uma said, uncertain of what he was going to say next. 'How exactly would you achieve that?'

'There're loads of ways. We could charge a nominal fee per LEAP. Say, one hundredth of one penny. Given the billions of transactions, we'll make enough money to run the system. We could also licence LEAP out to companies and governments, and prohibit them from charging users for basic services like transport and recycling. But we don't need to work out the details now. That can come later, with your input, of course. All that you need to do now is accept the fact that, in order to roll this out for free to everyone around the globe, we have to generate cash, and lots of it, so we can continue providing it for free. Do you think you can live with that?' Ethan was watching Uma carefully. They were reaching decision time, and he was looking for any sign that his pitch wasn't getting through to her. However, Uma's face remained implacable. Worse still, she was silent, forcing Ethan to continue. 'Otherwise, if you can't, we're both wasting our time here. Nothing I will ever say can change your mind, but you will never get this to market in the way that you want to.'

Ethan sat down on the sofa. That was it. There was nothing more he could say. He had made his pitch. It was now up to Uma.

Uma thought about what Ethan had said. She hadn't really considered how they would roll out the technology, only that it would be done. She had just assumed that the money would be there. Besides, what choice did she have? Ethan was right. Who else could she find who could do this? She had spent over two years finding Ethan. He was many things she hadn't expected but, despite her revulsion at his unashamed love of making money, she had a grudging respect for his blunt honesty. It was a very Icelandic characteristic and made her trust him. Could she start again, looking for another investor? Her chest felt heavy at the thought.

Uma stared at Ethan. He looked terrible; the little colour that had returned to his cheeks following the meal and brisk walk had drained away. Exhaustion was etched across his face, dulling his eyes.

'I can live with your profit motive so long as my Laws remain intact and we exclude nobody from LEAP because they can't afford it. If you can live with that, then we've got ourselves a deal, Mr Rae.'

She held out her hand. Ethan stared at it for a few seconds, thinking about the impact of her touch in the amphitheatre. But he was also relishing the moment. It would secure the future of his charities for a hundred years and keep him busy for decades to come. He finally took her hand and shook it warmly.

'You won't be disappointed,' he said. 'When can we start?'

He never got to continue. Suddenly, waves of fatigue rolled over him. He was sweating profusely and felt sick. His stomach was taut, heart beating wildly. Ethan felt himself sinking into the soft leather and their handshake was wrenched apart. Uma knelt down at his side, smiling.

'Mr Rae, you need to get some rest. There's a lot of work to do. But first, we need to get you back to Reykjavík before people question your disappearance. It was bad enough that my sister saw you in public today.'

'Sounds good,' Ethan sighed, staring up at Uma. 'But, please, if we're going to be partners, can you call me Ethan? This formality is not my style.'

'OK, Mr ... Ethan. I will.'

But Ethan didn't hear. He was fast asleep.

Safe House, Reykjavík, Iceland

Present Day

13 November 2003, 22:05 hours GMT

Andreus Grond checked his rear view mirror as he inched the four-by-four along the deserted cul-de-sac, but the sheeting rain blotted out nearly everything, bar four smudges of light from the following Shoguns. He could feel the weight of the clouds overhead, brawling like obsidian nightmares as they spewed water onto the deserted street. Either side of him, the houses were set well back from the road, their normally colourful palettes muted by the relentless deluge. He drew up outside the very last property and stepped out into the storm, pulling his hood low. It was scant protection from the squalling rain which seemed to come at him from every direction, courtesy of a gale force wind blowing in off the Reykjanes Bay. He moved quickly, handing out the heavy duffel bags from the boot to his three travel companions, who had joined him at the rear of the Shogun. Grond kept a watchful eye on the street, but nothing moved, save for the others who were also silently gathering equipment from the two four-by-fours behind Grond's. As he slammed the heavy door shut, Grond checked the street one last time. Satisfied that no one had followed them, he rushed up the drive to catch his team.

The eight men spilled into the warm hallway like drowned rats, shedding bags and coats onto the wooden floor. Several headed for the kitchen, bottles clinking in their hands, whilst the rest made their way into the living room. Grond who had remained on the porch to check the drive, grimaced as he surveyed the chaotic scene: it was amateur hour.

'Hansen,' he barked. 'Garments in the back. We need to dry them out. 'Solberg, Jorgsson. Take all the bags into the sitting room. Pedersen, Christiansen. You help them. Strip every weapon. Then clean and lube each one. Olsen, Nielsen. You do the magazines. Wipe them down and reload. Beer to me. Nothing gets drunk until this is finished.' He nodded at the last man. 'You and Hansen are outside. Two hours, rolling guard duty. I don't want any surprises.'

The men exchanged surprised glances, and a heavily tattooed man stepped forward. Grond recognised him from the profiles he'd been sent: Erik Pedersen. Thirty-three. Ex-Jegerkompaniet. Arctic Ranger Company. His specialism was explosives. That, and the groups' spokesman it seemed.

'Boss,' he said, 'the men prepped everything this afternoon.'

'I don't care,' Grond said.

Pedersen shrugged, glancing again at his companions.

'Is that necessary? All that work for one college professor. I could grab her myself. Do we even need all this firepower?'

Grond turned to face Pedersen and looked him up and down, before reaching out a hand.

'Grond is it?' Grond said.

Pedersen's looked puzzled, as he took Grond's hand in his own.

'No,' Pedersen began. 'You're—'

His voice cut off into a surprised scream as Grond jerked Pedersen's arm savagely down. Unbalanced, the younger man fell forward and Grond used the momentum to cartwheel him onto his back before placing a knee across his throat.

'I'm giving the orders. If you have a problem with that you know where the door is. I'll divide your fee amongst the others.'

Pedersen choked out a response.

'I didn't hear you,' Grond said, releasing the pressure slightly.

'I'm good,' Pedersen croaked.

Grond stood up and turned to the others.

'Anyone else think they're in charge?' he said.

No one answered.

'Thought not.' Grond grabbed one of the dripping duffel bags and headed for the living room. Slowly, the assigned men grabbed the remaining bags and began emptying them out onto a large dining table: ten P80s, the Norwegian army's version of the Glock, one for each man plus a spare; ten sound suppressors; ten Heckler & Koch MP-5's, the snub nosed submachine guns gleaming dully in the low light; piles of magazines—four for each weapon, eighty in total; and finally, Grond's axe case. They silently began stripping the weapons and Grond stepped away, leaning against the doorframe as he thought about tomorrow's assignment.

The strange thing was, that Grond agreed with Pedersen. But for different reasons. He didn't mind the over-preparation. That was a sign of good planning. No, that wasn't his problem. His issue was that he preferred to work alone. Had done so all his career since leaving the army and going freelance. This job was no different. He alone could have achieved the required outcome, but suspected the real reason for this show of force was that whoever had hired him, wanted to make a statement: that they could send nine heavily armed men, right into the heart of a European capital city and kidnap Target One in broad daylight, executing anyone else in their way. Bullet to the head had been the instruction. To do what? Make it look like a mafia hit?

He had no idea who would want to do such a thing. All he did was execute his contracts and collect the fee. Which in this case was considerable: $5 million. It was ten times his normal rate and, once he deducted the team's share, he would net £3.8 million. Enough to pay his debts and finally ...

Grond swallowed hard, his palms beginning to sweat. He dared not think of the future. He'd been in this position too many times before, so he quickly closed down the thought, instead, busying himself with an inspection of the weapons and magazines. Satisfied he braved the storm and recced the perimeter of the house to check on Karlsen and Hansen. He knew it wasn't needed. Nobody had followed them. Nobody would be out in this train wreck of a storm, but it kept his mind off what came next.

When he returned to the house, it was to the smell of sizzling bacon and wood smoke. The men were gathered round the dining table playing cards, laughing and joking, but as he entered, they fell silent.

'Want to play, boss?' Solberg eventually said, clearing a space between himself and Pedersen, who shuffled aside reluctantly, rubbing his throat.

Grond looked at the table and froze as he took in the scene: Poker. His favourite. Just one game he reasoned, but already he knew where that would lead. He instinctively reached for the pendant around his neck and fingered it tightly, rolling it between his thumb and index finger. The glass felt solid, the contents grounding and he could feel his heart rate level out.

'Not for me,' Grond said. 'I'm getting an early night. Big day tomorrow.'

He left the room and paused in the hallway, regretting his decision. The cards were calling to him, but he fought the urge, again grasping the pendant tightly in his fist, thinking of Jane. It seemed to work, and he reluctantly made his way up the stairs as a roar of laughter followed him onto the landing.

'What a damn pussy,' he heard Pedersen say. 'Doesn't play cards and needs an eight-man team to kidnap one college professor. How hard could that be?'

The Pink Nipple, London

13 November 2003, 22:16 hours GMT

The thick mane of black hair cascaded over Jack Anderson's face, causing him to shudder involuntarily as the soft curls lightly brushed his skin. He breathed deeply in anticipation of what was to come, the intoxicating blend of scents and oils magnifying his senses tenfold. The slightest touch made him flinch, a mixture of pain and pleasure that was almost too much to bear. He groaned as she repeated the action, caressing his forehead, cheeks and lips.

Without warning, the woman suddenly jerked her head back, causing him to open his eyes in surprise. She smiled down at him knowingly and began to rotate her neck in a slow, graceful arc so that, at first, the ends of her hair barely touched his face. However, as the pulsating music built to a crescendo, her head moved faster and faster until it became a blur of black. The bead braids skilfully laced into the ends of her hair whipped across his face. She laughed with delight at his reaction but didn't stop. If anything, she increased her frenzied rotation.

The bitch was going to cut him at this rate.

'Hey, stop that! It hurts!' he cried out, a hot flush of anger washing away the warm glow in his groin.

The woman screamed with glee and continued to whirl her long braids.

'What the fuck!' he cried, unable to restrain himself any longer. Anderson tried to grab her waist but one of the bouncers stepped forward and shook his head.

'No touching,' he mouthed.

Anderson swore, glancing sideways, but the four other men in the private members lounge of the Pink Nipple were oblivious, their eyes fixated hungrily on the woman, wishing they were him. She stepped back into the centre of the dimly lit room and stood motionless, head down, arms loose, the light silk gown now saturated with sweat and clinging tightly to her clearly naked body beneath.

As Anderson looked on, the room was suddenly plunged into darkness before a piercing white light snapped on. As his eyes adjusted to the glare, he could just make out the woman, her athletic figure silhouetted against the bright light.

Intrigued, he leaned forward and waited to see what would happen next, his anger doused by the promise of more pleasure. The room started to rumble, the opening chords of Richard Ashcroft's *Why Not Nothing* grinding through his bones. The light was now behind him, reflecting off a line of water that fell from the ceiling. At first a few drops, it gradually grew in intensity until a solid sheet of water cascaded down to resemble a fine glass mirror, seemingly solid to the touch and, impossible to see through.

A clenched fist suddenly broke the surface, before disappearing behind the shimmering screen. Then, another came slicing through and another before, without warning, the woman's entire body burst through the liquid screen, causing him to sit back in surprise. She was gone as quickly as she had appeared, allowing the water wall to reform behind her retreating body. Once again, she spun into view, travelling in a wide arc. She was moving impossibly fast. All he could see was a blur of wet skin, boiling foam and spray as she broke the surface before disappearing.

The passes became more frequent, following a pattern. She would appear from the right, gracefully arc clockwise before re-entering the wall, always at speed. It looked like she was flying. Seconds later, she would re-emerge in the same place. As the song passed its climax, the rotations began to slow, giving him the opportunity to simply admire her. Her voluminous hair, which had covered up so much of her body earlier, was now contained by the heavy fall of water. She was tall and slim but also powerfully built, the water accentuating every highly toned muscle of her coal-black skin. An athlete, perhaps, or maybe a gymnast. No, she was too tall. She had to be a dancer. Elegant muscle tone. Not too heavy but built for endurance and power. It was her thighs that gave it away. Impossibly long but supple and muscular, effortlessly gripping whatever was rotating her. Her breasts always came first, the nipples erect from the cold water that now covered him in a fine, cool spray, her firm buttocks always last as they disappeared from his view 180 degrees later.

It was mesmerising. He didn't know how long he sat there watching the show as the woman moved through her routine. Gradually, imperceptibly, the flow of water began to slow until, finally, it stopped, and she stood there, staring at all five men haughtily, chest heaving, right hand grasping the thick pole that had propelled her through the water wall, legs apart, like a black gladiator, resplendent in all her naked glory.

Anderson couldn't restrain himself any longer and lurched forward, reaching out to grab the woman but the bouncer was ready. He intercepted Anderson, clamping a huge hand down on his wrist. In a practised motion, he swung Anderson in a wide circle, before slamming him back into the wall.

'No touching,' the bouncer hissed.

Anderson stared up at the man, his passion now replaced by a different heat. The man must have been two fifty pounds, six six in his socks but that didn't deter Anderson. He jerked his head forward catching the bouncer in his throat. At the same time Anderson drove his knee upwards into the man's groin who let out a slow moan and sank to the floor. Anderson kicked the bouncer repeatedly, driving his boot hard into the man's stomach. The woman screamed and ran from the room, the other punters close behind.

'I'll touch who I want,' Anderson screamed.

Behind him two more bouncers entered the room, all muscle, tight T-shirts and angry tattoos. Anderson turned to meet them, but an afternoon of drink had slowed him down. One of them tackled Anderson around the waist, driving him back whilst the second bouncer caught him with an upper cut to the jaw. Anderson sank to his knees.

'Is that all you've got.' Anderson swung his arms lazily at the two men as they circled him, raining blows down on his back and chest.

The third bouncer struggled to his feet and motioned for his colleagues to hold Anderson.

'Jack,' I've told you before,' he said. 'No touching. If you continue like this, we're going to have to withdraw your special membership privileges.'

'Fuck you Andy,' Anderson spat the last word out, 'I'll touch who I want to.'

'Not tonight you won't,' the bouncer said, nodding at his two colleagues who pulled Anderson to his feet and dragged him into the main club. It was still early, and the booths were nearly all empty, groups of women in various stages of undress chatting around their plinths. They continued past the reception area, through the main doors and out into the miserable night, flinging Anderson down onto the wet tarmac.

'Go home and sober up.' Andy said.

Anderson got to his feet and lunged towards the three men, but Andy was ready. His boot caught Anderson below the waist and Anderson folded to the tarmac with a hissing whimper.

'That's for earlier,' Andy said and disappeared back into the club with his two colleagues.

Anderson curled up, moaning softly, trying to control his breathing and in turn the pain, but time was the only healer. When he was eventually able to contemplate moving, his clothes were soaked through. He gingerly rolled onto his back and lay there, staring up at a pink silhouette of a woman with huge breasts, wondering what to do: there was no way they would let him back into the club and it was too early to go home. A soft, urgent vibration made him wince with pain and he carefully extracted the mobile phone from his jean pocket.

'Can you talk?' a familiar voice said in his ear.

'I've answered, haven't I?'

'I've got a job for you.'

Anderson groaned.

'It's my week off,' he mumbled, spitting bloody phlegm onto the wet road.

'It pays.'

'How much?'

'Two a day.'

Anderson sat up gingerly, thinking of the woman. A private show cost two grand. Five thousand for extras.

'Doing what?'

'Babysitting a college professor for the next two weeks. Twelve hour shifts.'

Anderson did the maths: Twenty eight grand was a lot of money for babysitting. But it would buy him a whole heap of shows.

'Who is she?'

'Don't know, don't care.' Patra was getting bored with the conversation. She had to assemble a four man team in the next hour. Her fee was dependent on it.

'Are you doing it or not?' she said. 'I can find plenty who will.'

'I'm in.'

'Good. Where are you?'

Anderson looked up at the neon sign.

'The Pink Nipple, down in Soho.'

'That's a bit upmarket for you Anderson. No wonder you've got no money.'

'Fuck you, Patra.'

'Go home. Clean up. A car will pick you up at 3:00 AM.'

Anderson groaned. That wasn't for hours.

'Where are we going?'

'Camden Town. From there who knows.'

Somewhere over the North Atlantic

13 November 2003, 22:26 hours GMT

Ethan watched Jorge clear away the remains of his earlier meal. He felt groggy and realised he must have fallen asleep shortly after take-off. He stretched in his chair and rubbed his right thigh to calm the throbbing pins. Uma had badgered him repeatedly about having them removed, using LEAP. She had reassured him it was an easy routine whereby they would replace his previously shattered bone with new bone, atom by atom. It sounded straightforward and would relieve him of so much discomfort. But he couldn't do it.

Along with his scarred back, the metal was the only physical reminder of that fateful night. Everything else had been lost. Sure, he had his photos to remind him what his parents looked like, but recently he had become aware of more important treasures that were simply fading away. The way his father used to smile. His mischievous wink that he only ever used with Ethan. How Ethan's mum would hold his hand, gently stroking his fingers. The way she smelt when she hugged him tightly every morning before he left for school. They were all melting away like winter ice in a spring thaw and he was powerless to stop it. The pain in his leg, on the other hand, was permanent. He found the metallic ache strangely comforting. It was the same with his back. The ragged scars were a constant source of discomfort, slumbering pinpricks of pain that rippled out across his skin whenever he thought of his parents. Or at least his failure to protect them. Ethan shifted uncomfortably in his seat as a fresh spasm duly obliged. Unlike his memories, they were going nowhere, and Ethan had no intention of losing such physical reminders of his carelessness.

He looked up as Robin entered the spacious cabin. His pilot looked concerned.

'Boss, that storm over the south-western seaboard is getting worse. Air traffic control at Keflavík is reporting wind gusts approaching a hundred miles per hour.' Robin sat down heavily in the seat opposite Ethan. 'Nothing can land in that. They're going to place us in a holding pattern just north of the Reykjanes Peninsula over the Faxaflói Bay.'

'How long do you think it'll last?' Ethan asked, worried at the prospect of any further delay in getting to Uma.

Robin shrugged, choosing his words carefully. He had worked for Ethan long enough to know that his boss liked absolute clarity when making decisions.

'It could be anywhere between two to six hours. Any longer than that, and we will need to return to London. The Challenger doesn't have sufficient fuel for a delay beyond that sort of time frame.'

'We need to get there faster than that,' Ethan said. 'What's the likelihood of the storm lifting before then?'

'None, I'm afraid.'

Ethan groaned. He should have stayed in London and waited.

'Do we have sufficient fuel for a transatlantic hop to Manhattan?' He could LEAP from there. Surely the police would have finished with Uma by then.

'Sure, we do. The Challenger's built for that.'

'Then do it. And call ahead to update Uma. Patch her through if she has any questions.'

His pilot nodded, disappearing back to the cockpit. Ethan stretched again. There was nothing he could do now except wait. He still felt disorientated from his rude awakening and, with over five hours to kill, could easily get some more sleep, but there was none to be found. As he had done on countless occasions before, he found himself thinking about LEAP. It had taken Ethan a while to get used to the whole concept; particularly the fact that his body wasn't transported. That instead, LEAP just scanned his atomic structure and then reassembled him atom by atom, using the scan as the blueprint—not only for what atoms constituted him, but for which ones went where. To comply with the first LEAP law which prohibited copying, the system disassembled his original atoms at the outbound gate for later use by whatever was being transported to that gate. Meanwhile, at the arrivals gate, he was literally being created using different atoms. Except it was even more extreme than that. The first scan was comprehensive, but from then on LEAP only recorded what had changed since the previous scan. It was a terrifying prospect to think he was no longer the same person. LEAP had forced him to challenge the whole notion of what 'self' meant, at least atomically.

Uma, on the other hand, was much more comfortable. As she had explained to him on countless occasions, this change was happening anyway at an atomic level. All they did was speed up the process.

'In the world of atoms, we are never the same person for more than a millisecond anyway,' she would say matter-of-factly. 'At any one moment, billions and billions of our atoms are altering, changing, evolving, reforming into different compounds, molecules and cells.' Ethan struggled to imagine what she meant. 'Imagine you're eating a bowl of cereal. The moment it hits your gut, everything is broken down by the acids in your stomach. Think about it. They will actually split apart the molecular structure of the various constituents making up the cereal and milk so they can be absorbed into your circulatory systems. The process lasts two, three hours and, once it's complete, anything that can't be broken down will be ejected by the body whilst the rest will be circulated as fuel to feed your muscles or as fatty tissue. At a molecular level, the cereal is now part of you. That morning, it was just corn, milk, and sugar. By lunchtime it was blood and muscle, absorbed into the collection of atoms known as Ethan Rae. Whoever the hell he is,' she would add, smiling mischievously.

'There isn't a single part of you here today, atomically speaking, that was part of you twelve months ago,' she reminded him. 'Even your brain gets a full makeover. The cells I'm using to actually think these words up weren't here nine months ago. LEAP's doing the same thing,' she would reassure him, 'just many, many times faster and in one go, replacing your entire atomic structure on an outward jump with a whole new one at your arrival point. It's still you. You're still Ethan Rae, identical in every single detail to the one that made the LEAP.'

The impact of LEAP on his physical body was easier to comprehend than the changes taking place within his head. He knew it was the same process at work, but nevertheless, it might be problematic for some people if they stopped for one moment to consider what was happening. On one level, 'self' was all about looks. Atomically, that was a simple conundrum to accept, because his physical body at the arrival point was always an exact copy of what was left behind at the departure gate. But 'self' was more than that. It was also down to what was contained in his mind—his brain, his consciousness. They contained his memories, his personality and the sum total of his experiences and how he perceived the world around him. Without those, he was no longer himself, regardless of what he looked like. So why did he struggle with the concept? He wasn't religious. It wasn't as if his spirit was being left behind at the departure gate and that he was, therefore, somehow a lesser being at his arrival point. He always felt the same. Thought the same. Reacted the same. And therefore, must be the same. Except, of course, how would he know if he was different? That was the truly unsettling bit. He wouldn't because there was no reference point. Except through how others reacted to him. He often found himself asking Uma obscure questions to reassure himself that he was still himself.

She would laugh at his concern. As usual, she didn't seem to have doubts, relying instead on cold hard scientific fact about what humans really are. 'Take love and fear,' she would insist. 'Atomically, they're simply neurochemical reactions to situations that produce physical responses. If you find yourself in a threatening situation, your body will produce adrenaline. This prepares your body for action. It makes your heart beat faster to introduce more oxygen into the bloodstream. Something you will need if you're running away. It dilates blood vessels in your leg muscles. Again, very useful for running. You will perceive this as an emotional response to the situation. It's just a hormone. A chemical compound derived from amino acids, which are made from molecules that, in turn, are formed by atoms. Love's the same. If you see your partner, dopamine neurons are activated and they flood the caudate nucleus.'

It scared Ethan slightly to think of all this chemical activity in his brain. Billions upon billions of cells, whizzing around chaotically in his head, seemingly without purpose but, somehow, making connections with each other that enabled him to, well, be and to function. That resulted in thoughts, emotions, urges and physical movements that allowed him to sit in his seat, breathing, worrying about Uma, being aware of Jorge re-entering the cabin and simultaneously thinking about what had happened today, all whilst contemplating the enormity of LEAP.

At the subatomic level, things got weirder still. Ethan knew enough basic physics to understand the individual composition of an atom; a central, positively charged core—the nucleus—and negatively charged particles called electrons that orbit the nucleus. Almost the entire mass of each atom was concentrated in the nucleus, which occupied only a tiny fraction of the atom's volume. In fact, atoms were mainly empty space. How empty was impossible to comprehend. Uma had informed him that if the nucleus were the size of a ping-pong ball, the electron cloud would extend over one kilometre in diameter around it and the electrons themselves, the size of dust particles. They would be virtually invisible in this space and most of this distance would be emptiness.

In other words, humans were very simple. At a subatomic level, he was 99.9999 percent empty space—he was virtually nothing at all.

Ethan swallowed hard. Was that truly it? The sum total of the human race. Nothing! Just a bunch of empty atoms recycling themselves into different combinations of complex chemical reactions. That paid no heed to life or death. That don't think or love or hate. That were completely oblivious to the consequences of their myriad combinations. Ones that created war, hunger, pain and pleasure. It was all deeply disturbing. Like staring into a deep abyss that, if you weren't careful, threatened to suck you in.

In his darker moments, when he was sick with grief at the loss of his parents, and his back was burning, Ethan was willing to accept such cruel logic. But for the rest of the time, he fought the finality of it, for one simple reason: if he succumbed, then everything became utterly meaningless. LEAP itself. Uma. Sally and James. Rae Enterprises. Green Ray, his new fund to pay for the launch of LEAP. Even his parents' death. In essence, his whole life meant nothing. Even though he could accept the science and rationalise the logic, he just felt that, for whatever reason, this particular collection of atoms called Ethan Rae was worth clinging on to. He had always had a distinct purpose, especially following his parents' death. And, he realised with a smile, especially now he had met Uma.

Ethan yawned. He simply couldn't keep his eyes open any longer and slowly made his way into the master bedroom of the aircraft. There was no bed, just his battered mattress, which Jorge had laid out earlier. He settled himself onto the thin material and lay there thinking. Of Uma and whether he should have stayed in London and waited for the police to leave. Of James and Sally. Of his parents. But most of all he thought about who could have possibly discovered their plans about LEAP. Eventually the blanket roar of the rear-mounted GE CF34-3B1 turbo-fan engines lulled him into an uneasy sleep. One inhabited by a dark figure that stuck to him like a summer shadow, appearing time and time again as his side, regardless of how many LEAP gates he jumped through.

San Francisco Airport, San Francisco

13 November 2003, 14:38 hours PST

God, his head hurt. Samuel K. Reynolds III gently massaged his throbbing temples and tried to concentrate on Bill Parsons, his Chief Financial Officer, who was only ten minutes into what he knew would be a ninety-minute monologue. He was regretting slamming those last shots of tequila the night before. Or was it in the early hours of this morning? It didn't matter. He had been having far too much fun at his latest haunt, the Fat Cat Club, to even contemplate leaving early for today's board meeting. He must have downed at least four shots in rapid succession which, normally, wouldn't have troubled him, but that was on top of the early evening magnums of vintage Krug champagne at the Blood Red Steak House, followed by countless bottles of 2001 Sine Qua Non Shiraz.

He reached for the jug of chilled lemon water and shakily poured himself a glass, being careful to avoid his father's eyes across the large boardroom table. He took a long swig, trying to concentrate on Bill Parsons, but it was no good. The hammers in his head had picked up the pace and their dull thuds slowly mutated into the piercing staccato of a pneumatic drill. Reynolds groaned softly but loud enough to interrupt his CFO, who turned towards him expectantly, waiting for his input. There was a long pause before Reynolds finally looked up.

'That's OK, Bill. Please continue. I didn't mean to disturb you.'

Parsons nodded knowingly and returned to his notes. This time, Reynolds couldn't avoid his father's angry stare. Samuel K. Reynolds II scowled at his son, who looked down immediately and scribbled something illegible on the yellow legal pad in front of him, thinking of his grandfather. He would have approved.

The hard-living creator of his family's fortune had been a legendary drinker who had spent as much time in the bars of the Mission District of San Francisco as he had building up Reynolds Air, the airline he founded in 1910. Reynolds glanced up at the portrait of the great man who glared angrily down into the large boardroom and, despite his sore head, he managed a smile. He still remembered the old man clearly, even though he had died when Reynolds was just twelve.

His most distinct memory was sitting on his granddaddy's lap on the wide veranda of the family summerhouse. It was north of San Francisco, on the edge of the Humboldt Redwoods State Park. Huddled in his wheelchair, crippled by years of hard living, the nonagenarian would spend hours recounting stories of his early years in Dayton, Ohio as an assistant engineer. Working alongside the Wright brothers, helping them to perfect the gliding machines that would eventually form the chassis of the world's first airplane. These stories fascinated Reynolds, particularly the names. They sounded so romantic: Kitty Hawk, Huffman Prairie, Nags Head, Little Hill, West Hill and, his favourite, Big Kill Devil Hill, from where the very first flight was made.

Samuel K. Reynolds I remembered that famous day in particular—Friday, 17 December 1903. 'The day the human race really took off', his grandfather called it, and would describe it to his grandson in great detail. How he could not sleep the night before with the excitement of the endeavour. The short drive up to the airstrip on that frosty but clear winter's morning, and the flights themselves. They made four that day. The first lasted just twelve seconds and took Orville Wright a distance of 120 feet. As the flimsy machine, powered by a twelve-horsepower engine, lifted off the ground for the first time, his grandfather would recount to the enraptured boy how he had known with certainty that his life had changed forever that day. How, looking out over the frozen field, he had, in that very instant, understood with great clarity that he would achieve greatness. That he would own a huge fleet of flying machines capable of carrying hundreds of people at a time. Machines that could fly enormous distances to all the far-flung places of the globe without stopping to refuel. He didn't know how. Just that he would. Why else would he be allowed to witness such a historical event—the day that man finally conquered the skies.

Reynolds' attention drifted back into the boardroom. Parsons was warming to his report, although you wouldn't have realised it from his deadpan delivery. A neat and exacting man, he enunciated every word precisely in an even but very soft monotone that forced his audience to lean forward in their chairs just to catch what he was saying. Reynolds detested him and would have forced him out long ago, but the finance man was a Reynolds Air veteran and had his father's ear. Whilst the old man chaired the Board, he was going nowhere.

'So, gentlemen,' Parsons said, 'our problems continue. Only last month, West Coast Airlines announced four new routes into LA, Santa Monica and also over to Las Vegas and Reno. All compete directly with our scheduled flights, but at prices fifty percent lower than our cheapest fare. It now means we are facing low-cost carriers on eighty-five percent of our domestic routes.

'Our international routes are doing no better. The terrorist attacks of September 11 decimated our long-haul routes across the Pacific. In addition, the SARS outbreak last year, combined with the latest threat of avian flu, means people are simply not flying at the moment. Passenger numbers have fallen by nearly thirteen percent in this last quarter alone.

'We are being squeezed at both ends: revenues are falling, but our cost base is rising. Insurance premiums for the last twelve months have nearly doubled. Security costs, for the month ending 31 March, totalled $167 million for the year.

'However, our greatest single overhead is aviation fuel: the price has effectively tripled over the past eighteen months. This is not going to improve any time soon, particularly if unrest in the Gulf continues, along with the threat of domestic turmoil in Venezuela and Nigeria.

'Bottom line, the last two years have had a huge negative impact on our finances. As you know, we incurred an operating loss of $937 million last year, and I predict the loss for this year will be near $2.6 billion. I will have an exact figure for you by the end of the month.'

There was silence in the large boardroom as the eight men absorbed the figure.

$2,600,000,000.

Reynolds' heart lurched. There was no way the company could have lost that much money. It represented over twenty-five percent of their current market capitalisation. At this rate, they'd be bankrupt in two years.

As if reading his mind, Parsons continued.

'The net effect of all of the above factors is that our recent financial results are unsustainable. Unless we make significant adjustments to our operating costs, Reynolds Air will have to seek the protection of the Bankruptcy Courts under Chapter 11.'

Reynolds' stomach somersaulted with alarm. Chapter 11 was a form of interim bankruptcy that allowed a company to keep operating as a business while shedding some of its liabilities, such as debts and other financial obligations. The downside was huge—it would wipe out all shareholder value in one fell swoop. Despite being a publicly quoted company, The Reynolds Family Trust still controlled fifty-two percent of the airline, which, even in the current environment, was valued at over $10 billion. Everything his granddaddy and father had worked for over the last century would be destroyed. Extinguished for all eternity along with the airline his grandfather had dreamed of creating on that frosty morning, nearly 100 years previously.

Reynolds' father broke the silence.

'So, what are you suggesting, Bill?'

'I may have a solution that just might work.' Parsons paused theatrically and looked round the boardroom. Satisfied he had everyone's attention, he began.

'For the past two months, I've had a team working on a scheme to compensate the employees for agreeing to permanent long-term concessions on salaries, pensions and other benefits. If they collectively agree to the reductions we are after, I propose we issue sixty-five million shares of Reynolds Air stock in the form of stock options to the remaining staff. These will vest over a five-year period. It's a great deal: the stock is currently trading at a historical low, which means the unions would be crazy not to recommend it to their members. If the share price recovers to even fifty percent of its previous average, there will be some very wealthy employees out there and this will, hopefully, speed up the rates of early retirement for some of our older staff members.' Parsons stopped abruptly, unsure of the reaction he was receiving from his fellow board members. 'That's it, gentlemen. Short and sweet.'

There was further silence in the large room as everyone considered his suggestion. Even Reynolds had to admit it was a good idea. Neat and tidy. Just like his CFO to offer a win-win for all concerned.

Reynolds' father beamed at the CFO. 'Sounds like a slam dunk to me. Any questions?'

He surveyed the room, blue eyes flashing brightly despite his eighty years of age. No one spoke. Reynolds couldn't think of any objection or clever question that might pick a hole in Parsons' plan. Suddenly, his headache took an uglier turn and Reynolds realised he needed a drink to soothe the hammers.

'Good. Well, pending some feedback from the unions, it sounds like a plan that the Board would be happy to put its name to. Any other business to discuss?'

'Ah, yes, sir. I have one more point to raise.' Parsons stood back up to address the directors of Reynolds Air.

What the hell does he have now? Reynolds thought.

'It's more symbolic than anything but will do wonders for our environmental credentials,' Parsons began, smiling benignly in Reynolds' direction. 'It concerns the table. Zak, Wright & Tuff, our PR agency, has suggested we mothball that, too.'

That was too much for Reynolds. His morning hadn't started well, but suddenly it took a decided turn for the worse. His hangover was manageable. The results he could cope with. Barely. But not this.

'The hell we will,' growled Reynolds, jumping to his feet and facing Parsons. 'What's gotten into you, man? This is Reynolds Air.' He smacked the palms of both hands down on the table to emphasise his point. The solid wood felt cool against his hot skin, and its texture was soft to the touch. The timber had gradually faded over the years, worn smooth by thousands of shirt cuffs, early-morning meetings and even sleeping staff, exhausted by the legendary takeover battles of the 1950s and 1960s when his grandfather had gone on a non-stop acquisition trail. Over the last seventy years it had remained a silent witness to his grandfather's planning and scheming. The risks he had taken. The vastness of his vision. To the successes, the failures, the fights, the blood, the sweat and the many tears that had been shed in the forging of a family dynasty which, at its peak, had made his grandfather the richest man in America.

'That's precisely why it needs to go,' Parsons said. 'It's a beacon for environmentalists all over the world to target Reynolds Air as an anachronistic dinosaur. Sixty years ago, your grandfather could do what he wanted. The airline industry had just entered its golden age of growth. Flying was the exclusive privilege of the wealthy. He could charge what he wanted. Your grandfather was the largest employer in San Francisco. For heaven's sake, he was godfather to the senator's son! He owned this State. But things have changed since then. For a start, we are now a public company with shareholders to consider. What's more, flying no longer has the caché it once had. It's a commodity these days, with a downwards price spiral that's unsustainable. Anything we can do to improve our image needs to be acted on. Besides which, we don't need a table this size any more. Your grandfather used it to intimidate everyone: other airlines; takeover targets; the banks; his staff; potential investors. But none of that matters anymore. We need to charm people, not frighten them.'

Parsons stopped, suddenly aware that even he may have overstepped the mark in front of Reynolds' father. He sat down, leaving the younger man standing there with his palms pressed to the table, his aggressive stance reminiscent of a charging male gorilla defending its territory.

Reynolds senior broke the deadlock.

'As much as I hate to admit it, Parsons, I think you're right. I'm not sure I would have put it so forcibly, but this table is symbolic of our past. One that no one here should be ashamed of, but one that certainly doesn't play a part in the future of this company. We need a new image and now is as good a time as any to start the process. I suggest we retire this relic quietly to the museum without fanfare. Any objections?'

Reynolds stood dumbfounded, staring at his father with disbelief. Had the old man finally lost his marbles? How could he be sanctioning this insanity? The table was a reminder to everyone at Reynolds Air that the family was still very much a force within the airline. That no decisions could be taken without their say-so. And his father was prepared to give all that up, with total disregard for his own son's opinion. A public humiliation to go with everything else this meeting had thrown his way.

'I object, Father. I object most strongly.'

His father frowned slightly, perhaps puzzled by his son's stance, but then smiled, sensing some theatre. Yet further evidence of his offspring's poor judgement.

'It's not up to me, son. This is a democracy, not an autocracy. If you object, we will put it to the vote. Everyone in favour of the table being mothballed raise your hand.'

The other directors raised their hands in unanimous agreement with the Chairman, who continued to hold his son's imploring gaze with a steely determination that belied his years. Without looking away, he continued, 'There you have it, son. Seven to one. I'm afraid you're outvoted on this occasion.' He softened his tone. 'Now, come on and sit down so we can finish this meeting. I'm getting thirsty and you know what my old man used to say, "Why wait till eight? It could be too late".'

He burst into fits of laughter, all the while maintaining unbroken eye contact with the younger man.

Something snapped within Reynolds.

'If that table goes, so do I. That's what you want, isn't it?' He screamed the accusation out, directing it at Parsons, who remained silent, his thin lips set tight.

'Now, calm down, son. No one's trying to force you out.' His father's tone had gained a darker edge now, reminiscent of Reynolds' granddaddy's infamous bark. One that was rumoured to make a grown man cry. 'We're all trying to do what's best for the airline. It's a table, for God's sake. We have much more important battles to fight and wars to win. Sit down and stop this nonsense.'

Reynolds suddenly felt suffocated. It was so hot in the room. No wonder he had a headache. His breathing felt laboured and sweat darkened the light blue shirt his housekeeper had left for him that morning. He had to get out.

'You haven't heard the last of this,' he growled. 'None of you have.' With as much dignity as he could muster, Reynolds collected his papers, being careful to avoid eye contact with his fellow board members. The walk took forever as he silently waded through the thick pile carpet that sucked at his black brogues like soft sand. Eventually, he felt the reassuring touch of cool steel on his hot skin and, without looking back, he stepped through the narrow gap in the door into the hall beyond.

Manhattan, New York City

13 November 2003, 17:45 hours EST

Nancy Taffuri smiled dreamily to herself and continued to trace out yet another large heart on the ink blotter in front of her. She tried to stifle a yawn, but it was impossible to resist. God, she was tired, but not because of her workload. Snapshots from last night bounced around her weary head, bringing back yet another smile to her chubby cheeks. She hadn't felt this good in months and was determined to sustain the unfamiliar feeling for as long as she could. Nancy wished she had something to do. It would have made the day move faster, and taken her mind off the dull ache, which continued to gnaw at her chest, threatening to spoil what should otherwise have been a perfect day.

Nancy glanced at the bottom right-hand corner of her PC screen and groaned.

17:46!

Barely a minute had passed since she had last checked.

Oh, well, just another fifteen minutes to go and she could head home for a well-earned rest. Her mind drifted back to last night.

Tess McGill, her oldest friend and a legal secretary at O'Neill and White, had called with an invite to the launch of a new daytime soap called *Frat Pack*. Her boss represented the production company and had received ten tickets. He only needed two and had given the rest to Tess, who had organised an all-girls' party. Nancy had jumped at the chance. Since her divorce, she never went out these days. Tess had arranged everything, starting with a stretch limo that had picked Nancy up at 18:30 and brought her into downtown Manhattan along with some secretaries from the law firm. The launch party started in the Meat Packers District at Draw Down, one of the hottest restaurants in New York. After a boozy buffet, they'd all headed out to York's nightclub, where Nancy had finally rediscovered her smile.

He was an extra in a new soap. Six feet two inches. Dark brown skin. A sexy goatee that reminded her of Johnny Depp in *Don Juan DeMarco*. That and his thick black hair, which was tied loosely at the back with a white bandanna. He was beautiful and, most importantly, made Nancy laugh, virtually from the moment he had come over to ask her for a dance until their passionate embrace earlier that morning when she had reluctantly allowed him to depart her warm bed, leaving Nancy in a state of exhausted euphoria.

She smiled again at the thought, continuing to trace out the heart she had started earlier. One slight doubt niggled away, though. He hadn't left a number. There was no way of tracking him down. She didn't even know his name. It hadn't seemed to matter last night. It had all added to the romantic mystery of the moment. So she hadn't bothered to ask. Even this morning, it hadn't occurred to her. He had promised to call, which was enough for Nancy but, as the day wore on, the realisation that she had no means of contacting him again had slowly given way to the dull ache in her chest. From lunchtime onwards, she had been praying on the hour.

Her PC bleeped once, the small yellow icon showing that incoming e-mail had appeared in her desktop toolbar. Nancy double-clicked the icon to retrieve it, but another screen popped up on her monitor. 'Security Warning. Open mail from known sources only.'

She impatiently dismissed the notification, carefully studying the full-colour image that had appeared on her screen. Actually, it was more like a cover shot for a magazine. It was him! He was looking straight at the camera, his beautiful dark skin glistening in the strong sunshine, long hair slicked back. It had been taken on a beach, possibly Hawaii, judging from the black sand that disappeared into the rolling surf behind him. God, he looked good. Better even than last night, if that could be possible. His powerful chest looked even broader than Nancy remembered, but the tight trunks didn't lie. Nancy flushed at the memory.

'Nice photo, Nancy. But didn't you know? Downloading porn off the Internet is a dismissible offence.'

Nancy whirled round to find Chuck Roberts, the night guard, peering over her shoulder. She glanced at the clock. It was past six. Her heart leapt. Time to go home.

'Go screw yourself, Chuck. He's my boyfriend. Besides, I didn't realise you got off on men. I always had my doubts, though.'

The security guard straightened up, smiling.

'No man is going to lay a hand on this baby,' he laughed, cupping his groin in both hands as he backed away from the desk. 'Women are my thing, and if you play your cards right, this could be all yours.'

'In your dreams, fat boy,' Nancy shouted back at him. 'In your dreams!'

The security guard stuck a curled tongue out at her and wiggled it back and forth, making a sucking sound between his teeth before turning on his heels and disappearing down the corridor, laughing his head off.

'Disgusting pig,' Nancy muttered under her breath and returned to her screen. She wasn't taking any chances this time and saved the photo both to her desktop and personal folder on the main server. She double-checked her handiwork just to be safe and, satisfied, shut down her computer before collecting her coat and heading for the lift, a big smile on her face.

San Francisco Airport, San Francisco

13 November 2003, 15:18 hours PST

Reynolds looked round the large exhibition hall containing the history of Reynolds Air. The whole museum would shortly be dismantled and transported 3,000 miles east to the new Steven F. Udvar-Hazy Center in Virginia to celebrate the centenary of flight. If the Board had its way, the table would make the long journey, too. He glanced down at the glass cabinet in front of him, where a yellowing document, deeply scored by numerous creases, was mounted on light-green felt. One corner had been torn off completely, and the ink was smudged in several places, but the type was still clearly legible after all these years; authorising a banker's draft for $20 million. It was the stuff of legend in the Reynolds family. How the young Reynolds had struck out on his own after ten years of working for the Wright Brothers. By then, he had become a chief engineer in the fledgling Wright Company. He understood all the subtleties of aerodynamics.

This knowledge not only allowed him to file his own patents, but also to defend his persistent breach of the Wrights' patents whilst he built up his own airline. Reynolds' grandfather ruthlessly exploited this weakness in the system over the next twenty years. He never settled a lawsuit, and lost many. Even when he did lose, compliance requests were ignored. He never paid the judgement fees until he absolutely had to. He would appeal constantly, using his understanding of both the patent laws and engineering to design subtle alterations into his aircraft. All with the sole intention of obfuscating and further delaying the court action whilst he built up his business.

Eventually, after nearly twenty-five years of almost constant litigation, the Curtiss-Wright Corporation, as it had since become, won a decision against Reynolds' grandfather's company recognising the Wright's patent as a pioneer patent entitled to very broad interpretation. The result, considered a landmark decision at the time, required Reynolds Air to make a one-off payment of $20 million, which, back in the 1930s, particularly following the Great Depression, was considered an astronomical sum. His grandfather loved telling the young Reynolds that particular story.

How it was the best $20 million he had ever spent because, by then, Reynolds Air was established and thriving on the west coast of America, ferrying passengers across the wide continent and exploiting the burgeoning trade routes to the west, including those to the emerging economic powerhouse of Japan.

'Thought I'd find you here.'

Reynolds jumped, startled by the silent approach of his father.

'I was only eighteen when he signed that,' said Reynolds' father. 'Had just joined the airline. Everybody was scared stiff at the time, including me. None of his managers could understand the change of direction and thought it would sink the airline. Patent infringement was a core part of their strategy, and a recognised means of growth to stay well ahead of the competition. But Poppa didn't care. Money meant nothing to him. It was a means to an end. And his end was to be the biggest carrier in the world. Defending endless rounds of patent litigation had ceased to serve that purpose. It was becoming a huge distraction, and he knew it was time to move on. So, he wrote the cheque, which nearly gave his bankers a collective heart attack. But he was right. It cleared the company for an Initial Public Offering free of all litigation worries, and helped pave the way for his acquisition blitz.'

His father paused and turned to face Reynolds, who continued to stare down at the letter.

'Son, you've got to learn to pick your fights better. Just like Poppa. He knew when it was time to move on. We've got a fight on our hands here. As important as any we've faced in our entire history, and now is not the time to tussle over a damn table.'

'But, Father, it's part of our heritage. It's—'

'No buts, son,' his father snapped. 'You listen carefully and you listen good, because I'm only going to say this once. You need to pull yourself together. The Board is asking a lot of questions and I'm not surprised. You look like shit. Too much time spent on the front pages of all the wrong magazines. You're getting a reputation out there, son, and it's not a flattering one. Hell, I'm no angel. I'm not averse to a drink myself, nor a bit of pussy on the side.'

His father's tone was flint hard. Even at eighty-five, he was still formidable. Reynolds could see flashes of his previous strength. Not quite to his grandfather's level, but formidable, nonetheless.

'This partying is getting out of control. If you were pulling up trees, you wouldn't hear diddly squat from me, but you're not. At the moment, you're presiding over one of the biggest corporate failures in American history.'

'That's not fair, Father,' Reynolds protested. 'This airline is facing a pretty unique set of circumstances that are not entirely of my doing. I'm—'

'I don't give a shit what the problems are,' his father growled, blue eyes blazing with anger. 'That's why we are in business. Do you think Poppa gave up when the US Air Force requisitioned his entire fleet of planes during the war at rates far below commercial rates? Hell, no. He spotted an opportunity and, whilst others fought to keep their planes, he cooperated fully with the Fly Boys. Christ, he even persuaded his pilots to fly for them. The Air Force never forgot that. We are now the biggest subcontractor for the US Air Force.'

He paused, but only momentarily—partly to catch his breath, but also to check that his son was absorbing the news. He wasn't disappointed.

'So, don't give me that crap. This blip will pass and flying will be cool again. Sooner than you think. In the meantime, you need to hang in there until it does and then we can continue as before.'

The two men stood in silence, staring at the glass case. After a moment, Reynolds' father began again.

'You're running out of time, kid,' he said. 'I'm not only fighting it in the boardroom, but at home, too. The trustees are getting nervous. They want to diversify out of the airline for all the same reasons our investors are trashing the share price. In the last five years, the trust fund has almost halved in value. Having all your funds in one investment doesn't look like a great strategy when the price keeps dropping. They're starting to talk about diversification, maybe into these new-fangled Internet stocks that have outperformed our share price by 50:1. The family is pushing them to make this decision. They're getting restless and blaming you. If you hadn't stuck to this one company strategy, they could be sitting on an investment portfolio of over $50 billion, not less than $5 billion. However, if they diversify, you have a problem. The Reynolds family will no longer control the airline, and then it really gets bloody. Our investors can start questioning why a Reynolds is running the airline; particularly one who is so publicly disinterested in the business. They will replace you, son, and with my blessing. I'm not prepared to sit over the demise of this family's wealth. Blood or no blood. Get your act together and start turning this airline around—and quickly.'

Reynolds senior had finished. There was silence in the exhibition hall, which, he had learnt over the years, meant his hot-headed son had heard him, loud and clear. Satisfied, and without another word, Reynolds senior turned on his heels, leaving his next of kin where he had found him, in silence, staring at the instruction from his grandfather to the bank.

Safe House,
Reykjavík, Iceland

14 November 2003, 02:05 hours GMT

Andreus Grond woke with a start and for a moment lay there, staring at the low ceiling in confusion, wondering where he was. And then he remembered: the card game had come calling, waking him from his sleep and drawing him downstairs much to the delight of his team who had whistled at him drunkenly as he entered the room. How much had he lost? Nearly half his fee. The wrench of shame blossomed out from his guts like knotweed until it threatened to strangle his lungs and heart in its malign embrace. He struggled into a sitting position on the long couch and winced at the memory. Across from him, Hansen was fast asleep in the armchair, Karlsen squashed in the other. Both were snoring loudly. Grond slowly made his way into the hallway and cracked open the front door.

A howling gale tried to wrestle the handle from his grasp. He shut it and recovered his coat from the floor, before trying again. The night was still black, and above him he could feel the strength of the storm around him. A ghost emerged from the gloom and his hand went to the P80, but it was only Jorgsson who nodded miserably at his boss, before disappearing round the back, presumably to find Solberg. Grond crunched down the drive, letting his hood blow back. Within seconds his shaved head was dripping wet. And cold. If it continued like this the rain would soon turn to snow. Grond considered the consequence of that on the operation, happy to be distracted from the gnawing guilt at losing so much money. He squeezed the glass pendant hard, wondering why it hadn't worked last night. He'd had a good run. It had worked for months. No bet placed, no cards held, but last night had felt different.

He'd been dreaming just before he'd woken. Of another lifetime. With Jane. They were at the beach, his favourite place. She was laid sideway to him, head propped on his stomach. They were looking out over an ocean. It was hot but not unbearably so and the waves rolled onto the beach, gently lapping at his feet. She was laughing at something he'd said about the bar he wanted to run. She couldn't imagine him serving people. His bar would be empty, just him, languishing on a hammock wating for customers he hoped would never arrive. Just one more job, he'd said. And then he would retire. Buy the bar. Relax and enjoy their life together. And then he'd woken up. He wasn't sure why. Maybe the screeches of laughter from downstairs. He'd laid there for long minutes, gripping his pendant, body dripping sweat, but the mind was a cruel bedfellow, and the next thing he remembered was standing in the living room, muttering, 'Just one game,' under his breath.

He stopped by the Shogun and laid both palms on the huge bonnet. At least he still had half his fee left. That should be enough, he thought. He just needed to stay away from the table which should be easy. All they had to do was get the woman and get out of Reykjavik. Making his way slowly back up the drive, he entered the house and laid back on the couch. But sleep was not going to come easily. He removed the locket and stared at the tuft of hair frozen in its glassy embrace. It had been a gift from Jane six months before she died. Grond lay there trying not to think of what had led to that black day, but it was too late. The memories were already upon him like rabid hyenas. He lay there, trying to shut them out, but the toxic arguments raged between them—some physical, all of them hurtful—driving a deep wedge between the two of them, until one day they had simply fallen silent. No longer given sustenance by the cold lips of his dead wife.

Grond stared at the ceiling, the finality of her suicide pressing down on him with a force ten times that of the storm outside. Eventually he fell into a light doze, but it was no release: Jane was sitting on the beach, cruelly laughing at him running a bar with no customers.

Mojave Desert, Nevada

13 November 2003, 18:30 hours PST

The sound waves reached the flock first, reverberating around the stark rock formations worn smooth by millennia of sand-laced winds. At first, the birds didn't react. The low boom was too far away to demand any action, just a communal acknowledgement of an unknown danger. Gradually, the noise intensified until the entire flock lifted clear of the shallow waters and eased into the blue sky. A colossal collective gracefully twisting and turning in the hot afternoon sun. But nature's conditioning had not prepared them for the black monster that suddenly appeared over the sheer rock wall. Moving at well over 200 miles per hour, its twin engines created a pulsating wall of noise that, for an instant, overwhelmed their group instinct, causing the tight formation to scatter. Terrified birds twisted and turned in the vortex of noise as the sleek intruder cut a swathe through their numbers. And then it was over. The intrusion faded as quickly as it had appeared and the flock effortlessly regrouped before settling onto the warm waters to continue their early evening forage for food.

Reynolds looked out of the window of the Sikorsky S-92 Executive, unable to concentrate. Parsons' detailed explanation of how he intended to win over the unions lay unread on the table in front of him. Far too much detail for his liking. At least his headache had eased, but that was cold comfort, given the blows he had suffered in the boardroom and later on at the Air Museum. He had stayed behind long after his father had left him, the harsh words ringing around his battered cranium. He would have stayed longer, but a timid curator had approached him to enquire whether the packers could interrupt his vigil to dismantle the displays in preparation for their long journey to Virginia.

Below him, the enormous flock scattered in slow motion, fanning out like the leading edge of a shock wave created by the blast from a nuclear explosion. Within seconds, they were gone, and Reynolds settled back into his leather seat while he studied the e-mail message he had received on his Blackberry during the board meeting.

'Team in place. We move today. Noël.'

Like all the other e-mails he had received from Noël, this one was cryptically vague so that no one reading it could possibly guess its meaning. But, to him, it was clear. It had better work, he thought. So far, he had committed over $160 million of his personal fortune to the project, and no one in Reynolds Air, including his father, knew what he was up to. To explain his frequent and long absences, he had organised a coordinated PR campaign that ensured his face constantly appeared on every worthwhile celebrity magazine in the country. It had clearly worked. Almost too well, judging from his father's reaction this morning. He only hoped he had sufficient time to complete his plans before both the Board and the Reynolds Family Trust Fund lost patience with their playboy leader, and displaced him permanently from his position as CEO of the world's largest airline. Without that platform, the last phase of his plans would fail. He had to hang in there for the next few weeks, hopefully weather the storm that would hit after the annual results came out, and then step forward with a solution to all their problems.

The next evolution of flight. One that would alter, in an instant, the dynamics that currently blighted both his family's airline and the industry at large. The delays would disappear, security concerns would fade, competition would be obliterated overnight and, of course, pollution would be history, not just for airlines, but for all forms of surface transportation. Shortly, he would be the toast of the environmental lobby. However, most importantly, he could charge what he wanted. A return to the golden days of flight when all but the very wealthiest individuals regarded flying as a distant dream. His grandfather would have been so proud of him, not only for the commercial success that would follow, but for the sheer audacity of his plans.

He would finally secure his place in history alongside his grandfather. His name would be mentioned in the same breath as all the great industrialists of the last century. Men like Ford, Rockefeller, Watson—who engineered IBM's rise—and, of course, his grandfather. No one would ever again question that Samuel K. Reynolds III didn't have the balls for big business, the scale of vision required to change the course of history, indeed altering how society lived. He shivered in anticipation. It was so close, but first he had to overcome one last hurdle.

Reynolds looked out of the window again and caught sight of the graveyard ahead, still a dark blot on the bright landscape. He felt the powerful engines ease back as the pilot began his descent.

Not long now.

He slipped both his Blackberry and the slim report into the leather briefcase beside him. Even at this distance, the glare of bright sunlight on bare metal caused him to squint. Reynolds had made this trip countless times during the last twelve months, passing over the huge plot each time, and it never failed to impress him. As they drew closer, the glare slowly subsided, dulled by the desert floor that formed the wide roads that criss-crossed the vast storage facility.

He pressed his face to the Perspex for a better view. Row upon row of abandoned aircraft were now visible. Planes of every description: Saabs, Embraers, Gulf Streams, Lears, Lockheeds, Bombardiers, ATRs, Fokkers and, of course, the big transcontinental planes. The huge Airbus A300s capable of carrying over 250 people; the Boeing 777-200 Extended Range, including the more familiar 767 and 757. Reynolds smiled to himself. Every major carrier was represented and even some of the low-cost carriers who had been beaten at the short-haul game by some of the more fleet-footed newcomers.

These temporary storage facilities had experienced an unprecedented uptake in demand following the World Trade Center disaster as airlines all over the world, eager to conserve their dwindling cash reserves, had turned to these huge open-air warehouses. It was a sad sight, seeing so many idle aircraft grounded on the desert floor, some of which he knew had never even carried a single passenger, having been sent directly from the production lines to yards like this one in the Mojave Desert. A choice location, given its low humidity and compacted surface set like concrete, that could support even the largest planes without having to be paved over. If Reynolds had his way, this would shortly become a permanent graveyard for housing all the fleets of the estimated 11,000 airliners that currently flew the globe.

Eventually, the aluminium sentinels petered out to be replaced by the hot earth of the desert, but not for long. Reynolds felt the helicopter slow to a standstill. It hovered like a giant insect in the fading light as the pilot waited for clearance to begin his descent onto the large H below them. They were less than thirty feet from the external perimeter fence of 'the graveyard', as Reynolds had started referring to it, and while they waited, he caught his first glimpse of the research facility that would shortly change his destiny. The unassuming single-storey building was almost invisible in the gathering darkness, its brown roof the same colour as the arid landscape that spread out for hundreds of miles in every direction.

As the pilot began his descent, Reynolds could see a small figure in a white lab coat waiting for him on the ground below. The man was bent double to protect his eyes from the mini-hurricane that buffeted him. However, as the Sikorsky touched down gently, he straightened and rushed towards the helicopter. Reynolds grabbed his bag and made his way purposefully towards the exit.

Mojave Desert, Nevada

13 November 2003, 18:45 hours PST

'Mr Reynolds, I really don't think that's a good idea. We are some way off perfecting the Qubit structure. It hasn't been tested yet. It's very unstable. We need more time.'

'Time, Crouch, is one resource we have little of at the moment,' Reynolds retorted as he marched down the narrow corridor towards the main laboratory. His CTO scurried along behind him, struggling to keep up with his boss' long steps. He was a small man, barely five feet six inches, and he looked unkempt in an oversized lab coat that had turned a dirty grey over the preceding days, a forgotten accessory and unavoidable victim of its owner's unrelenting schedule.

Reynolds burst into the main lab, causing several technicians to whirl round in annoyance, but they turned back to their screens, reassured by their boss' trademark entrance. Reynolds hardly registered their presence as he strode towards the centre of the room and stopped in front of a leather-backed chair. It was larger than all the others, as was the desk in front of it, and was clearly the designated command seat for the centre.

'So, when are we going to start?'

'I'm sorry, sir. What do you mean?' Crouch said.

'The hack,' Reynolds said. 'When are we going to start? I've never seen one before. Why the hell do you think I flew down? To shoot the breeze with you?'

'We've already started.' Crouch smiled proudly, pleased to be ahead of his boss for once.

It was Reynolds' turn to look slightly mystified, which quickly turned to annoyance.

'I specifically requested that you wait,' he growled at his CTO. 'How could you possibly start without me?'

'I've waited for you, sir. It's—'

'But you just said you've already started,' Reynolds interrupted. 'Make your mind up, man. Which is it?'

By now, Reynolds was on his feet, pacing energetically backwards and forwards.

'Both. These things take time to set up. We actually began the hack over six weeks ago.'

'Six weeks!' Reynolds thundered. 'Why didn't you tell me sooner?'

Crouch smiled patiently, just as a parent would react to the rants of an angry child. It was too much for Reynolds, who was still smarting from the humiliation his father had heaped on him in the boardroom. He flushed with anger at the memory. In San Francisco, he lived in the long shadow of his family name, suffocated by his father's constant meddling in the boardroom, battered by the family squabbles over the Trust and the relentless scrutiny of the market. However, here in Nevada, he was his own boss. No shareholders or family members to answer to. This was his show and he could do what he pleased.

'Don't fucking patronise me, Crouch,' Reynolds snapped at his CTO. 'I specifically requested that you wait for me. Where is everyone, anyway? Where are the hackers?' he snarled. 'Don't tell me you've already finished.'

The small man seemed to visibly shrink. His gaze swept the room. All eyes were on him as his team paused in their work to witness his humiliation.

'Christ, I don't ask for much,' Reynolds continued. 'It's taken over two years to get to this stage, not to mention the small matter of $160 million. This was supposed to be the moment we get our hands on the final key, and you've gone ahead without me.'

A few beads of sweat trickled down Crouch's temples, before disappearing into the grey collar of his once-white shirt. He licked his dry lips nervously, wondering what all the fuss was about. He hadn't seen Reynolds this agitated in a while. In fact, thinking about it, he had only ever seen him like this on one previous occasion—the day of their first-ever meeting, when Reynolds had pitched his proposal to the then Head of Advanced Quantum Physics at Yale University. His ideas had sounded preposterous, and still did, but Crouch couldn't deny Reynolds his fierce passion, particularly the desire to return Reynolds Air to its rightful place as America's largest company. He remembered him droning on about his granddaddy's achievements and, at the end of the session, Crouch was still unclear how Reynolds intended to achieve his objectives, whether in this lifetime or the next. In fact, he thought Reynolds was a crackpot billionaire pursuing an insane pipedream and he would have curtailed the discussion much earlier but for one small detail that interested Crouch a great deal.

Money: Reynolds had proposed an annual research budget of $50 million, which represented a hundredfold increase on Crouch's current situation, or any alternative one, for that matter. It guaranteed to propel him into a unique position in his field and Crouch had promised Reynolds that he would give him an answer the very next week. However, that afternoon, as he sat in one of the many interminable department budget meetings, Crouch's life flashed before him. He saw an endless succession of under-funded posts, where his focus was more on balancing next year's stationery budget rather than unravelling the mysteries of the very essence of life.

He had called Reynolds that same day and, within the month, was busy creating the Quantum Center in the barren landscape of northern Nevada. Within six months, he had poached over ninety percent of his own staff from Yale, all on vastly increased salaries. But they were still doing what they loved. As was Crouch. Except now he was in charge, apart from when Reynolds swooped in for his weekly meetings and for about an hour, the facility descended into chaos. However, when he left, things returned to their collegiate calm, a state of cerebral order that Crouch encouraged and, in fact, craved. It was a world of deep thinking and philosophical discussions where time was confined to its rightful place, moving slowly, almost imperceptibly, as some of the most brilliant minds in their field sought to unravel the mysteries of the atomic world.

'I've waited for you, sir. The rest was preparation for today,' Crouch said.

'But where are the hackers?' Reynolds repeated.

Crouch winced. His boss had watched way too many movies.

'That's not how we do it, sir,' he stuttered. 'There's no way I would attempt a full attack on their systems. It would be suicidal. These days, everything is so well defended. They will have firewalls, AV control, IDS, software sensors, spyware detectors, scanners. You name it. Any number of these defences would pick up an attempted hack. Once that happened, they would lock down their network so tightly that nothing could get in. No, we have had to be far more subtle. The secret is not to be seen.'

'So, what have you done?' Reynolds sounded more curious than angry now.

'Social engineering,' Crouch said.

'Social what? What the hell does that mean?'

'It's simple, really. We haven't even bothered to hack their systems. We've gone for the weakest link in any organisation's defences—its people. It has allowed me to deliver a Trojan horse onto one of their machines and make it my slave. This console here is now its master,' Crouch said, tapping the keyboard in front of him. 'And from here, I will infiltrate their network completely unnoticed.'

Reynolds frowned. What the hell was Crouch on about? All this jargon. Social engineering? Trojan horses? Slaves? Masters? Reynolds could feel his blood beginning to boil again.

'Speak English, damn it!' he barked at Crouch. 'Just cut to the chase, man. When can we get our hands on the keys?'

Crouch didn't even try to explain this time. Instead, he dou-ble-clicked an icon on his screen and, in an instant, a colour photo-graph appeared, depicting a muscular, well-oiled man staring sugges-tively into the camera.

Reynolds let out a lecherous wolf whistle.

'Who the hell is that?' he sniggered, like a small schoolboy. 'Hey, Crouch, I didn't realise you were into the male escort scene. You should come up to San Francisco more often.'

'This is Tom, our Trojan horse. The picture is actually a software program I wrote. We delivered it via email and when opened, it allows me to take control of the machine it was opened on. Remotely, of course. What has taken the time is persuading someone to accept this picture via e-mail and open it on their workstation. We finally made a breakthrough last night. Hence, the call for you to come down today.'

'So, who did you find?' Reynolds asked. Even he could understand that explanation.

'Her name is Nancy Taffuri. She works as a receptionist and, at approximately six p.m. Eastern Standard Time, she opened an e-mail from Tom containing a copy of this photo. We now have control of her PC. From here, we can infiltrate the network without being noticed.'

'Are you sure this will work?' Reynolds said, a little disappointed at the benign nature of the attack. He had envisaged something way more interesting.

'It should, but just in case, I've created a little diversion, which is more up your street. Ten minutes after she has opened her e-mail, the program also sets in motion the sort of attack you probably had in mind.'

'I thought you just said that a full-frontal attack wasn't advisable.'

'It's not an attack, just a diversion. Nor is it designed to get into the network, just to keep their IT bods focused on the wrong thing. It'll keep them busy looking at the outside and not at the inside, where all the action is happening.'

'So, what does that entail?'

'Whilst we've been setting up the Trojan horse, I've also been as-sembling a small army of computers to attack their systems, both in

London and New York. At the last count, we had over 22,000 PCs under our control waiting for my command.'

'To do what?' Reynolds said, failing to keep the excitement out of his voice. This was more like it.

'To attack their website and e-mail systems so they can't send or receive anything.'

'But we don't have that many computers, unless you haven't told me something, Crouch?'

'No, they aren't ours. They belong to other people from across the country, mainly home PCs. You know the sort of thing. A cheap computer for the kids so they can play games, listen to music, surf the web. They're very easy to take over. Kids love downloading things, especially if they're free. Just like the little program I created and attached to a few music download sites.'

'But how did you infect so many computers so quickly?'

'Easy. The kids do it for you. They share everything with their friends. It's a simple multiplier effect. One download can easily get sent to ten other machines and, in turn, they're sent out to ten others. In no time, you're on a few thousand machines.'

Reynolds whistled. He was impressed.

Crouch continued.

'Once on the machine, I have complete control of it, including the ability to make it send out a continuous data stream to a specified destination—in this case, their mail and web servers. The stream is actually comprised of thousands upon thousands of small packets of data. Each one is only a few kilobytes in size. A single machine wouldn't do much damage, but multiply it by a few thousand and suddenly you have a deluge of data hitting their servers. The result is always the same. The server will shut down.'

'Christ, Crouch! Where did you learn all this stuff?' Reynolds asked, half listening, his thoughts still with the twenty-odd thousand computers under his command.

'At college. It actually helped pay my way. Back then, everyone did it.'

'Did what?'

'Hacking. It was all small stuff, really. At least to begin with. Hacking home PCs for suspicious wives spying on their husbands. Getting delivery addresses for rival pizza parlours. However, my operation soon grew as my reputation—'

Crouch stopped. Something didn't feel right. His boss never allowed him to speak for so long about his work. Normally, he would cut in. Reynolds had no interest in the details or how Crouch got to the result. All he cared about was that he got there. Quickly.

Crouch looked round.

Reynolds was standing a couple of yards away, deep in conversation on his mobile.

Philistine, thought Crouch as he began tapping away at the keyboard. He didn't have to wait long. Within minutes, he heard Reynolds' heavy footfall.

'Crouch, I'm going to have to leave you. Trouble back at the ranch. There's been a security incident on the East Coast and they've shut down every airport north of Philadelphia. It's a mess. The press wants to interview me. Angry passengers to mollify. Disillusioned shareholders to empathise with. You name it.' Reynolds paused, lost in thought before continuing, 'So, how long will this take?' He nodded at the screen.

'Hours. Could be days. Maybe weeks. It all depends on their internal security.'

'Jesus Christ, man! We don't have days. I'm running out of time here. If Reynolds goes into Chapter 11, I'm finished. This installation is history. You're history. We need to move fast. Very fast indeed. I need a breakthrough. Work at it, man. Work till your fingers bleed. We need that key—today.'

'It's not that easy, sir. We need to move carefully. One false move and we'll be locked out of their network for good.'

But he knew before he had finished the sentence that it was futile. Reynolds was already gone, striding out across the large room back to the helicopter pad.

Crouch stared at the screen, his fingers frozen above the keyboard. No wonder Reynolds was so agitated. Crouch suddenly saw himself sitting at a table in a windowless room, arguing about stationery. There was no way he was going back to that life. Not if he could help it.

He pressed a button on the phone in front of him. Within seconds, a female voice answered.

'Prof. Crouch's office.'

'Kath, it's me. I need you to hold all my calls. Cancel all my meetings for the next forty-eight hours. Can you also have my meals brought to me at the usual times?'

'Of course, sir. I'll have one plate of chicken and boiled rice delivered every six hours starting from nine this evening. Will there be anything else, sir?'

'No, that's it.'

There was an uncomfortable pause on the line before his secretary continued.

'OK, I'll speak to you the day after next. Goodnight, sir.'

His secretary was used to these strange working schedules. She had long ago learnt to accept that her boss would literally work for forty-eight hours straight, lost in his strange world of mesons, photons and lasers.

Crouch cut the connection and turned back to his screen where a cursor blinked expectantly. The professor undid his top button, loosened his grubby tie, and cracked his fingers.

'Right, then. Where are you?' he muttered under his breath.

It was going to be a long night.

Route 41, Reykjavík, Iceland

14 November 2003, 14:15 hours GMT

The afternoon looked washed out, the limp sun already being pulled inexorably below the horizon. Anderson checked his watch. He'd forgotten how short the days were at this time of year, where day met night before day had barely begun. He stretched his tired limbs in the front of the Jeep and looked over at his companion who looked similarly fatigued. Anderson had made the mistake of falling asleep in his flat after making his way there from The Pink Nipple. The limo driver had woken him, before driving to a town house in Camden where the rest of the team were already assembled. After a medical—which included some sort of scan—they had waited for hours, until about 9:00 AM when the same driver had collected them and driven to a private airfield north of London. The flight had been bumpy, their plane fighting the remnants of a huge storm that had delayed their departure until after 11:00 that morning. He'd barely slept, none of them had, and was awake as they began their final descent over the Vestmannaeyjabær archipelago. The private jet hugged the southwestern shore of Suðurland, the Southern region of

Iceland, before landing at Keflavík International airport. It was barely a stone's throw from the Naval Air Station, and Anderson smiled at the memory of three lay overs after the horrors of his Afghan tours. They were a blur of Brennivín—a foul-tasting Icelandic schnapps made from potatoes and flavoured with caraway—long days, and even longer nights. The army had turned a blind eye to their exploits. That is, until it had stopped turning a blind eye, and hot anger boiled through his veins at this memory. He'd enlisted straight out of school and loved the camaraderie, the exercise, even the discipline. It had provided a structure to his life that he had missed as a child and, in turn, he had repaid them with the best years of his youth. Until that one mistake. And now here he was. Babysitting college professors for pimp money, whilst his friends toured the world. All over a silly argument. A simple misunderstanding.

The Jeep had entered the outskirts of Reykjavík and he recognised landmarks from his previous visits. Little seemed to have changed and eventually they pulled up outside a large building. The driver looked over at him. He was pushing his late thirties but looked fifty; too many late nights.

'The professor is on her way. Remember, you stay outside. I'll cover the downstairs, whilst she goes upstairs with the other two man team. Any questions?'

'Have you met her?'

'Nope. I arrived with you, remember?'

Anderson did remember, he just didn't care. He was beginning to feel slightly nauseous, the effects of the previous night finally hitting home.

'Well, I hope she's worth it,' Anderson said, cracking the door open. Arctic air chilled the cabin and he inhaled deeply trying to clear his head.

'See for yourself,' the other man said. 'She's here.'

They both got out and waited for the approaching Jeep, which pulled up beside them. Two men jumped out, followed by a petite woman. She was wrapped in a blanket to fend off the worst of the cold afternoon, black hair springing everywhere. As she stepped onto the kerb, their eyes met and Anderson smiled but she barely registered him, her face etched with fatigue and worry. She continued past him, up the stairs and seconds later, was gone, swallowed up inside the building along with her three bodyguards.

'Fuck,' Anderson muttered to himself. That's all he needed. Guarding some frigid ice queen when he could be back in London at the Pink Nipple. Well, soon he would. With the proceeds of his babysitting, he was sure as hell going to tear that place to pieces with his partying. He climbed back into the Jeep, just as a large Shogun appeared at the end of the street.

Reykjavík, Iceland

14 November 2003, 14:20 hours GMT

Grond feathered the brake of the Shogun and dialled Hansen, who answered straight away.

'We're here. Stay with both teams at the house. I'll go in with Jorgsson, Pedersen and Karlsen. If we need help, I'll call you, but it looks straightforward. There's one man outside; three have entered with Target One.'

He cut the connection and then placed a further call to the airport, or more precisely, to a small charge placed on the fuel tank of a mothballed jet in one of the private hangars. It would pull every policeman from Reykjavík out to Keflavík and leave a clear route down to the harbour. No one would suspect a sea escape. Grond glanced over at Pedersen who scowled back, clearly sore about last night, but Grond figured they were more than even: Pedersen had pocketed the lion's share of his losses; Jorgsson and Karlsen the rest. Which is why they were sitting with him in the Shogun. After waking, Grond had lain there, thinking about the card game. No one could repeat the run of bad luck he'd just experienced. Maybe he should try and win it back? After all, it was nearly £2 million. But that was risky. What if he lost even more of his fee? The realisation had brought him out in a cold sweat but had also prompted another thought: what if these three didn't made it today? For it to work, he just needed to separate the teams. It wouldn't be quite the show of force that he suspected the contract wanted, but as Pedersen had repeatedly pointed out last night, one man could grab this woman. That man would be Grond, once he had cancelled the debt.

'Everyone ready?' Grond said, tapping the accelerator. The Shogun grumbled down the deserted street. As they pulled up alongside the Jeep, Grond attracted the attention of the passenger, a surly looking brute who looked like he hadn't slept in days. The man wound his window down and Grond pointed to the rear of the Jeep.

Puzzled, the man leaned out and looked down the street, whilst Grond retracted his window. He was now barely eighteen inches from the other SUV.

'What?'

'Your tyre,' Grond said. 'I think it's flat.'

The man swore and got out of the vehicle, this time kicking the tyre, before returning to address Grond.

'Looks fine—'

The bullet caught Anderson square in the forehead, jerking his body back into the Jeep as he slumped to the tarmac. Grond holstered the P80 and calmly parked the Shogun, before entering the building with his team. A man was sitting at the reception desk but was way too slow and paid for it with his life, slumping onto the desk, a smoking hole between his eyes. Grond motioned for Jorgsson and Karlsen to take the stairs. Tapping Pedersen on the shoulder, he nodded at an open door leading off the hallway. Grond had recced the building extensively and knew the layout intimately—there was a room along this corridor that would be perfect for dealing with Pedersen. He could tackle the other two after they had recovered Target One.

Pedersen made his way over to the doorway and stepped through, with Grond close behind.

'Check each room,' Grond said. 'She may be down here.'

The first room was a stationery cupboard, the second, a restroom and the third, a lone panel, as high as a man, bristling with dusty fuses.

All were empty. The last, at the end of the short corridor, was marked, "Pump Room".

'If she's not in here,' Grond whispered, 'we'll join the other two. You go first. I'll follow.'

Pedersen gripped his P80 and nodded. Cracking the door open, he slipped through, closely followed by Grond, who latched the door behind him. They were in what appeared to be a boiler room with pipes running round the perimeter, many steaming. It stank of sulphur and was suffocatingly hot. A College of Geothermal Studies needed a lot of hot water. This was the nerve centre, receiving water from the nearby Nesjavellir Power Plant. A tangle of metal and dials faced them, reaching up to the ceiling and running for twenty feet in both directions, before leading off down further corridors. Grond stayed by the door. He nodded for Pedersen to take the first corridor and mimed with two walking fingers that he would check the other way.

Pedersen frowned. The room was clearly empty.

'Why would she be in here?' Pedersen said, turning towards Grond. He slowly raised his arms, staring at the P80 now pointed at his chest.

'Slowly does it,' Grond said, wedging himself behind a large drum.

'What are you doing?'

'You didn't think I would just let you walk off with my money, did you?'

Realisation dawned on Pedersen's face. He tensed, estimating the percentages.

'I guess not.'

Pedersen sprang left towards the corridor, firing as he fell, but Grond was ready, squeezing off one shot as he crouched behind the drum. But not for long. Behind him, the pipes suddenly starting spewing boiling steam into the room. Grond screamed and broke cover, firing blindly in Pedersen's direction as he threw himself against the spaghetti of pipes opposite. Then silence, just the sound of whistling steam behind him and his own curses—he was normally more decisive. Would never engage in conversation with his targets. He was losing his touch.

He peered down the corridor. A bullet had caught Pedersen high in the throat, ripping through his skull and exiting the crown of his head. Grond unpeeled himself from the hissing metal and examined the pipework that was boiling vapour into the corridor like a bank of demented kettles. Pedersen's bullets had torn multiples holes in at least four and they were now ballooning super-heated steam into the room, creating a scalding-hot barrier between Grond and the exit. He removed his coat, wrapping it over his head like a hood and dropped to his knees, edging forward, but it was hopeless. The volcanic condensation was already burning through the thin material. He retreated and sat back against the pipes, thinking. Unless he isolated the pipes he was stuck, leaving Karlsen and Jorgsson still alive with Target One. The thought sent him scurrying down the corridor in search of the stopcock.

One Liberty Plaza, New York City

14 November 2003, 09:30 hours EST

Ethan stared out over Lower Manhattan, mobile in hand, wondering whether he should try Uma again. It was a beautiful cloudless day, in stark contrast to the storm clouds that continued to rage in his head and that had accompanied him on the short drive from JFK into the city. He wondered for the thousandth time whether he should have stayed in London, unsure what was worse: his unfamiliar indecision or total feeling of helplessness? The latter, he decided, and pressed Uma's speed dial. Nothing. He pocketed the phone and shielded his eyes from the bright sunshine that sparkled off the thousands of windows that made up the cityscape in front of him. From his vantage point, he could see right across the Hudson River to the Jersey shore beyond and, further west, right out into New York Bay, where the Statue of Liberty resembled a miniature doll. Below him, Ground Zero had begun its transformation. Previously, a vast brown-earth construction site had scarred the surface, but it had now completely disappeared, replaced by the dull grey of concrete and single-storey construction buildings as New York prepared to honour its dead with a new tower.

The scene brought memories flooding back of the first time he had seen this view. It felt like yesterday—his booming headache, Uma matter-of-factly telling him about LEAP—but it was actually over twelve months ago: October 4th 2002, the date LEAP had first been introduced to him. So much had happened since. A whirlwind of activity as they rushed to bring her teleportation device to market. Days, nights, weekends had all blurred into one long marathon while Ethan had created the infrastructure capable of launching Uma's vision onto an unsuspecting world. This is what he did. Had done on countless occasions before. The big difference, this time, was that everything had been performed in a shroud of secrecy. Now, it seemed that their secret was out. Uma was in danger and he couldn't get to her. His gripped the mobile tightly.

'Any ideas?'

Ethan turned towards the man sitting behind a tiny desk, partly obscured by two enormous screens and piles of paperwork that covered every inch of the surface.

'I'm sorry, Shane. What did you say?'

'We were trying to work out who was responsible for this cyber-attack. Any ideas?'

Ethan forced himself to concentrate.

'Nope. Besides which, are you sure that it wasn't just a random attack?"

Even as he asked, Ethan realised how unlikely that was.

'No, this was a carefully coordinated operation. I have the stats to prove it.'

Shane Williams, Chief Security Officer of Green Ray, stood up and walked over to a long desk that ran down the entire side of his office. He was a short, stocky man with a permanent frown etched across his face, as if the weight of the entire world's security rested on his shoulders. He flipped through piles of computer readouts before finding what he was after.

'Here it is.' He returned to where Ethan stood, smoothing the creased paper out in front of him. 'At seven last night, the main servers started to receive random hits. A few hundred to begin with, but that grew exponentially. By seven fifteen, we were receiving over a million packets per second, and then it went off the scale. It took us down. Nothing can cope with that type of load.'

He continued to leaf through the graph paper.

'That continued until seven this morning, and then it stopped. One second, a deluge. The next, absolutely nothing ...'

Ethan nodded, half listening. He wondered whether he should try Uma again.

'I've never seen such a sustained and coordinated DDoS attack. Whoever organised this was very sophisticated.' Ethan dragged himself back into the discussion. The attack was simple. Ethan had encountered many through several Internet Service Providers he had acquired about two years ago. Better known as Distributed Denials of Service, it was a technique employed by cyber gangs to target high-profile websites, such as airlines, banks or online retailers. There was nothing sophisticated about them. Basically, the targeted website was bombarded with millions of requests which either made them crash or slow down so much that nothing could really get in or out. The bottom line was that legitimate shoppers or users were denied access and the attack would continue until a ransom was paid. Too much adverse publicity was at stake, so the site in question had quietly paid up and the gang had moved on to its next target.

'It feels like a shot across the bow.'

'Most definitely,' Shane said, rummaging through piles of paper before he found the one he needed. 'Our initial analysis suggests they did not design it to upset our internal network or machines. More a show of brute force designed to consume all our bandwidth connection to the Internet.'

'Christ, I wonder what's going to be next?' Ethan couldn't help but think of Uma's call from earlier.

'Well, given what happened to the journalists and then Uma's offices, we need to be vigilant over the next few days.'

'How on earth did you find out about the offices?'

'It's my job to know these things,' Shane said, pleased at Ethan's reaction. 'That's why you pay me the big bucks. I called in two additional teams last night to watch over Uma for the next two weeks. They were meant to LEAP. In fact, I had them scanned but the attack put paid to that. They flew out from a private airfield this morning after the storm had dissipated. They're with her now. She'll be OK.'

'Don't you think that's a bit of an overreaction?' Ethan said, both perturbed at the way Shane was talking and slightly alarmed that he hadn't suggested it earlier. He could have—no, he should have—phoned it in from the Challenger last night or even from London. Christ, he wasn't thinking straight, just reacting to each situation as it presented itself. Ethan was also relieved. He had way more confidence in Shane's men than in the local police. Even Baldursson's team, who were trained for such eventualities. Shane's men were ex-military. Usually Special Forces. They could definitely handle themselves.

Shane looked over at Ethan, the furrows on his brow even deeper than normal.

'Two people died yesterday. We knew something like this might happen, so let's stop pretending that it was a random attack. We now need to work out whether these people are simply flexing their muscles or actually trying to get at LEAP. So far, I would hazard a guess that it's a show of strength.'

'You don't think they got through the firewalls?'

'I need to spend more time analysing the results. We're going to be out of action for two to three days whilst we sort this out.'

For a moment, Ethan was too shocked to say anything.

'Everything? LEAP as well?'

'I'm afraid so.'

'What? Everywhere?' he repeated. 'Including here?' Ethan's heart dropped at the thought of having to fly back in the Challenger. How would he get to Uma now?

Shane nodded.

'But I need to LEAP to Reykjavík.'

'I'm afraid that's out of the question,' Shane said. 'We're going to have to perform a complete system overhaul to make sure nothing breached the network defences. That'll take time. So, you need to lie low. Take a break. Catch a baseball game or something.'

Ethan stared at Shane with incredulity. He didn't even like baseball.

'There's very little you can do here until we've given the system a clean bill of health. Besides, it's nearly the weekend. By Monday, this will all be sorted and you can get back to work. I'd start with getting some sleep. You look like shit.'

Before Ethan could respond, his phone buzzed. He hurriedly pulled it from his pocket, almost dropping it as he did. It was a text from Pike. Christ, he had completely forgotten about the sale.

'Retention accepted. Deal done. Funds transferred. Green Ray Fund stands at £33 billion.'

Ethan barely had time to absorb the news before his phone rang again: Uma!

'Where have you been?' he said, failing to keep the agitation out of his voice. 'I've been trying—'

He fell silent, listening intently. As he did so, his face drained of colour.

'Slow down. I can hardly make you out. They killed who?'

His CSO looked up sharply.

'Shane's here. I'm putting you on hands free.'

'—shot him. Point blank. His head. So much blood.' Even over the phone's loudspeaker, they could hear the panic in her voice. 'They're in the offices. Trying to find me.'

'What are you even doing there after last night?'

'I came back to tidy up.'

'By yourself?' Ethan said. 'Where're the police?' he asked more softly.

'They've gone.' Uma's voice was barely a whisper. 'No one's here.'

'Can you call them?'

'They won't get here in time,' she said, clearly choking back tears. The line went dead for a few seconds. Ethan thought they'd lost the connection, but suddenly there was a loud bang followed by a muffled cry. 'Ethan, help me.' Uma was sobbing freely now. 'They're right outside.' She sounded hysterical. 'I think they want to kill me.'

Ethan tried to keep his voice steady.

'Can you get to the LEAP chamber?'

'I tried. It wouldn't work.'

He could see Shane shaking his head. They'd already started to shut the system down.

'We'll reboot it. Give us two minutes.'

His CSO was already busy tapping away, his face a mask of concentration and anxiety.

'It's too late. I've barricaded myself in the far offices. Please,' she pleaded. 'They're outside.'

Ethan's heart sank. He heard splintering wood in the background, followed by another muffled scream. Then the line went dead. This time, it stayed silent.

'Uma. What's going on?' There was no answer. 'Uma!' he tried again.

It was no good. He had lost the connection. He redialled once, twice, but each time it went straight to voicemail.

'Shane. Get me out there right now!'

'Is that a good idea? I me—'

'Uma's in danger.'

'I understand, but what can you do? I sent four men out to guard Uma. And they were armed. You realise,' he finished as calmly as he could, 'they're probably all dead.'

'And if we don't do something in the next few minutes, Uma will be too.'

'It's not just that,' Shane said. He had never seen Ethan so angry. Even during the most pressured situations, he simply never lost his temper. Instead, he would get calmer. Even more analytical, searching for solutions until he found one. It wasn't logical to follow Uma into so much danger. That much was obvious to Shane, but for once Ethan wasn't thinking coherently. Quite the opposite. He was being irrational. Shane tried one more time. 'The system is halfway through a shutdown. I can't guarantee your cellular integrity if I send you now. It'll take hours to test everything thoroughly.'

'We don't have ten seconds,' Ethan snapped back, surprised at his own reaction. Part of him agreed with Shane. It was madness to leap out there blindly, not least because he had no idea what he would do when he got there. He wasn't a fighter. It made more sense to call the police, but there wasn't time—those men were in the room with Uma right now—and all he could think of was Uma's terrified voice. The skin on his back tingled in agreement at the thought of losing someone else. He had to protect her, and that was all that mattered. 'I need to go now.'

'But Ethan, we can't be certain you will be safe. We could lose you as well.'

'I'm willing to take that risk.' He turned away and began punching numbers into his phone. 'Robin, it's Ethan. I need a private jet out of Keflavík airport.'

There was a slight pause.

'In the next thirty minutes. I don't care what time it is. Get me a plane.'

He cut the connection and looked over at Shane.

'Well, have you got me a jump window?'

Shane dropped his head in resignation. He knew from bitter experience that Ethan had now made his mind up. The fact it was the wrong decision was irrelevant. There was simply no sense in arguing. He had better focus his energy on rebooting the system.

Department of Geothermal Studies, Reykjavík

14 November 2003, 14:51 hours GMT

There was someone bent over him. He couldn't tell who. The face was blurred. Indistinct, but also familiar. However, it refused to solidify. He felt nauseous and for a second, thought he was going to vomit. His head hurt. Everything did. Just like after his very first jump, only much worse. What was he doing on the floor? He didn't remember falling over. Had he knocked himself out?

Something was tickling his face. It felt feather light. Smelt good too, but he couldn't place it. He brushed it away. The last thing he remembered was the look on Shane's face through the viewing booth as he prepared to make the LEAP. A mixture of fear and concern. Even after their initial argument, Shane had kept on at him, citing all the reasons he shouldn't make the jump until he'd been reduced to a simmering silence as the process began. And then nothing. Ethan must have blacked out.

And now he was in a strange room, doubled up on the floor. Suddenly his vision cleared, and he realised where he was; it was one of the inner offices at the Geothermal Department. The place was a mess. Upended bookcases. Toppled filing cabinets. Papers everywhere. He blinked. Uma was bent over him, her delicate features creased with worry. And there was something else in her expression. She looked scared. Her lips were moving, but he couldn't hear a thing. She helped him into a sitting position, where he tried to clear his head. Slowly, muffled sounds became anxious questions.

'Are you OK?'

'A bit groggy.' That was an understatement. He felt like his whole body was about to split down the middle. 'The worst jump yet,' he muttered, glancing over at her. That look again. Fearful eyes. She was talking again, but he didn't hear. He was staring over her shoulder at the figure of a man crumpled on the floor, his head bent at an unnatural angle.

'Who the hell's that?'

'You don't remember.'

'Remember what? I passed out.'

Uma couldn't hold his gaze.

'You killed him.'

He hadn't expected that.

'How?' His voice was devoid of emotion.

'With your bare hands. You snapped his neck. Like a twig.' She motioned with her own to emphasise the casualness of his act.

'I've never killed anyone,' he whispered, almost to himself. But even as the words left his lips, he realised it wasn't true.

'You seemed to know what you were doing.'

Ethan looked down at his hands. He wasn't sure what he was looking for, but they seemed fine. Not the hands of a killer.

He searched his memory again but came up with nothing. His reaction to this wasn't normal. He barely felt anything, except perhaps a surge of power at the thought of what he had just done. He had just killed a man.

'You were screaming my name, except—' Uma stopped herself, puzzled. Ethan's hands looked different. Really different. These hands were much larger than she remembered. Thicker too. Ethan's were slender. More angular. Long fingers. Delicate almost. The hands of a pianist. And it wasn't just his hands—his whole figure seemed fuller. More solid. Muscular, like a bodybuilder. But his face looked the same. What was going on?

'We need to get out of here,' Ethan said, completely oblivious to Uma's reaction. 'There could be others.' He nodded at the dead man.

He held out his arm. Uma stared at it in shock. Ethan had not touched her since they'd met. At least not intentionally. Now he was taking her hand. She hesitantly held hers out. He took it without pausing. It was strong. Easily enveloping her own. She felt herself being led through the offices. Out of what was left of the main door. And then onto the landing. She avoided looking at the ruined painting of her father. She might not be able to see him but could feel his accusatory stare boring into her back. The plan wasn't meant to happen this way, she reminded herself. They'd been so careful. And now it was all beginning to unravel, just as he had warned her it would.

Ethan descended the spiral staircase that ringed the large hallway below. Uma followed fearfully. She knew what was coming. Ethan hadn't noticed yet. She wondered how he would react. Perhaps he wouldn't, just like before when he'd stared at the dead man on the floor. She kept her eyes down, reluctant to look out over the banister at the Obelisk. But she felt herself drawn to it. It was unavoidable. And, of course, her glance confirmed the worst. The white was now blood red. Not just the tip, but the whole column. Dripping red.

'What the hell is that?'

Ethan had stopped and was looking out over the banister, down into the hallway below.

'You really don't remember, do you?'

He stared at her blankly before looking back at the impaled body on top of the sculpture. It was splayed, spreadeagled, as if caught in some macabre freefall. The man had died painfully, his face contorted in an angry scream, his lifeless eyes now looking right at Ethan.

'How could I have done that?'

Uma didn't respond. She was remembering the ease with which Ethan had disarmed the man before dropping him with a sidekick to his chest. As he lay, bent double with pain, Ethan had grabbed a handful of the man's jacket and trousers, jerking him upwards, high above his head like a demented weightlifter. He had purposefully carried him to the edge of the balcony, and then paused, before casually tossing him onto the deadly pyramid below. The man's terrified scream had trailed off as his own body weight carried him down the cold hard metal, finally stopping after it had nearly severed him in two.

'We need to go. I had Robin reserve a private jet out of Keflavík. We'll be in London before you know it.' He turned and continued down the stairs.

Ethan paused beside the pyramid before stooping to retrieve something from the blood-soaked marble floor. He held a bloodied set of car keys aloft. Next, a mobile phone, which he wiped clean on his jacket. As he did so, his own rang.

'I've got her,' he said. 'Yes, she's fine. Sure.' He handed Uma the phone. 'It's Shane,' he said before turning to continue his search of the hallway.

'What the hell have you done to Ethan?' she said.

'I had no choice. You were ... Ethan was ... The system was down. I had to improvise.'

'What on earth does that mean?'

'Well, I ... uhm ... wasn't sure ... speed was ... uhm ... well I ... I sent the minimum ...'

'The minimum?'

'Yes. There was limited bandwidth. Time. Processing power. It's the only thing I could think of.'

'Shane, what exactly did you do?'

Ethan, who was now standing by the door looking out into the street, turned towards her. Uma realised with a start that he was holding a gun. Where had that come from?

'I relied on the last transfer. I used Anderson. One of your guards. His body, at least. The rest is Ethan.'

'Jesus, Shane. Which bit?'

'Well, his head. His brain.'

Uma fell silent, her mind whirling with the implications of what Shane had done. What he had unleashed? The LEAP Laws were in tatters at their first hurdle.

'Where's Anderson?'

'Dead, I think.'

At least they didn't have to deal with that conundrum. Not that it would have mattered. This person was neither Ethan nor Anderson.

'I had no choice,' Shane said, his voice tight with emotion. 'Your life was in danger.'

Uma didn't know where to begin.

'What else could I do?' Shane continued.

'Something's gone wrong. It's not Ethan.'

'Well, strictly speaking, that's not true. His body is just cells and—'

Uma stared at the mobile.

'That's not what I meant,' she snapped, but Shane wasn't listening.

'—which we can reverse out once this is over. I've a full copy of him here. He will be fine.'

'And what the hell do we do with ... him?' She stared at the thickset man by the door. He had shouldered the firearm and was beckoning impatiently for her to finish the call.

'I've got to go,' she snarled at Shane. 'We'll finish this later.'

San Francisco Airport, San Francisco

14 November 2003, 07:01 hours PST

Through the darkened windows of the office, a huge silver 747 was framed in the doors of a colossal hangar. As Reynolds suppressed a yawn, the plane turned majestically, continuing its slow trundle out towards the waiting runway. Just behind, two 767s waited patiently in line for their monstrous cousin to begin its take-off routine. They wouldn't have to wait long. On a clear morning like this, at rush hour, each of the airport's four runways could handle upwards of thirty movements per hour. One plane every two minutes would be spat up into the blue skies above San Francisco. Over 100 planes, half of them belonging to Reynolds Air. Reynolds smiled to himself, turning back to the awkward conversation the other two occupants of his father's office were having.

'Bill, how could you have misjudged their mood so monumentally? Only yesterday you claimed they were eating out of your hand. What's gone wrong? And why so quickly?'

His father posed the last question quietly, just like he had done a thousand times with his son. That's when he was at his most dangerous. The quieter he got, the greater his anger. Even though it wasn't directed at him, Reynolds felt his stomach lurch slightly at the icy tone. Parsons cleared his throat. He didn't look so self-assured today. In fact, Reynolds doubted whether he had ever seen the man look so uncomfortable. He couldn't ever remember his father talking to his right-hand man in such a manner. Reynolds settled back in his chair to enjoy the fireworks.

'Well, sir,' Parsons began, his voice almost a whisper. 'I'm not sure. The TWU has rejected the proposal out of hand and, what's more, seems to have stirred up doubt in the minds of the Air Line Pilots Association and the Association for Flight Attendants.'

'But why? What's the basis for their stance?'

'They don't feel the deal is equitable. Plain and simple.'

'Why not? That doesn't make sense. Equitable compared to what?'

'They're comparing it to what the Reynolds family and the other shareholders stand to gain if the airline pulls through and sees the upside on their stock. In short, they want more. A lot more.' Parsons licked his lips, pausing in that annoying way that Reynolds had come to hate over the years. When he did that, you knew something was wrong. It was always accompanied by the slightly superior, almost gloating tone that finance people tended to adopt when they were going to deliver bad news. Reynolds' father waited, staring at his CFO. 'They want twenty percent of the airline's stock for agreeing to all the concessions.'

Reynolds burst out laughing.

'That's insane. On current prices, that's worth what? Nearly two billion. And where do they expect that to come from?'

'The family trust.'

Reynolds hooted with derision.

'But that will cut our stake below the majority voting rights. Besides which, the beneficiaries would never agree to it.'

'Oh, you can keep the votes. They want the stock.'

'Well, they can all go to hell,' Reynolds exclaimed, before looking questioningly at his father.

'Not so fast, Samuel,' admonished the old man quietly as he stared thoughtfully at his CFO for several seconds before continuing. 'They've got us, haven't they, Bill? Why the hell didn't we see this one coming?'

Reynolds looked puzzled.

'What do you mean?'

'Go on, Bill, explain to him what the problem is.'

'I'm afraid your father's right. Their position is actually much stronger than you think. If you don't agree to this transfer, they won't cooperate on the concessions. The airline will most likely go into Chapter 11 and you will lose everything.'

'Well, if they don't agree to the concessions, then half of them will lose their jobs.'

'Half of them will lose their jobs, even if they agree. The whole idea is to cut staff numbers. They feel like they have nothing to lose. No, that's not quite right,' Parsons corrected himself. 'They have plenty to lose, but they're betting that the family has even more to lose. If you reject their request, it is likely that the airline will go into Chapter 11 and you will lose all your shares. However, if you accept, they will give you all the concessions you want. And in turn, a fighting chance of pulling through.'

Reynolds senior laughed gently, shaking his head.

'What's so damn funny? They have us over a barrel.'

'They do. It's a beautiful piece of negotiation. Absolutely beautiful. So simple. We've been well beaten this time.'

'Bastards. We can't let them get away with it.'

'Oh, but they have, son, they have.'

'Well, what are we going to do?' Reynolds said.

'Relax. Admire their moment. You need to learn when you have been beaten. Accept that, on this occasion, we have been outmanoeuvred.'

'We can't take this lying down. We need to fight.'

'Drop it. There's nothing we can do. The unions have won this time.' Reynolds' father turned to his CFO. 'Bill, let them sweat for a few days. In fact, leave it till next week to get in touch. They'll have the entire weekend to worry. Call them all Tuesday to get their representatives in and reject the deal. Say it's too much.'

'What, an outright rejection? Or do I have some leeway?'

'No more than ten percent.'

'Ten percent!' Reynolds exclaimed. 'That's preposterous.'

'No, it isn't,' his father snapped back.

'Granddaddy would never have allowed that to happen.'

'He didn't need to. He owned the airline in its entirety and it was growing like hell. Unlike now. We are experiencing the worst slump in aviation history and are a public company with institutional shareholders to consider. We are stuck and they know it.'

Reynolds felt his phone vibrate and glanced down.

Crouch! The man's timing was unbelievable.

He stared at the screen, wondering whether he should answer it.

'Are you going to get that or look at it all day?'

Reynolds swallowed hard and put the receiver to his ear.

'What is it?'

'We're in business. I've secured the code. The data checks out and it's now on our servers. We have our answers. It's so simple. I don't understand how we could have missed it.' Crouch's voice quivered with barely suppressed excitement. He sounded like a kid in a sweet shop.

'Good. It's about time. When can we start testing?'

'Right away.'

Reynolds cut the connection and glanced at his father.

'Can we continue, or do you have any more calls to make?'

'Just one, but it can wait 'til later.'

His father glared at him, turning back to Parsons to discuss how to sell the new deal to the Family Trust, but Reynolds wasn't listening. He and Crouch were a step closer now. And not a moment too soon from the sound of it. Shortly, he wouldn't need to negotiate with anyone. No unions. No shareholders. No family members. Nobody. He would be untouchable. He smiled to himself. Just one more call to make. He needed to neutralise the competition. There was no point in having a rival consortium in the market when he went public.

His grandfather would have been proud of him.

Reykjavík, Iceland

14 November 2003, 15:05 hours GMT

U ma stepped out onto the street, suddenly reluctant to leave the building she had prayed to be free of only minutes earlier. She had nearly died in there. The sound of splintering wood filled her ears as she remembered how the heavy door had finally disintegrated in front of her. A man was stood in the entrance, carefully fitting a silencer to the large gun he was holding. His eyes sought her out. Cool. Detached. Business-like. He raised both arms to fire. But that was his final act. In a blur, she saw him drop his weapon as both his hands went to his neck. But it was too late. The next second, he lay slumped on the floor. Behind him stood Ethan. His eyes cool, detached, business-like.

Up ahead, Ethan was holding the bloody key fob above his head, pressing it repeatedly. A black Jeep, perhaps four or five vehicles beyond where he stood, suddenly flashed. A man was slumped against one of the monster tyres. He looked vaguely familiar. Ethan stepped over his outstretched legs without a second glance and climbed up into the huge four-by-four. The engine roared into life and for a gut-wrenching moment, Uma thought he was going to drive off without her. She hurried down the pavement, pausing at the prone figure. It was Anderson. Or at least the part of him she knew as Anderson. She had only met him once, on her way into the building. His lifeless face was large, like his body. And heavily scarred from too many fights. Otherwise, he looked unremarkable except for the neat hole in the centre of his forehead. Where had she seen his clothes before? Of course. Shane had used them. Why not? They were already here at the LEAP gate. Less to transfer. And they already fitted the body. Despite her abhorrence of Shane's solution, his breach of the LEAP laws, the scientist in her couldn't help but admire the simplicity of his quick thinking. It was, in essence, the logical conclusion of teleportation. They only really calculated the scale and form of a transferee's body anyway. There was no point going further since everyone was the same. Biologically speaking. Scale and form were the important components. That's what defined someone. Visually at least. That and their memories. Uma shuddered. What had Shane said? He had just sent Ethan's brain. And combined it with Anderson's brawn. She remembered the brutal efficiency with which Ethan had dispatched her two assailants. Anderson was clearly a fighter. She swallowed hard. Even if this person had Ethan's brain, something wasn't right. He wasn't behaving like the man she knew. And if it wasn't Ethan, who was it?

'Are you going to stand here all day?' he called down to her. 'It'll be dark in an hour.'

'Sarcastic as well,' she muttered under her breath as she rounded the Jeep and hurried up into the cab. 'Do you even know how to get to the airport?'

'Of course,' he said, edging the huge Jeep out into the chilly afternoon where a light snowfall was beginning to frost over the grey surroundings. The large tyres crackled on the icy road, which Ethan negotiated with a practised skill.

Uma glanced over at him. How did he know how to drive like that? Ethan had rarely been to Iceland. Maybe twice since she had met him. Once using LEAP. And Anderson? Did he know how to drive these icy roads?

'Call Fredrik.'

'Who?'

'What is with you today?' he said. 'Do I have to do all the work round here?'

'I've no idea what you're talking about.'

'The Chief. The Viking Squad.'

The penny dropped. Ethan was referring to Fredrik Baldursson. He had only met him once, as far as she was aware. At the Reykjavík Technical College on the first night she had met Ethan and introduced him to LEAP. And they certainly hadn't been on first-name terms. She was damn sure Anderson had never met Fredrik. What had Shane done? Who else had found their way into this man's memory?

'You didn't call him earlier, did you?'

Uma shook her head. She hadn't had time. The police had grilled her for an hour before taking her home. By then, she had forgotten.

'I'll call him now,' she said. 'What about?'

'Mmmm, let me see,' he said. 'Why don't you invite him to dinner next week when this mess has cleared up?'

Uma stared at him in amazement.

'We need an escort. I've got a feeling we haven't seen the last of these jokers. He also needs to know what's been going on. Best deal with the awkward questions now, not when we're in London.'

'What do I tell him?'

'Tell him someone took a pot shot at you. He'll be over here so fast it'll melt the permafrost off Oraefajokull!'

'Are you always this pleasant to be around?'

'Are you always this pleasant to be around?' he mimicked in a whiny voice. 'I'm not paid to be pleasant. Just to save lives.'

'Then I guess this amounts to a really bad day at the office for you,' she said.

'You're alive. What more do you want?'

Uma ignored him, punching Fredrik's details into her phone. It seemed to ring for ages. She was just about to try again when Baldursson's voice boomed out through the tiny speaker.

'Umi. You as well. I've been telling everyone there's nothing to worry about. Unless you were planning on taking a flight out of Keflavík this afternoon!'

What was Fredrik talking about?

'I'm not following you.'

'You haven't heard?'

'Heard what?'

'An aircraft has just blown up in the private jet arrivals hangar. Made quite a mess. We've had to close the airport and suspend all flights.'

'That's where we're heading,' Uma said, her mind whirling. Was this related to the attack at the Department?

'What an earth for?'

Uma filled him in on what had happened since her arrival at the Geothermal Department. The attempt on her life. The shootings. Their subsequent escape. She didn't mention Ethan. Baldursson didn't interrupt once. When she had finished, the voice that filled the speaker was now business-like and suddenly Uma felt more secure.

'Where are you now?'

'On Route 41.'

'Be more precise, Umi.'

Uma looked out of the window.

'We're about five minutes from the aluminium plant at Hafnarfjordur.'

'OK. You're about fifteen klicks from our roadblock. It's at the junction where 41 meets 43.'

'The one that goes to the Blue Lagoon?'

'Precisely. That's where we're turning everyone back. Wait there. I'll send two extra teams up to meet you.'

Uma thought for a second. Whilst she was sorely tempted to accept Fredrik's offer, especially with the way Ethan was behaving, it made little sense. By the time the teams were dispatched, she and Ethan would be at the roadblock. 'We'll be fine,' she said, glancing at Ethan, who ignored her. 'We'll be there inside fifteen minutes. The traffic is really light.'

She cut the connection and filled in Ethan.

'How did they know we were going to the airport?'

'You think the attack at the Department and the explosion are connected?'

'What do you think? We have a private jet reserved out of Keflavík. One hour later, the private arrivals hangar is blown up.'

Uma didn't respond. She had a feeling it wouldn't make any difference. Anderson, Ethan, or whoever the hell he was, didn't want her input.

Ethan removed a mobile from his jacket and stared at it.

'Give me your phone,' he demanded.

'You think they bugged us?'

'Just give me the damn phone.'

Ethan snatched it from her grasp, retracted the window, and tossed both phones into the freezing afternoon.

'Now what?'

Ethan held up a bloody mobile he had recovered from the floor of the entrance hall.

'That's not what I meant. What are we supposed to do if they know our next move?'

'Hook up with Fredrik's men. If we can't fly today, we need their protection until this settles down and Shane reboots that infernal machine of yours.'

An uncomfortable silence descended on the cabin, interrupted only by the monotonous roar of the powerful engine and the flip-flapping of the forty-four-inch tread on the frozen road. Visibility was terrible. Black clouds hugged the landscape, indiscriminately dispensing snow squalls onto the desolate lava fields that lay either side of the raised road. To her right, Uma caught glimpses of a steel pipeline that danced across the frozen magma and, every so often, criss-crossed a gigantic transmission line. Periodically, it disappeared underground, but always rejoined several hundred yards further on, bursting from the earth like a giant silver snake. As the lava plain gave way to a steep incline, both the pipeline and the pylons converged with the road and were soon running level with her window.

'Hello. What do we have here?'

Uma dragged her eyes away from the racing metal and glanced back. Her heart skipped a beat. She could no longer see the road behind them. A rusty ventilation grill now stared back at her through the rear window. It was so close she could see the scratches and indentations on the dull steelwork. As she watched, it pulled out and started to overtake them as another black Shogun appeared from nowhere to take its place.

'Ethan!'

'I've got them,' he said, his eyes glued to the rear-view mirror.

The first vehicle drew level, its blacked-out windows towering above Ethan's door. Uma leaned forward to look up at the cab, but the darkened glass stared dully back. Without warning, the four-by-four swerved towards them, causing Ethan to brake sharply and veer to the edge of the raised road. Ethan laughed maniacally as he over-exaggerated his recovery, swerving dramatically back onto the tarmac.

'Come on, boys. You'll have to do better than that,' he bellowed, knocking the gear into sports mode and punching his foot to the floor. The engine roared with approval, leaping forward and eating up the road in front of them. Uma screamed. She didn't even have time to brace herself for the impact. The Jeep smacked into the base of the huge Shogun's rear bumper at over fifty miles per hour. Their vehicle bucked savagely as the impact triggered both airbags. For a moment, the windscreen was obscured by the twin explosions as Ethan blindly fought to keep the steering under control. As the nylon fabric settled around them, the road reappeared, but the Shogun was nowhere to be seen.

Ethan let out a whoop, smacking the steering wheel repeatedly. 'That'll teach them.'

'What the hell's wrong with you?' Uma screamed, turning to search for the Shogun through the rear screen.

'What's your problem, lady? Now they know not to mess with—'

Uma's scream cut him off as Ethan's eyes flicked to the mirror. Neither of them had time to react this time as the second Shogun rear-ended them in an explosion of crunching glass and grinding metal. Uma's head smashed into the side window. As her vision faded, all she could hear was a maniacal laugh. It seemed to continue for an age, growing in size until it filled her entire head. She felt completely helpless in its frenzied embrace. And then finally it stopped as Uma slipped into unconsciousness.

Mojave Desert, Nevada

14 November 2003, 07:15 hours PST

The phone continued to blink red in the darkened room, ringing with a persistent metallic beep that demanded it be answered. Eventually, a hand appeared from under the duvet and blindly groped around the small table beside the bed before finally closing around the slim body and drawing it under the covers.

'I gave strict instructions not to be disturbed,' a muffled voice, groggy with sleep, grunted into the mouthpiece. 'What part of that don't you understand?'

'Sir, I know you asked not to be disturbed, but we've got a problem.'

There was an urgency in the man's tone. One that suggested things were not as they should be. The listener clearly thought so. The hand suddenly reappeared and pressed a small switch on the wall, bathing the room in a soft warm glow. Crouch emerged from under the covers. He blinked uncertainly in the light before rubbing sleep from his eyes and recovering his thick glasses from the side table with the practised memory of the partially sighted. Satisfied, he sat up and turned back to the phone.

'What is it?'

'Well, I'm not sure. I think you need to see it for yourself.'

'I'll be right there,' Crouch returned the handset to its cradle. His eye caught the digital readout of the clock.

07:17

No wonder he felt terrible. He had only been asleep for fifteen minutes. He threw back the covers but sat on the bed for a full minute before making his way unsteadily into the small bathroom, where he urinated noisily as he stared absentmindedly into the mirror above the toilet. Unruly tufts of black hair sprouted in all directions across his bulbous head, complementing the scraggy wisps that sparsely covered his chin and cheeks. Crouch didn't even notice. His mind was on other things, although, as he finished his hurried ablutions, he straightened his tie and buttoned up the top button of his long-suffering shirt before making his way back into the bedroom and out into the corridor.

The laboratories were at the heart of the desert compound, which had been intentional. Regardless of your location, you were never more than a short walk from the centre of operations and, within a few minutes, Crouch found himself outside the command centre. He paused before entering, suddenly nervous about what he would find inside. However, when he did finally swipe his index finger across the security scanner and the double doors parted with a whoosh of escaping air, nothing could have prepared him for the desolation that greeted him.

The entire room was devoid of human life, save for two white-coated individuals hunched over the command console in the middle of the room. However, this was not what had caught Crouch's attention. His eyes were on the screens. Every single one was blank, their empty faces staring silently back at Crouch. That was what unnerved him. They shouldn't have been blank. They should have been alive with activity, busily processing the fruits of his earlier labour. That the screens were devoid of life was bad enough, but what caused his stomach muscles to contract with fear was the silence. In fact, Crouch could not remember the control centre ever being so quiet. It was normally whirring with the reassuring hum of thousands of fans cooling busy processors. But not this morning. The huge room was deathly still.

Crouch slowly made his way across the large hall. The two men looked up and moved aside as their boss stood beside them, staring down at the black screen in front of them. Crouch eventually broke the silence.

'How long has it been like this?'

'Ten, fifteen minutes max,' replied Silverstein, the man who had called the professor earlier. He was a nervous type and shifted uneasily from side to side, waiting for his boss' next question.

'How did it happen?'

'I'm not sure. One moment, everything was fine. The very next second ... this,' he nodded down at the silent screen.

'And the rest?'

'It seemed to happen almost instantaneously.'

'A power cut, perhaps?' his colleague ventured. Crouch recognised him. His name was Ginsky. He had been at the Centre for only three months.

'Not a chance,' Crouch snapped. 'This place is rigged with three back-up generators.' He thought for a second. 'Was there any warning before they went dead?'

Ginsky looked at Silverstein imploringly before his colleague, who was clearly the designated spokesman, passed the professor a single sheet of A4 torn from a notebook.

'This. We have no idea what it means. It appeared on each screen seconds before they cut out.'

Crouch looked at the paper and let out a loud groan before slowly sinking into his seat. He put his face in his hands and sat there shaking his head, mumbling something inaudible.

The two men exchanged quizzical glances before Silverstein placed an uncertain hand on the professor's shoulder.

'Sir, are you OK? Is there anything we can do?'

Crouch jumped as if he had been electrocuted before leaping to his feet and turning on the unfortunate man.

'Get out of here. Both of you,' he screamed. When they didn't move, he shouted again. 'I said, get out! Do you understand? Get out! Leave me in peace. I'm not to be disturbed. No calls. No interruptions. Nothing. Nobody should enter this room unless I say so.'

Silverstein and Ginsky just stood there, staring at the professor incredulously. Crouch collapsed back in the chair. The silence was deafening. Eventually, Silverstein turned and made his way across the deserted room, followed closely by Ginsky. They looked back as they left, but the old man was still sat there staring at the blank screen. Every now and again, he glanced down at the sheet of A4 in front of him and shook his head.

Route 41, Iceland

14 November 2003, 15:30 hours

The seat beside her was empty. Uma felt her stomach lurch with panic for the second time that day. Where the hell was Ethan? In the distance, she could hear firecrackers popping haphazardly all around. Occasionally, the Jeep gave a small kick as if someone was rocking it. She sat up, groaning, and rubbed her temple. It was swollen and hurt like hell, but at least it wasn't bleeding.

Ethan was nowhere to be seen.

Fear tickled her spine. What if he had abandoned her? What would she do? Uma smothered her growing panic and gathered her bearings. Directly beneath her lay the lava field. It was so close she could have touched it. Uma realised they were on the steep slope that lay either side of the elevated road. She heard more cracks and peered through the back window, or at least what was left of it. Incredibly, it was still intact, but the glass was warped and glazed over from the earlier impact. That's when she saw Ethan. He was crouched behind one of the monster tyres. Using it as cover. Every so often, he would stand. His hand would flash and then he would duck down again. She couldn't be sure what or who he was firing at because the slope was too steep. All she could see were angry black clouds advancing across the dark sky.

The driver's door suddenly swung open. Ethan appeared in the cab, his face flushed red from the cold. Or was it from excitement?

'What have you done?' he yelled at Uma. 'This lot really wants us dead.'

'Who are you shooting at?' was all she could manage.

Ethan threw his gun onto the dashboard, slamming the Jeep into reverse. Uma was thrown forward as the large vehicle lurched backwards, fighting the slippery slope. Gravel plumed up behind them before the rear tyres caught the firmer tarmac. The Jeep shot back at speed. Fifty feet away two jet-black Shoguns were parked up diagonally across the highway, effectively blocking their route back into Reykjavík. The vehicles lit up with small flashes. Uma instinctively ducked low in her seat as shots peppered the Jeep. Ethan didn't even flinch as he floored the accelerator. Uma risked a glance through the rear window. She could see figures scrambling to get back into their vehicles. Already one of the Shoguns was moving, quickly picking up speed.

'Can you shoot?'

The question caught her off guard. All she could do was stare dumbly at Ethan.

'The gun,' he said, recovering the heavy weapon from the dashboard. 'Have you used one before?'

She shook her head.

'But you can drive, right?'

'Of course.'

A violent jolt caused the Jeep to lurch sharply left, drawing them close to the pipeline, which had suddenly reappeared. Uma stared at the gun in Ethan's hand. Did he honestly expect her to use that? A dark shadow appeared in her peripheral vision. One of the Shoguns had pulled alongside the Jeep, almost level with her window. It hovered beside them, waiting. Without warning, her window silently retracted. She had no time to react. Ethan's forearm appeared in front of her. Two explosions boomed beside her head. The passenger window of the Shogun starred in two places but didn't shatter. The Shogun swerved towards them. Ethan mirrored the manoeuvre to avoid a collision, but not fast enough. The Shogun slammed into the side of the

Jeep, causing it to veer wildly across the road as he fought to control the sideways shunt. The other vehicle appeared on Ethan's side, barging straight into them with even more force. This time, Ethan nearly lost control of the huge vehicle as it bucked hard to the right. Pebbles and small stones spat out from the offside tyres as they fought to maintain traction on the wet surface. She felt the back end going and realised they were teetering on the edge of the slippery bank above the dead lava fields. In desperation, Ethan accelerated. The powerful engine responded. They surged forward ahead of the Shogun, back into the middle of the road.

Ethan started swerving erratically, trying to prevent the other vehicles from pulling alongside. It made no difference. The Shoguns stuck with them, appearing time and again at either side of the Jeep with increasingly forceful shunts. Uma wasn't sure how much longer they could keep this up. Another jarring collision brought them close to the edge of the road. Frantically, Ethan swerved hard right, back across both lanes. He fought to control the steering as the Jeep bounced and bucked over the rough terrain skirting the edge of the road. Sure enough, one of the pursuing Shogun's appeared alongside them and steadied itself for the next shunt. This time, Ethan was ready. As it swerved towards the Jeep, he slammed his foot down. The servo-assisted braking system kicked in. The Shogun shot past them, its driver also braking whilst tracking left to avoid the fatal plunge down the steep slope. But Ethan had judged his trap well. The Shogun had no room to pull out. The back end started to slide down the bank as the driver fought in vain to recover his grip on the relative safety of the cinder slope. It sideswiped an outcrop of lava, which punched the Shogun back up the slope. For a fleeting moment, Uma thought it would claw its way back onto the road, but Newton's Law was not to be denied twice. The whole vehicle tipped slowly onto its side. Slowly, almost balletically, it overbalanced before smashing into the rocks.

There was a blinding flash, followed by a deafening boom. Ethan threw the Jeep hard right to avoid the diesel explosion that blossomed up the slope and into their path. He whooped excitedly.

'One down,' he yelled. 'I don't think they will fall for that trick again. I need—'

Uma suddenly grabbed his arm, causing the Jeep to pull left.

'Hey. Watch it.'

'Look,' she cried, pointing ahead. 'The roadblock.'

Sure enough, up ahead, a line of cars three vehicles deep was stretched across both lanes. Baldursson's message must have got through because Uma could see men running to move cars. Already the front ones had pulled aside to clear a way through for them.

'We're going to make it.'

The other Shogun suddenly appeared beside the Jeep. Ethan tried to pull ahead, but it was no use. There was a new urgency in its onslaught, as if sensing they had one more chance before their prey reached safety. Uma glanced nervously at the speedometer. They were doing over seventy. How could Ethan stop in time? She could see soldiers emerge uncertainly from the cars they were trying to move, standing, watching, weighing up whether to run or finish their orders.

'I need you to hold the steering wheel.'

Uma stared at him.

'We need to slow down.'

'Can you do that?'

She nodded.

'When I say go, grab it. Let's see if we can shake these bastards for good.'

He retracted both windows. Freezing cold air filled the cabin.

'Ready?'

Uma could barely hear him above the roar of the wind.

'Now,' he shouted.

She leant across as he disappeared out of his window, emptying a full magazine into the side of the Shogun. Nothing happened. Surely, he knew it was reinforced. Uma struggled to control the Jeep. And then she realised what he was trying to do. The tyres. He was trying to blow the tyres.

'Damn it!' he yelled, pulling himself back into the cabin and replenishing the magazine.

Up ahead, policemen and soldiers were now abandoning the road-block as the two vehicles hurtled towards them.

'OK, one more time.'

As he tried again, the rear passenger window of the Shogun slowly retracted and a dull black muzzle appeared barely two feet from Ethan's head.

Route 41, Iceland

14 November 2003, 15:36 hours

'Watch out,' Uma screamed, veering towards the Shogun. Ethan only just pulled himself back as they crunched into the side door. She saw the gunman jerk back as if attached to an elastic band, his gun flashing fire into the ceiling of his own vehicle. Uma tugged at the steering but it wouldn't respond. Jeep and Shogun were now one, barrelling towards the roadblock. The gunman reappeared at the open window. He was wearing some sort of balaclava hood, his smoking barrel pointing into their cab. Uma couldn't separate the two vehicles. They were stuck fast. Ethan reacted first. He punched the brakes with all his might. The Jeep tore free and slewed sideways. For a second, Uma thought they were going to tip, but driving was clearly one of Anderson's skills. He calmly adjusted the steering, bringing them to a gentle stop.

Up ahead, the other driver was not so lucky. The huge vehicle bucked wildly as its driver tried to recover. But it was too late. It suddenly jackknifed ninety degrees sideways. As the point of no return passed, the force of its own velocity flipped the Shogun savagely through a full 360 degrees. Once, then twice, three times. Uma lost count. It started to disintegrate before her eyes in a shower of sparks and flying metal. Men scattered in all directions. The wounded monster smashed into the gap recently created by the two lead cars.

The impact punched the second line of vehicles sideways, scattering glass and car parts high into the afternoon gloom. It finally came to rest, wedged deep into a black and white four-by-four. For a moment, there was an eerie silence. Men crawled, groaning, from smashed cars as others rushed to help them, their urgency driven by the unmistakable odour in the air. Even fifty feet away, Uma could smell fuel. She tried to get out of the Jeep, but Ethan held her back.

'Bad idea,' he mouthed at her. 'It's gonna blow.'

She ignored him and tried to open the door, but he restrained her. She attempted to pull free when a blinding flash lit up the gloomy day. Uma wasn't sure what came next. A deafening boom or the blast of fiery air that swept over their Jeep.

'Jesus Christ,' muttered Ethan as a holocaust of burning metal engulfed the central reservation. On either side, cars were scattered like autumn leaves, spilling down the embankment onto the lava fields. As they watched, one exploded in a fireball of liquid gasoline that punched the vehicle high above the road. It landed on another Jeep that quickly succumbed to the intense heat. In no time, a fresh wave of smaller explosions rocked the landscape until the entire width of the highway became a twenty-foot high kaleidoscope of raging fires and billowing smoke.

'Can't we help?' begged Uma, tugging at her door in vain.

Ethan didn't respond. He reversed the Jeep further back to escape the searing heat and acrid smoke that was threatening to engulf them.

'Please stop,' she sobbed. 'We need to help.'

'There's nothing we can do,' he said. 'No one could have survived that.'

Uma fell silent. He was right. They were so engrossed in the spectacle that neither of them noticed the third Shogun emerge from the smoke. It was travelling fast and hit them hard, ploughing deep into their rear bumper. The impact threw Ethan and Uma against the dashboard. For long seconds, neither of them moved as the Shogun pressed home its advantage, driving them toward the waiting flames.

Uma came too first, but just sat in her seat trying to process the hellish nightmare around her as thick black smoke enveloped the Jeep. She could feel the heat but couldn't see the flames. And then suddenly the smoke cleared. The raging fuel-infused fire turned hungrily in their direction.

Ethan groaned softly.

Panic-stricken, she tugged at his arm.

'Ethan!'

Behind her, the Shogun's engine roared.

She slapped his face frantically. Finally, he opened his eyes. For a long moment, he just stared ahead in confusion. Recognition finally dawned. He sat up, shaking his head groggily, willing his limbs to respond. His foot punched the gas pedal, but nothing happened.

Ethan turned the ignition. Silence.

'Come on. Damn you!'

He tried again. No reassuring growl greeted them.

Uma cracked the door open, readying herself to run, but fell back into her seat as a hail of bullets peppered her window. Twenty feet behind them, a hooded figure was crouched low, shielding himself from the flames. As she watched, he calmly reloaded his weapon and waited. Behind them, the Shogun's huge engine roared triumphantly. Just one more push and they would be in the fire. And then the sound she had been praying for—the Jeep's engine suddenly spluttered into life. For an agonising moment, Uma felt it fade. Then it finally caught and they started to move. Slowly at first, as if the tyres had melted to the road. Ethan jerked the wheel hard right, turning them away from the inferno. Up ahead, the hooded figure held his ground, his gun flashing frantically. Their windscreen starred over, a jagged line running from Uma to Ethan, who kept the steering straight. At the last moment, Uma closed her eyes, wincing at the crunch of metal on bone.

As they picked up speed, a high-pitched screeching filled the cabin. A shower of sparks fanned out from behind the Jeep like a deranged Catherine wheel, spewing higher as they went faster. Uma looked back, terrified, but the lone Shogun wasn't following them. As she watched, a figure appeared from the vehicle and started running towards them, his gun spitting brightly in the fading light.

'Come on,' she shouted above the metallic whine, urging the damaged Jeep forward.

'I can't go any faster. He's caught under the wheels.'

Ethan swerved crazily, trying to dislodge the body. He made a beeline for the central reservation. Beneath them, a series of staccato explosions peppered the cabin. Bullets ripped through the rear passenger seats into the ceiling of the Jeep.

'Jesus Christ, it's his bloody magazines.' Ethan wrenched the Jeep onto the raised section of the road and the high-pitched shrieking tapered off. Up ahead, a small maintenance bin appeared. Ethan rammed into it at speed. As the plastic disintegrated underneath them, the Jeep tipped crazily before thumping down onto the central reservation. There was a slight jump beneath them as the Jeep picked up speed. It was some seconds before Uma realised the shrieking had stopped.

'What do we do? We'll never make it to Reykjavík.'

Ethan suddenly pulled hard right.

'Where are you going?'

'Call Fredrik. Tell him we're holed up at the Blue Lagoon.'

'I don't understand.'

'You said it yourself,' he said. 'If we get stuck on the highway, we'll be sitting ducks. We can hide out at the lagoon. The whole area is littered with lava mazes. Get Fredrik to send some of his best boys up in a 'copter.'

Uma grabbed her mobile. Before calling, she glanced back at the billowing roadblock where the remaining Shogun had begun to move slowly in their direction.

San Francisco Airport, San Francisco

14 November 2003, 07:40 hours PST

'But, sir, he gave strict instructions not to be disturbed.'

'I don't give a shit what he said. I need to speak to him right now. Put me through.'

The secretary sighed.

'I'm really sorry, sir. I can't. There's been some sort of incident in the main control room. The professor is trying to put it right as we speak.'

'What sort of incident?' Reynolds said, suddenly nervous.

'I don't know. Some sort of power failure, I think.'

'Jesus, what the hell are you talking about? Put me through right now. I need to speak to him directly.'

'I can't. It's more than my job's worth.' Kath Parker had already received a graphic description of Crouch's outburst from Ginsky and was quite sure what would happen, even though she was disobeying her boss' boss. 'However, I will make it a priority to have him call you as soon as he becomes available.'

Reynolds admired her tenacity and made a mental note to have her transferred up to San Francisco. He needed a gatekeeper like this. At this precise moment, though, he needed to speak to Crouch more.

'Look, lady, if you don't transfer me right now, I will have you escorted from the building before you have the chance to put this phone down. Now, think carefully about what you do next. You're just about to make a very important career decision.'

Kath Parker stared at the receiver.

They did not pay her enough for this.

'Right, sir. I'll put you through. Do you mind holding for two minutes whilst I locate him? I've a feeling he won't be picking up his calls.'

'Good decision,' Reynolds said. He settled back into his leather chair, staring at the large TV screen in the corner. He had installed it to watch the Giants play, but this morning his PA had changed it to the local news channel at his father's request. The story had been running intermittently all morning and, as he watched, the familiar shot of the studio suddenly cut to an even more recognisable view. The exterior of the Reynolds' building at San Francisco Airport. He could actually see the corner windows of his own office. It felt strange to be watching himself on live TV. A reporter stood in frame, chattering into her microphone whilst, behind her, an orderly group of pickets from the ALPA and the AFA stood with placards. A large one read 'RA. Grounded until further notice'.

The reporter was speaking again, this time to a serious-looking man with large spectacles. He looked like a lawyer to Reynolds.

'I have the head of the legal faculty at USF, Professor John Forge, here with me this morning. He is a national expert on corporate bankruptcies, particularly those of airlines who have used the protection afforded by Chapter 11 of the Bankruptcy Code. Professor,' she asked, turning towards the grey-haired man beside her, 'what do you think the ramifications of this strike could be for RA?'

'Well, Joanne. It's serious. Like all the airlines, RA has struggled terribly since the events of 9/11. If this strike lasts too long, I imagine it could force them to seek the protection of the courts. They have no choice. For one thing, they will be haemorrhaging cash until they sort this out.'

'The market certainly seems to think so. This morning alone, RA's stock fell a full forty points. It is now trading at its historically lowest level since coming to the market in 1954. It's been a cruel fall from grace for a company that was once not only the largest in America, by quite some distance, but also the most valuable.'

The reporter turned back to the professor.

'John, let me ask you one more question before we return to the studio. If you were the CEO of RA, what would you do to get them out of this mess?'

'Fuck you,' Reynolds said as he muted the screen and stared at the phone.

Christ, where the hell was Crouch? This was ridiculous.

'Sir, I have the professor for you.' The woman sounded breathless, as if she had been running. 'Just one second. I will connect you.' There was an audible click. Reynolds leant forward in his seat expectantly.

'Crouch, are you there? Your secretary said there was a problem. You haven't scrambled someone, have you?'

There was silence on the other end of the phone. Reynolds adjusted the volume control of his speakerphone and tried again.

'Crouch, what's going on there?'

'It was a honey pot. They saw me coming a mile away. I got sucked into it.' Crouch's voice sounded muffled, as if he were talking to Reynolds through a blanket.

'What the hell are you talking about?'

'Pooh Bear. They set a trap for him. I fell for it.'

'Speak English, man. You're talking gobbledegook again.'

'It's all over, I'm afraid. They won. We lost.'

Reynolds sat up in his chair, suddenly concerned.

'What do you mean, they won? What's over?'

'They sent a message.'

'Who sent a message?'

There was the rustle of paper in the background.

'Pooh Bear has hundreds of them. What am I?' He sounded like he was reading.

Reynolds stared at the phone. What the hell was going on? It sounded like the old man had finally lost it. There was silence again.

'For God's sake, man, speak to me. What th—'

His door opened slightly as an elderly face appeared.

'I have your father on the other line, it's—'

'Not now, goddamn it. Can't you see I'm busy?'

'He said it's urgent.'

'Get out of my office,' Reynolds screamed at his startled assistant, half standing out of his chair to wave her away. He turned back to the speakerphone and took a deep breath.

'Now, Crouch. Take me through this slowly. What the hell is going on there?' Reynolds' outburst seemed to have momentarily snapped the professor out of his delirium.

'Who's that? Who are you shouting at?'

'It doesn't matter. Look, can you explain to me what is going on?'

'I thought it was too easy.'

'What? What did you think was too easy?'

'The download. I got through too quickly. They normally take days, sometimes weeks. I should have trusted my instincts.'

'Are you trying to tell me we got the wrong information?'

'Oh no. I got the right information, all right. The information they wanted me to have. They set a trap, and I sleepwalked into it.'

'What sort of trap?'

'A type of honey pot.'

'A honey pot?'

'Yes, a trap that security experts set up within companies. It's used to monitor hackers as a way of tracking them down. It's made to look like part of the company's network, but instead it's fake. I haven't seen one in a long time.'

'How do you know all of this?'

'They left a message.'

'What? The one about Pooh Bear. Sounds like a dumb joke to me.'

'It's a joke all right. And it's on us.'

There was silence on the phone again as Reynolds sat there thinking.

'So, what's the big deal? We got into the wrong part of the system. Why can't we try again?'

'That's impossible.'

'Why? Because of their security? Because they will expect an attack now?'

'No. Worse than that. When we downloaded the code, I brought something else across with it. A worm, I think.'

'A worm?'

'Yes. A piece of software similar to the one I attacked their servers with. It was undetectable. It must have been on a timer or triggered by something we did. Anyway, it spawned this morning.'

'How bad is this?'

'As bad as it can get. They fried our systems. There's nothing left.'

'Can't we repair them?'

'I can't even turn them on. This will take months to sort out, if ever.'

Neither man spoke. Reynolds stared at the muted reporter, still talking to the eminent law professor on the TV, the pickets milling about behind them, waving their placards. To the left of the screen, the RA stock price was graphically illustrated, its precipitous downward plunge matched only by the feeling in Reynolds' gut.

There was a quiet knock on the door. Reynolds hardly heard it. The knock came again, this time a little harder. He looked up with a flash of irritation.

'What did I tell you? No dist—'

Reynolds paused mid word, eyes fixed on his father.

'So, our family business is going to hell, but you're busy on another phone call. I had to come and see for myself what is more important than that,' he said, pushing the door shut quietly. 'Please continue.' He nodded at Reynolds, who had recovered his composure.

'Crouch, I will call you back. Something's cropped up.'

Reynolds lifted his finger from the speakerphone and nodded at his father, who had settled himself into a chair opposite.

'So, are you going to tell me what is going on?'

Reynolds remained silent. He had long ago learnt that the best form of defence against one of his father's interrogations was to say nothing. That way, he couldn't incriminate himself.

'I've been watching you recently. What are you up to? All these trips to a deserted air base in the Nevada desert. Liquidating your share portfolio. What is it? One hundred? Two hundred million so far? That's a lot of cash, son. What are you planning? A new business?'

Reynolds couldn't believe his father had known something was going on and his face said so.

'So, you thought the old man had lost his touch, hey?' his father grinned. 'Are you going to enlighten me? I think I have a right to know.'

'You wouldn't believe me if I told you,' Reynolds said, trying to maintain his gaze.

'I trust that whatever you're planning is a little more stable than the airline business.'

'It's fantastically stable. People want it badly. In fact, so much so I can charge what I like for it. Also, there are no competitors.'

'Hmm,' his father grunted. 'Impossible. If there are no competitors, there is no market. And without a market, you have no buyers.'

Reynolds stared at his father. The old man still hadn't lost his touch after all these years.

'There is one competitor, but I'm just about to take them out. Today, in fact. By tomorrow, I'll be the sole player in the market.'

'Ah, a monopoly. Your granddaddy would have enjoyed that,' the old man laughed. 'Are you going to tell me what it is?'

But Reynolds wasn't listening. He was thinking about what his father had just said. Of course! That was it. There was a way out of this mess. How simple. How could he have missed it? Christ, he needed to move quickly, before it was too late.

Reynolds jumped up from his chair, grabbing his mobile.

'Father, thanks. You've just solved a huge problem for me. I'll be right back.'

'Where are you going?'

But it was too late. His son had already crossed the room in three strides and was halfway out of the door.

'To make my granddaddy proud,' he yelled back, and then he was gone, leaving the elderly man sitting, half turned in his chair, staring after his departing son.

Blue Lagoon, Iceland

14 November 2003, 16:25 hours GMT

Like countless others before them, Ethan and Uma made their way up from the car park along a winding footpath enclosed on both sides by fifteen-foot walls of crusty black magma, frosted white by a light dusting of powdery snow. The dark path was illuminated by round metal cylinders sunk into either side of the block paving every ten feet or so. Although she had travelled this path hundreds of times, Uma was too preoccupied with her recent ordeal to notice the surroundings. Ethan had barely said a word, leaving Uma to relive every moment of the last few hours. The burning bodies. A blood-soaked obelisk. Her near death. And then rescue. Shane riding roughshod over the LEAP laws at the first opportunity. Her father would have had a field day with that one. The thought angered her. It was too late to unwind the past. Shane's actions had created this man beside her. Someone who looked like Ethan. But wasn't. A man she didn't know but who had saved her life. Repeatedly. Ethan couldn't have done half of what this version had managed. She felt a pang of guilt at the thought. As if she was betraying the old Ethan whilst at the same time admiring this new one—although she could do without his boorishness. And that was the problem. Shane had merged Ethan's brain with Anderson's brawn, yet this person was displaying a personality, knowledge and skills that Ethan simply didn't possess. Did they belong to Anderson? If so, then something had gone horribly wrong with LEAP. Or had it? Who knew the effects of merging two people? She suddenly had an image of Ethan throwing the hapless gunman off the balcony. Ethan could never have done that. It must have been Anderson. How much of that man had come across? Was Ethan decaying inside there? Was the real Anderson taking over? Whatever was happening, he seemed unstable. Unpredictable. Not great traits given their predicament. She needed this man to keep her alive until Baldursson got to them.

As they turned a sharp bend in the path, a large glass structure suddenly loomed up in front of them. It was brightly lit from the inside, double doors wide open. Ethan slowed, unholstering his gun as they entered the deserted building. Uma suppressed a shudder. Public places rarely felt right when they were empty, and this was no exception. Everything looked like it had been hurriedly abandoned. The tills in front of them were silent. A fluffy whale lay on one, a lump of souvenir lava by another. They advanced cautiously past the well-lit gift shop and through the large restaurant, their footsteps awaking echoes on the dull grey slate. At the far side, they paused beside the double doors leading out to the lagoon.

'What do we do now?' Uma said.

'Do you hear that?' Ethan said, looking up. The unmistakable thump of helicopter blades penetrated the hall. 'It must be the cavalry. Let's go.'

As Ethan disappeared through the doors, a bottle of ketchup exploded on the condiments counter. Uma whirled round. At the canteen entrance, a man was standing, dressed in black. His smoking weapon raised. The gunman from the Shogun? But where were the rest? The man, his bald head shiny bright under the overhead lights, was already moving, sensing Uma's hesitation. He was heavily muscled, disproportionately so.

The movement broke the spell and Uma fell backwards through the door, her overloaded senses catching snippets as she scrabbled to her feet. Freezing air, blinding fog, above her a deafening roar and ahead, Ethan floated ghost-like in the milky gloom. Uma followed, arms pumping, lungs bursting as she tried to catch him. And then he was he gone. Uma heard a large splash and launched herself blindly into the white void.

She gasped with shock as she hit the hot water. It was boiling. Uncomfortably so. Uma tried to keep moving, but her clothes dragged like an anchor. She ripped her heavy sweater off, then her jeans and finally, her shoes. Uma began to move faster. Putting distance between herself and the lights of the centre. And the gunman.

She kept low, head just visible, nose above the water, mouth below, thick hair fanned out around her like black seaweed. A wall of dense vapours swirled above her. Part freezing fog, part hot steam mixed with soft snowflakes; the combined effect was like staring into a snowstorm through the raised headlights of a car. Ethan was nowhere to be seen. Again, that feeling of panic. His presence was a reassurance. He seemed to know what he was doing. When he was around, she felt safer. Uma fought the urge to shout his name out.

Uma had forgotten about the lake. It was like a hot bath. Except, it wasn't like a bath at all, or hot tub, for that matter; the temperature was in a permanent state of flux, alternating from hot to very hot and, on occasions, almost scalding her. It was a strange sensation as hot pockets of geothermal fluid washed over her. Slimy goo pulled at her feet like watery clay, squelching up through the gaps between her toes. Memories flooded back of long forgotten visits with her father. Come rain, shine, dark or snow. Always on a Sunday. In the evening, when the facility was shut to the public. A small perk he loved. Having the entire lagoon to himself. They would float for ten minutes, sometimes longer, letting the water work its wonder. Melting away the stresses of the week. Eventually, they would slowly make their way to a rocky outcrop on the eastern side of the lake, out towards the power station. It would be a perfect place to hide until help arrived. Even close up on a clear day, it was easy to disappear in the hot rocks. Night-time, combined with the thick fog and steam coming off the lagoon, would provide the perfect camouflage. They would be impossible to find. All

Uma needed to do was keep the lights of the centre behind her and eventually she would hit the outcrop. But first, she had to find Ethan.

Uma moved cautiously, almost crawling on all fours, so her head remained low. A small indistinct target, almost invisible in the swirling steam and mist. Ethan was nowhere to be seen, as if the lagoon had swallowed him up. A dull splash from the direction of the main building made her jump. What the hell was that? She couldn't even tell how far away the noise had been. The fog deadened everything. It could have been twenty feet or six inches. She had no idea, although the thought that someone might be standing less than an arm's length away was disconcerting to the point of panic. She paused, trying to control her breathing, resisting the urge to cry out for Ethan.

A barrage of shots crackled through the silence. They sounded muffled in the fog. Otherworldly almost. All from the centre. More shots in response, followed by several small explosions. A man screamed out. Others shouting. In Icelandic! Then she remembered the helicopter flying overhead. Of course, Fredrik's reinforcements. They would be free soon. Uma felt strangely shielded from them. As if they were playing out in another dimension entirely. She wasn't sure whether it was the darkness, the fog, or the heavy water. But she felt wonderfully secure. As if nothing could harm her so long as she stayed in its hot embrace. Another muffled splash broke the spell, causing Uma to jump. This time, she wasn't certain where the sound had come from. It sounded closer, though. Too close. Again, the urge to call Ethan's name. She fought it, trying to rationalise the imagined danger. If the gunman was in the water, he would have trouble finding anything. She could stand right next to him and he wouldn't know unless she gave away her position. Nevertheless, she carefully backed away from the sound, moving further out into the lake.

'Getting a little jumpy, aren't we?' a voice whispered quietly in her ear.

Uma stifled a scream as she leapt up. At the same time, she lashed out, catching her would-be assailant with a satisfyingly heavy blow.

'You goddamn idiot,' Ethan hissed. 'You could have broken my nose.'

She couldn't see him, but sensed he was close by.

'Good,' she spat back. 'What do you expect? Creeping up on me like that?'

Ethan emerged from the gloom, and she noted with some satisfaction that his nose was bleeding. He looked her up and down hungrily, his eyes eventually settling on her white camisole. She sank back down into the water, her cheeks beginning to burn. What a pig, she thought. Ethan remained standing, staring down at her, arms unnaturally rigid, thrust down and out like a bodybuilder striking a competition pose. She couldn't believe it. He was posturing to her. Preening himself like an oversexed peacock.

'You'll get yourself killed stood there like that.'

He shrugged and dropped beside her, moving close so his face was almost touching hers. The transformation was instant. She was staring at Ethan again, Anderson's ugliness hidden beneath the surface. For the moment.

'Sounds like the cavalry's arrived.' He nodded towards the main centre. As he did so, their lips almost touched. She felt his elbow brush her forearm, and a different anxiety suddenly permeated the hot air. Uma edged back, acutely aware this wasn't Ethan. He was silent. She moved again as more shots and shouts came from the direction of the centre, now no longer sure who she was running from. He seemed to track each movement she made so that their faces stayed close.

Without warning, she suddenly felt his lips on hers. She was so shocked that for a second, she didn't respond. They were surprisingly soft. Gentle almost. Uma lingered as she melted into the moment, enjoying the sensations, but then she felt him pulling her camisole down, her breast crushed in a huge hand. Anderson! Uma pulled back, indignation rising like a hot geyser.

'Hey, cut it out,' she hissed through clenched teeth.

He didn't respond. Just grinned back at her like a naughty schoolboy.

She felt something soft brush against her neck.

'I told you. Keep your hands to yourself.'

Ethan held both hands up in mock surrender.

As he did so, Uma felt it again, but this time against her shoulder. And the contact was heavier. She instinctively swatted the back of her head.

That was strange. Her fingers came into contact with something solid.

Her heart lurched. As she whirled round, the slightest of breezes caressed the white cocoon surrounding them, causing it to separate and, for the briefest of moments, she could clearly see a full ten feet behind them.

'Fredrik,' she cried out, struggling to find her footing in the slippery sludge. Chief Inspector Baldursson of the Viking Squad didn't answer. And never would. He was floating peacefully in the milky blue of the lagoon, glassy eyes staring up into the night sky. He could have passed for any one of the thousands of bathers who came to unwind in the life affirming waters were it not for the thick blood welling up out of a savage cut to his upper body. The source protruded three feet into the night at a forty-five degree angle to his chest: a lightweight aluminium shank, the only clue that an axe head was buried deep inside his body.

This sight was not wholly responsible for sucking the shriek from Uma's lips. One body length from them stood a man waist deep in the hot waters, one guiding hand resting on the chief inspector's boots. The other held his gun. An undersized white T-shirt accentuated his muscular, squat body, which was otherwise unremarkable, save for the eyes. Cold and calculating, they stared impassively at Ethan and Uma.

The frame dissolved as the mists descended. Freed from the mesmerising hold of Baldursson's killer, Uma and Ethan sprang into furious action. Uma saw Ethan dive to her left. She went right, ploughing through the hot waters in an adrenaline-fuelled front crawl. Except that she wasn't moving. In fact, she seemed to go backwards. It took a few moments to register the iron-like grip on her right ankle. She fought hard, kicking, scratching and screaming, but it made no difference. A heavy fist smashed down into the side of her head and as she lost consciousness, all she could think of was Ethan ... He had abandoned her to this monster. When she had needed him most.

Blue Lagoon, Iceland

14 November 2003, 16:45 hours GMT

A ndreus Grond allowed himself a rare smile and kissed the small pendant around his neck. Jane would have been proud of him. With good reason: he was working alone again, had cancelled his debt, been offered a second fee for the removal of Target One's business partner and recovered a situation that, just one hour earlier, had seemed lost. After finally breaking out of the boiler room, Grond had quickly discovered Karlsen's and Jorgsson's bodies. That was the good news, but Target One had disappeared. He had summoned his remaining five men to the college and split them evenly between the three Shoguns, before sending two teams towards the airport—that is where he would have headed. Once he'd received confirmation from Olsen that his hunch had been correct, he'd followed, more slowly, in time to see Hansen and Christiansen's Shogun plough into the roadblock. Assuming that one of Target One's protection detail were still alive, Grond had dispatched Solberg to kill the driver whilst he had tried to disable the Jeep by ramming it. It had so nearly worked and then, suddenly, the last of his eight men was gone. Buoyed by the fact that he would no longer have to share his fee, Grond had followed the badly damaged Jeep as it turned off the main highway towards the Blue Lagoon. An effective cul-de-sac, according to the map.

His mood had improved even more after discovering the facility was deserted. That was until the untimely arrival of the Icelandic police—the big policeman had put up quite a fight. The only further setback had been the weather. As he stood waist-high in the hot water, focused on Target Two's voice, preparing himself for the kill shot, a light breeze had parted the dense fog, allowing the man to escape. That had bothered him. Not the fact that he had escaped. No, it was the manner of his escape that seemed at odds with Grond's detailed research. Target Two was a desk-bound bean counter with no prior history of athleticism or military training. However, in the seconds following his discovery, the time when his targets were meant to freeze, Target Two had not hesitated. Grond had purposefully locked eyes with him, but the man hadn't been drawn in. Instead, he had calmly absorbed the scene and then just disappeared, melting away into the milky water almost nonchalantly. Grond thought of the college: Jorgsson impaled on the obelisk, Karlsen with his neck snaped like a twig. Had that been Target Two's work? He wondered what he had missed and whether it would cause problems later. Painstaking preparation was the bedrock of his success. It eliminated the unknown, which shortened the odds. Grond liked to stack those in his favour.

He looked down at Target One's limp body. She would be out for a while, giving him plenty of time to reach the car park and transfer her to the Shogun. He needed to hurry. The Icelanders would be wondering where their helicopter was. Pity it had been destroyed. It would have provided the perfect getaway, but that was now the past and couldn't be undone. All he could do was just keep calculating the odds and moving forward. Unless anything untoward happened, he would leave this godforsaken island in less than four hours.

But first he had to get out of this damn lake. The hot steam seemed to have a stultifying effect on his senses. His limbs felt weary and his movements were becoming more and more lethargic as he laboured on through the volcanic waters. The woman couldn't have weighed more than a hundred pounds, but she seemed to grow heavier with every step through the mud, which sucked heavily at his feet.

Without warning, the water to his right suddenly exploded upward into the night sky. On a different occasion, he might have reacted quicker, but the Blue Lagoon had made him sluggish. Out of the steaming eruption emerged Target Two, whirling a heavy baton above his head. Grond moved to defend himself, but even though Target Two was a good five feet away, it was too late. Grond's listless arms seemed to drop the woman in slow motion and, as he raised them to his head, the truncheon struck him full across the face. He felt his nose crumple under the impact, then pain as his nerve endings registered the blow. He sank to his knees, slowly looking up. Target Two was towering over him, two huge bright red straws clenched between his teeth.

Ethan stood over the still body of the hitman, waiting to see if it would move, but one blow had been enough. He spat the straws out. Discovered in the restaurant, they had seemed a great idea, but his innovation was heavily flawed. The thick, silica-based sediment had reduced visibility to zero, which meant he was blind once submerged in the water. Instead, he had used the thick fog as cover, staying hidden, tracking the slow-moving man. As he had drawn closer, Ethan sank beneath the water and counted him in. It had nearly backfired. When he had jumped up, the assassin was still a good five feet away, which had meant a mad scramble to reach him before the man could react.

Ethan turned his attention to Uma, who had been pitched into the shallows of the lagoon where she now lay, facing the night and moaning softly. Ethan stopped to admire what she had denied him earlier. The thin camisole was wet and pulled tight over pale breasts, her hard nipples clearly visible in the cold air. He felt himself stir and feasted his eyes for several more seconds, remembering the earlier reaction to his unwanted, but not entirely unwelcome, advances. He knew women and for a second she had melted into his kiss, her lips willing and compliant. That meant unfinished business as far as he was concerned, but for now, it would have to wait. There was work to do.

He couldn't be sure who was still alive in the visitor centre, but judging from the silence, they must be badly injured or even dead. That was both good and bad. It meant the police were down and out. But so too were the hired guns. And he had no idea whether reinforcements were on the way. For either side. Surely the Icelanders had sent more police. Once regular updates stopped, they would have had to dispatch another unit at the very least, particularly if there was any chance their precious commander was down. What a fool to come himself. It was very touching, but surely he could have exercised some restraint instead of charging in like the Light Brigade. Now Ethan would have to endure Uma wailing on about his untimely death.

Uma was now fully conscious but seemed completely perplexed by her surroundings. He roughly pulled her to her feet, where she stood, swaying drunkenly and mumbling incoherently. Something about Fredrik. As he firmly guided her towards the visitor centre, she suddenly stopped, looking back at the man slumped in the shallows of the lagoon, a pool of red blossoming out around him. She stood silently, clearly struggling to place him. And then suddenly, recognition swept through her slight frame. She stood up straight, fists clenched tight, face contorted with anger. But it didn't last long. Almost as quickly, she seemed to deflate. Heavy tears followed as her legs gave way, and she would have crumpled to the cold deck had Ethan not caught her.

'Oh, dear God. What have I done?' she cried, burying her face deep into his chest.

'Baldursson was just doing his job,' he tried to reassure her.

'But I made him come here.'

'Nonsense,' he said, but then he continued more gently as he felt Uma stiffen. 'Men like him are not forced to do anything. He came because he wanted to protect you.'

There was no response from Uma. Ethan didn't risk more platitudes, preferring instead to savour the pressure of her body on his. He pulled it tight, enveloping her petite frame in his muscly arms. It felt good, really good. Luckily, he had the foresight to turn slightly sideways, so she was pressed into his hip. They remained that way for many minutes, Uma silently weeping, Ethan secretly enjoying their tight embrace. Eventually, the sobbing slowed, to be replaced by violent shivering. Shock or cold, it was time to go.

'Come on. We need to get you inside.'

Uma stared at him dumbly, her eyes dull with grief. He didn't wait for an answer this time and instead scooped her up in his arms. She didn't resist, but as he turned towards the centre, she gave a small cry. Ethan followed her gaze, and thought he had stepped through one of Uma's LEAP gates.

The thick curtain of fog had melted away to reveal the steaming lake in all its nocturnal splendour, courtesy of a huge three-quarter moon that bathed everything in a luminescent glow. White tendrils of steam snaked up from blue milky waters over jet-black magma that ringed the small pool of water. In the distance, the smoking chimneys of the nearby Svartsengi Power Plant were clearly silhouetted against the clear night sky. Sixty feet from shore the chief inspector was rocking gently, the axe shank framed against the dark waters at forty-five degrees like a dinghy's mast. But this hadn't drawn Uma's cry. It was the assassin. He was sitting bolt upright and staring directly at them, the fathom-less pools of his eyes that had hypnotised Uma earlier, now glowing crimson in the lunar light. The moment stretched out unnaturally. No one moved. Then the man blinked and this time Uma screamed, an anguished cry that grew in strength, building on a wave of anger that crested in vengeful rage at the sight of Fredrik's killer.

Ethan calmly put Uma down on the wooden deck and walked towards the man. Even from this distance he realised, with grim satis-faction, that the truncheon recovered from one of the dead soldiers in the centre had caused more than just a flesh wound. Where the bridge of the man's nose met, the forehead was now a mass of crushed bone and gristle through which bloody mucus bubbled. At the very least, his injuries would require hospital treatment and probably plastic surgery to rebuild his shattered nose.

'That's for Fredrik and Uma,' Ethan muttered under his breath as he quickened his pace. The assassin gingerly traced around his oozing nose. He turned once again to stare at Ethan in puzzlement. Then a shriek of recognition pierced the quiet night. He leapt to his feet and rushed towards Ethan, who also broke into a run. At the very last mo-ment, the bloody apparition feinted left, clearly hoping to draw Ethan, but he resisted the invitation, instead dropping low and slamming his shoulder into the squat man's midriff. Ethan kept low, forcing his attacker backwards into deeper water before following through with an uppercut aimed at his bloodied nose. But instead of soft tissue, he swiped air. The next second, he felt his ribs crack as the killer drove a knee into Ethan's exposed chest. Ethan had no time to think about it as he parried a succession of heavy blows to his head. Piledriver upon piledriver delivered in a blur of flying fists that would have crushed a lesser man. As the attack subsided, Ethan leapt to his feet, unleashing his own barrage at the bloody gash. If just one hit home, this fight would be over, but Grond, sensing the danger, suddenly changed tack, leaping high out of the water and catching Ethan with a crunching heel kick that clipped his temple. White light seared Ethan's vision as Grond followed through with a front kick to his chest that lifted Ethan clean out of the water. As he floundered on his back, Ethan felt powerful hands close around his neck, forcing him deep beneath the hot surface.

He was now fighting a different battle as his unprepared lungs screamed for air. He started thrashing wildly, clawing at his attacker's wrists, trying to break free. Gradually he weakened until finally, in a shuddering fit, he fell completely limp, mimicking the final throes of drowning. Five seconds passed. Ethan counted slowly, willing his body to remain still, fighting the natural urge to gulp fresh air. Ten more, but there was no let-up in the pressure around his neck. He had another ten seconds left in him and then it would be all over. The dull ache in his chest boomed like a bass drum. His limbs screamed for oxygen. Then, finally, he felt fingers release their grip ever so slightly. That was all Ethan needed. He whipped his body sideways, driving an arm through the man's hands as he crowbarred them apart. And then he was free, clawing up towards the surface. He emerged, arms flailing like demented windmills, ready for an onslaught that never came.

Grond was crumpled in the shallows, blood welling up from a fresh cut on the back of his shaved head. He was clearly unconscious. Uma was standing over him, a large lump of lava clutched in both hands. She had lost her catatonic look and held Ethan's surprised gaze with piercing green eyes. As she raised her arms high above her head, Ethan stepped forward.

'When I need your help, I'll ask for it.' He prised the rock from her hands before hurling it far out into the lagoon and storming off towards the visitor centre.

By the time they reached the safety of the ruined restaurant, Uma was shaking uncontrollably. Ethan was already inside, forcing her to step over five bodies that lay crumpled by the entrance. Even up close, it was difficult to see which side of the fight they belonged to since they were all dressed head to boot in black. Around them lay the aftermath of a fierce firefight that had reduced the eating area to broken tables and burning chairs. She could barely see Ethan through the thick black smoke and hurried to catch up. As they approached the shops, two more bodies appeared, sprawled over the checkout desks. Ethan disappeared inside, emerging seconds later with two super-sized Blue Lagoon sweatshirts. They each shrugged one over their wet clothes, before hurrying through the silent turnstiles and onto the path that had brought them into the centre less than one hour earlier. But that's as far as they got. Arrayed across the entrance to the Blue Lagoon were five figures, all dressed in black and pointing snub-nosed machine guns in their direction.

New York City

14 November 2003 21:00 hours EST

The man tapped away on the keyboard, his face just inches from the glowing screen. He looked weighed down, as if carrying the entire world's weight on his narrow shoulders. Every now and then, he would swivel left to study several more screens covered in dense digits. To his right, a TV silently played out scenes from earlier in the day as reporters in different locations stood hunched against the Icelandic winter, trying to make sense of the smoking carnage behind them. He slapped the table in frustration and buried his head deep in his hands. He remained that way for many seconds before taking a deep breath and returning to his work.

'Any idea what went wrong?'

'Christ,' Shane exclaimed, upsetting a glass of water as he spun round to face Uma. 'When did you get here?'

She was perched on a low credenza behind his desk, arms folded, staring at her CSO. Shane met her gaze, clearly irritated at the delayed acknowledgement. He held it for several seconds but was no match for Uma's piercing eyes, hardened by the horrors of the afternoon.

'You seem nervous.'

He looked up, shifting uncomfortably in his chair.

'Damn right. I thought you were dead. Ethan as well, judging from the reports coming out of Iceland.'

'You still haven't answered my question.'

'I'm not sure what you mean.'

'You know exactly what I'm talking about,' she said. 'What did you send over?'

'I had no choice. Ethan thought you were in danger and—'

'Of course, you had a choice. You both did.'

'It's all I could think of.'

'Did you stop for one second to consider the consequences?'

'How was I to know this would happen?' he said, nodding at the TV as it panned across a blackened mountain of smoking metal.

'So many lives lost,' Uma said, swallowing hard as she fought back tears. 'My Fredrik. His men. Those policemen at the roadblock.'

Shane sank even lower in his chair.

'What the hell happened out there?'

'You had no right to do that.'

'We couldn't just leave you.'

'That thing you sent through has carved a trail of destruction across southern Iceland.'

Shane looked close to tears, but her hardened heart stayed a comforting hand as the image of Fredrik appeared before her, rocking gently in the hot water.

'What now?'

The question went unanswered as Uma stared in horror at the unwelcome vision; Fredrik's lifeless eyes, extended arms, the axe head embedded in his enormous chest.

'Delete him.'

'Who?'

'Ethan ... Anderson. Or whoever the hell he is.'

'Delete him,' he said, realisation dawning. 'We can't do that.'

'We have to. Anderson's dead; have you forgotten the second LEAP Law?'

Of course, Shane remembered the second law: If your physical body died in the natural world, your LEAP file would have to be deleted from the system. It was both a blessing and a curse, that once they'd scanned someone's atomic structure into the system, they used the scan of that person to rebuild the body at the destination. Atom by atom. The original person was disassembled and their atoms stored as building blocks for the next incoming LEAP. The obvious benefit was that they didn't have to transport someone, just a snapshot in time of everything that comprised the person in that moment, including the brain and all its memories. That's what had allowed him to merge Anderson's body with Ethan's head.

'But he's flesh and blood now. We're responsible for him. He's our creation.'

'He's an aberration you cooked up,' Uma hissed. 'That ... thing is just a bunch of atoms that you spat out of the system. Ninety percent of them are in the image of a man who was already dead. His program should have already been wiped. He has no rights. He's not human. He's a monster and needs returning to the atomic soup you brewed him from.'

'Who made you judge, jury and executioner?'

'Oh, for God's sake, Shane, don't you understand anything? You breached three of the Laws? You can't copy people. You can't keep dead people alive. You can't merge people. They exist for a reason. To prevent messes like him from occurring. What do you propose we do? Let him live?'

Shane nodded.

'OK, so what happens to Ethan, with his doppelgänger running about?'

Shane didn't respond.

'Do we just leave him in suspension? Or maybe we should wipe his program since he's as good as dead if we don't restore him.'

'I need to think about it,' he eventually responded.

'We don't have time. Every second will leave his evil twin on the loose, heading up one of the largest businesses in the UK. One who's lost a hundred IQ points and gained thirty pounds of muscle, with a mouth to match. How will you explain that one? Christ, this whole endeavour will be over before we even begin.'

Shane shifted uncomfortably in his chair, before giving the answer she knew he would. 'I'm really sorry, Uma. I can't do it. You wipe it. Him. I want nothing to do with this.'

'I already have.'

'What do you mean?'

'That killing machine you sent over. He's gone. I've wiped the program and restored Ethan. He's in my father's house sleeping. And that's where I'm going before someone wonders why I'm in NYC and not under house arrest in the centre of Reykjavík.'

She marched across the room before he could answer.

'You can't control this, you know,' Shane shouted after her. 'The genie's out of the bottle now. It will not be easy to put back.'

'You don't know the half of it,' Uma muttered under her breath as she slammed the door on him and stormed off down the corridor.

Reykjavík, Iceland

15 November 2003, 03:03 hours GMT

The entire night sky was lit up by a pulsating curtain of multi-coloured lights that advanced across the horizon like a ghostly shroud pulled along by some invisible force of nature. The leading light strings were moving incredibly fast and were impossible to focus on for more than an instant, twisting and turning like billowing sheets caught in a fierce gale. Teasingly, they would fade from view and then suddenly reform in the clear night sky before finally disappearing in a blaze of purples and reds over the horizon, the few lone clouds—now tinged with rose and light pink—the only witness to their spectacular demise. Directly overhead, the movement was subtler, as luminescent greens and yellows streamed delicately through the atmosphere, like soft silk carried gently on a summer breeze. They gracefully swayed backwards and forwards as if caught in the giant swell of an ocean's tidal pull, completely powerless to resist the elemental forces at work, but also clearly content with the natural rhythm being played out across the heavens.

The effect was truly mesmerising and had completely transfixed Ethan for the past half hour as he sat alone in an oversized lounger, looking up into the night sky through the bay window that formed the centrepiece of the living room. When the galactic fire show had first appeared, Ethan knew he was witnessing the fabled Northern Lights, the breath-taking result of huge plasma clouds of solar particles colliding with the earth's atmosphere. Before tonight, he had only ever viewed pictures and grainy videos taken by amateur photographers, but had never seen it first-hand. Despite the tragic aftermath of the last few hours, he felt a great sense of peace wash over him as he gazed up at the spectacular emission of light photons, humbled by the experience. Each particle had travelled millions of miles from the surface of the sun, driven outwards by the unrelenting solar winds, before crashing into the outer layer of gas enveloping the earth. It was a natural phenomenon that had occurred for billions of years and would doubtless continue for many more, long after mankind had gone.

For the first time since he had arrived in Iceland, Ethan appreciated the Icelanders' stoical acceptance of their place in nature. It was an understanding, born not only from centuries of struggle against an inhospitable environment, but also from observing the majesty of the elements in their most basic forms, both on the ground and in the sky.

Ethan could have studied the lights all night, but even they were no match for the waves of fatigue that overwhelmed him. Other than the dazzling pyrotechnics above, there was no good reason to stay awake. Fifteen feet below him, he could just make out the silhouette of two policemen slowly making their way back down the main lawn towards the front gate. It was a reassuring sight, as was the knowledge that six more troopers were also patrolling the grounds.

Ethan found the show of force reassuring, especially since they'd still not apprehended Baldursson's killer. Incredibly, despite his injuries, he had somehow made his way to the car park, overpowered two men, stolen a police car and disappeared. The vehicle had been discovered later, abandoned on the outskirts of Reykjavík. Shortly afterwards, a black Mercedes had been reported missing. CCTV footage from the visitor centre had provided their only breakthrough, recording everything in all its savage glory. The assassin coolly cutting down the chief inspector. The firefight that had taken the lives of eight other members of the Viking Squad. Uma rescuing Ethan from certain drowning. It was all there and had earned them both a grudging respect from the shell-shocked team who had witnessed the massacre.

It had been an intensely moving moment to witness them recover Baldursson's body from the Blue Lagoon. Ethan had been stood by the entrance to the destroyed dining hall giving yet another statement when three soldiers had entered with a heavy load loosely covered with a groundsheet. Behind them, their section leader followed, the murder weapon swinging from a bag gripped tightly in his right hand. Two others cleared a small space in the centre of the room, where they carefully laid Baldursson. Then all eight stood silently around the body along with Uma, heads bowed, hands clasped in front of them, whilst their leader administered what Ethan presumed were the last rites in Icelandic. The ritual lasted less than a minute and, having paid their respects, the grim-faced group broke up to begin their search for his killer. Within the hour, they'd recovered a pristine mugshot from the CCTV system. One camera had caught the killer almost face on, his piercing black eyes preserved in a DVD-quality still that had been distributed to all the relevant authorities. After that, there was very little to be done. A police doctor had given Uma and Ethan a clean bill of health, after which they were dispatched back to Reykjavík in a multi-vehicle police escort.

Ethan glanced over his shoulder at Uma on the couch behind him, her soft features gently illuminated by the lights of the Aurora. She looked so peaceful, the horrors visited on her earlier in the day temporarily held at bay by the sanctuary of deep sleep. He was tempted to reach out and stroke her cheek, but thought better of it. He didn't want to wake her, partly because she needed the rest, but also because he was slightly fearful of her mood. Following their return from the Blue Lagoon, she had insisted that they check up on the Interior facility. He had wanted to wind down. To relax and sleep, but she would have none of it. So, they'd made the LEAP. On their return, she had quizzed him repeatedly about the most inane subjects before disappearing to New York for almost an hour. When she returned, her mood had worsened. She seemed distant, almost resentful of his presence, and had crashed on the couch, leaving him alone and thoughtful.

He had tried not to read too much into her angry silence, preferring instead to dwell on their passionate embrace from earlier. Had they really kissed? He could scarcely believe it, but the memory of her soft lips melting into his felt real enough and had filled his every waking thought since the LEAP. He found himself grinning like a love-struck teenager, and not even the abrupt interruption of her pulling away had dampened his mood.

Ethan shifted on the soft cushions and stretched his legs. He was tired, but his mind was too active, churning through a whirlwind of possibilities that at some point slipped with him into a deep sleep. The last thing he remembered was a multi-coloured kaleidoscope of light shimmering protectively above his head.

He was naked. Outside, in the freezing cold. Standing in what seemed like a tear in the earth, perhaps ten, maybe twelve-feet deep. On either side of him, ancient lava gleamed dully in the light of a hundred billion stars arched overhead. He knew this place but couldn't work out how. Up ahead, a soft glow appeared, compelling him forward. He took tentative steps, his feet carefully feeling their way over sharp rocks littering the deep fissure. That was strange. The lava was moving. He could feel it silently pulling apart along its entire length, that ran for thousands of miles in each direction. But it wasn't just the rock face that was being forced apart. The entire landmass beneath him was stirring like an ancient giant awaking from a long slumber.

The light was getting closer now, forcing him to shield his eyes from the bright glare. His instinct was to run, but he was drawn towards it like a helpless moth. With a start, he realised where he was. In the fissure zone at Þingvellir, the site of Iceland's first parliament. Uma had taken him there on one of his trips to Iceland as they prepared LEAP for release. She laughingly called it downtime from their work and he had been happy to accompany her. In this maze of deep trenches and rifts, the on-land exposure of the Mid-Atlantic Ridge, the boundary point between the tectonic plates carrying North America and Eurasia, was at its most prominent. What had been their rate of separation? One inch every year as the plates slowly ripped Iceland apart. But the walls seemed to be receding much faster than that, as the trench suddenly plummeted outwards and downwards at a preternatural speed. Overhead, the stars had faded from view, but he no longer needed their comforting glow as the light swept towards him, a ball of iridescent white that burned his eyes. The sides of the trench had long since disappeared, and a thunderous roar now filled his ears. As the brightness completely enveloped him in its fiery embrace, he felt a surge of knowledge flow effortlessly through his synapses. It made his head hurt and he suddenly felt nauseous as the enormity and clarity of his newfound understanding overwhelmed him. It frightened him. No one could contain that much learning and he tried to turn and run, but it was too late. He couldn't move, his outstretched arms were frozen in space. Without warning, black specks began to dance across his eyes and he began to fade from view. It started with both hands, crawled up his arms and continued past the periphery of his limited vision. He did not feel any pain. In fact, his nerves had no feeling, rather like the sensation he had experienced after the operation following his accident twenty-five years before. When he had come round, the lower half of his body from the waist down had been completely anaesthetised and was, therefore, devoid of any feeling. He thought they had amputated both his legs until the postoperative pain came to haunt him a few hours later.

With his newfound intellect, Ethan was privy to his rapid disappearance as layers of anatomy were stripped away. First, his skin, from the epidermis, through the dermis, down to the subcutaneous tissue. Tendons, arteries, veins, muscle, cartilage and bone were all suddenly revealed in startling clarity. The breakdown was relentless and far too fast for the human eye to fully absorb. Except he could. Ethan focused on his wrist. The process had already reached the two main bones of his forearm, the ulna and the radius. First, the periosteum—the fibrous connective tissue sheath surrounding the bone—was stripped away. Then came the hard outer bone through to its spongy interior, and onward down to the soft bone marrow itself until, eventually, there was nothing left for him to see. His hand and wrist had completely disappeared. But Ethan remained calm and clear headed. There was no time to panic.

Through the oceanic roar of a thousand seas, he heard a ringing which interrupted the relentless progress of his vanishing act. He toyed with letting the phone go to answer machine, but the caller persisted, dropping the connection each time the service cut in. At this rate, the noise would wake Uma. He couldn't let that happen. But he couldn't move. In fact, he was no longer there. He had gone. Vanished from the face of the earth without a trace. His accumulated knowledge of a million millennia gone for good, his atoms scattered across the universe like the billions upon billions of life forms that had gone before him and would follow. He willed himself to reform, but the trillions of bits that used to be him were already hard at work building other things and ignored his cry for help.

And then, suddenly, it was over. Without warning, he reassembled at what seemed like warp speed, but not in the cold trench at Þingvellir. He was no longer standing, but sitting in a giant comfy chair. The temperature was warm and he was fully dressed. Everything had changed, but the phone continued to ring incessantly behind him, and then he realised he was back in the living room, the house still dark, the Aurora now gone, extinguished by the advancing dawn.

Ethan pulled himself up from the soft cushions and stumbled past the sleeping Uma, who stirred softly but did not wake. He nearly knocked the ringing phone to the floor in his haste to answer it.

'Ethan speaking,' he mumbled. 'Shane! Hi, I know. We've had our mobiles turned off. It's a long story. I'll tell you later. What's up? What do you mean, bad news? Oh, Jesus! When did this happen?'

Ethan was fully awake now, his heart pounding in alarm as he absorbed Shane's news.

'Yes, yes, I'm still here. Yes, I will tell Uma. She's sleeping at the moment, but I'll wake her right now. Yes, we will call you back immediately. OK. OK. I'll speak to you soon. Goodbye.'

He heard Uma stirring as the call ended.

'Ethan?' her voice was thick with sleep. 'Who was that?'

'Shane.'

An unruly mass of black hair suddenly appeared over the top of the couch.

'What did he want?' she asked anxiously.

Ethan swallowed hard before slowly looking down at her.

'I'm afraid he had some bad news.'

Reykjavík Harbour, Iceland

15 November 2003, 04:34 hours GMT

Sixty feet above the icy waters of Reykjavík Harbour, Captain Haraldur Sveinsson peered out into the darkness as he carefully manoeuvred the freezer trawler away from the concrete quay, its powerful Deutz engine humming softly in the wintry morning air. It was slow work. Just short of 300 feet, the *Selfoss* was the largest of its class in the Icelandic fishing fleet and capable of freezing up to eighty tons of fish per day, courtesy of its network of freezer cabinets that crisscrossed the ship's maze-like interior. For nearly two decades, she had fished the 200-mile zone around Iceland, the protected fishing grounds offering up an abundance of fish, including cod, haddock, saithe, redfish, herring and capelin. But today, that was not the purpose of her early morning departure.

Sveinsson became aware of a slight commotion on the starboard deck of the large trawler. He peered through the misted glass of the wheelhouse. Down below, he could see four of his crewmembers chatting excitedly, pointing back towards the jetty they'd just left. He glanced over his shoulder but, despite the elevated position of the bridge, could see nothing. No matter. He would soon find out what was going on and, sure enough, a few moments later, the clatter of booted feet on metal steps announced a breathless seaman who couldn't have been older than sixteen. Sveinsson recognised him immediately. He was the latest recruit to the *Selfoss* and had only been with the ship for two weeks. The bright yellow waterproof brace trousers and overjacket looked far too big on him, which only added to the impression that he shouldn't be there.

The young man seemed nervous and stood for several seconds by the open door, staring at the sole inhabitant of the warm bridge.

'Come here, boy. Move over here where I can see you.'

Still the young man did not speak, but this time he moved reluctantly away from the relative safety of the door to where the captain stood.

'Captain. Uh ... the others sent me,' he mumbled, eyes to the ground and anxiously trying to tear a woollen cap apart with his soft hands. 'To tell you—'

'Tell me what? Come on, boy. Spit it out. I haven't got all day.'

'There's a car floating in the harbour. They just spotted it off the starboard bow. We nearly hit it. There's no way you could have seen it from up here. The crew thought you might want to know. It's a hazard.'

The words tumbled out in a sudden splurge, and the young man stopped just as suddenly as he had started, clearly pleased to be free of his burdensome message. He made to leave, but the captain grabbed his arm in a vice-like grip.

'You're shitting me! A car, hey?' Sveinsson said. 'Don't tell me. It was towing a caravan, right?' His crew's sense of humour was legendary, and it was the sort of dumb joke they would pull on the latest addition to their team.

'Uh ... no, sir. No caravan,' the boy said, totally oblivious to his superior's scornful tone. 'Just a car. A black one. It looks like an old Mercedes. They thought you might want to ring it in.'

The captain laughed. He was in a good mood. The $100,000 sitting in the ship's safe guaranteed that. Crisp new one hundred-dollar bills.

One thousand in total. A nice neat number he had endlessly checked and rechecked. The money had a unique texture, and the smell of the cotton-linen blend fuelled an intoxicating desire to feel each note, long after the need to make sure they were all there. Two years' pay for two weeks' work. Tax-free as well. Now, that would put a smile on anyone's face. He would play along with his crew's childish jokes.

'They do, do they? Well, Jóhannsson, Már Haraldsson, will appreciate that, won't he? Let's ring it in right now.'

He knew the harbour master well and it was just the sort of mindless joke he liked, but as he picked up the intercom, there was a metallic click in his ear.

'If you make that connection, it will be the last thing you ever do. Now, put it down and concentrate on what I have paid you for.'

The intercom hit the metal deck with a loud clang.

'Christ, you nearly gave me a heart attack. What the fuck do you think you're doing snooping about like that?' Sveinsson half-turned to look at his assailant. 'And, for God's sake, put that damn gun down. There's no need for that up here.'

Andreus Grond let the P80 hang at his side, never taking his eyes off the older man who had recovered the radio mic. Grond raised his gun again.

'Did you not hear me? Don't make the call. No one needs to hear about the car. I would prefer it remained that way. At least, for the time being.'

'I don't care what you think,' the captain said. He had spent the last forty years at sea, and the sight of guns and the death they dealt no longer shocked or bothered him. If it was his time, he was more than ready. 'That car's a hazard.'

'Leave it. The vehicle will soon sink.'

'That could take five minutes. I can't risk it snagging someone's propeller shaft. It would shatter the blades and leave a boat out of the water for weeks. Long enough to bankrupt the man and his family.'

Grond shrugged and holstered the weapon, slowly walking round the front of the helm, so he now faced them.

Sveinsson let out a low whistle.

'My God, man. What happened to you?' he exclaimed at the apparition in front of him. The man who had handed over his big pay day less than forty-eight hours earlier had been impeccably turned out and sporting a healthy complexion. This one was covered in blood. It was everywhere. On his face, arms, hands and T-shirt. Even his jeans were bloodied, stained a dark black by the cut on his nose. For now, the flow had stopped, clotted over by a huge crust of blood that arched in an angry scab across the bridge of his nose. His eyes were swollen black slits—the surrounding skin already darkening—and the damaged blood vessels bruised into activity by the blow to his nose.

'A fight. In Reykjavík.'

Even the man's teeth were red, reducing his smile to a ghoulish leer.

'No shit. Who did that to you?'

'Some English hooligans, I think you say.' Grond enunciated the unfamiliar word carefully as he continued to stare down at the older man. 'They ambushed me on the way out of the city centre. You know what they're like. Can't hold their drink and at the end of the evening search out a good punch-up to finish their night off.'

Sveinsson didn't believe him for one second, but also knew that was as much as he was likely to get out of the man.

'We need to take care of that,' he said, nodding at Grond's nose. 'If it gets infected, you won't be getting off in Bergen, except in a body bag, and I want the rest of my payment.'

'I need to use the sat phone in your cabin to make a call.'

'Be my guest. It's your show.'

Grond slowly moved back around the wheel column towards the door. As he passed, Sveinsson let out a silent whistle. The back of the man's head mirrored the front, his nearly shaved scalp was bloodied red by a deep cut to his skull. It must have been six inches long, running right to left, and would need as many stitches. It was incredible that he was still standing. A blow that hard would have fractured the skull of most men.

The captain turned back to face the bow and, in doing so, noticed Jóhannsson still standing at his side, frozen to the spot. He had forgotten all about him. He suppressed a smile. The poor lad was scared witless, his skin the same pale pallor as the spectre that had just left his wheelhouse.

'God, boy. You look like you've just seen a ghost. Pull yourself together and tell your yellow-bellied friends that I'll report the car.'

The young man didn't move but, this time, his reluctance was not born out of shyness.

'Did you see his eyes?'

'I sure did, son. They have seen many deaths. Just make sure they don't witness yours.'

Reykjavík, Iceland

15 November 2003, 06:07 hours GMT

Ethan was standing in Uma's office on the second floor of her house in Reykjavík. Behind him, a star-shaped Polycom conference phone blinked intermittently on an antique table, the red light confirmation that the conversation was audible to Shane in Manhattan. In front of him, a large window running the full length of the room provided a bird's-eye view of the picturesque capital and its harbour beyond. Down below, Ethan picked up the sudden glow of a lighter in the gloomy morning as one of their guards lit a cigarette. It was extinguished just as quickly. He turned his attention back to the call.

Uma had not said a word since he had broken the news to her. She looked manic, shifting in her seat, hands clasped one moment, fingers drumming on the table surface the next. Energy crackled through her sparkling green eyes, which shifted between him and the phone. They looked dangerous and reminded Ethan of a volcano that was just about to erupt.

'Take me through this, Shane. What happened?' Ethan said.

There was a slight pause before their CSO's voice filled the room.

'Well, according to security, Eva was on her way home when she stopped at Zabar's on Broadway. She was with a girlfriend, a Miss Judy

Frieman, who waited outside, opposite the store at the intersection where 80th crosses Broadway. She actually reported the incident to the police, not that she was able to tell them much. Eva came out of the deli and was waiting to cross the road when an unmarked black Savannah Passenger Van pulled up in front of her. It was only there a matter of seconds. When it moved, she was gone. That's it. Her friend didn't even get a good look at the driver. Windows were blacked out. Whoever took her didn't get out of the van. The police were on the scene pretty quickly and took her friend's statement. We didn't know anything was wrong until the recording arrived.'

'What time was that?'

'Let's see.' There was a rustling of papers as Shane checked the delivery log. 'Ah, yes, the delivery was made at three p.m. Eva disappeared just before two.'

Ethan did the mental arithmetic. The times fitted almost exactly. The assassin had escaped from the Blue Lagoon at about 17:45 Icelandic time, making it nearly midday in New York. It was tight, but possible.

'Can we hear the recording again, Shane?'

'Sure thing. One moment.'

They could hear more activity in the background, followed by a loud click that made them both jump. There was a low hissing sound over the speaker box before an unrecognisable voice filled the room. Neither male nor female, there was no discernible accent and, to further disguise its true owner, the vocals had been altered extensively, so much so that it no longer sounded human. The pitch, timbre and tone had been lowered and slowed down to a point where all emotion and feeling had been stripped out, leaving a computer-generated monotone devoid of all personality. Ethan shuddered. If he had stopped to imagine a voice that matched those eyes from the Blue Lagoon, this disembodied growl would not have been far off.

'By now, you will have discovered that Eva is missing. We have her. You will get her back safely. However, we need something in return. The source code for LEAP, along with your quantum passwords to access the system. You have twelve hours.' There was a slight pause before the artificial tones continued. 'You will be contacted with details of where to send the information at midday New York time tomorrow.'

There was an audible click, and the line went dead.

Ethan looked at his watch. Christ, it was already 06:15 in the morning, 01:15 in New York, which meant they had less than twelve hours!

'Shane, how long would it take to provide the information they're after?'

'I can't get that information. No one person can.'

'What do you mean?' Uma said.

'Access to this information is only available to you and Ethan together, in person and, because of the lockdown, you both need to be here in New York with your Q-Passes.'

'A Q-Pass?'

'Hey, don't ask me. Ask Ethan. It was his idea.'

Ethan held up a small black device that he had fished out of his trouser pocket. It was oval shaped with a tiny LCD screen in the centre. To the left of the small readout was a single grey button, the size of a fingernail. Uma recognised the fob; there was an exact replica currently hanging around her neck and she traced its shape through her shirt.

'It's a passkey, right?'

'Sort of. It's part of a security solution we sell at Rae Security Group. In the trade, it's known as a two-key five-factor authentication system.'

'For God's sake, Ethan. Speak English!'

Despite the tension, Ethan managed a tired smile. For one moment, Uma sounded almost normal.

'It's designed to protect highly confidential information. In this case, certain components of the LEAP technology, including the source code and all current password details. Essentially, the only way to access them is by using a digital passkey, thirty-two characters in length, of which the first sixteen are contained on my Q-Pass,' Ethan waved the small fob at Uma. 'And the second string of numbers are contained on yours. To avoid you having to remember a sixteen-digit password, the Q-Pass actually generates the code strings for you, but, for extra security, they're randomly created every time you use it. That's the two-key part of the system.'

'What's to stop someone from stealing the fob and just entering whatever numbers come up?'

'Well, to work, they need both key fobs and would have to enter the codes within sixty seconds of each other.'

'So, they steal mine and then yours. They would be in business, right?'

'Not quite. That's where the other four factors of authentication come in. As added security, the holder of each Q-Pass would also need to undergo four of the security checks required to access a gate—palm reading, iris identification, body scan, and voice recognition. These are unique to each Q-Pass. Normally, the procedure can be performed wherever there is a gate but, because of the lockdown, we both need to be back in New York and that presents a bit of a problem.'

'What's the problem? We could make the jump and be back in fifteen minutes. No one would even know we have gone.'

'It's not that easy. We're currently involved in the biggest murder hunt in Iceland's history.'

'I went earlier and it wasn't a problem,' she said.

'Well, I wasn't thinking straight or I would have stopped you,' Ethan said. 'There's no way we can leave this house. We're surrounded by eight policemen who think we're safely tucked up in bed. What if one of them wants to talk to us and finds out that we're not here? It's just simply too high-profile to risk.'

'To risk what, goddamn it? My sister's life!' Uma slammed her fist down on the table. Ethan jumped, even though he had been expecting it.

'We don't even know who these people are,' Ethan said. 'For all we know, they could be terrorists. If they got their hands on LEAP, they would be untouchable. They wouldn't need to hijack planes. With this technology, they could travel anywhere with anything. Think about it.' He enunciated each word slowly, as if talking to a child. 'Anywhere they wanted. They could even transport a dirty bomb right into the

White House or any other seat of government, if they so wished. Are you prepared to let that happen?'

'Of course, I'm not,' Uma said, angered by Ethan's insinuation. What did he take her for? 'My sister's life is on the line here, and you're behaving like we have a choice.'

'Not exactly. I'm just saying that we need to tread carefully. We have no idea who we're dealing with.'

'So, what exactly are you proposing? That we forget about Eva?'

'That's not what I meant.'

'Well, it sure sounds like it. Too many people have died already and I'm not prepared to lose someone else, especially my sister.' Uma blinked back tears.

Ethan walked over to where she was sitting and placed an awkward arm on her shoulder. Uma suppressed the urge to pull away, the memory of their recent encounter in the Blue Lagoon all too clear.

'If it's any help, I know what you're going through,' he said. 'But it's not that black and white. Do you think for one second they will let us live if we hand over the codes?'

'Why wouldn't they?'

'Oh, come on,' he removed his arm. 'Of course, they won't. Why should they? It's too risky. They need us out of the way.'

'What possible threat would we pose once they have access to LEAP?'

It was too much for Ethan.

'I can't believe you're being so naïve. To begin with, we know too much. That's why I think they tried to kill us on the way to the airport but behaved so differently down at the lagoon.'

Uma stared at Ethan in shock, too stunned to respond.

'Ethan, how do yo—'

'Shane, don't interrupt,' Uma cut in, hitting the mute button. All she could think of was Anderson's ugly temper. There was no way they could let Ethan know what had happened the last time he jumped. If LEAP had malfunctioned, God knows how an Anderson-infected Ethan would react. 'I think he's on to something.'

'Go on,' Uma prompted, her mind lurching blindly for a logical explanation. There wasn't one, unless she had made a catastrophic mistake ... That simply wasn't possible. She had been so careful. Double, triple checking her routine before deleting the Anderson infected Ethan and then restoring Ethan from the copy that existed when he made the LEAP from New York City to the Reykjavík Technical College for his rescue attempt. The restored Ethan should have no memory of what happened on the road to the airport. The awful truth was that she had no idea what had happened. This was far worse than Shane's earlier blunder. At least they could explain that. But not this. Uma realised with a sickening feeling that there was no way they could ever launch with this hanging over the programme. Nauseating guilt cut through the half-formed thought.

In her shock, Uma had completely forgotten Eva. The room began to spin, and she felt her chest tighten as her tired mind pinged from Eva to the LEAP Laws, her father, dear Fredrik. And now Ethan. Or was it still Anderson? She stared at the man opposite with new eyes. Ones that had witnessed his cool calmness and frenzied rages.

He was speaking, completely oblivious to her blind panic.

'Up to now, I couldn't understand why they were trying to kill us one second and do God knows what with you the next. You said yourself that the Shogun was trying to push us off the road. There was no way we would have survived a high-speed crash. Christ, they even tried to shunt us into that fireball and nearly succeeded. Why was that? I think it's because they thought they had the source codes, until Shane fried their systems. When they realised what had happened, they sent that monster to kidnap you.'

Uma nodded slowly, unable to speak, dumbly trying to rationalise what was happening. How had Ethan's new memories from a different person infected the restored Ethan? Her biggest fear was whether Anderson could still be in there. But that was impossible. But then again, what do she know? This was definitely the old Ethan, she reassured herself hurriedly. Anderson would never have behaved like this, calmly sitting down having a half intelligent conversation. She forced herself to listen to what he was saying. There was the small matter of her sister's abduction. If anyone could sort this mess out, it was Ethan. Even an entangled one.

'When I clobbered him with the truncheon, he was taking you somewhere. It wasn't to kill you. He could have done that easily enough in the water. I got lucky and so did you at the lagoon. God knows what would have happened if the boys in black hadn't arrived when they did. As it was, he escaped, but must have raised an alarm, which is when they turned their attention to Eva.'

What he said made sense, but somehow it no longer seemed to matter. All that mattered was that these people had Eva. That Baldursson was dead. That a monster of their own making had killed others. That somehow a restored Ethan had been infused with Anderson's memories. None of these tragedies would have happened without LEAP. And she was helpless to undo any of them. Her father's unwelcome retort rang in her ears: 'Mankind needs to remember its place on this planet,' he would tell her. 'Our time here will be fleeting and, if we are not careful, will end sooner than even nature intended.' He used to get so angry, particularly when he read about some man-made disaster or atrocity. 'Mankind is on the edge of a precipice,' he would rant at her. 'If it isn't nuclear Armageddon that gets us all, then it will be something else of our own doing. A virus. Another world war. Biological weapons.' More latterly for him, it had been climate change. He had toured the world from the early 1970s, as soon as the scientific evidence linked the two together, lecturing on the dangers of manmade climate change. However, he had always fought Uma over releasing LEAP, right until his death. 'Man's travelling fast enough as it is towards oblivion,' he would argue. 'I'm not going to speed up that process.' Maybe her father had been right after all. She angrily tried to push the thought aside, but it refused to be silenced.

'Don't you see?' Ethan said, unaware of Uma's creaking resolve. 'We're in a much stronger position than you think. They need these codes. Without them, they're locked out of the system and they can't get their hands on LEAP. They're stuck. Just like killing us wasn't in their interest, neither will executing Eva do them any good. If they kill her, they're really stuck. I think they're bluffing. We can outmanoeuvre them here. We just need to think through how to respond.'

Uma realised with a shock that she half wished some of Anderson's personality had come across with the memories. For all his many faults, he would be doing something by now. And it would be foolhardy. And risky. And stupid. But at least they wouldn't be sitting around talking about it. He would probably be in New York already, doing what he did best.

'Bluffing!' she spluttered. 'Think! You want to sit here and play Russian roulette with my sister's life? This isn't a spy movie, Ethan. Eva isn't some expendable asset, and you aren't James bloody Bond.'

Uma began pacing in front of the long window.

'How many more people need to die before enough is enough? How many more?' she screamed at him. 'What if that monster had succeeded in kidnapping me at the Blue Lagoon? What would you have done? Sat around strategizing? I sure as hell hope not!'

Ethan scowled back at her. But Uma's mind was made up.

'No, it ends right here tonight. To hell with LEAP. No one else is going to die. There has been enough bloodshed already.'

Uma sat down again, chest heaving, eyes red from crying. She was completely drained.

Ethan tried again. 'I'm afraid it's too late now. We couldn't walk away, even if we wanted to. We're caught up in a chain of events that we might have started but which we are now powerless to control. It won't stop here, regardless of whether or not your sister lives.'

'You've got—'

'Hear me out.' Ethan held up his hands to silence Uma. 'This is not about me or you wanting to stop or continue with LEAP. I'm just trying to ensure we come out of this mess alive. Simple as that.' He smacked the table, causing Uma to jump. 'Given what has happened in the last two days, that looks increasingly unlikely once they have LEAP. They will try to kill us again, so we need to work out how we can survive. If we give up and hand this over, we have lost and will end up dead. Just like Fredrik and all his men.'

There was a deathly silence in the room.

'Do you see what's happening here?' he said.

Uma nodded blankly and slumped into the deep leather couch. The tension melted away and her clenched fists relaxed into hands again. No tears this time, just a silent acquiescence. Finally, she spoke. 'I don't want to lose Eva as well.'

'I understand.'

Something in Ethan's tone troubled Uma. How could Ethan possibly know what she was going through? He didn't have any family. He didn't even have any friends, just his damn deals. She wasn't even sure if this was Ethan.

'How could you?'

'You don't have a monopoly on losing people.'

'What, your parents?' Uma spat back. 'They died in a car accident. That's hardly the same thing. I'm directly responsible for all these people dying.'

Ethan grabbed the conference phone in both hands and hurled it across the room. It smashed against the door, chunks of plastic ricocheting off in all directions.

'So was I, goddamn it,' Ethan screamed at her. 'So was I.'

He rounded the table and advanced on Uma until he was towering over her. She shrank down into the oversized chair, her eyes wild with fear. For a moment she thought he was going to strike her, but just as suddenly, his fury passed and he slumped into the chair opposite.

'I was responsible for their deaths.'

'What are you talking about?' she said, her mind still reeling from his outburst. All she could think about was Anderson calmly throwing the gunman off the balcony at the college, snapping that man's neck like it was a twig. Ethan would have never lost his temper like that.

'I killed them.'

'Ethan, you're scaring me.' Was this Anderson talking? Had he killed his parents?

'I was driving the night they died,' he continued in a low whisper. 'I hit a car coming out of a junction. I misjudged the lights. My parents were killed instantly. The driver of the other vehicle died a few weeks later. I killed them all.'

There. His ugly secret was out and hung like a toxic cloud between them.

'When did this happen?' was all she could manage.

'I was fifteen. We lived in Saudi Arabia. My father worked for Shell. He was an oil man.' Ethan's voice was flat. No trace of emotion. As if he was reading a confession statement.

'You poor thing.' Her first reaction was to go over and comfort him, but something held her back. She couldn't be certain if this was even Ethan's memory. 'Why were you even driving?' she said, anxious to know if this was Anderson or Ethan speaking.

'We'd been out to celebrate my dad's birthday. He'd had a few drinks. So had I, just not as many. Mum couldn't drive. Women have no rights in Saudi, you know. That really used to piss her off!' He laughed hollowly at the memory. 'It wasn't just the driving. She couldn't work either, nor could she go anywhere unless her head was covered. She used to get so angry with Dad for moving her out there. We were in Scotland before that, which she hated as well. But she would have swapped Saudi for the wet granite of Aberdeen any day.'

Ethan smiled faintly at the distant recollection.

'What happened to you?'

'The other car was travelling so fast. Too fast, it seemed. I shouldn't have gone, I should have waited, but Dad wanted to get home. He had a big meeting the next day. I was rushing.'

'But were you old enough to drive?'

'As soon as I set off, I knew I wouldn't make it. You know that feeling when you commit to something but realise straight away that you won't make it but still keep going? I should have stopped. If I had, they would still be alive today.'

'Didn't the Embassy help you?' Uma asked with more concern, her suspicions beginning to fade. Ethan seemed so genuine, his recollection so precise and heartfelt.

'They were laughing in the back of the car at a joke Dad had just told. I didn't hear it because of the wind. It was a hot night, so we had the top down.' He wiped a single tear from his dry cheeks. 'They were having so much fun. That's the last thing I heard. Their laughter. Then we hit the other vehicle. It caught the back end of our car. My mother's side. Spun us round and round. I was thrown clear. They were trapped in the back with this bloody great four-by-four embedded in them.'

'Ethan—'

'The police showed me the photos,' he cut across Uma, desperate to finally get the words out. 'Of my parents. Crumpled up in the morgue. Mum's beautiful hair, black with blood and dirt and oil. They could have cleaned it, you know?' His voice choked to a whisper again. 'I'm still not sure to this day why they did that. To make me suffer?' He spat each word out. 'Did they think I wasn't suffering enough?'

Uma got up and walked over to Ethan. She cradled his head in her arms and held him quietly. She couldn't think of anything to say. Everything seemed so hopelessly inadequate. She tried again.

'Ethan, it was an accident.'

'There's no such thing as accidents,' he said, pulling away from her. 'I had a simple decision to make. Go or stay, and I made the wrong one, and it cost my parents their lives. I'm not about to let the same thing happen to you. I've made that mistake once before with the two people I ...' His voice trailed off.

'Ethan, don't do this to yourself.' Uma said, his sudden outburst once again challenging her seesawing doubts that this was Ethan's memory.

'No, I can't let this happen again. Not to you, especially after this evening. You've got to listen to me,' he pleaded. 'If we do what you're suggesting, we will all die.'

'It's not your decision to make.' Uma was beginning to get angry herself. Was this just a sob story? A crude act of manipulation to get her to go along with his scheme? She wasn't sure. Nothing made sense anymore. And as for Anderson ... she shuddered at the memory of his huge hands clawing at her breasts in the Blue Lagoon. All that mattered now was saving Eva before it was too late. 'It's mine and, rightly or wrongly, I have to put a stop to this now, before anyone else gets hurt.'

'That's exactly what will happen if you cede control of LEAP.'

'Well, that's a risk I'll have to take. You, of all people, should know about that.'

'Uma, please—'

'No, Ethan. Don't start this again.'

'Uma, it won't happen like that—'

'Enough,' she cried, leaping to her feet. 'I've heard enough. That is what we're going to do. If you don't like it, don't bother coming with me. Now, if you'll excuse me, I have to call Shane back to arrange the transfer of the source code.'

Uma marched towards the door, kicking the shattered phone out of the way. She jerked the handle back, causing the door to fly open and slam into the table. Then she disappeared down the stairs, leaving a shell-shocked Ethan staring after her in amazement.

Reykjavík, Iceland

15 November 2003, 07:36 hours GMT

'How long is this transfer going to take?' Uma said, pausing behind Shane.

'We're about two minutes closer than when you last asked me.'

'Can't we speed it up?' she urged him. 'It's already been five hours since that message was left.'

'I'm going as fast as I can,' Shane said, wiping his brow. 'I've cut every corner I know to speed this up for you.'

Uma continued her nervous pacing around the windowless room just off her office. In front of her, Shane was furiously tapping away on a keyboard. Every so often, he would turn to stare at the centre of the room, where the quantum decoder was transferring the source code for the entire LEAP system. Ethan and Uma had already completed the access routine and were now waiting for the download to occur. It seemed to be taking ages, but Ethan had decided that was more down to Uma's impatience. Since Shane had arrived from New York, her frame of mind had not improved. For the last hour, she had badgered Shane constantly. To his credit, Shane had remained calm, but in the last five minutes, his demeanour had begun to crack.

'Shouldn't be long now,' he suddenly announced, a look of relief on his large face. He stretched tiredly. 'The decoder is entering its final sequence. I reckon we've got another fifteen minutes and then you're on your way.'

Ethan checked his watch. It was 07:37 here in Reykjavík, which made it 02:37 over in New York. They still had to make a LEAP to New York to deliver the source code. A highly risky undertaking, particularly given their police escort waiting obliviously down below. If anything happened that substantially delayed their return to Reykjavík, he didn't dare think of the consequences.

He felt utterly drained following his confrontation with Uma and was totally at a loss about what to do next. He had never confided the secret of his parents' death to anyone and now he felt torn; it was as if someone had lifted an enormous weight from his shoulders, but the price was a gnawing anxiety in his stomach at the memory of what he'd shared. Then there was the course of action Uma had committed them to. She wasn't thinking clearly and was no longer listening to him. In fact, she had steadfastly ignored him since their argument. The last thirty minutes hadn't improved matters. He needed to put some distance between them. Perhaps it would allow her to calm down and for him to work out what to do next.

'I'm going to get a drink of water. Does anyone want some?' Ethan announced to the room, but neither Shane nor Uma even acknowledged his offer. After a few seconds, he gratefully exited into the welcome coolness of the corridor outside.

Ethan immediately felt better and stood there enjoying the silence.

Through the half-open door, he could hear Shane and Uma talking in hushed voices. They were saying something about him.

'Did you hear what he said?' he heard Shane ask Uma. He sounded worried. No, it was more than that. He was scared.

'Of course I did,' Uma replied. 'He remembers everything that happened yesterday.'

'I thought you corrected this?'

'I did.' Uma sounded defensive. 'Something went wrong.' There was a slight pause as Ethan heard someone tapping away on a keyboard. 'Look at the logs. I did everything correctly, but the impossible seems to have happened.'

'You're forgetting one thing,' Shane said. 'You're applying classical thinking to a new area of science. Atoms don't follow the laws of physics. They play by a different set of rules. Ones we haven't even begun to comprehend.'

'So, what do you propose we do?' he heard Uma hiss back angrily.

'I'm not sure we can do anything. You've already wiped the new Ethan from the system. What else can you do? Wipe the old one? And replace him with what, exactly? He's clearly become entangled with Anderson.'

'And adopted some of his personality traits,' added Uma, with a hint of disgust in her voice. 'You should have seen him smash the phone against the wall. He was totally out of control. It reminded me so much of Anderson in the Geothermal Department and on the drive up to the Blue Lagoon.' Through the door, Ethan could sense the emotion in her voice. She sounded like she was going to cry. 'I really thought he was going to hit me earlier. And all that stuff about his parents. Were those his memories or Anderson's? Or was he making that up?'

'I've no idea,' Shane replied. 'I know very little about Ethan.'

Ethan's heart lurched. They'd wiped his program! He could hear the fear in Uma's voice. What had he done to make her think he would lie about his parents' death? His instinct was to barge in and confront them, but something held him back. Uma muting the phone suddenly took on a new significance. Why hadn't they said anything to him? Confronted him? Or at the very least, told him what had happened?

He stumbled away from the doorway, down the corridor, his mind whirling with unanswered questions.

Shane looked over at Uma.

'You did the right thing to conceal it. I don't think it would do him any good to know what's happened until we have a chance to sort this mess out.'

'What if we can't separate him?'

'Even more reason not to tell him anything,' Shane said. 'This shit can seriously mess with your mind.'

'Do you know anything about Anderson?' If they couldn't explain why it happened, maybe they could somehow contain the damage to Ethan if they knew more about his new memories and personality.

'I pulled his file before you came over.' Shane fingered a light manila folder lying on the desk beside him.

'And?' Something in Shane's demeanour suggested all was not as it should be.

'He's your typical private security contractor.'

'Meaning?' Shane was clearly holding something back.

'Ex-Special Forces. Exercise nut. Highly trained in all weapons systems. Multi- lingual. His speciality was long stretches behind enemy lines. Commendations as long as your arm. He'd been active since enrolling at the age of twenty. Panama. The first Gulf War back in 1990. Somalia. Kosovo. Afghanistan. You name it, he was there. All deployments involving unconventional warfare.'

'What does that mean?' Uma said, thinking of Anderson's behaviour at the college.

Shane shrugged. 'You know. All the dirty stuff that never gets reported, but that everyone knows goes on behind enemy lines.' Uma shuddered. That would certainly explain his behaviour. 'There was one thing,' Shane continued. 'He was discharged last year.'

'Christ, Shane. What for?'

'We hire from a pool of ex-military, mainly Special Forces, for Rae Defence. Over the years, Ethan has found them to be the most reliable bodyguards. Very professional. Incredibly disciplined. But ...' Shane paused, suddenly unable to hold Uma's gaze. 'Anderson was highly recommended by everyone I spoke to. However, they described him as a bit of hot head.'

No shit, Uma thought, remembering his rages over the last two days.

'Always leaping first, asking questions later,' Shane said. 'A continuing problem with authority stretching right through his army career, but everyone was happy to overlook it because of his success behind the lines. I didn't think it was a problem because of the job we needed him for. He was just supposed to watch you before the launch. He wasn't even the team leader. Just one of two groups of four I detailed to provide low-level security on a rolling twenty-four-hour basis. Twelve hours on, Twelve off.'

'What was he discharged for?'

'It seems Mr Anderson's temper was worse than his ex-colleagues thought. I've done a bit more digging since he became entangled with Ethan the first time around.'

'And?'

'On his last leave, he claims to have caught his girlfriend flirting with another soldier in his unit. They were all at a disco on the Fort Bragg army base in North Carolina. It was supposed to be a celebration of the unit's return from a six-month tour in Afghanistan, arming the guerrillas.'

'Christ, Shane. What did he do?'

'Damn near killed the man. Hospitalised his girlfriend as well. Broke her nose. Fractured her arm.'

Uma stared at Shane in amazement. 'Why wasn't he prosecuted?' Uma said, remembering Ethan towering over her, eyes blazing, fist half raised. He had been about to strike her. She wondered what had stayed his arm. Ethan, perhaps?

'Neither of them would press charges. Said it had all been a horrible misunderstanding.' Uma pictured Ethan's eyes after he had snapped the gunman's neck. Cool. Detached. Business-like. No wonder they wouldn't talk. They had both known Anderson would kill them if they did.

'So why the discharge?'

'It doesn't say, but I can imagine that sort of behaviour didn't fit the Special Forces mantra. You've got to remember how tightly knit the units are. They need to be. They can't afford internal dissent in the ranks when they're behind enemy lines for months at a time. A transfer was out of the question. Especially given his history of temper flare-ups. I'm sure the Forces didn't need the adverse publicity either, so they buried it.' Shane shrugged. 'He probably struck a deal and was given an early discharge.'

Uma realised that none of this was Shane's fault. She could choose to blame him, but how was he to know that a temporary hired gun would somehow morph into the body of their CEO and threaten the whole programme? There was something else that stayed her anger. Something she couldn't even bring herself to tell Shane about. Where would she even start? That she herself had breached the first LEAP Law at the very first hurdle she had ever faced; just like Shane and Ethan had done. In an attempt to save someone she had also loved. She remembered it so clearly, as if it was yesterday.

Uma had been at her father's house, sat in the bay window overlooking the main road when she saw Fredrik walk slowly up the steep drive from his car, her father's rucksack in one of his huge hands. She had known something was wrong the moment she had seen him and had listened to his news without any reaction. That they were recalling the thirty or so rescue teams that had been searching non-stop for over three days. Her father had failed to return home after a routine afternoon hike up to the Þingvellir National Park. He loved it up there, exploring the maze of deep trenches produced by the relentless separation of the two tectonic plates carrying North America and Eurasia. 'History in the making,' he used to call it with a wry smile. She had sounded the alert later that same evening when he didn't return. It was cold at that time of year, dropping to minus five degrees in the evenings. With the wind, it could be many degrees below that and a storm was coming. Her father was a careful hiker. He respected the unpredictable Icelandic geology and weather and so had packed an emergency bag, beacon and rations to last a night, maybe two at a push, but not three.

He was almost certainly dead, but the search parties had found nothing except her father's backpack in a deep fissure, lying amongst the sharp rocks that littered the crevices. It had been their only clue. They had diverted every team to search the immediate area for a mile in every direction, but they found nothing. Fredrik had given her the rucksack right there in the house. She had gripped it fearfully, her mind already made up.

Later, when Fredrik left, she went straight to the LEAP chamber and restored her father from the very last version. It was recent—from a LEAP he had made the very morning of his disappearance. When he had stepped out of the chamber, Uma had embraced him tightly, refusing to let go as he laughed in his quiet way at her reaction to his arrival. She was weeping with relief, suddenly aware of every small characteristic. His familiar smell. Itchy beard. Gruff laugh. Sing-song voice that always sounded slightly amused, as if he was privy to a big cosmic joke that was playing out for his benefit and no one else's. Of course, when she told him what she had done, he was furious.

'You can't do this!' he had scolded her. 'It will upset the natural order of things.'

'But you might not be dead,' she had wept, all too aware of what he was suggesting. And also confused. Only the week before, they had made a monumental breakthrough with the LEAP system. One that effectively cleared the way for her to launch LEAP out to the market. She couldn't understand why he would want to miss that.

'Even more reason not to have done this. You can't have two of me running around!'

He had ordered her to transfer him back into the system and then delete his program. She had refused. What daughter wouldn't? But this had made him even madder.

'The line "With great power comes great responsibility" exists for a reason,' he lectured her.

But she would not be moved and eventually he had relented. They had talked for hours after that. About her childhood. His work. The joy he found in his study of geology. His crippling disillusionment with the Manhattan Project. His delight at having brokered the Reykjavík Summit. And his gratitude towards Uma for curing him of his terrible illness. They had laughed at the outfits she had made him wear when they had played dress up. How he would wander through the thick heather disguised as an ice troll pretending to chase her. Their weekly swims at the Blue Lagoon. His pride at her studies and growing interest in the environment. Looking back on their conversation months later, she realised he was saying goodbye. Even worse, that he had intentionally got lost. She had been too relieved to notice. Or maybe she had chosen to ignore it. Eventually, they had gone to bed. She was exhausted with happiness and had fallen into a deep but troubled sleep from which she had awoken many hours later to a loud knocking on the door. It was Fredrik again, coming to check up on her. She had greeted him with a big hug and the joyful news that her father had returned home the night before, tired but unhurt. He had looked at her quizzically as she had rushed round the large house, searching every room in vain as the dreaded realisation washed over her.

Many hours later when Fredrik, the doctors and nurses finally left her alone, she had searched in one last place. And, of course, her father was not there. His program had been deleted. In its place was a letter, thanking her for recovering his memories but also gently admonishing her for such foolish behaviour, that if it was his time to go, then so be it. That their long goodbye the previous night was a precious gift granted to no other in human history and that it had to be treasured as such. She had to mourn his passing like a billion others had done before and would do again. He asked her to respect his wishes and not restore him. Instead, she was to return his atoms to the earth to rebuild someone else. And that was it. Her father was gone.

But there was more. So much more in his note.

Her father couldn't stand by and watch her unleash LEAP onto an unsuspecting world—he wrote that if he did, they would end up with another Manhattan-sized problem from which there would be no turning back. He told her she must continue their shared dream of eradicating global warming. But without LEAP. That he had decided to delete LEAP for the good of mankind. She remembered standing there, utterly bereft at the finality of his act, wondering which was worse, his decision to die or to delete the LEAP program. How could he possess such a gift capable of doing so much for humanity and then destroy it knowingly? But he had only partially succeeded in deleting LEAP—the system wipe had failed. She had decided that day to prove her father wrong and launch LEAP to eradicate global warming. Within months, she had devised the LEAP Laws. Finding the right partner had taken longer. But once Ethan had come on board, everything had progressed smoothly, until they were ready to launch. And then it had all unravelled in spectacular fashion.

As she sat there waiting for Shane to complete the download routine, Uma wasn't sure what she was most angry about. The fact her father had been right all along or that she had let him down so badly. She realised that, sadly, it no longer mattered. James and Sally had been killed, her precious laws were in tatters, Fredrik was dead, her sister kidnapped, and now she was just about to hand the system over to people who no doubt would put it to the very uses her father had feared.

Norwegian Sea

15 November 2003, 07:39 hours GMT

The huge wave hit the *Selfoss* head on, breaking over the bow in a fury of white water and boiling bubbles. For a second, the trawler's front end completely disappeared under the turbulent breaker, where it seemed to hang, held by the ferocity of the storm, before breaking the surface and pulling free of the sucking ocean. There was no respite, however. Already, Sveinsson was preparing for the next big roller, positioning the trawler so that she hit the wave head on, driving through it and into the relative calm beyond. The entire ship groaned as metal sheets, rivets and structures were stretched and pulled to the limits of their tolerance. It sounded like the end of the world, but her captain wasn't bothered. She had survived far worse storms than this one and, so long as he kept his position, he could ride this one all night if necessary.

Down below, Grond wasn't so sure. From the precarious safety of his bed, he peered out into the flickering gloom of the tiny cabin and felt certain it had somehow detached itself from the ship. The few loose items from the metal wall-table had long since been tossed onto the grimy floor and were now sliding from one end to the other with each roll of the ship. Above him, the single light struggled to provide any illumination, but it was enough for Grond to realise that he was in for a very long night.

Christ, he needed some fresh air.

He cautiously sat up in the tiny bed and dropped his feet over the edge, just as the trawler went into another non-stop drop that seemed to continue forever before ending abruptly as it smashed into the hard ocean. It was too much for Grond, who retched violently, staggering towards the primitive bathroom in one corner of his cabin. Within seconds, the entire contents of the whisky bottle he had consumed earlier were sloshing about at the base of the bowl, leaving the hired assassin curled up in a foetal position on the floor, his stomach muscles heaving uncontrollably. But there was nothing left to bring up, and he grunted in pain as further spasms caught hold, threatening to rip the thin sutures from his grossly swollen nose. Through the pain, he resolved there and then that, if he ever actually got off this damn boat alive, it would be the captain's last trip.

After leaving the relative safety of Reykjavík harbour, the old man had come to see Grond in his cabin and calmly informed him that there was no anaesthetic. He had instead handed Grond a half-empty whisky bottle, along with an old-fashioned leather shaving strap to bite down on. Thirty minutes later, the captain had returned and guided his now-tipsy guest to the ship's medical quarters, where he had strapped Grond to the bed and then proceeded to straighten his damaged nose before stitching up the deep cuts to his face and head. By the time he had finished, Grond was half comatose, and babbling incoherently through a haze of pain and neat alcohol, the now empty bottle rolling noisily around the floor as the storm tightened its grip on the *Selfoss*.

As the contractions gradually subsided, Grond made his way unsteadily into the corridor, where the rolling motion didn't seem as bad. Perhaps it was the freezing cold gusts of air that filled the passageway or simply the fact that he was no longer in the claustrophobic surroundings of his small cell. For the first time, he was able to focus on the rhythm of the bucking ship. There was a definite pattern. He braced his legs as the trawler hit the next trough in the storm before softening his stance to face the unpredictable roll of the deck as it broke through the wave to face the next onslaught.

Grond studied the dimly lit corridor that stretched rustily away in both directions. Behind him, it ended abruptly, blocked by a locked steel door. Up ahead, raucous laughter spilled out from an open doorway and he gripped the pendant tightly: he knew a card game when he heard one. Grond stood there for what felt like an eternity, debating what to do. He couldn't go back to the cabin. He would surely die if he did, but the thought of losing more money filled his heart with terror. Except, he reasoned, the whole operation had been a disaster. While he had cleared his debts, other than the fee for the two journalists, he hadn't made any money either: Target One was still at large; Target Two still breathing. Maybe this was a chance to feather his retirement nest until he could complete the contracts, if they were still open. Buoyed by his idea, Grond set off slowly, testing his newly found sea legs, which, despite a confident start, gradually lost their early swagger. By the time he arrived, Grond was sweating profusely and stood swaying, like a drunken sailor, trying to brace himself between the metal frame of the door with both arms.

It was Jóhannsson, the youngster from the bridge, who first caught sight of Grond. He was sitting opposite the entrance, spouting elaborately about facing down the blooded gunman on the bridge, his bravado growing with each sip of the homemade Brennivín. However, as his story faltered, his fellow shipmates, one by one, turned to discover what had caused the dread to re-enter their young recruit's eyes. Gradually, the room fell silent.

Grond clumsily staggered to the table, pulling the only remaining chair behind him. He reached for his belt, but too late remembered he had no money. With a shrug, he realised he had other currency anyway, and placed the loaded P80 and his heavy Rolex watch on the table.

'Diamonds.' He motioned to the man sitting beside him, who carefully looked at the watch before staring impassively at his colleagues gathered round the table.

'Just one hand,' Grond mumbled to no one in particular.

One Liberty Plaza, Manhattan

15 November 2003, 03:01 hours EST

The fifty-second floor of One Liberty Plaza was in virtual darkness, save for the moonlight that flooded in through the floor-to-ceiling windows. It reminded Ethan of the moment he had glanced round to see what had startled Uma at the Blue Lagoon. The clear white light that had revealed the man-made basin in all its nocturnal splendour now spilled across the wide, open floor, casting long shadows beyond solitary piles of abandoned furniture left by the previous tenant. Ethan walked in a daze, trying to process what he had overheard in Reykjavík. He had barely spoken to either Uma or Shane after they'd finished the source code download. They had made the LEAP back to New York in complete silence. All of them pre-occupied. Ethan most of all. He had left them running a final check and had prowled the empty offices of One Liberty Plaza, trying to make sense of it all. What had they been talking about? How could Uma be afraid of him? Everything he did was to protect her. The gunman he had cut down just as he was about to pull the trigger. The other one who had fought like a tiger until Ethan had tossed him over the balcony. He had seen the fear in Uma's eyes but had put it down to simple shock. Of seeing someone die. It was quite natural. But who was this Anderson? And why had they deleted—what did they call him, 'the new Ethan'? Who the hell was the old Ethan? He didn't feel different. He remembered everything as if it had happened yesterday. But if they thought he was someone different, who had he become? Anderson? The old Ethan? The new one? Someone that Uma was clearly now afraid of. Could he trust his innermost thoughts? Were they even his? Did they belong to Anderson? How was he to know what belonged to which version? He suddenly felt dizzy under the onslaught of unanswerable questions. For an awful moment, he thought he was going to be sick and stopped to rest against the wall. He stayed bent double as his breathing returned to normal. Slowly, he began to feel better. His vision cleared, and he resumed his aimless walk through the dark building.

Ethan stopped still and looked upwards.

He felt sure a thin beam of light had just scythed across the ceiling up ahead. Christ, his nerves were so wound up he was seeing things.

But as he watched, another arc of light swept across his vision before being snatched away. It looked like the beam of a Maglite. He had used them a hundred times on his many tours of duty.

What the hell was going on? Was this a trap Uma's stubbornness had gotten them into?

His inclination was to shout out a challenge, but Ethan wasn't taking any chances this time. The lessons of the lagoon rang loudly in his head. Keep quiet. No noise! Remain still. Wait. He stayed motionless for a full two minutes, straining his eyes to see into the blackness, trying to glimpse the mysterious light, but darkness was his only companion. Of course, that meant nothing. Whoever was out there would be watching him, waiting. There were a hundred hiding places amongst the open-plan offices. He felt very exposed, standing there with no way to warn Uma and Shane of the danger. Time to return.

As he turned to retrace his steps, a whoosh of escaping gas, perhaps fifty feet away, was followed by a streak of fluorescence that looped lazily towards him through the gloom. He barely had time to react before it landed on his chest, which suddenly lit up with ten dancing points of light. His first instinct was to grab the tiny glowing projectile that had now broken in two, one end remaining attached to his jacket whilst the other had fallen away, where it was now hanging, suspended by a thin strand of thread. For a millisecond nothing happened, and then he felt himself crumple backwards onto the floor as if a mule had kicked him. Ethan couldn't move. His entire hand felt as if it had been immersed in a pan of boiling water, delivering a white wall of pain to his overloaded senses. The fireball blossomed out along his arm, burning his muscles. He tried to scream, but there was no sound to publicise his pain. His lungs couldn't work. Like every other muscle, they were spasming uncontrollably, twitching and contracting, a marionette in the hands of a manic puppeteer. He felt his bladder empty, but it barely registered as he fought to draw breath. It was no use. He was completely paralysed and could only lie there, staring up at the ceiling, where dozens of light beams now danced. In the distance, he could hear voices. Shouted commands? A bright light was suddenly thrust into his face. Someone screamed at him. Unintelligible. Still, he couldn't move a muscle.

And then, abruptly, the pain stopped. It felt as if a great weight had been lifted off his chest. He could breathe again and gulped down huge lungfuls of air. His hearing returned with a vengeance.

'—t move. You have been tasered. If you move, you will be stunned again. You don't want that. Each hit hurts more than the last. Do you understand? Blink twice if you understand,' the voice boomed.

Ethan complied.

'Good. Now, hold still whilst I scan you.'

Despite the pain, Ethan bristled at the absurdity of the command as he felt his right index finger being forced into a tube. Next, his left hand.

'It's him, all right. We have our man.'

Behind him, more shouted orders.

'We have Rae. Finish searching the rest of the offices and we'll get this one back to the secure area.'

Christ, Uma and Shane. He had to warn them.

Strong arms forced him into a sitting position against the felt wall of an office cubicle.

'Carroll, watch him. If he moves, juice him up again. The rest of you, come with me.'

Ethan tried to turn his head to follow the sound of running boots, but it was no use. He still couldn't move a muscle.

Shane had finished the download, and they were now both sat waiting for Ethan to return. Uma had already checked the corridor twice, but it was deserted.

'I'm going to look for him again. We need to get out of here.'

'I'll go. If he comes back, then you two can leave straight away. We can touch base later about untangling this mess when you've got your sister back.'

'Oh ... OK.' Uma sounded surprised as her CSO made his way round the table towards the door.

'Hey, Shane. Thanks for doing this.' She held up the small black metal box in her hands. 'I really appreciate it.'

Shane smiled sheepishly.

'No worries. I've got family as well. Let's hope it works. This whole scene has got way too spooky for my liking.' Shane paused at the door. 'I hope you get your sister back.'

Uma felt an overwhelming urge to hug him. She wasn't sure what to say and blushed.

'Sorry for being such a bitch earlier,' she blurted out, feeling even more foolish.

Shane gave her a huge smile, and then he was gone.

Uma sighed and sat down.

She wasn't sure her nerves could stand much more of this. She checked her watch again.

Time was running out. They needed to get out of here.

Ethan willed movement into his jellied limbs. All he could think about was warning Uma and Shane. Ethan reckoned he had less than two or three minutes before they were discovered, and then it would be all over. He looked up, his eyes the only part of his body that was moving freely. The solitary guard had his back to him and was totally preoccupied with watching his colleagues check each office. From the light beams on the ceiling, he reckoned they were still close. Maybe he had a little longer. Gradually, feeling began to return. First to his fingertips, then his fingers, and next his hand. He didn't know how much time had passed. It felt like an eternity, but the soldiers, or whoever they were, didn't seem to be in a great hurry.

His guard glanced at him but only fleetingly. His prisoner was going nowhere. Nobody walked away from a Taser stun for at least half an hour after being hit. Satisfied, he moved further up the corridor to help with the search. That suited Ethan fine. He was quite surprised at how quickly his frozen limbs were defrosting, although there was still no way he could have walked, or even stood up, but that wasn't what he needed to do. He could actually feel the hard metallic imprint of the mobile phone against his left thigh and, by now, was able to move his left hand and wrist freely. However, his right side, which had received the full discharge from the small dart, remained completely paralysed. He felt for his trouser pocket and slowly eased the small phone onto the floor. Ethan pressed three, the pre-programmed number for Uma. She answered it immediately. He could hear her, but only managed a hoarse whisper and groaned as she rang off.

Christ, he needed to be quick. If he wasn't careful, she would come out of the room looking for him.

He grasped the phone and leant sideways, slowly sliding down the cubicle wall to the floor so that his arm, skewed up towards his head, could press the mobile against his cheek. That was better. He dialled the single digit again, and Uma answered immediately.

'Ethan, where are you? Shane's looking for you. We need to leave. Now. The transfer is complete.'

'Uma,' Ethan croaked.

'Ethan, are you OK?' Concern swiftly replaced the irritation in her voice. 'You sound terrible. Are you ill?'

'It was a trap. They've got me. You must get out of here. They're coming—'

'Hey, you,' a voice could be heard bellowing in the background.

'Who's that?'

But Ethan didn't get a chance to reply. Another gaseous whoosh was followed by silence as the second dart delivered its agonising current. The phone spun out of Ethan's hand into the path of the returning guard, who angrily stamped down on the thin metal, crushing it under his heavy boot. He kicked the pieces away and pulled the almost unconscious Ethan into a sitting position before binding his hands with thick plastic ties.

Uma dropped the phone as the line went dead.

She sat still in complete shock, the severed connection deafening in its sudden silence. And then realisation struck. It was a trap. Ethan had been right all along. She was stuck on the fifty-second floor of a skyscraper surrounded by God knows who.

Uma felt sick, her heart beating wildly.

How could they ... she ... have been so stupid? Eva's kidnappers would have known where the LEAP code was and that they couldn't lay their hands on it.

Now she'd led them straight to it.

She should have listened to Ethan.

How could it end this way? After everything she had come through to get this far, only to walk into such an obvious trap. One, Ethan had tried to warn her about. LEAP suddenly seemed to matter a lot more than it had done earlier this morning. What else could she have done, though? She pictured her father's stern face, his judging eyes.

Volcanic rage burned away her helplessness.

It wouldn't end like this if she could help it. She owed that much to everyone who had already died, everyone who might die before the night was out. There was still one way she could escape. It was a long shot, but worth a try.

Uma grabbed the download drive and rushed to the door, remembering to kill the lights as she peered out. It looked clear. Emboldened, she stepped out into the gloom of the corridor.

As she carefully closed the door behind her, the latch dropped with a metallic click. It sounded very loud. She winced and hurried in the opposite direction Ethan had travelled. As she hugged the wall, a powerful beam of light suddenly cut through the gloom. It passed right through her in a wide arc, and for a moment she thought they had missed her.

'Hey, you,' bellowed a gruff voice behind her. 'Stop.'

Uma glanced back to see a black shape hurtling towards her. Behind him, another figure lifted a black cylinder to his shoulder. A gaseous whoosh broke the spell and Uma turned to run, barely noticing the green glow that looped over her head and disappeared into the carpet. She just kept running, focused on the door barely twenty paces ahead. It was slightly ajar. She could feel the heavy presence of someone gaining on her. He was so loud. Sounded huge. His breath ragged. His boots slamming into the floor. A crazed light beam slashing back and forth across her body. Fear lent her speed and strength. As she leapt towards the small gap, her pursuer made his move, lunging forward in an ambitious rugby tackle. He mistimed it marginally, grabbing the hem of her jacket. Uma felt the lining tear as the man crashed headfirst into the edge of the heavy steel door. He howled in pain as bone met hard metal and suddenly fell silent.

Uma's luck held. The lightweight Gore-Tex jacket easily slipped from her right arm as she felt herself being pulled down. In one fluid movement, she slipped through the narrow gap and grabbed the internal handles with both hands. She heaved the heavy door inwards with all her might and slowly, painfully, it slammed shut just as the second man arrived. He hammered on the metal in frustration, trying to find a handle, but there was none, its surface smooth and solid.

His headpiece crackled.

'Jones, report in. Anything?'

'Forster's down, but not out. We lost the girl. She escaped. We'll continue the search.'

'No need. We have what we came for. Return to the reception area now.'

'Aye, sir.'

Jones helped his section leader up, pressing a field dressing tightly to the five-inch-long gash in his forehead. As they made their way back up the corridor, something glinted in the bright moonlight. Jones stooped to pick up a solid lump of metal. On closer inspection, it looked like a computer drive of some sort that was unlike any he had seen before. It was about four inches in length, barely one inch thick, and felt heavier than its diminutive size would suggest. The woman must have dropped it. Well, at least they had something to show for their efforts. He pocketed the object and ran to catch Forster, who had already disappeared, the narrow beam of his headtorch jumping crazily backwards and forwards across the ceiling.

Reykjavík, Iceland

15 November 2003, 08:55 hours GMT

The frantic thudding started up again as two uniformed policemen looked on, their faces taut with worry. Around them, huge snowflakes gently settled on their thick coats, turning the black material white to mirror the low clouds above their heads.

'I think we should break the door down,' one of them muttered to no one in particular. Despite his gloved hands, the cold had long since permeated the thick fleece lining, and he clapped them together in a vain attempt to warm up.

'Here, let me have a go.' One of the policemen stepped forward and removed his Glock from its holster, before hammering against the wood with the butt of the gun. His subordinates glanced at each other knowingly. One grimaced in mock alarm. The other smiled back.

'Christ. Where the hell are they? We're going to have to call it in,' their boss grumbled. 'Are you sure you haven't seen anyone leave?'

'No one, sir. We've watched it all night,' replied the younger of the two men, stamping his feet to keep warm.

His boss grunted in acknowledgement and raised the Glock again for another assault. However, it wasn't necessary. Through the door they heard a latch being drawn and, seconds later, a narrow crack appeared, revealing Uma's drawn face.

'Yes, officer. Can I help you?'

'Miss Jakobsdóttir! Sorry for disturbing you. The station has been trying to call you for the last hour. They got no response and asked us to check up on the house. Is everything OK in there?'

'Of course! I was sleeping. As you know, the last few days ... they've been rather traumatic. I must have slept right through it.'

'And Mr Rae?'

'How would I know? He left three hours ago.'

There was silence as the young officer absorbed Uma's words. 'Gone!' he said. 'Where?'

'Back to New York, I think. His pilot drove him to Keflavík. You look surprised. He said he would tell your men.'

'Tell us? We didn't even see him.'

'Is there a problem, officer?' Uma responded in kind through the narrow opening. 'I understood we were both free to go.'

'You are,' the man said. 'No, there's no problem. It's just that we were meant to be watching the house. At what time did you say he left?'

'I'm not sure.' Uma paused, thinking. 'About five a.m. Maybe later.'

The officer turned to glare at his men, who both shrugged in denial. He turned back. 'Well, I've had at least two men watching the house all along and they didn't see anyone leave.'

Uma smiled through the crack in the door.

'Well, maybe they missed him. Perhaps they were ... you know ... resting.'

An awkward silence chilled the already frigid air between them. 'Look ... Captain?'

'Lieutenant.'

'Lieutenant. I appreciate your concern, but I really need to get some rest. Please inform your central command not to disturb me again. If I need anything, I will call you.'

With that, she shut the door, leaving the three men standing there staring at the five shallow indentations in the door. The senior man carefully holstered his Glock before turning to his colleagues.

'How the hell am I going to explain this?' he said, being careful not to raise his voice. This was bad enough without letting the woman hear him acknowledge his men's incompetence. 'You let the Englishman walk right out of the house under your very noses. We will be the laughing stock of the station.'

'But sir, we were—'

'Save your excuses for the captain,' he said. 'Don't just stand there. Get back to the Jeep and see if you can manage to watch her whilst I call this mess in.'

They all turned and made their way down the drive, still arguing.

On the other side of the door, Uma slid to the floor, listening to the raised voices fade away. She felt terrible about getting the two young policemen into so much trouble, but she really had no choice. Somehow, she had to make them believe Ethan was no longer in Iceland.

Almost on cue, the phone in her hand rang, making her jump. She checked the caller ID and answered it.

'Robin, thanks for getting back to me. What have you got?'

'Like taking candy from a baby,' the pilot said. 'They barely glanced at Ethan's passport when I presented it to them. They actually seemed pleased to see me ... I mean, him ... go.'

Uma laughed out loud. It felt good.

'When you return to New York, can you wait for my instructions?'

'Will do,' Robin said. 'I'll speak to you later.'

The phone line went dead. Uma sighed with relief but remained slumped against the door. It was a very small victory in a long night of setbacks.

Deep down, she knew there was nothing else she could do. Ethan was probably dead or, at least, seriously injured. And her sister was still kidnapped. The thought of Eva lying face down in a gutter almost made her weep. She dared not return to New York and couldn't really report anything to the authorities. Who would believe her, anyway? Since losing the source code in New York, she was effectively stuck in Reykjavík, totally marginalised, with her only bargaining chip now in the hands of an unknown but all-seeing enemy. Maybe that was why she felt so calm—all she could do was await her fate with as much dignity as she could muster, safe in the knowledge that she had done everything possible. The forces arrayed against her seemed much like the tectonic plates slowly but gradually tearing her beloved Iceland apart. They were unstoppable and largely unseen. It was pointless to resist that sort of force.

Uma stood up and wandered into the living room. A miniature of the Age of Man sculpture dominated the centre of the room like a white sentinel, throwing its long conical shadow across the room. She stared at it guiltily, remembering her father's oft-repeated lecture about mankind remembering its place on the planet. She couldn't even get that right, going against his express wishes, hoping to prove him wrong. In doing so, she'd allowed the LEAP technology to get out into an unsuspecting world. And now the entire plan was unravelling before her eyes.

Uma suddenly felt exhausted and slowly made her way upstairs, full of trepidation at the prospect of sleep and the nightmares it might bring. However, she needn't have worried. Despite her total exhaustion, Uma lay wide awake thinking of Eva, of poor Fredrik, of Anderson, of Ethan and his terrible secret. She knew Ethan's parents had died in a car crash, but had he been responsible as he claimed? Or was that one of Anderson's memories merging with his own? Even if it was Ethan's memory, his furious reaction had still terrified her.

The image of Anderson/Ethan raising the unfortunate gunmen above his head and tossing him down onto The Age of Man rose unbidden. She shuddered at the memory. Everything had derailed so quickly. It was hard to believe that less than three days ago she had been looking forward to the launch of LEAP, a new technology that would begin the long overdue process of reversing centuries of carbon emissions. She had been oblivious to the chaos that would shortly overwhelm them. All of them had been. Except Ethan. He had obsessed about someone trying to steal LEAP from the first day they had shaken on their deal. His assumption had always been that someone would try. He had planned accordingly. Not only that—he had realised what was happening and had tried to warn her. But she had chosen to ignore him. Now it was too late. Close friends and family were dead. Her

LEAP Laws lay in tatters. Ethan was lost to her. Replaced by ... by a man she didn't recognise. They clearly couldn't leave him like this. The whole programme was at risk. Who was she kidding? There was no coming back from this, even if they did succeed in disentangling Ethan. Assuming, of course, he was even still alive. They were playing with forces they knew nothing about. Tinkering with the very building blocks of life. Yet again, she found herself agreeing with her father. He had been right all along. Mankind wasn't ready for this type of technology.

At some point, she must have drifted off into an anxious half sleep filled with a kaleidoscope of memories from the past week. Of fading bodies and smoking landscapes. Of familiar faces that kept morphing into Ethan, who was one minute angry, the next calm and analytical, then indecision and uncertainty seemed to cripple his every thought. He knew her as a friend, lover and mentor and there was no escape from his omnipresence, however hard she tried to shake him off. There was simply no hiding from him in her dream until a ringing phone interrupted their eternal game of cat and mouse.

Uma opened her eyes with relief. The shrill tone was a welcome release from her nightmares, but very quickly, a new anxiety overtook her. Who could be calling so early in the morning? She rolled over and glanced at her watch.

19:00!

She'd been asleep for nearly ten hours.

Uma checked the caller ID, but it was blank, and she answered it cautiously, half expecting the metallic tones that had so scared her earlier.

'Uma, is that you?' a familiar voice enquired.

'Shane? You're still alive?'

'I beg your pardon.' He sounded tired. 'That's one hell of a greeting.'

'I thought you were dead,' she blurted out. 'You know. After last night. I thought both of you were.'

'No, I'm very much alive. I presumed they had detained you as well, otherwise I would have called you earlier.'

'Who detained you?' she asked, suddenly afraid of learning the identity of his kidnappers.

'Homeland Security, of course.' It wasn't just fatigue in his voice, she realised. Every word he spoke was laced with fear. Her frayed nerves soaked it up.

'Shane, what are you talking about?'

'That's where I've been since last night.'

'Where?' she asked stupidly, struggling to process his news.

'Homeland Security. Down at their offices on 3rd Avenue, just off 42nd Street.'

'The Office of Homeland Security?'

'I assumed you were there as well, receiving the third degree in one of the other interrogation rooms.'

'No, I escaped back here. After losing the source code, I ...' Uma sat up, her mind whirling with Shane's news. 'That means they must have Ethan as well.'

'I presume so, although I haven't seen him.'

Uma started to cry. At first, silent tears, then great sobs of relief as realisation dawned on her that Ethan might be alive.

'Uma, are you OK?'

'Yes,' she replied tearfully. 'I'm OK.' Uma wiped her tears away. 'I thought everyone was dead. That it was all my fault.' The questions rose unbidden, one after another. 'How did they find us? What were they doing there? Do you think they were behind the web attack?'

'I've no idea,' Shane said. 'Maybe not. They asked an awful lot of questions though, particularly about Ethan.'

'What on earth would they want with him?'

'Beats me. Maybe they kidnapped Eva?'

Shane's suggestion was so obvious, but hearing it out loud shocked Uma into silence. Were the US government behind Fredrik's death? The attack at the Blue Lagoon? Eva's abduction? Last night?

Shane was talking, but she barely heard him.

'Are you near a screen? I've something to show you. It came in this afternoon, and I think you need to see it.'

Uma tried to concentrate on what he was saying. 'See what?'

'I would rather not say,' he said. 'I've watched it a few times already and still can't believe it myself.'

Something about his tone frightened Uma. She breathed deeply, trying to control her rising panic.

'OK,' she said, full of dread. 'E-mail it over then.'

'The file's too big. I'll stream it to you off the main server. If you can get to your PC, I'll send a link now.'

Uma made her way back up to the top floor and into the large office where they had heard the fateful recording by Eva's kidnappers. While she waited for the PC to boot up, her eyes drifted to the conference phone Ethan had destroyed earlier. Since waking, she had forgotten all about the mess she had created, but the sight of the broken plastic brought it flooding back. She recalled what had scared her so much. It was his eyes. She had seen them before. The eyes of a cold-blooded killer. Her relief at hearing Ethan was still alive was now tempered by the realisation that they couldn't hope to put right what they'd done to him with LEAP. Worse still, the longer Ethan was held by the security services, the more difficult it would be to resolve later on. She forced herself to focus on Shane's latest crisis.

'OK, I'm ready. What have you got to show me and why the secrecy?'

'You'll understand soon enough.' He sounded business-like but slightly nervous as well, just like the time Uma had confronted him about merging Ethan with Anderson. 'Click on the link I e-mailed over. It will connect you to the main server.'

Uma sat mesmerised as the footage unfolded. As it finished, she pressed play again and then again. Halfway through the fourth replay, she closed the link and sat there in shock, silent tears streaming down her face.

'I'm so sorry to hit you with this.' Shane sounded relieved, as if the showing had transferred his burden to Uma. 'Unfortunately, there's more. I've been doing a bit of digging since I saw this and thought you might want to see something else. I'll e-mail it over right away.' Uma didn't respond. 'Uma, are you there?'

'Yes,' she said dully. 'It makes no sense.'

'I know,' he agreed, 'but the next bit of footage might fill in some gaps. Here it comes.'

Twenty minutes later, Uma emerged from the office and made her way down to the living room, deep in thought. She dialled a number on her mobile and waited, but not for long. Over the loudspeaker she heard the cheerful tones of Robin Greg, Ethan's pilot, answer on a surprisingly clear line.

'Robin. It's Uma.'

'Good morning. Or, should I say, good evening? What can I d—'

'Where are you?'

'In New York. I've just finished mothballing the Challenger for the night.'

'Robin, I know you've only just left here, but I need you back in Reykjavík as soon as possible. I'm sorry for the short notice, but I need you here now.'

The pilot's cheerful tone didn't alter. He was used to unusual requests from his boss, and Ethan had given him strict instructions that the Challenger was at Uma's disposal. Even so, her requests were strange in the extreme. First, to impersonate his boss and fly all the way from Reykjavík to New York City. And now, minutes after landing, she wanted him back in Reykjavík. Until today, she had never once called him in eighteen months. He'd always presumed it was because of her green credentials. If she was asking him to fly back and deposit several more tons of CO_2 into the atmosphere, it must be serious.

'No worries. I'll make my way back to JFK now. We'll be airborne in the hour and with you in five.'

'Thank you so much.'

The line went dead, leaving Uma standing in the bay windows looking out over a silent white night. Without warning, everything had changed once again. An alternative course had presented itself to her in far greater detail than perhaps she should have been allowed to see. It was a lucky break but, all of a sudden, her invisible enemy didn't seem quite so invincible or immovable as before. For the first time in a long time, maybe, just maybe, there was a chance to rescue what had been, until Shane's phone call, a lost cause.

Manhattan, New York City

15 November 2003, 14:32 hours EST

The room was completely empty, save for a dull grey metallic desk in the centre, either side of which sat two plastic chairs facing each other. A dishevelled figure was slumped in one, staring down at the cold, hard surface of the table, his head supported between his hands. Behind him, a wall clock ticked loudly. Without warning, the door swung open and two men entered, chatting away. One placed three cups of coffee on the table, whilst his companion sat down and produced a small recorder from his jacket pocket before pushing one of the steaming cups towards their prisoner, who ignored him. All three remained silent for nearly a minute, maybe two. Finally, the seated man cleared his throat, pressed the 'Record' button and began in a soft voice.

'Ethan Rae, you have the right to remain silent. If you give up that right, anything you say can and will be used against you in a court of law. You have the right to an attorney and to have an attorney present during questioning. If you cannot afford an attorney, one will be provided to you at no cost. During any questioning, you may decide at any time to exercise these rights, not answer any questions or make any statements. Do you understand these rights as I have read them to you?'

Ethan glanced up at the agent, his face impassive.

'How are you feeling?' continued the man in his soft voice. 'I understand Tasers can deliver quite a punch, particularly these new prototypes.'

His colleague sniggered loudly.

'And I understand you were hit twice. You know, you really shouldn't have made that call. It won't help your case one bit.'

'And what case is that exactly?' Ethan asked. 'Why am I here?'

The agent took a long sip of his coffee and smacked his lips. 'How about unlawful entry into the United States, for one? We have cause to believe that you were present on US soil with the sole purpose of committing terrorist activities in contravention of the Patriot Act.'

Ethan sat up. He hadn't expected that.

'Ah, so we have your attention,' the softly spoken man said, clearly pleased his words had made some impact. 'Before it wanes, let me paint a picture for you and maybe you would like to explain it to me.

'On 14 November, at precisely 04:42 hours, you entered the US at JFK. Less than eight hours later, we intercepted a call through our airbase at Keflavík, that you had been discovered at the Blue Lagoon just outside Reykjavík.'

'So, what?' Ethan said as casually as he could, although he felt anything but relaxed. His worst fears about someone discovering LEAP through a simple mistake like this were being confirmed. 'You might consider that sort of behaviour unusual, but I could have easily returned to Reykjavík in that time span. The journey from NYC to Reykjavík is only five and a half hours. Besides, I was the victim in Iceland,' he concluded.

The thin man smiled, clearly pleased at the answer.

'You're missing my point entirely. I'm not questioning how fast you got to Iceland or what you did there. What I'm struggling to ascertain is why there's no record of you having left the States to get there and why there's no record to explain your return less than twenty-four hours later.'

'That's it?' Ethan couldn't keep the surprise out of his voice. 'All this is about my papers?'

'I don't think you appreciate the seriousness of your situation, Mr Rae,' the other agent said. 'Might I remind you that our country is currently at war and faces considerable danger from undesirable foreign nationals seeking to enter this country, both legally and illegally?'

But Ethan wasn't listening. He was way ahead of his captors. He realised the banality behind the reason for his interment hid the real problem. Eva's kidnappers had smoothly removed him from the picture. He'd be held here for God knows how long—certainly long enough to take him well past the launch of LEAP. How had Homeland tracked his movements so precisely? How did they know he would be in New York in that building at that hour? Someone must have tipped them off. He began turning through the list of potential candidates who could have given away his location and realised with a shudder that there were very few. Perhaps only two. Uma and Shane. The thought left him nauseous, but Ethan had learnt long ago that the least likely options often hid the truth. Twenty-four hours ago, he would have dismissed such a suggestion, but the conversation he had overheard in Reykjavík changed everything. Uma didn't trust him anymore. He was clearly a liability now that he had become entangled with Anderson.

Despite all the evidence to the contrary, something still left him questioning whether Uma would betray him like this.

The agent was still rambling on about national security, and he forced himself to listen. Anything was better than facing the possibility of Uma's betrayal.

'We,' the agent said, glancing over at his colleague before continuing, 'have been tasked with ensuring that any such people who do, face the full weight of the US legal sys—.'

'How did you find me?' Ethan cut in, suddenly desperate to remove Uma from his own line of enquiry.

The two men exchanged surprised looks. This was not going to plan. Most prisoners broke down completely at this point. It had not been uncommon for some to even cry. This one was different. Interrogees were not supposed to ask questions—that was their job.

'How did you find me?' Ethan repeated the question, this time a little more forcibly. 'Who told you I was in New York?'

'Mr Rae, considering the trouble you're in, I have to say that is not the question I expected.'

The other agent leant forward in his seat.

'You know, Mr Rae, in the big scheme of things, exactly how we tracked you down is irrelevant. All that matters is that you appear to have entered the US illegally. My job is to understand why you left and re-entered the US without going through the normal channels. My job is to find out what you were hiding, and whether it constitutes a terrorist threat. If I believe that it does, then you could go to jail for the rest of your natural life.'

Ethan shrugged, but inside he was struggling to control his emotions. He had no doubt that someone had tipped this man's agency off as to his whereabouts, but it was a moot point. By detaining him, they had, in effect, taken him out of the equation. Permanently. Was Uma capable of such an act?

'I'd like to see a lawyer,' he demanded suddenly, pushing himself away from the table.

The agent relaxed. Everyone had a button. It was just a question of finding it.

'Ah, Mr Rae. The answer I'd been expecting earlier. Of course, we can arrange for yours to be contacted. Until we do, you're to remain here within this facility. Given the circumstances of your apprehension, the danger of you skipping the country is simply too great.'

The man stood up and nodded towards Ethan with the faintest hint of a smirk. He recovered his recorder and newspaper before following his partner out of the room, leaving Ethan staring after them, his fists clenched tight, mind reeling from the knockout blow the agent had just delivered.

It was worse than he could have imagined. His chest felt tight and the walls suddenly pressed in on him from all sides. For a moment he was back in another cell, beginning a similarly indeterminate jail sentence that he thought would never end. The prospect both terrified and angered him in equal parts. He could still feel the dull ache in his right leg as the pins slowly healed his shattered femur. The ripped flesh on his back had taken almost as long to mend in the stifling heat of the small, windowless room that he was confined to twenty-four hours a day, seven days a week. On that occasion, his confinement had also felt arbitrary and just as abrupt. Except back then he had been a teenager, left to mourn his parents' deaths in absolute solitude, the guilt of his act leeching into his soul across the long hours that stretched into interminable days, then months, and finally years until it had become a suffocating burden which no amount of time could release him from.

Now his mind whirled with irrelevant questions. But only one haunted Ethan: Was Uma capable of betraying him? He could hear the fear and disgust in her voice as she recalled his behaviour at the Blue Lagoon to Shane. Clearly, she no longer believed that he was capable of leading LEAP. Was that the reason for locking him away here? That made sense, he reasoned. But why not talk to him first? Her failure to do so baffled him. He could only put it down to who she felt he had become. Clearly, she thought him unreliable. Dangerous even. He was now someone who threatened the very existence of LEAP. Her actions, if indeed it was Uma, left him safe but completely powerless to interfere with the launch. She had no awkward questions to answer about his reckless behaviour. It was a brilliant move, he realised ruefully. One he would have been proud of but, however he rationalised her act, it still hurt deeply. No, it was worse than that, he reminded himself, suddenly angry at his willingness to excuse the obvious. His initial instinct had been correct. He felt betrayed. And foolish for letting her in. For confiding his innermost secret and, worst of all, beginning to envisage a future with her. One that was no longer wracked with guilt. He smacked the table in frustration before helplessly sweeping the coffee cups into the mirror opposite.

Agent Drew Forbes studied his prisoner through the two-way glass, deep in thought. That hasn't gone quite as he had expected. What was going on here? Why was the UK's richest man creeping round the top floor of a deserted tower block in downtown Manhattan without the correct papers? And now he was losing his cool in a way that was completely at odds with his reputation as an unflappable businessman. He fingered the thin report that one of his agents had hurriedly compiled on their famous guest. It wasn't much, but the little they had painted a picture of a brilliant negotiator who never displayed his feelings, let alone lost his temper. So much for the public persona. It was amazing what the threat of incarceration could do to a man. Rae's reaction to finding out they were part of Homeland Security had been quite extraordinary.

In here, reputation and riches counted for nothing. Ethan Rae had been found on US soil without the necessary entry clearances and Forbes had been tasked with getting to the bottom of it. And what about the woman who had disappeared behind that metal door? He had no doubt it was Uma Jakobsdóttir, Rae's current business partner. His men had all confirmed that it was her they had been chasing. She was the person who Rae called after being Tasered. Forbes pressed a recorder in front of him and Uma's urgent tones filled the room:

'Ethan, where are you? Shane's gone to look for you. We need to leave. Now. The transfer is complete.'

'Uma?'

Forbes presumed that was Ethan's voice. It sounded husky, barely audible.

'Ethan, are you OK? You sound terrible. Are you ill?'

'It was a trap. They've got me. You must get out of here. They're coming—'

Over the recording, he could hear the muffled shout of the guard before the line went dead.

They were currently tracing the call, but he had no doubt it would lead them to the fifty-second floor. If so, how had she managed to elude them in an empty room? And why was it protected by a six-inch steel door? The room looked more like a safe, but it had been empty and, despite one of his crews searching the entire floor, there had been no sign of the missing woman. And what had she dropped? It was something none of his technical boffins had seen before.

He suddenly had a thought and pressed the play button on the recorder again: 'The transfer is complete.'

Maybe they had been transferring whatever it was to the drive his team had recovered.

He turned to one of his men sitting beside him. 'Myers. Can you bring me the box that the woman was carrying? I want to study it some more and maybe present it to Mr Rae. It might get a response from him.'

'Yes, sir, right away.'

The man exited the room, leaving Forbes leaning against the glass, staring at Ethan who was now sitting, unmoving. Exactly as they had found him.

Manhattan, New York City

15 November 2003, 17:30 hours EST

'Forbes, is that you?' The voice sounded breathless.

'Yes, Myers. What can I do for you?'

'I'm down in the evidence room. You know the black box you asked for?'

'Yes.'

'Well,' he paused before continuing, as if steeling himself to deliver news that would not be well met. 'It's not here.'

'What do you mean?' Forbes said. 'We bagged it at the offices. I saw it being done.'

'I'm telling you it never made it here. There's no record of it being signed in.'

Forbes stared at the speakerphone in silence.

'Sir, are you still there?'

'I am.'

'What would you like me to do?'

'Trace it back. Go to the point they bagged it and find out what happened to it. And don't come back here till you find out what's going on.'

'Yes, sir.'

The line went dead.

He sat there deep in thought. This was becoming stranger by the minute. In his fifteen years working for immigration, he had never known a job bag to disappear, but it fitted the profile of this strange case. Whilst tip-offs were usual in this business, Ethan Rae was a first. Billionaires simply didn't come into contact with his office. There was no need because they had all the necessary paperwork. Something else had been troubling him about this case. The timing. What possessed someone to enter New York and the next moment return to his original destination, only to come back less than twelve hours later? It didn't make sense, but Forbes was determined to get to the bottom of it.

He pressed a button on his phone.

'Yes, Mr Forbes?'

'June, any word from our friends in Iceland yet?'

'No, sir, nothing as yet.'

'Well, please ring them and see what's holding them up. I need that information in the next hour.'

'Yes, sir.'

'Oh and, June, can you please bring the Rae file through? I'm going to be working on it tonight.'

'Yes, sir.'

Forbes cut the line again.

'Right, Mr Rae,' he muttered. 'What are you hiding?'

Bergen Harbour, Norway

17 November 2003, 13:42 hours CET

The steps were slimy with grease and dirt, as he descended carefully into the depths of the ship. Twice he nearly slipped on the steep gradient, which would have meant a twenty-foot uninterrupted fall to the unforgiving metal plates beneath him. But that wasn't what concerned Police Inspector Erik Harket. He was more concerned with the putrid smell that assaulted his nostrils. With every step, the odour grew stronger, as did the heat, until he felt he was descending into the very pit of hell itself. Eventually, he reached the last step and pulled a crisp white handkerchief out of his pocket, which he pressed over his nose and mouth in a vain attempt to lock out the stench. Next, he removed his thick black trench coat and carefully hung it from a rusty hook beside him. It was still blisteringly hot, but there was nothing he could do. Instead, he turned to survey the grisly reason for his presence. Already the homicide team had cordoned off the area, which left very little room at the bottom of the ladder-like steps. Barely twelve inches from where he stood, a pair of hobnailed boots protruded from under a red cotton sheet. He tightened his grip on the handkerchief and made his way round to where two men were painstakingly dusting the metal walls of the trawler. He knelt down beside the sheet and slowly peeled it back.

Haraldur Sveinsson's sightless eyes stared up at him. Just above them, in the centre of the old man's forehead, was a neat hole where the bullet had entered. His attacker must have been close. Even Harket could see the burn marks from the weapon's flash as it had exited the barrel. Beyond his immediate vision, he was aware of the near-perfect pool of crimson blood, fanned out around the captain's head almost like an ornate Renaissance picture frame.

'There must be a bullet,' Harket murmured under his breath.

'You're right, Erik,' someone replied directly behind him. 'It's embedded in the deck. As soon as we have moved him, we will extract it.'

The police inspector swivelled on his heels and, still crouching, smiled up at one of his most senior detectives, Jon Furuholmen.

'I wondered where you were.'

'I've been here for about two hours.'

Harket stood up and turned to shake his hand.

'Do you think he was already dead or was he shot here?' he nodded at the metal beneath his feet.

'Difficult to say. Judging from the position of some of his limbs, he clearly fell down the stairs, but until we have the autopsy, I wouldn't want to hazard a guess.'

'What else have you got?'

'Well, quite a lot, actually. A likely suspect. A likely motive,' replied Furuholmen wearily. 'However, do you mind if we continue this discussion on deck? I'm slowly suffocating in this heat.'

Within five minutes, both men were gulping down huge lungfuls of crisp sea air as they stood on the deck of the *Selfoss*. In front of them lay the picturesque harbour of Bergen, fishing boats bobbing in the cold grey waters of the North Sea. Behind them lay the white peak of Ulriken, glistening brightly in the morning sun. However, already the clouds had obscured its six brothers, and Harket knew that, by lunchtime, the small harbour would be cloaked in rain squalls and, possibly, snow flurries. He shivered involuntarily and pulled the tall lapels of his trench coat tightly around his neck. To his left stood three men dressed in faded yellow oilskins. One, a young boy, was crying as his fellow crew members tried to comfort him.

'He found the body.' Furuholmen nodded at the sobbing youth. 'It's their captain. They had been allowed ashore for two days. A treat, really. The crossing from Iceland was one of the worst they had experienced, and the captain gave them an extra day's shore leave to recover. Big mistake, it seems. They had picked up a passenger in Reykjavík. A nasty piece of work, by all accounts. The crew reckoned he had been in a fight or something when he arrived on board. Covered in blood. I've already rung one of my contacts in the Icelandic police department with a description. He's looking into it for me. Compulsive gambler, apparently. He did nothing but play cards from the moment he arrived to the moment they docked on Sunday evening. However, he wasn't very good. They,' Furuholmen nodded at the men who stood comforting the boy, 'cleaned him out, apparently. He kept writing IOUs because he had nothing on him. They seemed to think he took the captain out. When they landed on Sunday evening, he opted to stay aboard. Said he had something to talk to the captain about. The safe in the captain's quarters might be a clue. Open and empty, I'm afraid.'

'Wasn't there anyone else on board who might have seen or heard something?'

'Yes.' Furuholmen opened a well-worn notebook and leafed through it. 'An engine hand. His name was Erik Nilsen, a Norwegian.'

'Was?' Harket grimaced, already fearing the answer.

'I'm afraid it's a double homicide. He was also shot. Point blank. Back of the head. Poor bastard probably didn't know what hit him.'

'Christ, this is all we need,' Harket muttered under his breath. 'Cancel all leave. Get a good description of this guy from the crew. See if our Icelandic friends can help us. Get the bodies out of here. Contact the next of kin. Let's see if we can hunt this one down quickly for a change.'

He climbed up onto the gang walkway before carefully exiting the ship. As he walked back along the cobbled path leading away from the harbour, he glanced back at the *Selfoss*. During their brief exchange, the trawler had become framed against a darkening sky as huge grey storm clouds raced in from the north. He had been right. The weather was coming in really fast and it looked bad.

633 Third Avenue, Manhattan

1 December 2003, Time unknown

'5,062, 5,063, 5,064, 5,065.'

'Thirty minutes to lights out,' bellowed a metallic voice through the speaker on the wall above his head.

Right on cue. Just 215 feet to go and another mile completed. The room was exactly ten feet long, which made 528 trips across the concrete floor—264 one way and 264 the other—exactly one mile. Since entering the cell, Ethan had religiously jogged it five times a day. Once when he arose, twice before lunch and twice more before lights out. The five-times-daily summons to prayer had been his life during ten years of imprisonment. It had determined the natural rhythm of his day. Whilst all around knelt in supplication, he had exercised. He had no use for their god. What mercy had it shown him? Running calmed his mind, relaxed his limbs, and had provided an invaluable lifeline for the years spent in solitary confinement. The discipline had returned effortlessly on the first day in his new home, and he had embraced it with the same fervour. First a mile, and then fifty sets of ten press-ups, followed by a similar repetition of sit-ups. And finally, the same number of pull-ups, alternating between an overhand and underhand grip.

He felt fitter than he had done in years and vowed if he ever got out of this place, he would continue the regimen. 'If' was the big question. Since his incarceration, he had spoken to no one except the two agents he had met on the first night. He now remained silent in the face of their relentless questions, determined to win their crude war of attrition. The questions never varied. What was he doing in the United States without a passport? Did he have links to any known terrorist groups? What had he been doing in Iceland? How was he connected to the deaths at the Department of Geothermal Studies? Or the pile up on Route 41. Or the destruction at the Blue Lagoon. What was his relationship with Uma Jakobsdóttir? He just ignored them, sitting there with calm indifference, head in hands, waiting for the sessions to end. Deep down, he sensed the Americans had absolutely nothing on him. They clearly didn't know about LEAP. Their only interest seemed to be his lack of papers.

And that was where cell time became a battleground of a different sort to the one he had endured in Saudi. The punishing workouts were his only respite from the time he now dreaded. The endless hours of inactivity in which to ponder his growing belief, however unpalatable, that Uma was behind his internment. He was certain beyond any doubt that it all had to do with the LEAP malfunction Shane and Uma had clearly presided over and chosen to keep from him. They no longer trusted him or his ability to take LEAP to market. Something catastrophic had clearly happened to LEAP. That somehow, he had become entwined with another person called Anderson. He shuddered. As he had always known, they were tampering with science they knew very little about.

He relived his encounter with Uma in the Blue Lagoon every day. He couldn't help himself, regardless of what he now felt about Uma or she about him. Her gentle lips on his. Lingering. No, melting into his mouth. The softness of her breasts as he lovingly caressed them. It was so much more than he could ever have hoped for, until Baldursson's dead boot had interrupted their passionate embrace. The tenderness of their moment seemed completely at odds with what she now thought he had become. Uma was clearly terrified of him. Disgusted even. He was at a loss to explain what he had done to cause such fear in her voice.

What if Uma was right and he was actually someone else? If that was true, he couldn't trust any of his memories. Not the oldest ones. Not the most recent one. Nothing in between. The night of his parent's death. His ten years in jail. The rise of Rae Enterprises. His first sight of Uma at the lecture. His first LEAP. And the whirlwind of their race to launch LEAP. He had never spent so much time with one person. Wouldn't have believed such happiness was possible until that fateful night when he had overheard Uma and Shane talking behind his back.

The hours spent alone were sanity sapping. He didn't know what he should remember. Nor what Anderson had been. And, in turn, whether his new memories were bits of both men, everything of one or merged snippets of things both had done. Had he even shared a kiss with Uma? Had he killed his parents? Or had that been one of Anderson's memories? Then, in the next thought, he doubted who he was. The conundrum would turn full circle and he'd start grinding through the endless possibilities again. No wonder his head hurt. Hot, searing pain that compressed his brain in a vice-like grip. Often he would pass out, waking hours later on the floor of his cell, screaming, head in hands, fingers clawing at his scalp.

Sleep offered no respite from his daily torment. All it promised was a succession of night terrors filled with strange beings that followed him constantly from one nightmare to the next. They were always indistinct. Invisible even. But he could feel their presence. Feel their eyes on him. Watching. Waiting. Plotting. Ready to steal his ideas. His woman. His memories. His very being. But when he confronted them, they would start to laugh and, as he got closer, they would disintegrate before his eyes. Disappearing into the night like dust particles in a storm. Images of women who would torment him with hollow promises of love. Of a future together. But he would always catch them out before the night was done, entwined in the arms of another man. Sometimes it was Shane. Often it was Ethan. Other times it was Anderson. But Ethan and Anderson were always the same person and he would wake, crying pitifully like a baby, bathed in sweat, holding his blanket just liked he had done when he was a small child.

When he was awake, his relentless routines were his only comfort, and he pursued them until his breath tasted of blood and his muscles spasmed with cramp. But at least it numbed his mind and the relentless questions that had no answers he could trust.

'5,278, 5,279, 5,280.'

Ethan finished the mile with a weary flourish. He rose like a basketball player and smacked the ceiling with the palm of his hand. He dropped to the floor and pushed out ten press-ups in rapid succession before flipping over to repeat the same number on his stomach.

'Lights out in ten seconds,' the voice boomed over the speaker.

Ethan got back to his feet, head down, waiting. Without warning, the lights clicked off, plunging the cell into darkness. He remained that way for many minutes, steeling himself for the long night that lay ahead. And then finally he moved, except this time he wasn't counting towards a target but prowling like a caged animal, fear and doubt propelling him back and forth across the short space, his mind reconsidering every option. But just like every waking moment since the first day of his incarceration, he kept running into roadblock after roadblock. He continued to pace his small cell, because even the Gordian knot of his mind was preferable to the horror of sleep and the faceless monsters it would bring.

Mojave Desert, Nevada

10 December 2003, 02:33 hours PST

As the solitary figure entered, room lights suddenly sprang into life, extinguishing what remained of the night. She abandoned her thick woollen coat on the floor before grabbing a bottle of water from a nearby table. It was empty. Cursing softly, she made her way over to the small kitchenette on the far side of the large studio where she filled a tumbler. She took two or three small sips before opening the fridge, and then stood, absentmindedly scanning the shelves for something to eat. Eventually, she settled on a large bowl of fresh fruit and a mug filled with Reese's Pieces. As she turned towards the settee, a slight movement caused her to glance over at the black leather lounger.

'Jesus Christ,' she exclaimed, dropping her midnight snack at the sight of a familiar figure curled up on the large seat. Everything shattered on the hard tiles of the kitchenette, shooting fruit, broken glass and chocolate candy pieces out across the floor.

'Surprised to see me?'

Eva just stood there in shocked silence at the sight of Uma in her empty apartment, in the middle of the Nevada desert.

'Sis! Thank God you're alive,' Eva said, recovering her composure. 'I thought you were dead. The reports from Iceland said that you had just disappeared. Something to do with that strange man I saw in your office that day. How, what ...' Eva's voice trailed off.

'Don't bullshit me, Eva. I've seen the CCTV footage.' *And more besides,* Uma thought darkly, but that would have to wait. She wasn't sure she was ready to have that discussion.

Her sister frowned.

'What footage?'

'The video footage of when you supposedly got kidnapped. Our security people got hold of it from one of the shops on Broadway. Interesting viewing, especially the bit when you opened the door of the van and climbed in. I have to say, it didn't look much like an abduction to me. Quite the opposite, in fact.'

For an instant, Eva's face flashed with anger but a mixture of relief, anxiety and worry soon replaced it as she burst into tears.

'That's not true. They had a gun on me. I had no choice. They threatened to shoot me unless I got in.'

Uma had to give it to her. She was an excellent actress.

'Eva, you opened the door yourself. It's on camera. There was no abduction. It was a set-up.'

'What do you mean?' her sister protested. 'I was kidnapped. They threatened to kill me.'

'Eva, you can stop the charade. I've seen the building logs. Someone posing as me entered Liberty Plaza on eight separate occasions during the last year. There's no use denying it. Our security team compared the logs to my actual whereabouts. I was abroad on every single occasion.'

Once again, Eva's composure cracked for an instant, her face frozen in anger and then she laughed, her tears drying up as quickly as they had appeared.

'Quite the little Sherlock Holmes, aren't we, sis?' Eva carefully negotiated the remains of her supper and walked over to the long sofa, where she collapsed theatrically into the soft cushions. 'It's the first time in my life when having an identical twin has served me well. I sailed through all your little security tests,' she exclaimed triumphantly.

Uma was unsure of what to say next. She wanted to say that Eva wasn't her identical twin—wanted to scream it out but couldn't. Eva would never believe her. Even now, Uma was struggling to accept it and had been dreading this confrontation with her sister. With good reason. What Eva didn't know was that posing as Uma shouldn't have been enough. Ethan's security was way more sophisticated than that. It could tell anyone apart, even identical twins from the same egg. The small imperfections in their fingerprints. Slight variances in their eyes. And, of course, their DNA structure. That should have been the clincher. Twin DNA differences were subtle, but significant. Small mutations called Single Nucleotide Polymorphisms would have formed in their mother's womb after or before the human blastocyst had split in two to create Uma and Eva.

All these differences should have been picked up when Eva entered Uma's offices and again when she entered the LEAP chamber, but on every single occasion, the system had let her through. Same fingerprints. Same eyes. Same DNA. There was only one explanation. One that Uma was still unwilling to accept.

She had made Shane test their DNA again and again until on the twentieth occasion he had refused. 'Just accept it,' he had grumbled. 'No one has identical DNA.' And he was right. That was why they had based the LEAP security on it. They didn't need anything else because every individual on the planet had a unique set of DNA from every other person, which made it perfect for policing the LEAP gates. It prevented anything and anyone from using a particular transporter. It was like a security password. An unbreakable one, in effect, because the only way to crack it was to introduce someone's DNA into every cell being replicated, which, of course, was impossible.

Unless they were an exact copy.

'How the hell did you find me anyway?' Eva continued in that bored tone she often affected with people. Uma felt herself bristling with anger.

'Tracker device on the source code download. You didn't think we would just hand it over. It was triggered the moment you ran the routine. I've been watching this facility for the past two weeks, waiting for an opportunity.' And of course, thinking endlessly about the DNA discovery she had made. She remembered laughing at Ethan's suggestion that Uma and Eva were copies. Back then, it had sounded so ridiculous. But she now had the evidence. And there was only one explanation. Her father must have copied one of them at birth. But why? It flew in the face of everything he had endlessly lectured her about. How could that same man both reject eternal life and delete the LEAP programme, but also make a copy of another human being? But which one of them was the copy?

'What took you so long?' Eva said, completely oblivious to Uma's turmoil. 'This place is hardly Fort Knox.'

'Why would it need to be since you thought you took us out?'

'Touché. Although I'm surprised you got this far.' Eva said, frowning. 'Samuel is very particular about security around here, especially after you melted his server room.'

'I did what you did,' Uma said, thinking about the iris scan she had sailed through. Yet further proof of what she was struggling to accept.

'I never thought you had it in you.'

'Nobody suspected a thing. Why should they? One elderly gentleman even opened up your room for me.'

'But—'

'Why did you betray me?' Uma cut across her. 'Your own sister. What were you hoping to achieve?'

Eva stared at Uma long and hard before answering.

Uma swallowed hard, suddenly fearful that her sister was piecing the puzzle together. Working out that twins couldn't defeat iris scans?

'You remember that day I visited your office?' Eva began. 'There was a man there. Heavily bandaged. Filthy clothes. I recognised him at the time but simply couldn't place him. It wasn't surprising, considering the state he was in. And then it came to me a few days later. Ethan Rae. The reclusive British billionaire. I saw a picture of him in one of the society magazines. Looked a little more attractive, but it was undoubtedly him. What I couldn't work out was why one of the richest men in the world was in my sister's office. It just didn't make sense. And why was he in such a mess? That was when I started digging a bit. Eligible bachelors are my territory, not yours. I only meant it to be a bit of fun at first until I discovered what you two were really up to.'

Eva wandered over to the large refrigerator and recovered a plate of raw carrots, one of which she nibbled. She looked quite animated. Uma looked around and suddenly realised that the room was a replica of her sister's apartment in Manhattan, right down to the smallest detail. All the furniture was identical and had been laid out in exactly the same manner as in New York. Even the blood-red velvet curtains were the same, as was the horrific abstract art on the walls. Whoever had moved her here had gone to a great deal of trouble. How could two exact copies have such different tastes?

'It was incredibly easy, really, and quite exciting. Dressing down to look like you. Boy, that was a challenge! It reminded me of when we were kids and pretended to be each other. Your clothes caused me the most trouble. That and not wearing any make-up, but I soon got the hang of you after visiting a few charity shops in the Village. After that, it was a simple matter of calling you a few times on the pretence of meeting up for lunch and, once I discovered you were out of town, I made my first visit. I went down at five p.m., just after your PA had left. The receptionist never batted an eyelid. Nobody did. She actually let me into your office on the first occasion because it was locked, and that's when I discovered what you were doing.'

Eva had moved over to the bed and sat down, her eyes flashing with excitement at the memory. 'I couldn't quite believe it at first.' She almost seemed to be talking to herself. 'Still can't, in fact, but it's clearly happening. Of course, when I found out, my next challenge was to work out how to lay my hands on it.'

'How could you betray your own sister?' Uma said. 'Your own blood?'

'That's rich coming from you. If anyone should be complaining, it's me. You stole my heritage. Decided to keep it all for yourself. By rights, half of this is mine, but you never mentioned it, and I figured you were never going to, so the decision to betray you—' Eva held up both hands and feigned speech marks with her two index fingers '—was really quite easy.'

'You never took any notice of Papa's work. You hated Iceland, just like Mama. You have no interest in the environment. What on earth would you do with LEAP?'

'Christ, sis. You can be so fucking naïve sometimes.' Eva's voice crackled with anger. 'What interest?' She jumped to her feet and advanced on Uma. 'You're sitting on the greatest discovery in the history of mankind and you ask me what interest I have? We could have been partners. Made billions.'

'But I don't want to make money from this.'

'But I do. No one gives a shit about the environment. Global warming is a load of rubbish anyway and, even if it wasn't, I will be long gone from this earth before it makes any significant impact on how I want to lead my life.'

We can't be copies of the same person, Uma thought.

Eva turned and sat back down on the bed again, her voice calmer.

'What a waste. To think that you wanted to give this away. For nothing!' Eva shook her head incredulously. 'It made my decision to take it from you even easier. I just needed a partner who shared my vision. I found Samuel at a ball in New York. Complete luck, really. A one-night stand with the CEO of one of the oldest airlines in the world. All he talked about was getting out of the business and finding something else that would make money. It was the perfect fit and, most importantly, he has the vision. The ambition to do what you don't dare do. Thanks to your little black box, we will shortly be launching our own version into the marketplace.'

'Eva, I can't let you do that! It's not what Papa would have wanted.' But Uma couldn't help wondering if she had any idea what her father would have wanted. With his hollow words and cruel contradictions. The man she thought she knew was now a total enigma to her. During the last few weeks, she had endlessly questioned every conversation she had ever had with him, trying to discover some hidden undertone to explain what he had done. Was she the copy?

'Papa's dead, sis. He's in no position to dictate what I do with his little find.'

'But I am,' Uma said. 'I can't let you do this.'

Eva snorted with derision as she reached for the phone. 'And what exactly are you going to do about it? In two minutes,' she said, picking up the receiver, 'security will be here. By the time you're free, we will have launched to the public and it will be too late.'

'Do you know how many people have died in the last few months because of LEAP?'

'Oh, come on, sis. It's a bit late for the guilt trip.' Eva said. 'Samuel promised me that no one would get hurt and I trust him. He's from one of the oldest and wealthiest families in America.'

'And I'm being naïve?' Uma exploded. 'Jesus Christ, Eva, listen to yourself. I presume you're going to tell me he's not responsible for Ethan's disappearance either.'

Eva laughed. 'Actually, that was us. We set up the whole thing. I made the recording. Samuel tipped off Homeland. It was so easy.'

Uma stared at her sister in disbelief.

'This isn't a game, you know.'

'Damn right it isn't. I'm deadly serious about becoming the richest woman in the world. Now, if you don't mind, I've a call to make.'

Eva punched digits, but a metallic click caused her to look up in surprise. Uma was holding a small black pistol in both hands, the barrel pointing shakily in her direction.

'For Christ's sake, sis. Do you even know how to use that thing?'

'Of course I do!' Uma said, remembering how she had frozen when Ethan told her to take his gun.

'Yeah, well, knowing how to use a gun is one thing. Actually pulling the trigger is an entirely different proposition.'

'Eva, I'm serious. Don't make me do this.'

'So am I, sis.'

'Hang up the phone or I'll shoot.' Uma was nearly hysterical.

'OK, sis, have it your own way,' she replied, half turning with the phone resting on her shoulder. As she did, Eva suddenly dropped to one knee and, from a crouching position, launched herself at Uma's gun. The move caught her sister completely off guard. Uma tried to jerk the barrel away, but Eva held on firmly. Without warning, Eva suddenly released her grip, causing Uma to fly backwards. Eva followed through and sank her knee deep into Uma's stomach. For a moment she lay there trying to draw breath as Eva lunged towards the gun that had spun out of Uma's grasp. Ignoring the pain, Uma grabbed Eva's trailing legs, who began kicking out wildly, raining painful blows down on Uma's head and shoulders. Uma hung on grimly, locking her arms round Eva's waist, trying to pull her back. In desperation, Eva grabbed a fistful of Uma's hair.

Uma screamed and released her sister's legs to protect her head. As she did so, Eva suddenly relaxed her grip and scrambled towards the gun. Uma launched herself at Eva's back, just as she spun round, holding the small weapon. The momentum of her jump knocked Eva backwards with Uma on top. There was a thunderous explosion and the two women collapsed to the floor. Unmoving.

Geneva, Switzerland

10 December 2003, 11:45 hours CET

Grond took a sip of espresso that the bank concierge had brought him earlier and licked his lips. It was delicious, and a great improvement on the crap served up at the various motorway cafes he had stopped at on his journey across Scandinavia and down through Germany to his final destination on the shores of Lake Geneva. Then again, it should be. The boutique private clients' bank he was sitting in charged a fortune for managing his business affairs, but it was a small price to pay for the "no questions" policy they operated in return.

He stared at the flashing cursor on the screen before him and expectantly typed in the name that had consumed most of his waking hours for the last few weeks: on the *Selfoss*, in Bergen as he had recovered, and more recently in the hire car. As he hit the return button, a message appeared in the top right-hand corner of his search page:

Results 1—10 of about 9,810,000 for "Ethan Rae".
(0.07 seconds)

He was impressed. Nearly ten million hits, which made Ethan Rae one of his most famous targets. Grond loved the Internet, particularly

Google. Search against any famous person and within seconds you had an immediate biography plus a history of their recent movements: which countries they had travelled to, for how long, where they stayed and even who they had visited. Today was no exception. Right below the Wikipedia entry was a *Times Online* article that made him smile for the first time since arriving in Bergen.

A Grey Day for Rae

American authorities in New York confirmed today that they're holding the British billionaire Ethan Rae on a number of charges, including entering the country—

He clicked on the link and was instantly taken to the extended story.

—arrested ten days ago ... no charges brought ... held in the 7th Street offices of the Office of Homeland Security ... concluding their internal investigation, which is likely to last upwards of twelve weeks ... no bail.

Bingo!

He sat back in his chair, staring at the screen. A high-security prison in the heart of Manhattan was not the easiest target, but Grond had little choice. For the first time in his eighteen-year career, he had failed to carry out a hit. Worse still, he had not been able to top up his retirement pot. He needed this job.

Grond closed the link and turned to the large metal deposit box on the table beside him. First, he removed several bundles of US currency and counted off $50,000 in $100 bills, which he placed with the remaining cash he had recovered from Sveinsson's safe. Combined, it now totalled close to $135,000 and was more than enough to finish what he had started in Iceland. He placed the thick wad of notes into a brown leather holdall on the floor, and then casually flicked through a pile of passports until he came to the distinctive blue of his destination. He checked the expiration date and slipped the small booklet into his coat pocket. Satisfied, he locked the long box before pressing a buzzer on the table. There was a gentle knock on the door of the viewing room as the same bank official who had brought him his coffee earlier entered.

'I've finished. Can you return this, please?' Grond greeted the young man in perfect German as he handed over the heavy container.

'Yes, Mr Bauer. Do you require anything else today?

'No, thank you. That will be all.'

Grond followed the man back into the plush waiting area and, within five minutes, was standing outside the ornate building where, what was left of his life's deadly work was deposited. He checked his watch. Connecting flights to New York left tomorrow morning, so he had some time to kill. The thought made his heart beat a little faster in anticipation, or was it fear? He turned towards the lake and threaded his way down through the quiet streets, normally thronged with tourists and A-listers enjoying the city. As Grond made his way across the Pont du Mont-Blanc, he stared out over the lake. The water looked cold and grey in the dull afternoon light and reminded him of his incarceration on board the *Selfoss*. Never again, he thought. From now on, all future trips would be by land or air. He shuddered and continued crossing the bridge. As he passed the Île Rousseau, his gaze was drawn to a flashing neon sign on a nondescript building to the left of the Four Seasons. He stopped, fingering the pendant, as the Mont Blanc Casino flickered invitingly at him. The problem that had haunted his drive down from Bergen was suddenly upon him—the fact that he hadn't fulfilled either contract. Worse still, even if he successfully killed Target Two, he was still way off what he had expected. What he needed. The bulk of the contract had been for the kidnapping of Target One, the woman, and that opportunity had been lost. She had disappeared from the face of the earth, presumably taken out by another contract. Besides which, as he had already surmised, entering a Homeland Security prison was not without risk. If he could win the money now, he wouldn't need to fly tomorrow. He could retire. The cash liberated from Sveinsson felt reassuringly heavy in his bag—easily enough to stake his attempt.

'Just one hand,' he promised himself as he strolled purposefully across the bridge towards the Mont Blanc Casino.

Mojave Desert, Nevada

10 December 2003, 03:32 hours PST

The prone figure on the floor didn't move. It was never going to, and beside it, a woman cried quietly as the man looked on. He had never seen a dead body before and was uncertain what to do. Stare? Look away? Leave the room and let her grieve? He was still debating the best course of action when the woman looked up from the floor and smiled at him almost pleadingly. He felt compelled to say something, but what?

'I'm sorry about your sister,' he offered. 'This wasn't meant to happen.'

'Thank you,' she sobbed, seemingly unaware of Reynolds' uncertainty. 'It was an accident. She pulled a gun on me. We fought. It went off.'

She dissolved into another flood of tears, and Reynolds helped her over to the bed where she sat, giving him the first uninterrupted opportunity to study the body.

As far as he could tell, the bullet had caught her in the throat, travelled right through her head and exited out of the top of the skull.

It was a complete mess, and already a big pool of blood had formed, matting her thick hair so that, in the bright light, it looked wet. Her face was snow white. Even in death, it looked identical to the woman sat on the bed. He knew Eva had a twin sister, but the likeness was uncanny.

Reynolds couldn't help himself.

'How the hell did she find us?'

The woman on the bed looked up. If the callousness of his question surprised her, she didn't show it.

'I triggered a tracking device in the download when we uploaded the information.'

'Clever. And did she tell you anything else of interest?'

'Yes, actually. She said that a lot of people had died. That Ethan Rae had disappeared and that he might also be dead.'

Reynolds didn't reply, but just stood staring at Eva.

'Samuel, we spoke about this right at the beginning. You promised me no one would be harmed.'

Reynolds smiled reassuringly.

'And I stand by what I said. No one has died and no one will get hurt. Mr Rae isn't dead, merely imprisoned at the pleasure of the Office of Homeland Security in New York City. We tipped them off about his night-time jump when he came over to deliver the code. Your sister should have been picked up at the same time. How on earth did she escape?'

'She didn't say.'

'Well, it doesn't matter, although this might have been avoided.' He nodded at the dead body. 'I have to say, my money has been well spent. Our only competitor, with both the resources and the know-how to beat us to market, is stuck in New York on terrorism charges. He won't be getting out of there for a long time and when that eventually happens, he will be tainted goods. We will have a complete monopoly.' Reynolds' voice had grown in pitch whilst he spoke, but hurriedly trailed off as he finished, suddenly conscious that he was showing way too much excitement given what had just happened.

He stared at the body whilst Eva sat on the bed sobbing quietly, but he couldn't contain himself for long.

'You know, this little incident really complicates things for us.'

Eva didn't reply.

'I mean, we can't call the police. How will we explain it? They will ask questions, you know. Damned awkward questions. Not only about her, but about what she was doing here. What we are doing here. The last thing we need is adverse publicity. We're launching in a week's time. Nothing can derail that. It is my ... our,' he hurriedly corrected himself, 'passport to greatness. You already said it was an accident.'

There was silence in the room and Reynolds thought that he might have overstepped the mark, but Eva's reply completely floored him.

'We could always put her through the scanner,' Eva said.

Reynolds stared at her in surprise.

'I beg your pardon?'

'You know, put her through the scanner. Transport her, but not send her anywhere.'

'But she's your sister. Wouldn't you want to give her a proper burial?'

'I think it's quite fitting actually. It is a burial of sorts. Her atoms would re-enter the atmosphere, probably much like she intended.'

'Wouldn't she be missed, though?'

'By whom? Mama and Papa are dead,' Eva said, beginning to cry again. 'Rae's in prison. Uma didn't have any other friends. Her work consumed everything. She won't be missed.'

Reynolds laughed out loud. It was brilliant. The body would be removed and there would be no evidence. Why hadn't he thought of that? 'Oh, you're good! You are really good.' Reynolds could barely contain his excitement. 'We need something to carry the body in. There are some trolleys that the cleaning crews collect the sheets and towels in. I'll check the transporter room to make sure it's clear.' Reynolds turned and headed for the door. 'You wait here. We're so lucky this place is deserted.'

'She planned it that way,' Eva said, her voice dull with grief. 'Came when the building was empty. She's been watching it for weeks.' She stifled a sob. 'I didn't really know her that well. We were separated just months after our parents' divorced. Their idea of a marital compromise. I saw her during the summer holidays, but that was it. Just six weeks a year, and then we went our separate ways. She stayed in Iceland with her rocks. And I lived in Manhattan with Mama. Parties, shopping and boys. Christ, we were so different. I'm amazed we ever spoke, and now she's gone.'

She looked up for Reynolds' reaction, but there was none. He had already gone, and she was left alone, staring at her sister's body. She looked so peaceful, laid there as if she was sleeping. But the pooling blood told a different story. She would never wake up. Was gone for good. There was no going back now.

Manhattan, New York City

15 December 2003, 18:34 hours EST

Drew Forbes stared at his notebook. He had reviewed it countless times but even accounting for the advantages of private air travel, he was struggling to explain how his prisoner had managed to get from downtown Manhattan to JFK, boarded his aircraft which, incidentally, had no record of having left American airspace, flown to Iceland, got himself caught up in a massacre at the Technology College, the mother of all pile ups on Route 41 and yet more death and destruction at the Blue Lagoon. All before returning to the States. Over the past two weeks, Forbes had spoken with the Viking Squad on numerous occasions and built up quite a detailed picture of Ethan Rae's movements in and around Reykjavík right until the moment a commander in the Viking squad had dropped him off at Uma Jakobsdóttir's house at precisely 01:32 Icelandic time, on 15 November. That would have made it 21:32 NYC time, on the fourteenth. The surveillance team watching the house had been told by Uma Jakobsdóttir that Rae had left the house at about 05:00 that same morning. Passport control at Reykjavík Airport had stamped his passport at

06:34. However, less than two hours later, in New York, one of his agents had apprehended him on the fifty-second floor of One Liberty Plaza.

It clearly wasn't possible, and time was running out. Rae's lawyers were arguing he had de facto diplomatic immunity on account of his quasi-governmental role within the Foreign Department. Forbes knew he didn't have long before he would have to release his famous prisoner or come up with a damn good reason for holding him longer.

However, despite all the pressure and mystery, Forbes' gut instinct was that he was on to something big. It wasn't often they picked up celebrities through the Office of Homeland Security. It was normally deadbeats. Political prisoners on the run from their national governments, or impoverished immigrants without papers or money, chancing their luck to gain a foothold in America. Ethan Rae was neither of those, and the circumstances of his apprehension had intrigued Forbes sufficiently to lead him to this point. In fact, so much so that he had widened the search by involving both the CIA and FBI in his investigation. Maybe they would pick something up. He hoped so. Unless he came up with something concrete in the next seventy-two hours, Rae would walk.

Forbes glanced at the clock above his door and groaned.

It was nearly seven o'clock.

He would be in trouble on a whole other front if he didn't get himself home shortly. It was his eldest son's church play this evening, and there was no way he could afford to miss that. If he left now, he could just catch the second half. He reluctantly stood up and recovered his jacket from the back of his chair. Ethan Rae could wait for another day and, maybe tomorrow, he would be ready to give Forbes the break he so desperately needed. As he pulled the door shut, his phone rang.

He checked his watch again and cursed. He was going to be late anyway. Decision made, he returned to his desk.

'Forbes here.'

'Drew. It's me.'

Forbes instantly recognised the southern drawl of his former colleague down in DC. They had sat next to each other for over ten years at the CIA overseas intelligence unit before their career paths had separated, Forbes to pursue more field-based work, Danny Ebert to continue his upward trajectory within the intelligence unit.

'Danny.' He grimaced, realising that any chance of catching his son's performance was disappearing fast. However, something in his former colleague's tone stopped him from cutting the call short. He sounded excited. 'Any answers for me?'

'I sure have,' he responded lazily, dragging each word out beyond the point of patience, but Forbes didn't care. He may have spoken slowly, but Danny Ebert had one of the sharpest minds Forbes had ever encountered. He would only call because he had discovered something about his prisoner. 'Your Mr Rae is a hard person to track down. In fact, I would go so far as to say he has spent a considerable amount of money and effort to conceal his true identity.'

Forbes' heart skipped a beat. He sat down at his desk and flipped the phone to speaker mode.

'I'm listening.'

'Well, it's very strange. Mr Rae checks out perfectly until about fifteen years ago. Then he disappears off the radar. Until that point, he'd been as clean as a whistle. Not even a parking ticket to his name.'

'OK.' Forbes couldn't hide the disappointment in his voice. 'But why the sudden disappearance?'

'Well, to begin with, I wasn't sure, but for reasons best explained later, I ended up in the Far East. That's when I hit the jackpot.'

Forbes leant towards the speaker in anticipation.

'First, his name isn't Ethan Rae.' There was a long pause on the line, which Forbes resisted the temptation to break. Danny would tell his story at his pace. 'At least it wasn't his name until 17 October 1988. The name was registered at the Riyadh Ministry of Identity by an English lawyer called Charles Ratcliffe on behalf of a twenty-five-year-old Mark Brown.'

'Never heard of him,' Forbes said, willing Danny to speed up.

'Nor me, but I ran the name through the ISI records and this is where it gets interesting.'

'How on earth did you get access to the records of the Saudi Intelligence Agency?' Forbes exclaimed.

His friend guffawed loudly.

'We can thank 9/11 for that. Since the Towers came tumbling down, the Saudi Royals have been fighting a rearguard action with our intelligence boys, particularly given that so many of the bombers were Saudi nationals. The consensus is that, with a little more cooperation from our Saudi brethren, we might have stopped the attacks. As it is, we now have unprecedented access to all of their security files and intelligence documents. Basically, nothing is off limits, except with respect to the direct family of the King himself.'

'And what did you find?'

'On 1 October 1978, a Mr Mark Brown was sentenced to ten years' imprisonment by a sharia court for the manslaughter of his parents and a young Arab man by the name of —' Forbes could hear a rustling of paper in the background '— Nawaf Al-Dossary.'

'What?' Forbes exclaimed. 'He killed his parents?'

'Not exactly. He was driving the rental Jeep that was involved in a head-on collision just outside Riyadh. His parents were killed instantly. Mark Brown and the driver of the other vehicle were both critically injured. According to the local papers, both of them died several days later in hospital, and the matter was considered closed. Simply a tragic case of death by misadventure. It hardly registered in the English press. Mark Brown's father was an oil man working for Shell, and neither he nor his wife had family in England, so it slipped under the Reuters radar. However, the official records tell a different story. Apparently, the Arab boy died, but Mark Brown didn't.'

'But why cover it up?' Yet another mystery to add to his growing list.

'I'm afraid Brown just hit the wrong vehicle. Unfortunately for him, the driver happened to be the only son of a local sheikh. A member of the Saudi Royal family, albeit a minor one, but royalty, nevertheless. When his son died, he wanted blood and young Brown was simply in the firing line. The sheikh insisted on an investigation after first persuading the local authorities to declare Brown dead. They found that

Mark Brown had traces of alcohol in his blood. Nothing excessive, not even dangerous, but without the glare of publicity, the court threw the book at him, gave him fifty lashes and ten years of solitary confinement in a maximum security jail in northern Saudi. He was only fifteen.'

'Jesus Christ.' Forbes couldn't help himself. 'Wouldn't it have raised a diplomatic outcry? Jailing a fifteen-year-old British national. In solitary.'

'Not really. Everyone thought he was dead.'

'How could they get away with it?' he said, thinking of his own son. Jordy was a similar age to Rae was when he was imprisoned. He glanced at the clock. There was no way he could make the play now, but if he rushed, he would get home in time to hug him. Tell him how much he loved him. Forbes forced himself to listen, suddenly anxious to end the call.

'You have to remember that Saudi went through quite a difficult period in the late 1970s, early 1980s. For a time, it was quite unstable. King Faisal had been assassinated only three years earlier and his half-brother Khalid, who succeeded him, had no great interest in politics. Until his death in 1982, the Kingdom was beset by political infighting as the tribal elite manoeuvred for control of the country. Nobody cared about a fifteen-year-old kid with no immediate family to protect him, particularly if a local sheikh was out to get him.'

'But didn't the court protect him?'

'It's not that straightforward. Criminal cases in Saudi Arabia are heard by the General Sharia, who interprets the sharia, or Islamic law.' Danny seemed to be getting slower, stretching each syllable to breaking point as he showed off his research skills. Forbes bit his tongue. He had earned the right. 'Many of the laws are vaguely worded, which means individuals can be arrested and imprisoned on religious or, in Brown's case, political grounds. Once arrested, detainees are held incommunicado and denied any contact with family members or even their lawyers. Not only that, but it is likely that he knew very little about his case. He most definitely won't have attended his trial, and probably wasn't even informed he had been convicted.'

'Christ, it sounds barbaric. Poor bastard. How did he survive it?'

'Our Mr Rae is nothing if not resilient,' Danny continued. 'He was badly injured in the initial crash and had the whip to contend with. If they used a metal tip, which was common in Saudi prisons, it would have stripped the skin from his back.' Forbes felt nauseous at the thought. The urge to hug his son intensified. 'He spent a good nine months in a high-security army hospital just outside Riyadh where he was allowed to recover before being carted off to the Al-Ha'ir Prison, a Saudi Arabian maximum-security prison facility located approximately twenty-five miles south of Riyadh. That's where he spent the next nine years. It's a tough place for anyone, especially a foreigner. I'm surprised he survived.'

'Danny, this is incredible, but how does it explain Rae's skulking around One Liberty Plaza in the middle of the night?'

'Hold your horses, Drew. I'm just getting started.'

Forbes groaned. At this rate, his wife would be asleep by the time he got home.

'The reason I ended up in Saudi is because of something I found out about Mr Rae and his relationship with the British press.'

'Go on,' Forbes pressed as gently as he dared.

'Well, our Mr Rae has always been a big mystery to the British press. No one has ever been able to work out how he built up one of the most successful private businesses in the world. There have always been big questions about where he actually got his start-up capital from.'

'And?'

'Well, it's not clear. Any investigation barely registered with the public. In their eyes Rae could do no wrong.'

'I know that much.' Forbes couldn't help himself. Maybe Danny had exhausted his supply of golden nuggets. 'His charity work, right?'

'Not just the foundation.' Forbes heard more rustling in the background. 'I've found a little bit of interesting information about Mr Rae's finances courtesy of a contact in Curaçao. Again, you can thank 9/11 for this as well. Since the attacks, we have forged some pretty strong links with all the offshore banks and can find out virtually anything we want. Always off the record, of course, but nevertheless enough for our needs. Shortly after Rae returned to England, he received several large payments from abroad totalling nearly £10 million. They actually came via Curaçao.'

Forbes was silent for a moment, hardly daring to ask the next question. Had Danny Ebert just found the smoking gun that would enable to him to detain Rae beyond the end of the week? This sounded like money laundering.

'And where did it come from?'

'Impossible to say. I tracked it back to a Swiss outfit in Geneva which, in turn, had received the funds from Saudi. That's what led me there in the first place.'

'And I don't suppose you know who sent the money?'

'Not yet, but I'm working on it.'

'Do you have enough for me to detain him for further questioning?'

'I think you already know the answer to that one,' Danny said. 'Most of this information has been released to me off the record. It's—'

Forbes was way ahead of him. '—inadmissible.'

'Not only that,' Danny concluded. 'Whilst interesting, I'm not sure it adds up to any more than a hill of beans.'

Forbes sighed heavily, suddenly overcome with exhaustion. His former partner was right. They didn't have a thing to explain Rae's connection with any terrorist group or other subversive activity. It was just further mysteries piled on top of known mysteries about Ethan Rae.

There was silence on the phone.

'Look, Drew. I can only give this another day, and then I will have to leave it. My section leader is becoming highly suspicious of all my overtime.'

'Danny, you've been more than helpful. I owe you.'

'Anytime, buddy. Speak later.'

The phone went dead, but not for long. Seconds later, the LCD readout lit up, glowing brightly in the dark office. Even before Forbes looked, he knew it was his wife's mobile phone number. This time he didn't even bother to answer, but grabbed his bag and left the room, his mind whirling with the strange news he'd just heard.

Grand Central Station, Manhattan

16 December 2003, 18:30 hours EST

At this time of day, the streets were thick with weekday commuters streaming into Grand Central Terminal on 42nd Street. For many, it offered a welcome refuge from the icy wind that was tearing down Park Avenue, allowing them to emerge, tortoise-like, from their thick hats and scarves as they scurried into the cavernous building. In their hurry to escape the frigid evening, very few dared stop at the concession kiosks lining the pavement outside the entrance. All except for one solitary figure. Grond was standing by one stall, staring at the racks of magazines and newspapers, face covered by a dark hoody, forcing the throng of people to sidestep him as they rushed into the station.

'Hey, buddy,' shouted the ruddy-faced owner from behind his wooden stand. 'Are you going to buy that paper or stare at it all day? This ain't a library, you know?'

Gunmetal eyes, heavy with fatigue from lack of sleep, quietened the irate man, then continued their surveillance of the passers-by. A familiar movement drew Grond's attention and, without a word, he

joined the crowd moving west along 42nd Street. Several feet in front
of him, a figure, all but hidden by a heavy blue trench coat with its
collar pulled high, plodded along the pavement. For a few seconds, he
disappeared from view, swallowed up in the early evening crush, and
Grond's heart skipped a beat. He couldn't afford to lose his new target
now. His plan depended on it. Not the plan he'd wanted but now he
had no choice. Geneva had put paid to that and Grond felt nauseous
at the thought: $3 million. The number hovered over him like a guil-
lotine blade as he fingered the pendant, fearful of the arguments he
would have had with Jane over such an amount. It had filled his last
six days with nightmares and his nights with sleepless visions: of his
wife hanging from a rope above their bed; of his safety deposit box,
now empty, drained by the inexplicable losing streak at the Mont Blanc
Casino; of Ethan Rae languishing in a Homeland Security cell, now
Grond's only way to rebuild his retirement pot.

Grond breathed a sigh of relief as he caught sight of his prey up
ahead, doing what he had done every evening that week—stopping at
the same deli to pick up the same pizza: double crust, Italian sausage
with extra-hot pepper, before continuing to the eighteenth floor of
his apartment tenement between 11th and the West Side Highway on
42nd Street. Inside was spotless, Grond knew. He had visited it three
times in the last week, after the occupant had left for work. He was
a tidy freak. Everything was in exactly the correct place. Grond had
wondered whether he was ex-military. A reject, perhaps, who couldn't
cut the pace at bootcamp and had instead made a career out of the
prison system. Everything about his life seemed meticulously planned.
His uniforms were scrupulously kept. As was his personal appearance.

As they moved west, Grond was able to drop back as the office
buildings made way for apartment blocks and the crowds thinned out,
replaced by a scattering of people caught up in their early evening
rituals. He waited patiently whilst the target performed his own. The
mandatory pizza stop was followed by his weekly collection of five
pressed shirts from the laundrette. Eventually, the man arrived at his
destination and Grond continued his vigil outside to let him settle
down, get changed, and start his pizza. Kind of a last supper, he rea-

soned. Grond had chosen him as carefully as time would allow. There were ten guards on the rota that covered the target's floor. Six were married and, therefore, excluded immediately. The rest were single, but one was six feet three and weighed in at 190 pounds. That left just three to choose from. All had similar builds, but Grond had chosen Mr 42nd Street because of his apparent love of routine. He was perfect.

At exactly 18:40, Grond made his way up to the eighteenth floor, rang the buzzer of Apartment 1802 and waited patiently. He heard the latch being drawn and, within seconds, was staring at his penultimate target, now in jeans and a white T-shirt, holding a half-eaten slice of pizza.

'Hi, buddy. Can I help you?' the man said.

'Yes, my name is Gerry Bronson. I'm carrying out a building survey. Could you answer a few questions for me?'

His target looked uncertain.

'It won't take two minutes. Here's the list if you would like to look at the questions first.'

As Grond handed the paper over, it slipped from his hand and floated towards the floor.

'Here, let me get that for you.' The man stooped to recover the sheet and Grond made his move. Withdrawing a small syringe from his coat pocket, he plunged the needle deep into the man's exposed jugular vein.

'What the f—'

But he never finished his sentence. Delivered intravascularly, the effect of the suxamethonium was instantaneous. Grond's target collapsed to the floor as the powerful drug locked down every single muscle in his body. Grond stepped over him into the apartment, quietly shutting the door. He stared down at the jerking guard dispassionately. The effects would last two, maybe three minutes but, unless he received medical intervention, the man was as good as dead as his respiratory system shutdown, starving his brain of oxygen. Continuing into the living room, Grond placed his case on the table, unclipped the lid and opened it out to reveal a cosmetics kit that any Hollywood make-up artist would have been proud of. He glanced down at his watch—18:42. He was on right on schedule and now had just over thirteen hours before he was due back on duty at 08:00 the next morning.

633 Third Avenue, Manhattan

16 December 2003, 21:30 hours EST

The colour TV beamed down at him from a metal cage that now served as Ethan's pull-up bar. It had appeared three days ago following one of his routine interrogation sessions. At first, he had been suspicious of its presence. It just didn't tie in with the Americans' reluctance to disclose any information to him. However, after a day of watching wall-to-wall news, he realised it was simply a new front in their war of attrition. They were providing tantalising glimpses of the outside world and the damage that had been done to his reputation. He had watched daily briefings on the legality of his detention without charge and had even seen an interview with his UK-based London law firm, who were clearly placing a great deal of pressure on the American authorities. Ethan embraced the new distraction. It meant less time to think between his sets. And that could only be a good thing. He could handle the amateur hour presented by the two agents. However, Uma's behaviour tormented him. Any distraction from that was worth its weight in gold.

As Ethan completed his three hundredth stomach crunch, he glanced up at the ever-present TV. Two seated presenters were mouthing silently to each other, but that was not what caught his attention. Behind them, a banner headline scrolled across the screen.

'Beam me up, Scottie—teleportation takes a step closer to reality'

Slightly rattled, he lay still, watching the segment.

'You're right, Janet. For the past few weeks, a story has been circulating the Internet that someone has developed a new form of travel that is not only totally green but exceptionally fast. Apparently, it will be announced tomorrow in Virginia at the centenary celebration of the first flight made by the Wright brothers.'

Ethan swallowed hard, a knot of apprehension forming in his gut.

'What do you reckon, Joanne? Do you think it's true?'

Her colleague laughed and shrugged dismissively.

'I doubt it, Janet. This has happened a few times before—a story has swept the Internet about a new form of travel but, on each occasion, has proved to be a lot of hot air.'

'Well, this one seems to have a little more substance than most. I'm getting unsubstantiated reports that it is backed by Reynolds Air, the venerable airline that has been having troubles of its own recently.'

'It has certainly helped the stock price. Since this story was leaked over a week ago, the share price has risen fourfold and is currently trading at a ten-year high. Quite a comeback from the dark days of only four weeks ago when, at one point, it looked like RA would be put into Chapter 11.'

'Let's hope for them that there is some element of truth in all of this, otherwise this could just about finish them off. In other news this week, scientists in Australia have announced a break-through in—'

Ethan lay there, unable to move. In his endless attempts to justify his wavering belief that Uma wasn't behind his incarceration, Ethan had comforted himself that it would take months, if not years, to turn the source code they had released to the supposed kidnappers into a fully functioning prototype. The longer nothing happened, the more likely it was that Uma couldn't have been involved. Until now. The only way they could have moved so quickly was with Uma's help. Yet even now, he refused to believe it. A tiny part of him clung on to the notion that Uma wasn't behind this rush to market. That a bankrupt airline had, in fact, kidnapped Eva and forced Uma to hand over the keys to their kingdom.

Ethan punched the wall in frustration, barely registering the pain as the rough cement bit into his knuckles. There was nothing he could do except watch whoever was behind his incarceration launch LEAP to the rest of the world in less than twenty-four hours' time.

Steven F. Udvar-Hazy Center, Virginia

16 December 2003, 22:47 hours

The plane looked ominous in the low lighting, its dull black fuselage stretching away into the gloom until it disappeared entirely, swallowed up by the cavernous hangar. Either side of its tiny wings, barely fifty-five feet from tip to tip, hung the massive Pratt & Whitney J58-1 turbojet engines, each capable of generating thrust in excess of 32,500 pounds. The incredible power load was matched only by the speeds to which they could push the SR-71 Blackbird. Over twenty-two hundred miles per hour and four times faster than the cruising speed of most commercial jet airliners. Reynolds stood admiring the space-age plane before turning to study the Concorde behind him, its unmistakable hooked nose-cone tipped down towards him like the beak of an enormous sea gull. This particular bird could cruise at speeds approaching 1,300 miles per hour.

Both planes were incredible achievements of engineering and two of the premier exhibits at the new Steven F. Udvar-Hazy Center outside Dulles Airport in northern Virginia. It was hard to believe that the Blackbird had entered service in 1964, with Concorde only five years later. That was just six short decades after the Wrights had managed seven miles per hour on their first flight. A two-hundredfold increase in just over sixty years. It was truly unbelievable. His grandfather would have marvelled at them had he been alive to witness the breathtaking speed of these technological wonders. But now, shortly to be supersonic dinosaurs.

A shiver of anticipation tickled up Reynolds' spine as he dared to think of the future. Tomorrow, everything in this brand new museum would be well and truly confined to the history books, as far removed from his new form of travel as the pen and paper were to computers. He turned and made his way through the vast structure towards the northern end of the hangar, where they had constructed the stage for tomorrow's celebrations. The 10:30 start was chosen to coincide with the first flight by the Wright brothers so that everyone could count down to the moment, exactly 100 years earlier, when they had achieved their historical breakthrough.

Because of the connection through his grandfather, Reynolds Air had always been invited to take part in the celebration, but Reynolds had decided it would be the perfect moment to make his announcement about the next chapter of travel. At first, the museum's trustees had been reluctant to alter the running order but, as Reynolds' teaser campaigns—released on the Internet over the past three weeks—had begun to generate interest in the centenary event, they had relented. It was far in excess of what the organisers had hoped for and, as more networks from around the world picked up the show, they had happily granted Reynolds his every wish.

A movement to the right made him jump. He smiled as an old man emerged from the shadows behind a display cabinet.

'Father, you surprised me. I thought I was the only one down here.'

'You and me, son. Just you and me,' responded the old man, walking slowly up to Reynolds. 'Son, I've been meaning to talk to you over the last three weeks but haven't really had the chance, what with the surge in the stock price and this show to organise.'

He cleared his throat.

'I guess I owe you an apology. And a big thank you. The Trust's stock is secure. We have diversified out of Reynolds Air, as you suggested, but I have to say, not to the extent you demanded. The airline seems to be safe. Stocks trading at a ten-year high. Whatever you have got planned seems to have done the trick.' He turned to Reynolds suddenly. 'Son, I hope reality lives up to all the hype.'

'It will, father.' Reynolds said. 'It will, but I would advise you to divest more stock. Tomorrow's announcement will depress the share price.'

'So you keep telling me. That doesn't make any sense to me. Why would you want to do that to Reynolds Air?'

'Hey, father, it's not just Reynolds Air that will be affected. All airline stock will sink. In fact, I would say the entire transport sector will get quite a battering come Monday morning.'

'I don't suppose you will share with your old man what exactly you have got planned for tomorrow?'

'No, sir. This is my moment. You had yours. So did Granddaddy. Now it's my turn. Tomorrow you will find out what all the fuss has been about.'

His father looked frail in the half-light, slightly stooped at the waist and probably carrying fifteen to twenty pounds of extra weight. His white hair had lost its lustre. Reynolds had often dreamt of this moment, but now that it had arrived, he felt hollow, sad almost. The shift of power acknowledged silently by his father with no great fanfare. Just a moment of quiet realisation between the two men.

Reynolds placed a hand on the older man's shoulder.

'Father, you need to slow down. You don't need to work these hours. Put your feet up. Relax a bit. Spend a little more time with Mama. God knows you deserve it. Now, go to bed and rest. Tomorrow's going to be a big day.'

With that, he turned and marched confidently towards one of the exits, his father already forgotten as he practised the opening lines of his presentation to the world.

Manhattan, New York City

17 December 2003, 06:55 hours EST

The uniform fitted perfectly, as it should. It was an exact copy of the one Grond had discovered in Mr 42nd Street's wardrobe four days earlier. He had taken it to a tiny little shop run by an ancient Chinese man, a gifted tailor on East 55th down in the garment district, who had made the copy for him. However, the garments were merely window dressing to what Grond was truly capable of. When needed, he could adopt any persona he wanted to: a guard, cleaner, waiter. Anyone who would help him get within touching distance of his target without being noticed. However, his greatest creations were when he actually needed to be someone else. Then he had to perfect the 'look'. The walk, the talk, their mannerisms and, of course, their physical appearance. For that, preparation was everything. This was no exception.

He had been practising his new target for over five days now. He learnt the man's accent from numerous taped conversations at the pizza parlour, the paper stand and several on his home phone, which he had called three times over the last week, once to sell him insurance and two wrong numbers. It was an easy one. A thick Brooklyn accent complete with 't's becoming 'd's and run-together words. Also, his mannerisms. The guard had an annoying habit of sucking his teeth when he talked, as Grond had observed in the pizza parlour, and tended to constantly run his right hand through his thick black hair, which was always slicked back. The guard's walk had been filmed from all angles on numerous videos Grond had taken of the man returning home from work and were now playing on a continuous loop through his DVD player.

Height and bulk were important and had played a part in his choice of target since he needed someone within two inches of his own height. He could compensate to some extent by stooping or inserting thicker soles but, beyond that, it became noticeable. He had estimated the man's weight at 180 pounds and hadn't been far off when he finally weighed him. The body came in at 172 but, importantly, Grond now knew it was mainly in his gut and chest and had accommodated with plenty of padding in the uniform. He kept glancing back into the mirror and smiled. It was impossible to tell the difference, particularly now that he had added his blue-coloured contact lenses and the prosthetic front teeth that compensated for the man's substantial overbite and buckteeth.

The face was always the greatest challenge and, as usual, Grond had not disappointed. This part of the transformation had taken the best part of twelve hours to assemble. It had felt like a marathon given his fatigue, but also strangely cathartic. It was the first time he had felt in control since stumbling out of the casino six days ago and as he studied himself in the mirror, he smiled with satisfaction.

'Purrfect,' he mimicked in his new Brooklyn accent.

On top of the make-up case were two frontal photographs of his target's face, whilst to the left and right were profile shots. Proportion came from the man himself who had watched the gradual transformation like some eyeless dummy. To capture his likeness, Grond had applied a layer of alginate to his face. Quickly, because it dried in two minutes. Grond had taken care to block his nostrils, just in case the suxamethonium hadn't done its job. This was the last imprint of his 'live' face and, beyond the cast, he had no further use for the guard. Then the plaster went over the top, layered carefully to form the hard casing that would prevent the alginate from ripping or tearing when it came off. Then it was a case of waiting for the mask to set. That had taken three hours, which had been put to good use practising the man's slouching walk.

At exactly 22:30, he had carefully peeled off the mask. The man was white by then, his chest unmoving, rigor mortis already setting in. The mask now formed a perfect imprint for the silicon skin that Grond poured in, being careful to ensure that it reached every area of the mask. Another wait, and the face cast was ready. Now he had a perfectly proportioned canvas to copy and, for the remaining five hours, had carefully absorbed the man's face onto his own, applying the self-adhesive prosthetic silicon that had allowed him to fill out where necessary, particularly around the cheeks and lower neck, which were much thicker than his own.

The differences were now microscopic and would be revealed only through a close inspection that he certainly would not grant anyone. His peaked cap, when pulled low, virtually hid his eyes. Besides, he would be relieving the night shift, who would be blurry with fatigue.

Grond checked out his identification, pulling the rest of his disguise together. Gun. Thick gloves. Black trench coat with the collar pulled high to protect him from the bitter cold outside. He was ready. He closed the make-up case and checked his watch again. Perfect timing. He had exactly fifty-five minutes to make his way over to the East Side, collect breakfast, dump his make-up case at the Grand Central Terminal and still be at the East Side office complex of the Office of Homeland Security for the start of his day. He was already in character and realised, with a surge of relief, that he was going to complete this kill within the hour. And this was it, he promised himself. The last job. After today he was done. Taking one last look around the apartment, he carefully closed the door and made his way to the elevator, where a middle-aged woman bade him good morning without raising an eyebrow.

Steven F. Udvar-Hazy Center, Virginia, USA

17 December 2003, 10:25 hours EST

'Camera One in position.'

'Good to hear it. What about Two? John, are you ready? We're going live in forty seconds.'

High on the gantry, almost 150 feet above the ground, John Hawkins smiled appreciatively as he looked out over the vast hangar that continued for almost three full-size football pitches in front of him. In the distance, he could just make out the object of his focus, a white stage that stretched almost the entire width of the building. It all looked tiny from up here, particularly the full-scale replica of the first plane that the Wright brothers had flown almost exactly one century previously. At least he could just make it out. The people standing near it looked like ants, and he glanced down at his viewfinder for a better view. Ali Williams, their presenter for the day, came sharply into focus, causing Hawkins to smile again. Barely twenty-five, she was almost six feet in her heels, had bleach blonde hair, model features and a smile to match her ambition. All the cameramen loved her and, boy, did she know it. John never tired of photographing her and, right on cue, Ali looked at him and delivered one of her killer smiles.

'Good to go, boss. Don't worry.'

In readiness, he reversed the zoom and Ali Williams grew smaller as the image returned to normal. Airplanes of all sizes, from all walks of use across the past 100 years came into view, including military aircraft, commercial and light-sport aircraft. The huge Boeing B-29 Super Fortress, *Enola Gay*, that had, in effect, ended the Second World War appeared, the 200-foot wingspan dwarfing everything around it. Smaller planes were now visible, particularly those suspended from the massive arched trusses that curved gracefully to the ground on either side of him. Finally, the image was still, and he heard his boss over the earpiece.

'Looks good, John. Pan in like that for the beginning and we'll have a great start. Camera Three, are you ready?'

The third cameraman acknowledged his readiness. He was located on the elevated walkway that ran parallel to the two tiers of suspended craft and, consequently, was much lower. His job was to film the presenters on stage, including Reynolds, the CEO of RA. He had a big announcement to make, something about the next phase of flight, and Hawkins could see him pacing energetically on stage, waiting for the red light that would signal a live transmission.

'OK, guys, we've got 10, 9, 8, 7, 6, 5 ...'

An assistant producer in front of Reynolds continued the countdown with his right hand, lowering each finger theatrically until he was left with one that he raised dramatically, giving Reynolds the thumbs up as the red light appeared.

'OK, guys. Let's give our audience a good show. We'll start with Camera Two for the long shot.'

In his cell, Ethan watched, transfixed, as the TV screen zoomed in towards the stage, where upwards of 500 people sat expectantly. Ali

Williams finished her brief introduction as the long shot was completed, and the scene switched to a slightly different angle, a much lower shot of Reynolds beaming beside the podium. Even 200 miles away, Ethan could sense Reynolds' pent-up energy.

'Good morning, ladies and gentlemen. It's hard to believe that one hundred years ago, my grandfather stood in a frosty field with the Wright brothers, witnessing the first motorised flight. History being made before his eyes. A truly momentous day for mankind, which, over the last century, has fully harnessed the gift of flight in all its glory and misery. As everyone now knows, within a few years of that day, my grandfather went on to found Reynolds Air and, over the course of the next sixty years, turned it into the biggest airline in the world. During this golden period of flight, the company made my grandfather a rich man and at one point RA was the biggest company in the world. But that was before my time. The last twenty years have seen a less glamorous period for aviation, for both airlines and passengers alike: falling profits, rising costs, a drop in passenger rosters. You name it. The airline business has been plagued like no other since the turn of the century, beginning with the horrific attacks on the Twin Towers. This has since been followed by a fall-off in passenger numbers that has yet to recover, except at the cheaper end of the market.' Reynolds almost spat out the word 'cheaper,' causing him to pause as he wiped his mouth. 'Of course, it has been no better for passengers. Flying isn't what it used to be. Delays are now commonplace. It's no longer an "experience" for most of our customers, but an endurance test that people take out of necessity rather than pleasure. Quite frankly, I can't see an end in sight, which doesn't bode well for the airline industry.'

Reynolds saw his father shift nervously in his seat on the front row, a puzzled frown on his face.

'That's why I've spent the last five years looking for an alternative. Something that is faster, cleaner, safer. Not necessarily cheaper, but a way of travelling about that suits our increasingly global lifestyles. Perhaps the need to work in Manhattan, but maybe live in London whilst taking weekend holidays in Beijing.'

Ethan flushed with anger; Reynolds was even stealing his marketing slogans.

'And I'm pleased to say I've discovered one, or at least my team of scientists out in the Nevada desert has done so. They have come up with a new form of transportation that has zero emissions, gets you from point A to point B almost in the blink of an eye, and crucially does not require you to go near an aircraft terminal.'

Reynolds heard the crowd rustle in anticipation as he continued.

'I know we are here today to celebrate the first hundred years of flight and, most importantly, to honour the brave men and women who risked their lives in the early years to perfect the flying machines that have made flight what it is today. Men like my grandfather. However, after what I show you here this morning, I think you will all agree that we may also be drawing a curtain on flight as we greet the next wave of transportation. One fit for the twenty-first century and beyond.'

Ever the showman, Reynolds paused before continuing, fully aware of the hum of voices around the cavernous hangar as his audience turned to each other and whispered excitedly.

'Now, before I demonstrate our discovery, I would like to welcome an integral part of my team onto the stage. This person, along with myself, is almost single-handedly responsible for our discovery. Please, everyone, join me in welcoming Doctor Uma Jakobsdóttir, the daughter of the famous Icelandic environmentalist, on stage.'

Ethan sat there, unmoving, struggling to comprehend what he was seeing. The screen seemed to move rapidly away from him until he felt as if he was viewing it through the wrong end of a telescope. The commentary fell silent and then, suddenly, the whole image rushed back at him, growing bigger and bigger until Uma, who had turned to face the camera, was staring right at him, only him. Her sparkling green eyes were enormous, and they continued to stare at him unblinking,

cold, and heartless. He had been right all along. Eva's kidnapping. The
insistence on giving up LEAP. The required trip to New York to hand
over the source code. All against his instincts. It wasn't an airline that
stole LEAP. It was Uma.

She had betrayed him. Sold him out to that flyboy buffoon. The
whole Eva drama had been a diversion. It wasn't the government coming after them. Or some unknown force. It was Uma. Stringing him
along. Wrapping him in her web of lies. Ethan had told Uma things he
had never shared with anyone else! And his reward? Imprisonment.
Struggling to keep his sanity. Someone else sharing his body. Ethan
paused as another dread realisation hit him. Was the Anderson merge
even true? Had that been part of the diversion all along? Of course it
had! Uma had known he would be listening at the door in Reykjavík.
She had set him up to sow doubt in his mind. LEAP hadn't gone
wrong at all. It was simply a trick to put him off. But how could Shane
betray him? Ethan felt his uncertainty disappear, washed away by the
sight of Uma on stage. In its place, an unfamiliar feeling swept over
him: loathing.

He barely noticed the soft click of his cell door. It was only after it
had fully opened with a clang that he glanced over. One of the guards
stood there with a food tray. Ethan stared at him in surprise. The man
was unmoving, staring back.

'I've had breakfast,' was all Ethan could manage before turning back
to Uma. She was still standing at the lectern that Reynolds had just
vacated.

'It's an extra meal. A little surprise. Good behaviour, they said,' the
guard drawled in his thick Brooklyn accent.

Ethan ignored him. Uma was speaking, something about it being a
great honour to stand up on stage alongside one of the oldest families
in America.

'Hey, you gonna take this off me?'

Ethan sighed with frustration. He jumped off his bed and snatched
the tray from the man's outstretched arms, eyes still on the screen.
Uma was explaining the challenges they had overcome to bring her
creation to market. Some preternatural instinct made him glance back

towards the guard. He was still standing there. But that was not what drew his gaze. It was the overextended barrel of a gun pointed at Ethan's head.

'Boss, you need to come and see this. We've found the Jakobsdóttir woman.'

Forbes looked up from the table that was covered with the detritus of his investigation. Around him were whiteboards containing detailed timelines depicting Ethan's movements in the days leading up to his arrest.

'You've found her! Where?'

'On TV.'

Television!

'What do you mean?' Forbes said, jumping to his feet and following the man out of Evidence Room One into the main office, where several agents were gathered round the small television that Forbes had allowed them to watch ball games on their late night shifts. As he reached the screen, two of his men stood aside so he could see. The unmistakable figure of Uma was staring into the camera.

'Where is this?'

'Virginia. It's in the new centre that opened yesterday to celebrate the hundred-year anniversary of flight.'

'Call the Virginia field office. Get two men out there.'

Uma cleared her throat and began to address the assembled crowd.

'Ladies and gentlemen, I'm delighted to announce the launch of a new form of transportation, one that will redefine travel as we currently know it. As part of the demonstration, Mr Reynolds is going to make a trip, from this stage in Virginia to his HQ in San Francisco.'

Reynolds stood back smiling as confused chatter broke out around the vast hall. It been a masterstroke of Eva's to impersonate Uma. In one move, he had totally avoided any accusations of illegality and also enhanced his green credentials immeasurably by involving a recognised environmentalist on his team.

Eva was still talking, and Reynolds turned his attention back to what she was saying, even though he could have given the speech himself, they had practised it so often.

'Now, don't jump to conclusions. The process won't take long and, as you can see, we have already prepared a reception for Mr Reynolds in San Francisco.'

As she spoke, a huge screen to her right unrolled silently from scaffolding that crisscrossed the long stage and, almost instantly, a close-up of Reynolds' office in San Francisco appeared. In the centre of the screen stood a short, squat figure.

'Professor Crouch. Can you hear me?'

'Loud and clear, Ms Jakobsdóttir, loud and clear.'

'Good. Now, Mr Reynolds, would you step this way please?'

They both made their way towards the back of the stage, where part of the backing cloth rose silently into the air to reveal an empty room, maybe ten feet by ten feet.

'Now, ladies and gentlemen, this is the Transporter. As you can see, it's very small and can comfortably fit in your home or office. For the purposes of this demonstration, we have built this out of Diamond Glass, a durable abrasion-resistant polycarbonate sheet that's virtually unbreakable. And completely transparent, so you can reassure yourselves that no trickery is involved. From here, you can travel anywhere in the world. In this case, to San Francisco, which, as you know, is well over two thousand miles away.'

John Hawkins, who was tracking the couple across the stage, whistled with derision.

'They're fucking joking, right?' he snorted under his breath. 'Hey, Stu, is this a spoof? Are these guys serious? I've never heard so much crap in all my life.'

'Hawkins, shut the fuck up! We're live. Our job is to record. If this joker wants to commit commercial hara-kiri on national prime time TV, that's his choice.'

Forbes stared at the screen in blank amazement.

How was it possible?

It would certainly explain the ease with which Ethan Rae had seemingly jumped 2,600 miles to an island in the Atlantic Ocean. However, he didn't have time to react further. An agent sitting to his right suddenly looked up.

'Boss, we have a problem on the top floor.'

'What do you mean?'

'Ethan Rae's cell, sir. Someone's tripped the silent door alarm. There's no authorised entry scheduled, but the door opened over thirty seconds ago. A guard detail has already been dispatched. They want your instructions.'

Forbes looked over in surprise, reluctant to leave the mesmerising scene unfolding before his eyes.

'There's got to be some mistake. Has anyone checked the CCTV cameras on his corridor?'

'Cameras two and three are out.'

'They can't be disabled from the corridor, they're in two-inch-thick steel cases.'

'Control thinks they have been turned off, sir. What do you—'

He never finished his sentence because his boss was already halfway across the large office. As Forbes reached the exit, he shouted behind him.

'Tell them to wait for my orders! Jones and O'Shea, come with me.'

Grond stood in the doorway, staring at his target, slightly puzzled. Something seemed wrong. He realised with a start that the man who had evaded him so nonchalantly at the Blue Lagoon was much bigger than this one. The millisecond delay gave Ethan his chance. Turning towards Grond, he instinctively threw the cup of coffee at the guard, who howled in agony as the scalding liquid drenched his face. Grond staggered into the cell, clawing at his cheeks. His gun clattered to the floor and the heavy door swung shut.

Again, Ethan reacted first. He dived to recover the weapon, grasping the black metal with relief, but, as he turned to face his assailant, it was his turn to pause. The guard's face was horribly disfigured, drooping like soft wax on a candle held too close to a fire. Around his nose and left cheek, great scabs of skin hung limply where the man had clawed at the hot water. Ethan's indecision almost cost him as the guard, with a practised speed, brought his heavy truncheon crashing down towards Ethan's head. All Ethan could do was parry, screaming in pain as he felt his radius crack under the force of the blow. He barely had time to recover as the guard followed up, swinging the heavy plastic down onto his head once again. Ethan tried to dodge the lethal cosh, but this time he was too slow and the truncheon caught him a glancing blow to his right temple. He collapsed backwards onto the floor, momentarily stunned.

Grond calmly recovered the pistol and held the long barrel to Ethan's head. He stood there for several seconds, staring down at the groaning man, and then glanced back at the door.

He was locked in. There was no escape for either of them now.

Grond smiled, an unfamiliar sense of peace washing over him at the sudden realisation that he would never be leaving this cell. He felt weightless as all his debts melted away and Jane's laughing eyes appeared on the beach. He kissed the pendant before placing his gun on the pillow, along with his cap and jacket. There was no sense in rushing now. He was going nowhere.

He turned back towards Ethan, who was cradling his shattered forearm, sobbing with pain. Grond strode over to him, dragging the lightweight truncheon from its wrist strap.

'Remember me?' Grond said, staring down at Ethan, who glanced up, puzzled by the heavy Norwegian accent. 'No matter. I have a score to settle.'

He began circling Ethan, who turned with him, trying to keep the guard in his line of his sight. Suddenly, Grond jumped lightly to one side, drawing Ethan with him before nimbly sidestepping to the other. Ethan couldn't recover fast enough and, within two strides, Grond was behind him. As Ethan turned, he felt the truncheon slip under his chin and tried to counter with his good arm, hoping to protect his neck, but it was too late. One second, he was upright and the next, almost horizontal, staring up at the guard, his legs stretched out in front of him.

'Thought you had escaped me, did you?' Grond grunted with satisfaction as the truncheon bit deep into Ethan's larynx. Ethan reached up with his good arm and tried to dislodge the man's grip on the heavy plastic, but it was useless. He tried to push up with his legs to relieve the pressure, but his feet kept slipping on the smooth floor and he was forced into a sitting position. Above him, Reynolds and Uma were talking about the security of the system. About how it was based on a person's unique DNA sequence and therefore was impregnable. From far away, he heard Uma's sing-song accent proudly announce that, without a DNA match, no one could travel unless their details were recorded in the system. All it required was a sample of blood. From nowhere, her bloody fingers nudged another piece of the puzzle into place. The day Ethan had met Uma for the first time. She had cleaned the cut to his hand after the stage invader had rammed into him and pocketed the tissue. With his blood. His DNA. That was how she had been able to transport him less than thirty minutes later. Uma's deceit had begun from the moment she had met him.

The dull ache of despair throbbed deeply within his chest as his lungs spasmed uncontrollably, greedily trying to gulp down air that wasn't there. They fought for breath, retching wildly as the uneven pressure of the truncheon allowed tantalising gasps of oxygen into his lungs. It wasn't enough. Nowhere near enough. The burning sensation in his chest grew unbearable.

Ethan's body and instincts took over. He heaved himself up into a half crouch and, for a moment, the tension in the truncheon relaxed. Pressing forward his advantage, his good arm reached up and tore at the man's face, ripping great chunks of plastic from his neck, chin, nose and cheeks. Grond stepped backwards to recover the initiative. The impact was decisive. Ethan's body could not maintain the upward push, his depleted muscles collapsing with the effort of holding the position. As he sank to the floor, he made one final despairing lunge at the man's face. Desperate fingers closed around a fistful of hair that he yanked down with all his might. It came away far too quickly, leaving his glazed eyes staring at a thick, black, oily wig.

Ethan registered the now smooth head and the hooked nose with an angry scar across the bridge. Instead of the black pits that had so transfixed Uma at the Blue Lagoon, soft blue eyes stared down at him. They looked so peaceful, angelic almost, and totally at odds with the violence they were witnessing. A deep primeval spasm surged through Ethan's body, but this time, nothing happened. He was spent.

Grond sensed the end, too. All the tell-tale signs were there. The target's eyes were glassy and swollen, his lips blue, the veins in his neck and head congested with starved blood. Grond exhaled triumphantly and applied the full lock on the truncheon. Ethan's whole body shuddered and then slumped to the floor just as Reynolds opened the glass door and stepped confidently into the transporter room.

Reynolds' heart was beating so fast he thought it was going to explode. His moment had arrived, and he walked confidently into the centre of the glass room, where he turned and stared back at Eva and the assembled crowd, some of whom were on their feet, staring back.

At first, nothing happened. Maybe ten seconds passed. Someone in the crowd laughed in derision, voicing what many were thinking, including Hawkins on the high gantry above. Then, as everyone watched, Reynolds suddenly disappeared. One moment he was there, looking back at everyone, and the next he had gone. Hawkins heard the producer swear through his earpiece and then there was pandemonium in the hall as everyone started yelling simultaneously. Some of those in the front row ran onto the stage to get a better look. One tall man actually pulled the door of the room open and ran in, charging around as if he were looking for something, but there was nothing to see. Uma, meanwhile, had moved back to the centre of the stage and was staring up at the screen. At first, no one paid her any attention but, on camera, the producer had recovered his composure and had cut to Hawkins' shot of Uma in the foreground with the large screen behind her. As the seconds ticked by, people fell silent in the room and began looking up at Professor Crouch on the screen. Finally, you could have heard a pin drop in the hangar as everyone stood waiting expectantly. They must have stood there for one, two minutes staring at the screen, but nothing appeared.

All Hawkins could see was the dumpy form of the professor in San Francisco staring uncertainly into the camera, clearly unsure what to do. He shifted uneasily from side to side and, eventually, made his way over to the duplicate glass room in Reynolds' office. He carefully turned the handle and, eventually, after what seemed an age, entered the room. However, a lifetime of clumsiness caught up with the professor as he stepped forward. The doorway had been cut out of the glass panel, which meant that there was a four-inch-high step-over for Crouch to clear. He never got close. His right foot caught the high lip and, almost in slow motion, he tumbled forward into the transparent room, his glasses spilling from his face and sliding across the shiny white floor. The old man had not hurt himself, but was clearly stunned. He got to his hands and knees and crawled forward, one arm outstretched, carefully feeling for his glasses, the emblem of RA clearly emblazoned across his back.

In Virginia, the fall was like a release valve as the entire crowd burst out laughing at the sight of the comical figure crawling around the white room. Several journalists leapt onto the stage and made their way over to Uma as she stood transfixed by the sight of the professor scrabbling blindly round the room. Within seconds, several more journalists joined their colleagues. High above the pandemonium that had broken out on the stage, Hawkins could hear Stu, his producer, screaming into his earpiece for Ali Williams to get her butt onto the stage to interview Uma Jakobsdóttir, who was standing calmly in the centre of the scrum, a smile on her face. Behind her, a banner gracefully unfolded from the gantry above, causing the camera to pan back to get a better view of the huge plastic tarpaulin that engulfed the entire back of the stage with just four words: THE RACE IS ON

In the cell, Grond turned towards the door as shouts penetrated through the thick metal.

'Ethan Rae. Stand down. We are opening the door. We are heavily armed and will not hesitate to use force.'

Grond unhooked his gun and stood against the basin, waiting, as the heavy metal swung cautiously open and the first guard came into view. Grond's gun hissed. The impact of the bullet at such close quarters sent the man flying back into his colleague. Within seconds, the cell erupted in crackling flashes as bullets ripped into Grond. As he collapsed to the floor, his knees seemed to sink into something soft. It wasn't the cold, hard concrete of a cell. Puzzled he glanced down and his lips broke into a smile at the sight of the sandy beach glistening in the glare of a midday sun. Behind him, there was a soft tinkling laugh which he would have recognised anywhere. He turned. Jane was sitting on a high stool, a cool drink beside her on the counter.

Grond jumped to his feet, a great sense of peace washing over him as he realised where he was: home. No contracts. No casinos. No people. Just him and his wife on a beach by themselves, in an empty bar where the sun never set.

Unknown

17 December 2003, 16:47 hours GMT

A blanket of darkness enveloped Reynolds so completely that, at first, he thought he had his eyes closed. He put a hand to his face. They were open but unseeing. Had he gone blind? He reached out in front of him. Nothing. The air felt cold, though. Really cold. He shivered involuntarily and rubbed his hands together. He put them to the floor. It was rough to the touch and uneven, like it had been laid in a hurry. Was he outside? Unlikely. The darkness was too complete. This was a pitch black from the innermost cavern buried far from natural light. A blackness so impenetrable that it felt oppressive, folding in on him like a heavy weight that stifled his breathing in the stale air. He sat motionless, listening, but couldn't hear a thing except the silence amplified by the night. He began to sweat, despite the temperature, and realised he was beginning to panic. He forced himself to calm down, breathing deeply and trying to think clearly. He was fully clothed. They were the same garments he had been wearing moments earlier. He pinched himself hard. The sharp pain felt reassuring. He felt OK. Emboldened, he stood up, half expecting his head to bang into something, but the way was clear.

He stood for a full minute, maybe two, listening, thinking, and then he remembered. His watch had a push-button backlight to illuminate its face. As this thought trickled into his mind, so did the next: his mobile would have a backlight as well. He pulled it from his pocket and released the digital lock. A blazing light seared his retinas, causing him to drop the phone. It took several seconds to clear the flashing white spots from his eyes. When he did, a reassuring glow greeted him. He stooped to recover the phone, which he held out in front of him like a torch. It wasn't much, but it was enough. He was in a room. Barely six inches in front of him was a wall, unfinished, like the floor. He reached out and walked right, trying to find the corner and possibly a way out. He wasn't disappointed and, within a few paces, was forced right again and then finally came the reassuring solidity of a doorframe and, higher up, a light switch. He flicked it on.

Reynolds was standing in a windowless room with breeze-block walls painted white. Above him, a row of bright fluorescent tubes glared down, causing him to lower his eyes. Opposite was a small table. Other than that, the room was completely empty. He sighed in frustration. It clearly wasn't his office in San Francisco. Nor did it look like any other room in the Nevada complex. What was going on? He glanced down at his watch. It had already been ten minutes since he'd left the museum. The crowd would be getting restless. He needed to get out of there.

He checked his mobile. The signal bars were non-existent. Swearing softly, Reynolds turned towards the door and froze. Tacked to the back of the door was a white envelope.

'Mr Samuel K. Reynolds III,' he mouthed silently.

Inside was a single sheet of white paper. One side was covered with neat handwriting. He quickly scanned the text before staring at the neat signature in bewilderment, realisation dawning.

'Uma?' he snarled, slamming the letter down on the table.

He ripped the door open and hurried down the unlit corridor into a larger room. Opposite was a small spherical containment chamber which looked like a doorway to somewhere. He leapt in and a semi-circular panel slid closed, leaving him standing in pitch black. For a split second, he panicked again just as a dim halogen flickered into life above his head. Seconds later, the opposite panel retracted, and Reynolds gasped in surprise. It had been cold in the room but his light suit was no match for the frigid cold of an Arctic winter which cut through the thin material like a knife through soft butter. As his teeth began to chatter, he stared out onto the barren winterscape.

Reynolds slowly sank to his knees.

'Noooooooooo!' he screamed, but no one heard him in the frozen wasteland that Uma had delivered him to.

Bellevue Hospital, Level 1 Trauma Center, Manhattan

18 December 2003, 10:00 hours EST

'Good morning, everyone. My name is Joanne Greer. Welcome to the Thursday morning business round-up delivered right from our studios here in New York City.'

'And I'm Chuck Grogan,' her smiling anchor boomed out, before turning to his colleague. 'Well, Joanne, there is only one story dominating the headlines today, and I'm sure that all our viewers at home are all still catching their breath following the extraordinary scenes at the Steven F. Udvar-Hazy Center down in Virginia yesterday morning.'

'That's right, Chuck. We actually have Professor John Forge here with us in our San Francisco studio. For those of you who haven't been following this story over the last few days, he is head of the legal faculty at the University of San Francisco as well as a national expert on corporate bankruptcies, particularly airlines.'

The right-hand corner of the screen above the man and woman magically morphed into a shot of a slightly portly man, who sat there combing down his iron-grey hair with his hands. He was breathing hard and looked like he had been running.

'So, Professor, where do we start? Yesterday was quite astonishing. I'm not sure I've witnessed anything like it in over twenty years of broadcasting. What do you make of it?'

'Good morning, Joanne. You're right. It was quite unbelievable.'

'Before we continue with some questions, perhaps Chuck would like to fill in those viewers who might not have heard the news.'

'Well, if they haven't, I'm not sure where they've been for the last twenty-four hours. We are referring to, of course, the centennial celebration of flight held down in Virginia at the brand new Steven F. Udvar-Hazy Center. It was here, at precisely ten thirty Eastern Standard Time yesterday morning, that Samuel Reynolds III, the CEO of RA, the distinguished airline founded by his grandfather over eighty years ago, made the outlandish claim that he had not only discovered teleportation but managed to commercialise it for use by members of the public. If that weren't enough, he then proceeded to demonstrate the technology by announcing he would ... I'm not sure what he called it ... teleport ... jump ... from the East Coast over to his office in San Francisco.'

The large presenter stifled a laugh before continuing.

'Hey, you'll have to forgive me here, folks. I'm still struggling to take it seriously and I saw it with my own eyes ... I'm sorry ... Where was I? Oh, yes, he then managed to disappear from a glass room, but never turned up on the West Coast. In fact, he hasn't been seen since.'

'I'm not surprised, Chuck. Maybe he saw his stock plummet after the fiasco,' the anchor woman added, turning to address another camera.

'Professor, it was like a scene from the Magic Circle. What do you make of it all? Why would the head of one of the biggest airlines in the US risk ruin by pulling a stunt like that? What would he have to gain from it?'

'That's an interesting question, Joanne, and hopefully I can spend the next few minutes explaining to your viewers what his motives may have been. I think there was actually some method to his apparent madness yesterday.'

'OK, Professor, you have our attention now. I take it, however, that you're not trying to suggest he had discovered the secret of teleportation?'

'Not quite, Chuck. I'm referring to his motivation, not the validity of his claims. You have to remember that one month ago Reynolds Air was going bust. It was, literally, days from collapse, possibly hours. The unions had them over a barrel on a stock-for-jobs swap, which would have significantly dented the Reynolds family shareholding. The shares were trading at a ten-year low. There was no good news for RA on the horizon, either, in the short to medium term. To put it bluntly, they were in a mess. Had they gone into Chapter 11, the family would have lost its entire shareholding.'

'Let me get this straight, Professor,' Chuck cut in. 'You think Reynolds realised the airline was gone and he was just trying to prop up the share price? To string out the inevitable?'

'Partly,' the professor said. 'But I also think he was a little more calculating than that. As you know, we've been tracking RA's stock movements over the last six months and actually saw the stock trade at a ten-year high last Friday. That, in and of itself, was a remarkable reversal of fortune, given everything that has been happening in the airline sector, which has taken a real battering since 9/11. It was also a significant milestone for the Reynolds family, which, at the time, held ninety percent of the family's wealth in the airline. They certainly had a vested interest in seeing the stock price rise. In fact, I would even go as far as to say they were trying to protect the family trusts by bolstering the airline's stock price in the short term.'

'Professor, that's quite a claim to make.'

'Well, we have some pretty compelling evidence here,' John Forge continued. 'As part of our research, we have also been tracking the buyers and sellers in RA. Last week, the stock was the most heavily traded stock on the NASDAQ. One of the most active traders was the Reynolds Trust itself. They disposed of over seventy-five percent of their holdings. Who wouldn't? The stock was trading at a ten-year high.'

'So, you think the Reynolds family perpetrated this ... this ... fraud to bolster the firm's share price, knowing full well that the airline was going out of business, and in the weeks leading up to yesterday diversified out of the airline into safer investments?'

'Sounds about right. The figures bear it out. By my very rough calculations, the various Reynolds trusts we know about made a paper profit in excess of ten billion dollars over the value of their holdings even two months ago. That's quite an incentive, don't you think?'

Both anchors whistled in appreciation.

'It certainly is. That's a fantastic sum of money. But surely, that approach was incredibly risky. I mean, it's not as if he tried to hide the fraud. It must be the most blatant one on record.'

'It certainly seems that way, but they'd absolutely nothing to lose. The airline was gone anyway and, with it, most of the family's wealth.'

'I understand that, but how on earth were they hoping to get away with it?'

'Well, so far they have, in the sense that the money is theirs and the main perpetrator has disappeared. I would imagine he will be the most wanted man in America come Monday when the markets reopen.'

'That's right. The NASDAQ authorities have taken the very unusual step of suspending all trading in RA stock for two days until next Monday. I expect there will be quite a bloodbath when the first bell rings.'

The professor laughed sarcastically.

'That's an understatement. The airline is dead and buried. In fact, the Stock Exchange will probably delist the stock first thing to avoid any more bad news.'

'But surely, the SEC will get the money back? If they can't get Reynolds, won't they go for the trusts?'

'Reynolds isn't the only thing that will have disappeared. I would hazard a guess and suggest that the entire proceeds will have disappeared by now. Offshore accounts. Blind trusts. You name it. It'll take years to track it down. The best the SEC can hope to achieve is to bring some very heavy fines. That will all come out later. In the short term, they need to find Reynolds.'

'Do you think they will find him?'

'Who kn—'

'And you have no idea where he is, of course?'

Uma jumped at the voice behind her and turned away from the TV.

'Agent Forbes. You startled me. You really shouldn't creep up on people like that.'

'I'm sorry. That wasn't my intention. My office said you had come straight here from the interview rooms. I just came over to see that everything was OK.'

He walked over to the cooler in the corner of the well-furnished waiting room.

'Water?'

'Sure, that would be nice.'

Forbes brought the cup over to Uma, who gratefully sipped the cold liquid.

'So,' Forbes tried again. 'Any idea where Reynolds is?'

Uma managed a wary smile. She had been asked this question a hundred times since yesterday morning and was beginning to feel like a parrot.

'Not a clue,' she said. 'I had no idea any of this was going on. Reynolds kept it all to himself. I was just an employee. No stock. No options. Nothing to gain from this.'

'That's not entirely true, is it?' he said, studying her carefully. She looked tired.

'What do you mean, Mr Forbes?' she said, trying to control the slight tremor in her voice. Had they discovered something? Is this why they had sent an agent so early? To confront her with some new evidence? Did they know?

'Well, you certainly had an agenda,' he tried again.

'Maybe,' Uma relaxed. They had nothing and the agent knew it. 'I didn't break any laws.'

'But you had a vested interest in the company going bust.'

'No, I didn't,' she said. 'I just wanted to raise people's awareness of what mankind is doing to the planet. What better way than at the centenary celebration of flight? It's one of the most potent symbols of man's systematic and wholesale destruction of the atmosphere.'

'And you had nothing to do with the stunt Reynolds pulled? All this nonsense about solving teleportation?'

Uma snorted with derision.

'You're kidding me, right? I thought he was nuts. A crazy rich kid pulling some elaborate stunt to promote his failing airline. To be honest, I didn't really pay much attention to what was going on. I was pretty focused on my own stunt, as it were.'

'And what good do you think it achieved?'

'Well,' she said, 'in the last twenty-four hours, we've had over twenty million hits on our website. I could never have achieved that level of publicity before yesterday.'

'Do you think it will do any good?'

'I hope so,' she said. 'It's probably the only way we will change people's behaviour. Through education and persuading them to alter entrenched habits that, maybe twenty years ago, they wouldn't have thought twice about. That, in turn, will pressure governments and, who knows, we might end up with genuine change, just like the disarmament and non-proliferation treaties of the 1970s and 1980s. They resulted from grassroots campaigns. Everybody said it would never happen, but it did and that came after years of lobbying and campaigning by people like my father.' She almost choked on the last word, but recovered quickly. Nothing could be gained from opening that can of worms. 'It made people aware of the dangers,' she continued, 'which forced the politicians to listen. The dangers of climate change aren't going away, you know.' The words flowed effortlessly now, and it felt good to think that her so-called stunt had reached so many people. And that perhaps she had planted a seed of doubt in their conscience that with time would germinate. It was nowhere near as effective as LEAP or as fast, but ... at least no one would die, she kept reminding herself. 'In fact, the environmental problems are just going to get worse and worse, until it might be too late. Hopefully, I can change people's minds and behaviour enough to make a difference. Take a look at the website, Mr Forbes. It's - you might learn a thing or two. Who knows, it might even make you alter some of your own habits.'

'Excuse me, are you Miss Jakobsdóttir?'

They both turned as a tall man entered the waiting room. Judging from his white coat and hospital name badge, Uma assumed he was a doctor. He looked extremely tired.

'That would be me,' she said.

'Reception just paged me. What can I do for you?'

'I wanted an update on one of your patients, a Mr Ethan Rae.'

'Are you a relative?'

'No, just a close friend.'

'I'm sorry, ma'am. That's confidential information. We can only share it with immediate relatives of the family.'

'But—'

Forbes stepped forward.

'That's OK, Doc. She's with us.'

The doctor warmed up immediately.

'Oh,' he responded, smiling sadly at Uma. 'Why didn't you say so? I'm Doctor Scott.' He moved towards Uma and shook her hand. 'I'm head of the Trauma Center here at Bellevue. It's one of the best in the country, so Mr Rae is in good hands. Unfortunately, the prognosis is not good.' The doctor paused for a second to let his words sink in. When he continued, his voice was grave. 'Mr Rae is in an extremely critical condition. He has suffered severe brain damage following a catastrophic reduction in the amount of oxygen reaching his brain. That's not surprising, given the ferocity of the attack. Having studied the initial CT scans we have performed so far, I would say he was clinically dead for at least a full minute before being resuscitated, and that is what has caused the damage.'

'Is he conscious?' Uma asked hesitantly, afraid to hear what was coming next.

'No, of course not,' the doctor said. He saw Uma's face drop and continued more gently. 'He's in a coma. A deep one.'

'How deep?' was all she could manage.

'We've tested him extensively over the last few days. On our coma scale, if fourteen is fully conscious and zero is totally unresponsive. Mr Rae is a zero.'

Uma's heart skipped a beat. *Zero!*

'How can you be so sure?' she said. Zero sounded so final.

The doctor shifted uneasily, unable to meet her gaze. 'The tests. His eyelids are fully closed, even with pain prompters. His motor responses are totally unresponsive. As are his pupil reflexes. And corneal reflexes. There's no brainstem activity. And his breathing—it's non-existent without the respirator and has no response when we intubate.' His voice trailed off.

Uma slowly sank down onto the couch.

'Will ... will he recover?'

In the long silence that followed, Uma didn't move, struggling to process the doctor's words.

'I wish there was better news, but if the brain is denied oxygen for that length of time, there is virtually nothing we can do to bring it back.'

The doctor lapsed into an uneasy silence again until Forbes broke it.

'Thanks, Doctor. I really appreciate your time and also all your efforts to get Mr Rae over here so promptly yesterday. If there is anything more that can be done, I'm sure your team will attempt it.'

'I'm so sorry that I couldn't be the bearer of better news.'

He turned to leave, and was half out of the door, when a small voice stopped him in his tracks.

'Can I see him?'

'I beg your pardon, ma'am?' doctor said, turning back towards Uma.

'Can I see him?' Uma repeated.

'Well, I have to say that he is in critical condition. Under —'

Forbes nodded at the doctor, who picked up his unspoken assent.

'— normal circumstances I would have to say no but, on this occasion, I don't see why not. Would you like to come with me?'

Uma stood up and turned towards Forbes.

'Thank you, Agent Forbes, for all your help. I appreciate what you have done for us ... me, I mean.'

And then she was gone, leaving Forbes staring at the television as the professor continued to enthusiastically expand on where Reynolds could have disappeared to.

The Interior

18 December 2003, 15:28 hours GMT

Reynolds stood on the threshold of the chamber and looked outside. It was a beautiful afternoon. The sky was a deep blue. There wasn't a cloud to be seen. The sun was very low, skirting the edge of the horizon and casting deep shadows over the white landscape. He reckoned there was probably another ten minutes of light before the Arctic night returned, unchallenged. He shaded his eyes against the low glare, stepping forward over the lip of the door. He didn't even notice it closing noiselessly behind, not that he would have cared. He was not going back. There was no going back. Uma had seen to that. He stumbled slightly as the smooth soles of his black brogues slipped on the icy crust of the frozen snow. There was no wind today but, despite the balmy evening, he could already feel the cold envelop him, rising from the ground to suck greedily at his warm body. He pulled the lapel of his suit jacket around his neck tightly and hunched his shoulders instinctively, before straightening. *Not this way,* he thought. He wasn't going out like this, cowering in the cold like a defeated dog. He was walking out proud, head held high, safe in his own knowledge that he had played his hand to the best of his ability. Reynolds let the jacket swing open. He turned back to look at the low, squat building of the facility he had just emerged from. It reminded him of the Nevada labs, its single-storey, plain-white exterior almost invisible against the icy backdrop of the desert interior. The recollection caused him to pause a little longer than he intended as the last few months flashed before him. The race to steal the LEAP technology, Reynolds Air, Eva, the sweet smell of victory so close he could taste it, and then Uma. Those events seemed such a long time ago already. But it no longer mattered. It was all gone, a distant memory, all sucked away in an instant, leaving him in this frozen wasteland on the last leg of his journey. Perhaps this was his moment? He wasn't so sure anymore.

As Reynolds turned, the sun slipped beneath the horizon. One moment he was standing in orange sunlight, shielding his eyes from the low glare, an instant later, the light had disappeared to be replaced by night; the stars flickering on overhead like millions of light bulbs, advancing across the wide arc of sky in hot pursuit of the sun's re-treating glow. Within seconds, he was left staring at the majesty of the night sky. With no light pollution to fade the glow, the full grandeur of the stars overwhelmed him. It was breathtaking, and far exceeded the odd flickering pinpricks he was used to seeing, even in the Nevada desert. Above him, the dense swirl of powdery lights resembled a thick cloud of billowing steam that spiralled across the entire night sky. He shivered in awe, looking towards the horizon where the sun had disappeared.

Perhaps it's a good day to die after all.

He strode out purposely, being careful to the keep his balance in the icy snow. This time, he didn't look back. There was no point now. This was his moment.

His grandfather would have been proud of him.

Bellevue Hospital, Level 1 Trauma Center, Manhattan

18 December 2003, 10:32 hours EST

Uma stood facing the doctor across the bed, trying to focus on his face rather than on the unmoving figure in front of her. It should have been easy. He had kind eyes. Healer's eyes. Unselfish eyes that asked nothing from her and promised life in return. Except that she couldn't concentrate, because the shadow of impending death was cast long in the hospital room. She felt her gaze drawn downwards.

Ethan lay unmoving, his skin a deathly pallor, face bruised and cut from the brutal fight in the cell. His throat was covered so Uma couldn't see the real cause of the damage, but it was clear that nothing was right. Beside his bed, the mechanical whoosh of the ventilator patiently pushed air through three tubes that disappeared into his mouth. Her earlier resolve crumbled as she studied the ugly mess before her. *The LEAP Laws are there for a reason*, she reminded herself forcibly. She was already dealing with the consequences of ignoring them: first to save her father and more recently to keep the programme on track, trying to play the role of a god. Tampering with forces she knew nothing about. All in pursuit of some foolish dream to save mankind. And what had she achieved? A trail of dead bodies. She had killed her sister. Dear Fredrik was dead. And now Ethan. She choked back a sob.

'... has suffered a traumatic asphyxia that has effectively caused a catastrophic reduction in the quantity of oxygen reaching ...'

The doctor was doing his best to explain why Ethan was unlikely to recover, but Uma wasn't listening. He was as good as dead. Because of her naïve belief that she could change the world for the better. Such a waste. Her father had been right all along.

The mere thought of her father made her heart ache with a mixture of deep sadness and boiling anger. What had he done to her? And what did that make her and Eva? Designer babies? One for her father and one for her mother? She suddenly felt an even greater affinity with the man lying in front of her. Were they both copies? The only two in the world? Freaks of nature? She kept reassuring herself that, if she was the copy, she was no different than anyone else. No one person remained the same atomically for more than a millisecond. But it didn't work. She was simply a science experiment. A test tube monster created by her father. Or was Eva the copy? Original or copy. It made no difference. A sudden realisation left her reeling. Had she killed herself? Had she intended for that to happen? Was it some deep-seated primeval instinct that had kicked in the moment she found out that she was an exact copy of her sister? The decision to take the gun. To draw it. What had she hoped to accomplish?

But why had her father done it? She had asked herself that question a thousand times over the past few weeks. Had it been to appease Mama when they split? She had been a difficult woman, even in marriage, but her father had never stopped loving her. He hadn't wanted a divorce, or so he'd claimed; it was her mother's idea. According to her father, she couldn't live in Iceland with its dark winters and bleak summers. But maybe her father had lied about that as well. That was the deepest cut; having to live with her father's hypocrisy. It made a mockery of the man she had admired so much. His moral certainty was the very essence of who he was. And who she had wanted to be. It permeated everything he ever did and said. His disillusionment with the Manhattan Project. His breakthrough at Reykjavík in '86. His love of geothermal studies. And, of course, the environment. Take that away and what was left? *Nothing*, Uma thought bleakly. *Nothing except lies.*

Uma looked up. The room was empty, the doctor long gone. She took Ethan's hand from under the sheets. It was cold, uncomfortably so, and brought home the finality of his condition. Ethan was never coming back. Not tonight or at any time in the future. In that instant, Uma realised she couldn't abandon him. She owed him that much. He had stood by her from the start, even after the accident. In Iceland, he had saved her life repeatedly. Even later he had put her first, patiently trying to persuade her not to transfer LEAP over to her sister's captors. She remembered their kiss. For a second, she had melted into Ethan's embrace. And how had she repaid him? With this. *But the LEAP Laws exist for a reason,* an unwelcome voice in her head screamed silently. She no longer needed her father's lectures to remind her of that. She was experiencing it first-hand. Nothing good had come from tampering with them. That was why she had decided to bury the programme and focus on saving the environment the traditional way, just like her father had done.

Until that is, she had stepped into this room and seen Ethan lying here, just one flick of a switch from oblivion. And knowing that she had the means to save him, but couldn't. Or wouldn't ...

'Excuse me, ma'am. We need to carry out more tests, and I would like to complete them tonight.'

Uma looked up and saw the young doctor standing in the doorway.

'Of course, I will be out straight away. Just give me a few more minutes alone with him.' The doctor looked uncertain. She had already overstayed her welcome. If his boss found out, he would be in all sorts of trouble. 'Please?'

He nodded in resignation and turned away, telling himself that just five more minutes wouldn't do any harm. As he walked back to his office, he glanced through the smoked-glass window to the room. The woman was still holding the man's hand, but now it was clasped tightly in both of hers, and her head was bowed. For all the world, it looked like she was praying.

EPILOGUE

The Interior, Iceland

8 February 2009, 11:30 hours GMT

The squat building had been visible on the horizon ever since the sun had inched its way over the horizon at around nine. *It didn't make sense, though,* Sverrir Ingólfsson thought as he checked his position, trying to work out who was at fault. His map? His compass, perhaps? Or was it him? Had he miscalculated and wandered off course? It was easily done. The white desert offered no landmarks to map a course by, so he was totally reliant on the sky and his magnetic companion. However, each computation returned the same answer and his various maps showed no structures in this part of the world. He had been tempted to call in just to check it out, but that wasn't allowed. No help was allowed. Those were the rules. He could only use the Sat Phone in cases of life of death.

Ingólfsson cursed under his breath. He had better be right. If not, it would totally screw up his schedule and jeopardise his record-breaking attempt. A solo trek across Iceland's vast Interior without air support to resupply his dwindling provisions. What he needed, he carried. As if to emphasise the point, the shoulder harness bit deep into his chest as the 125-kilo sledge reminded him of its heavy presence. He was already four days in and progress had been excellent, until this morning and the unwelcome sight.

'What could it be?' he asked out loud, his deep voice breaking the unearthly silence of the vast landscape. He always spoke on his long treks. It kept him company. Kept him sane.

Maybe it was a scientific outpost monitoring volcanic activity? Or a tourist hut? Ingólfsson doubted that. He had chosen his route carefully. Moving east to west, it passed through some of the most inhospitable parts of Iceland that were completely inaccessible for ten months of the year. What could it be? He would find out soon enough. Before sunset if he set a good pace. He estimated the distance to be two miles, three at the most. Best not think about it. It would use up valuable energy. He shifted the shoulder straps slightly and set off at an easy pace, sliding over the soft permafrost with a practised nonchalance born of a lifetime on skis.

At 5:24, Ingólfsson punched the release catch on his shoulder harness, savouring the few seconds of weightlessness before gravity reminded his tired body of its own load. He didn't rest for long. He only had an hour before sunset. Just enough time to strike camp and explore. Not that there was much to see. The building couldn't have been more than forty feet square. There were no visible signs of a door, or even any windows.

He was on his third circuit when his eye caught sight of something fluttering in the light breeze. He couldn't believe he had missed it before. It was protruding from the snow that had drifted to head height at various points against the building. A piece of dark blue material with bright pink dots. Ingólfsson could have sworn it looked like the end of a tie. He tried to scrape the snow away, but it had iced over and his thick mittens slid harmlessly off the hard packed ice. He didn't dare expose his bare hands. Even on a sunny day like this, the wind chill was running at minus twenty degrees. Definitely not worth the risk. Ingólfsson unstrapped an ice pick and short-handled shovel. They felt feather light and he was soon hacking away clumps of ice around the mysterious material.

He had been right. It was a tie. A silk one.

'SALVATORE FERRAGAMO,' he heard himself mutter, his tongue struggling with the unfamiliar words. He continued digging, grunting with the unfamiliar effort despite his equipment. The ice pick suddenly sank deep into the compacted snow. He must have hit an air pocket. Sure enough, he could see a small chamber six inches into the ice. Beneath it was more material. Ingólfsson tried to withdraw the metal head of the ice pick, but it was caught fast and, despite his best efforts, refused to budge from whatever was now trapping it. He swore softly and shoved his gloved hand deep into the crevice. That was better. He was able to worm his arm down deep. Right up to his shoulder. Shifting his weight to get a better purchase, he jerked backwards. Nothing happened. He plunged both boots deep into the side of the drift and pulled again. And again. Absolutely nothing. The ice wall refused to budge. One last attempt and then he would have to get on with striking camp before he lost all light. He tugged with all his might and without warning, a large section of ice suddenly shattered into a million diamond pieces, sending Ingólfsson sprawling onto his back. He sat up, spluttering, brushing away the light powder from his sun visor.

'Jesus Christ,' was all he could say.

Ingólfsson reached into his jacket and pulled the Sat Phone from its holster as he continued to stare, transfixed by the bizarre sight.

A businessman was crouched in front of him. Black brogues. Dark blue suit. White shirt and, of course, the garish tie. He didn't look peaceful. His frozen visage was scowling, almost scornful. He hadn't died comfortably. His hands were frozen into angry claws and his icy fingers looked red raw, as if he had been scratching at something.

'How in God's name did you get out here?'

The man stared back at him, his sightless eyes white with ice. Ingólfsson hacked more snow away from the body and, within minutes, had cleared much of the drift to reveal a semi-circular chamber directly behind the frozen corpse. It was clearly a door. To one side was a panel. It looked like an entry point and the metal was badly scratched. Ingólfsson glanced at the damaged fingers.

'Poor bastard must have been trying to get back in.'

He stood for a few minutes in silence, head bowed out of respect for the unknown man crouched at his feet, trying to picture the desperate nature of his final few minutes as he realised he was going to die. He needed these memories to propel him forward, knowing that if he stopped, he would die. Unnoticed. Undiscovered. With no proper burial. Alone. In some desert wilderness with no one to witness his last moments on earth. He shuddered at the thought, took one last look at the dead man, burnished the image on his mind for later use, collected his equipment and made his way back to the sledge. He was already worrying about the call he would have to make and whether it was an allowable communication under the strict rules of the Interior Trek. That and the lost time that would eat into his precious schedule.

To Be Continued in Green Ray, Book 2 of The Race is On Series and which you can download on AMAZON NOW!

What Next?
Did you enjoy LEAP! You can be the difference.
As an Indie Author, reviews are **THE** most powerful tools in my quiver when it comes to getting attention for my books. It's the only way I can compete against the financial might of the big publishers who can command unlimited budgets for advertising and an army of marketeers to promote their writers.

However.

I have my own army.

An army that the big boys would love to get their hands on.

My faithful readers.

An honest review of my book is worth a thousand ads. And ten thousand marketeers! It provides social proof of my writing to other readers and more often than not, persuades them to hit the BUY button.

So, if you enjoyed this story, I would be eternally grateful if you tell others what you thought about LEAP on the book's Amazon page—it can be as short as you like. Just scan the QR code below or type the following into your browser: https://geni.us/LEAPreview

Thank you so much.

Fancy some exclusive swag?

Building a relationship with my readers is the very best thing about writing—I'm blessed to call many my friends and a few even help me with my writing; spotting typos, correcting research errors, suggesting plot improvements or simply agreeing to join my infamous ARC teams!

I email a newsletter every three weeks with details of new releases, special offers and signed giveaways.

Oh, and the odd snippet about my life in Leeds and that of my writing buddy Max—an aged, often bad tempered, but very lovable brown Labrador.

In return, you'll receive the following gifts, which are all exclusive to my club and can't be obtained anywhere else:

1. A free novella called MAD, explaining why Uma's father created LEAP and how Uma became a copy of her sister. It's a doozy and one of my favourite stories, although the plot nearly cleaved my mind in two!

2. A short dossier that answers some of the questions that you might have as a reader about LEAP, including what is made up and what is actually fact. And how I merged the two.

3. A chunk of chapters that didn't make the final draft of LEAP, including the reasons for deleting them. I really didn't want to, in fact I loved them, but my evil editor made me—loud sigh—she was right. Drat, I hate being wrong!

4. My date and time ss which I created to track the timelines in LEAP—sounds small, but endless hours were poured into this baby and I want you to see the blood, the sweat and the tears in those 1,080 cells as I worked to create a sense of urgency across Reykjavík, London, New York, Nevada, San Francisco, Bergen and Geneva. See if you can spot the intentional error. Only one eagle eyed reader has so far.

If you want to unsubscribe at any time, it's simple to do and I promise never to share your details with anyone. To join the club and receive the novella, chapters, dossier and ss, **for free**, scan the QR code below or type the following into your browser: https://ocheaton.com/leap-mad

I've dreamt of becoming a writer for years and, like many, believed there was at least one book in me. Having passed that hurdle, I've discovered there're loads and look forward to sharing future stories with you as I create them.

OC

Leeds, England

The Race Is On series

I've listed the complete Race Is On Series below

MAD, prequel novella

1986. Reykjavik, Iceland.

Brilliant quantum scientist Jakob Arnasson is on the brink of im-
mortality. After years of fervent anti-nuclear activism, he has finally
brokered a nuclear disarmament summit between two of the world's

greatest powers: the USA and the USSR. But on the eve of the talks, Jakob is forced to use his LEAP teleportation device to save his own life — an action that has far-reaching consequences. It resets his memory to the day of his first "leap", in 1954.

Thrust into a future-altering weekend without any recollection of why he should be there, Jakob's responsibilities suddenly multiply when the CIA recruit him for a dangerous covert operation to save the talks.

And just as he looks set to lose everything, a much greater threat appears on the horizon...

MAD is free and ONLY available on my website. To download MAD, just scan the QR code below or type the following into your browser: https://ocheaton.com/leap-mad

LEAP, Book 1

You've just read this!

Green Ray, Book 2

No good deed goes unpunished...

Six years after the near-catastrophic hijacking of LEAP, Uma Jakob-sdóttir is determined to find a safer path to environmental salvation. So, with her father's invention back under wraps, Uma turns her attention to the $85 billion-dollar Green Ray fund with the intention of renewing the planet—minus any teleportation.

But when the capabilities of LEAP are discovered by the U.S. government, it sets its sights on using the device to protect the country against economic collapse. When the White House proposes a new set of rules for LEAP—ones which would only allow the teleportation of goods, not people—Uma's objections are steamrolled by powerful forces.

Then the President's life is endangered, and the rules of the game suddenly shift again—leaving Uma in ethical turmoil as she races to stop the full power of LEAP from being unleashed on an unsuspecting world...

To buy Green Ray from AMAZON, just scan the QR code below or type the following link into your browser: https://geni.us/K8SbJA

ATOM INC, Book 3

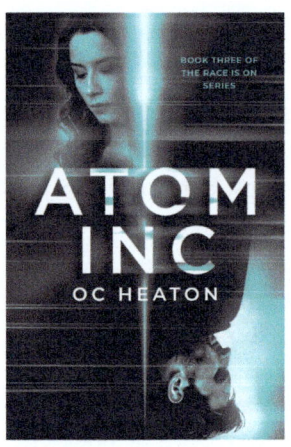

No one is above the Laws...

Seven years after its conception, LEAP is finally about to spell the end of global warming. For Uma and Ethan, this means personal and professional triumph – but quantum teleportation is an unwieldy beast, held back by those fighting to dominate the new world order.

As LEAP's roll out slows to a trickle, a greater threat emerges when a stealth attack on US troops leaves thousands dead. With the finger of suspicion pointing to a LEAP copycat, Ethan and Uma are forced to condone a breach of the Laws to reverse the massacre.

As LEAP's new rival continues to show their hand, Ethan is dragged back into a nightmare he thought he had escaped. One that may finally claim his sanity, and that pushes Uma to the limits of hers, to defeat an evil that no longer plays by the rules.

ATOM INC hits AMAZON on 29th February 2024 – To pre-order ATOM INC NOW, just scan the QR code below or type the following link into your browser: https://geni.us/6zpC

About OC Heaton

I write what I love to read—big issue technothrillers, with a side of sci-fi, that are super well researched inside a complex plot full of twists and turns.

When I sit down to write a book, I have three non-negotiables:

1. It needs to concern a current or recent real world issue that I can deeply research (I love research!) and weave my fictional story into. Hopefully, so tightly that you struggle to spot where one stops and the other starts.

2. It has to have a complex plot full of twists and turns that'll leave you guessing right until the end.

3. It must contain grey characters, even the good guys. This makes sense to me. First, as a reader I hate stereotypical/one-dimensional characters and second, grey is real life, right?

When I'm not writing I relax in my hometown of Leeds in the UK with the love of my life and our two daughters. And Max—my aged, often bad tempered, but lovable Labrador—who features a lot in my newsletters. It rains a lot in Leeds but that works out well for me—loads of time for research and, of course, writing!

Here are some ways that you can talk to me:

Email: oc@ocheaton.com

Web: www.ocheaton.com

Facebook: https://www.facebook.com/ocheatonauthor

Instagram: https://www.instagram.com/ocheaton

Dedication

To the one and only love of my life, Lillian. And, of course, our girls

Acknowledgements

M y thanks go to my partner, best friend, adviser and sounding board in this latest adventure, Lillian Ayala. Your love, enthusiasm, patience and wisdom know no bounds.

I am also extremely grateful for the assistance I received from the following individuals whose input helped me shape, write and eventually publish *LEAP*: Chris Wood, Jo Gledhill, Phil Carr, Martin Grange, Katie Kingston, Edward Kingston, Tamara Bootherstone, Julie Hoyle and Naomi Ayala.

Copyright